EDGAR RICE BURROUGHS
UNIVERSE ™

A century before the term "crossover" became a buzzword in popular culture, Edgar Rice Burroughs created the first expansive, fully cohesive literary universe. Coexisting in this vast cosmos was a pantheon of immortal heroes and heroines—Tarzan of the Apes®, Jane Porter®, John Carter®, Dejah Thoris®, Carson Napier™, and David Innes™ being only the best known among them. In Burroughs' 80-plus novels, their epic adventures transported them to the strange and exotic worlds of Barsoom®, Amtor™, Pellucidar®, Caspak™, and Va-nah™, as well as the lost civilizations of Earth and even realms Beyond the Farthest Star™. Now the Edgar Rice Burroughs Universe expands in an all-new series of canonical tales written by today's talented authors!

A PRINCESS OF MARS

SHADOW OF THE ASSASSINS

CEDGAR RICE BURROUGHS UNIVERSE™

The Edgar Rice Burroughs Universe is the interconnected and cohesive literary cosmos created by the Master of Adventure and continued in new canonical works authorized by Edgar Rice Burroughs, Inc., the corporation based in Tarzana, California, that was founded by Burroughs in 1923. Unravel the mysteries and explore the wonders of the Edgar Rice Burroughs Universe alongside the pantheon of heroes and heroines that inhabit it in both classic tales of adventure penned by Burroughs and brand-new epics from today's talented authors.

TARZAN® SERIES
Tarzan of the Apes
The Return of Tarzan
The Beasts of Tarzan
The Son of Tarzan
Tarzan and the Jewels of Opar
Jungle Tales of Tarzan
Tarzan the Untamed
Tarzan the Terrible
Tarzan and the Golden Lion
Tarzan and the Ant Men
Tarzan, Lord of the Jungle
Tarzan and the Lost Empire
Tarzan at the Earth's Core
Tarzan the Invincible
Tarzan Triumphant
Tarzan and the City of Gold
Tarzan and the Lion Man
Tarzan and the Leopard Men
Tarzan's Quest
Tarzan and the Forbidden City
Tarzan the Magnificent
Tarzan and "The Foreign Legion"
Tarzan and the Madman
Tarzan and the Castaways
Tarzan and the Tarzan Twins
Tarzan: The Lost Adventure (with
    Joe R. Lansdale)

BARSOOM® SERIES
A Princess of Mars
The Gods of Mars
The Warlord of Mars
Thuvia, Maid of Mars
The Chessmen of Mars
The Master Mind of Mars
A Fighting Man of Mars
Swords of Mars
Synthetic Men of Mars
Llana of Gathol
John Carter of Mars

PELLUCIDAR® SERIES
At the Earth's Core
Pellucidar
Tanar of Pellucidar
Tarzan at the Earth's Core
Back to the Stone Age
Land of Terror
Savage Pellucidar

AMTOR™ SERIES
Pirates of Venus
Lost on Venus
Carson of Venus
Escape on Venus
The Wizard of Venus

ERBUNIVERSE.COM

ERB UNIVERSE™

Swords of Eternity Super-Arc

Carson of Venus: The Edge of All Worlds
by Matt Betts

Tarzan: Battle for Pellucidar
by Win Scott Eckert

John Carter of Mars: Gods of the Forgotten
by Geary Gravel

Victory Harben: Fires of Halos
by Christopher Paul Carey

Victory Harben: Tales from the Void
Edited by Christopher Paul Carey

The Dead Moon Super-Arc

by Win Scott Eckert

Korak at the Earth's Core

Pellucidar: Land of Awful Shadow

Tarzan Unleashed

Other ERB Universe Books

The Land That Time Forgot: Fortress Primeval
by Mike Wolfer

Mahars of Pellucidar
by John Eric Holmes

Red Axe of Pellucidar
by John Eric Holmes

Tarzan and the Forest of Stone
by Jeffrey J. Mariotte

Tarzan and the Dark Heart of Time
by Philip José Farmer

Tarzan and the Valley of Gold
by Fritz Leiber

EDGAR RICE BURROUGHS UNIVERSE™

A PRINCESS OF MARS®

SHADOW OF THE ASSASSINS

ANN TONSOR ZEDDIES

Includes the bonus novella

JOHN CARTER®
OF MARS®

SWORDS OF THE MIND

BY
GEARY GRAVEL

EDGAR RICE BURROUGHS, INC.
Publishers
TARZANA   CALIFORNIA

ERB Universe Creative Director: Christopher Paul Carey

Special thanks to Michael Croteau, Geary Gravel, Janet Mann, James Sullos, Cathy Wilbanks, Charlotte Wilbanks, Mike Wolfer, Bill Wormstedt, and Ann Tonsor Zeddies for their valuable assistance in producing this book.

First paperback edition

Published by Edgar Rice Burroughs, Inc.
Tarzana, California
EdgarRiceBurroughs.com

ISBN-13: 978-1-945462-69-6

- 9 8 7 6 5 4 3 2 -

To the next generation:
Michael and Julia, Eleanor and Jon,
Margaret and Dave, Tim and Erin
And the one to come:
Thomas, Roland, Jasper, Eli
With all my love and hope

CONTENTS

THE PRINCESS GOES TOO FAR

A SOLITARY FLIER SOARED ABOVE the tawny moss of the dead sea bottom beyond the outskirts of Helium, steered by its lone pilot. Her dark hair tumbled free in the wind of her passage, streaming behind her like a shining black banner. She stood braced at the controls, in an attitude of ease and grace, her lithe young body riding lightly on the deck of her craft. Her flying harness betrayed no rank, save by the supple fineness of its manufacture, but the exquisite workmanship of her craft, and the symbol of Helium painted on its prow, announced the presence of Dejah Thoris, the princess and fairest daughter of Helium.

She used every trick of flight that she had learned to urge the little craft to its maximum speed, joying in the keen chill of the high air. Soon the twin towers of Helium diminished behind her. Her father, Mors Kajak, Jed of Lesser Helium, had exacted a promise that she would not go beyond the point where she could still see those towers—but how could she know that, when the towers were behind her, and her attention focused always onward?

She had reason to seek solitude and speed this day. She was trying to outrun the mood she had fallen into after her brother, Kajan Dan, departed on his latest adventure, a survey mission into the wildlands beyond the canal. His expedition planned to extend the exploration of Barsoom's resources that earlier generations of scientists had begun. Dejah Thoris had longed to join the expedition, but Mors Kajak had forbidden it. The jed explained that he could not permit both of his heirs to be out of reach at the same time, leaving Helium bereft should some accident prevent their return. Dejah Thoris accepted his word. Yet her brother's departure had left her feeling that she had been too long confined within the city walls. In her heart rose an unsatisfied longing to do great deeds for Helium, worthy of her mighty ancestors.

It was this longing that caused her to strain at the bounds of her father's command. She had watched her brother's fleet, gay with pennons, disappear across the dead sea bottoms in the direction of the canal. She followed in his imagined wake, until the towers of Helium were mere specks of red and yellow on the horizon, and the breaking of her promise to Mors Kajak was but an eye blink away.

Directing her gaze steadfastly forward, she spied the line of darker green where vegetation marked the edge of the canal. She wondered if, by rising higher, she might be able to see both the canal and the towers, thus keeping her pledge without turning back quite yet.

In the instant between thought and deed, her reverie was shattered by a powerful shock that sent her flier careening, its deck slanting at a perilous angle. She lost her grasp on the controls, sliding sideways across the deck until her trajectory was halted by a stunning crash into the bulwark. Now, indeed, she was grateful that she had clipped her flying harness to the deck bolt, in spite of the rebellious impulse that had urged her to leave herself unencumbered.

Unable to regain her feet on the tilting deck, she dragged herself back to the controls. As she grasped them, she saw that blood trickled from her left hand, spotting the deck. A long and wicked splinter of the iron-hard skeel wood of the gunwales was still embedded in the tender skin of her inner arm. Only the jeweled bracelets that adorned her had prevented it from slicing open the entire length of the limb. She plucked the splinter free before the shock could stop her, and clung to the controls while pain shadowed her vision.

But a princess of Helium is not to be daunted by the sight

of blood. Raising her head, she drew in deep breaths of the thin Martian air and shook off her momentary faintness. Once again the little ship darted forward in level flight. Whatever had caused the shock had not permanently damaged its capacities. Once she had leveled off, she had time to search for the source of the interruption to her flight. It did not take long to find it. A splintered hole marred the bow of the flier and was clearly the source of the fragment that had wounded her. Something had struck her little craft with tremendous force.

Another such something shrieked past her in the air, just as she realized what must have caused the damage. Acting instinctively, she turned the nose of her flier skyward so impetuously that once again, the deck tilted beneath her and nearly threw her to the side. She strained higher and higher, tossing her little ship from side to side and tipping it edge-on to her former direction of flight, to present a narrower target.

Leveling off at such a high altitude that she could now see the twin cities far below and behind her, like clusters of jewels on the drab fabric of the terrain, she gazed toward the green canal and saw what she expected. Puffs of smoke rising from the canopy of vegetation showed a conflict in progress. Somewhere in the midst of that distant conflagration, fierce hordes of green warriors battled travelers on the canal. The projectiles that had smashed into her hull and screamed past her in a near miss were bullets fired from the deadly radium rifles of the green men. It was unlikely they had targeted her. The rifles had a range of hundreds of *haads*. A stray bullet could speed on to strike a target far beyond its intended aim.

Nevertheless, she knew it was well to proceed with caution. She was the scion of countless generations of fighting men, and so her instinct was to go forward rather than to retreat, to meet the combatants and offer succor. But prudence, and her promise to her father, tugged her back. She had only her personal weapons, and no means of calling for assistance from Helium. She brought her craft about to return home.

And once again, the impact of enemy fire jolted her off course. Two more projectiles narrowly missed her as she fought for control. This was no accidental strike. Someone on the ground below was targeting her. She swerved and dropped nose-first toward the ground, and heard another bullet whistle past, far above her head. She saw the flash of the gun far below, and as she dropped swiftly, a lone green warrior became visible, galloping toward her astride a massive thoat.

When he realized that she was turning back in his direction, he raised his rifle above his head and shook it at her, before leveling it to fire again. She had no rifle on board, but her radium pistol hung in its usual place at her belt. Zigzagging, she dodged more bullets from the green man before she could draw the pistol and aim it.

It occurred to her that the thoat would make an even easier target than its gigantic master. But even in danger of her life, she could not bring herself to harm a creature that had no share in its rider's murderous intent. She aimed at the warrior's torso, just below the crossing of his harness straps, sought a moment of balance on the swaying deck, and fired.

She could not at first see the effect of her shot, for the green warrior's final volley exploded at her ship's bow, scattering deadly splinters everywhere. Violently tossed off her feet, she fell low enough that none of the shrapnel pierced her, but it took her some time to rise and regain control of her vessel. Swinging about to determine her enemy's position, she saw that he had fallen to the ground and lay motionless, while the riderless thoat made off in the direction of the canal.

She banked her craft like a leaf on the wind to speed toward Helium. To return was easier to wish for than to put into action. Her prized airship had been damaged to an extent that could not be determined while in flight. She was fortunate that the green warrior had not struck the buoyancy tanks, but she guessed by the erratic, limping motion of her ship that the rudder was less than fully functional. The warrior had not been firing strategically, or she would now find herself shattered on the ground. Rather, he had aimed at her personally.

"Ironic," she said, patting the damaged bow, "that I spared his steed, but my own faithful ship has suffered in my place!"

Once she had the flier on a steady course and believed herself out of range of more stray bullets, she took time to untwine a length of the silk with which she must decorate the most prosaic of harnesses, and wrap it around her arm to stanch the bleeding. Even with this precaution, plentiful drops of red stained the deck, enough to cause alarm when she reached her destination.

The moment she alighted, warriors tending the sky harbor leaped to her side with expressions of concern. She fended them off.

"I am well. Tend to my ship; it will require cleaning and repair. As for me, I need only that you take me at once to the jed. May the gods of my ancestors grant that he is in the city!"

Relieved by assurances that Mors Kajak had just returned from a council meeting, and was in the family quarters, she hastened to meet him.

The great jed sprang to his feet with an exclamation of alarm as she entered. Instantly spying her wounds with the keen eyes of a commander for his troops, and the concern of a father for his child, he swept her up in his powerful arms and carried her to a couch softened by abundant furs.

"My father! I am perfectly well!" she protested. But, in truth, she was not sorry to be supported and comforted. The shock of the wound, to one so tenderly raised, was severe. Yet, as Thoria, consort of the jed and mother to the princess, hurried to summon assistance, Dejah Thoris struggled to sit up.

"You must hear my news. I was injured by a stray bullet. Green men have attacked travelers on our side of the canal. They have crossed into the lands of Helium. I fear the green raiders have already done their worst."

Leaving her side only for an instant, the jed strode to the door of the family rooms, where guards awaited his orders, and sent for a map. With his aid, Dejah Thoris pointed out the location of the plumes of smoke she had seen. Then, at last, she allowed herself to relax and to be tended by the women whose calling it was to dispense the famed healing salves and medications well known to the red race. Soon her arm was washed, anointed, and bandaged. Wrapped in silks, she fell into a healing slumber, with her mother watching at her side.

As soon as he determined that the princess was being cared for, Mors Kajak left the room to order an immediate sortie of armed ships under the command of his odwar to go to the aid of the beleaguered travelers; or, if they were already lost, to deal with any of the green men who might remain in the area. His orders given and set in motion, he returned to his wife and sleeping daughter.

He gazed down at Dejah Thoris with an expression in which were mingled the fond father and the stern leader.

"By my calculations," he said to his wife, "her position when she made her observations was at the very limit of the boundaries I had set for her—or more probably, somewhat beyond it. Why must she strive against the gentle constraints we place on her, only for her protection?"

"Indeed," replied Thoria, "she is her father's daughter. Is it really surprising that the same spirit of courage and freedom dwells within her breast? It has been many years since my jed and chieftain brooked any constraint—and even in your youth, only Tars Tarkas, greatest of jeddaks, dared command you. Our daughter is long past her hatching, and it is only natural for her to begin to test her powers in the world."

"You speak truth, as always, my princess," said the jed. "But I would that she might test those powers in the sphere best suited for her talents and experience—not hurtle rashly into dangers too great for her. I would not see the treasure of Helium scarred like an old panthan."

"May our ancestors forbid it!" Thoria exclaimed. "And yet,

had she not strained against your limits, we might not have received news of the raid until it was too late to respond."

Mors Kajak sighed. "Yes, she was bold and swift in action, like a true heir of Helium. But my heart is glad to see her returned to your care, and I could wish her recovery be not too rapid, lest she fly away too quickly."

"She needs a challenge worthy of her mettle," Thoria said.

But to this, the jed made no reply.

After a long sleep, Dejah Thoris awoke much refreshed. As her father had feared, she was all too ready to spring back into action. She could hardly be induced to wait for her arm to be treated and freshly bandaged before going to find Mors Kajak and inquire about the fate of the rescue mission.

The jed was in conference with his senior warriors and counselors, so Dejah Thoris went first to the hangar to see if repairs were being made to her beloved airship. She found the hangar area in a great turmoil, and her ship as yet untouched. The warrior who normally took charge of the maintenance of her vessel was apologetic.

"The jed has ordered all ships of war to be placed in fighting trim, provisioned and armed for a major expedition," he said. "All craft that will not go with the fleet have been given a lower priority. I'm sorry, Princess. It will be my honor to repair your ship as soon as my duty to the jed allows."

"Thank you," Dejah Thoris replied graciously. "Of course, the jed's commands must take first place."

She apprehended the jed as he left his council chamber. "Father," she cried, clinging to his muscular arm, "tell me, I beg, what is happening this day? All the palace is in an uproar. I hear rumors that the noble jed goes forth to battle."

The jed moved as if to throw her off impatiently, but checked himself, his eyes softening as they dwelled upon the daughter of Helium.

"First tell me, child, how did you sleep? Have your injuries been well tended? Your welfare is everything to me."

Dejah Thoris laughed gaily. "It was a scratch! No more than the bruises the newly hatched get in play, or the attack of a peevish sorak. Quickly mended, quickly forgotten. Not worthy the attention of a jed on his way to conquest."

"Hardly conquest, Princess. Say rather, punishment. Your encounter with a stray bullet yesterday brought it to my attention that we have been far too lax with our green neighbors. They wax bold and dare to think they can enter the lands protected by Helium with impunity. It is time we taught them a lesson. Three days from now, we will set forth and scour the lands on the far side of the canal. We shall drive the green men back to their ancient cities. There let them lick their wounds for many days before they dare harass travelers again in our lands."

The dark eyes of the princess glowed with excitement. "The damage to my craft is still unmended," she said. "Give order, I pray, that my ship, too, will be made battle ready and armed with weapons, to accompany your fleet."

Now the mighty jed frowned, even as he gazed upon the beauty before him. Yet his voice was gentle.

"The offer of your ship is generous, but unnecessary. Helium owns many ships of war and need not take the pleasure craft of the princess."

Dejah Thoris raised her chin defiantly, eyes flashing. "You misunderstand me. I offered not my ship, but myself with it. Your son is far away and cannot accompany you to war, but you have another heir to stand at your side."

Mors Kajak took his daughter by the shoulders and set her at arm's length. His look was stern. "Did you not hear my words when I told you that I could not spare both you and Kajan Dan for the scientific expedition? Helium would never forgive me for risking her greatest treasure in such a minor campaign.

"I spoke earlier of a stray bullet, for that is how you described your encounter. On examining your craft, however, I see that you were struck both fore and aft. Do not expect me to believe that you turned tail out of prudence. I see how it was. After a stray bullet struck you from behind, you turned and engaged the enemy. Is it not so?"

Dejah Thoris searched for words to excuse herself. "But father—" she exclaimed, finding her voice. "That seemed the prudent course of action, rather than fleeing while the enemy continued to aim his weapon unchecked. I thought it wiser to stop the attack, since I could not outrun it."

Mors Kajak was not to be swayed. "Had you been true to your promise to stay within safe limits, you would not have needed to make such a choice. A promise is meant to be kept in spirit, not to the technical minimum. You knew my wishes, but found a way to circumvent them. Your responsibility to city and ancestors is not to be carried out in battle, but rather to guard and inspire your people here. I have spoken."

With flushed cheeks and downcast brow, Dejah Thoris watched her father stride away, already issuing orders to his retinue in preparation for the foray—another venture in which she would not be included. She bit back the words of argument she longed to speak. She knew well that no persuasion would change Mors Kajak's mind when he spoke with the voice of command.

2

AN UNEXPECTED EMBASSY

EJAH THORIS THOUGHT OF SEEKING SYMPATHY from Thoria, but the excitement and bustle of preparation reached even to the private quarters of the jed's consort. Moreover, she knew that Thoria would be mentally occupied with her own concerns over her husband's journey into danger. Now was hardly the time for a daughter to voice complaints of her father's treatment. Dejah Thoris needed to get away from the palace and distract her mind. Unable to fly, she could think of only one haven: the Hall of Beauty.

She summoned a pair of servants and sent one to her mother with news of her planned excursion. The other was ordered to accompany her to the Hall of Beauty, bearing her exercise harness, fresh silks, bandages, and salves.

It is unknown whether other cities of Barsoom boast such an institution, but Helium's Hall of Beauty is a cherished feature among the stately buildings in the central city, near the palace. The graceful marble building, surrounded by gardens, has existed for generations—and, given that a Barsoomian generation can be equal to what the denizens of Earth would call a millennium, that is time immemorial. Always has it served the same purpose: to provide for the red women of Helium a protected space for recreation and refreshment. Warriors guard the doors, but no man is permitted to enter, save on festive occasions when a competition or an exhibition is presented to the public and all are welcome.

Within, all was grace and beauty. The splashing of fountains made music in concert with groups of musicians playing gay tunes. The centerpiece of the hall was a great oval pool of blue stone, lit from within by radium bulbs and from above by a skylight that focused the pale Martian sunlight to create an atmosphere of comfortable warmth. Within its temperate waters, lithe forms sported joyously.

Swimming is a rare skill on Barsoom, due to the scarcity of open, pure water. Few would swim in the canals, with their cloudy waters that have passed through so many haads of open land and carry much eroded soil and detritus. None dare swim in dread Iss. The swamps of Toonol are home to many savage creatures before whom no warrior would wish to be found naked and unarmed. Many of the red race never learn to swim at all, and it is rare for green men to encounter more water than serves to wet their lips. Yet, thanks to the Hall of Beauty, as well as the baths in the inns of hospitality where male strangers may take the plunge, the people of Helium are capable of at least rudimentary flotation.

Leaving her harness and other accoutrements in an alcove, Dejah Thoris surveyed the pleasant scene, deciding which pastime would best soothe her spirits. She cast an eye over the sparring circles, where young women engaged in mock combat with skeel-wood versions of the slender blades carried by Martian females for self-defense. She did not trust herself to such games in her present mood. Sore at heart that her father would be engaging in real combat with no one of his blood to stand beside him, she found no joy in academic exercises with a lesser blade.

Turning her eyes elsewhere, she lit upon the ranks where others took part in playful contests of archery. This was more to her taste. She prided herself on her steady hand and skilled eye. She had not thought to bring her own bow of precious inlaid woods, but one of the communal bows kept for use in the Hall would do well enough. Entering the lines before the targets, she was hailed by friends and joined in the competition. At first she shot poorly, her concentration disturbed by unwelcome thoughts, but soon enough her focus cleared and her arrows flew unerringly to their goal.

After winning a few rounds and receiving the congratulations of her friends, her spirits lifted. She moved on to the area where young women exercised their strength and flexibility on aerial silks, swinging and turning high above a net woven also of silk threads in all the colors of the rainbow. This was almost as good as flying for clearing one's head, she found. To rise above the ground gave her a new perspective.

After a vigorous workout in the air, she was ready for a swim in the waters of the pool. Her servant, Susho Llan, met her at the edge with a length of silk to pat the water from her hair and skin. Then it was time for a light massage with scented oils before she donned her harness and ornaments again for the walk across the gardens to where the gates of the palace beckoned. Once again there was a spring in her step and a light in her eyes. How foolish she was to fear for the safety of a jed, and son of a jeddak! Mors Kajak would surely return victorious, as always. And how foolish to imagine that she, the daughter and granddaughter of mighty jeds, would not find her purpose in life. There were many bright mornings to come before she should voyage down Iss. No doubt one morning soon would show some deed worthy of attempting.

As soon as she entered the palace, she noticed even more stir and bustle than before. She was not left long to wonder why, for an older woman named Ela Dusa, one of Thoria's best-loved ladies in waiting, hurried to greet her. Clearly, she had been waiting by the entrance for Dejah Thoris' return, and not waiting patiently.

"Quickly, Princess," she whispered, beckoning to the servant to make haste. "Your royal mother has sent me to tell you that unexpected guests have arrived, and you must dress yourself to receive them with proper dignity."

"But the embassy from Zodanga is not expected for another week or two," Dejah Thoris said.

"These messengers are not from Zodanga. We've never seen them before. The lady Thoria has dressed in her finest, and requests that you do the same, just as we would have for the visitors from Zodanga."

She led Dejah Thoris to one of the less-frequented ramps to the upper floors, one normally used more by servants and guards than by the family. Dejah Thoris was discomfited by the glances of those she met along the way. Warriors of lesser ranks and others who might not have expected to see her in such close quarters stopped in surprise to salute her, bowing deeply. She could feel their gazes on her back even after she had passed them.

I suppose they are getting an eyeful of their princess, she thought. *And in my exercise gear, without adornment!* But her manner to them was universally gracious as she nodded to them and even spoke a word or two to those she recognized.

She felt relieved to reach the privacy of her own quarters.

"If you have no further need of me, Princess," said Ela Dusa, "I too must prepare myself to stand at your mother's side." She hurried away to the quarters kept for palace friends of the queen.

Dejah Thoris sighed, hastily divesting herself once again of her harness and piling it into the arms of the servant, along with the items she had brought with her to the Hall of Beauty. "Please put these away and bring me the new harness, the one with the opals and rubies. Or no—first run to my mother's rooms and inquire of her servants what she is wearing. Let me have my comb. My hair is in such disarray! Oh, why must these pestiferous visitors show up today, of all times! Like nasty ulsios sniffing for crumbs! But don't tell anyone I said that. If my mother should hear—I will be greatly displeased if you repeat that!"

She had seen the amused smile that Susho Llan tried to hide behind her hand.

Soon enough the fussing was over, and no one would ever have known that the Jed of Lesser Helium and his family had been surprised by this visit, as the ranks of the palace guard stood at attention, and the trumpets sounded.

"The princess comes! The princess and consort, Thoria!"

And then, "The princess comes! The princess, Dejah Thoris!"

Mors Kajak himself stood in ceremonial harness at the foot of the ramp, prepared to receive the ladies of his family. Thoria swept regally down the ramp to him, arm in arm with the young princess. Dejah Thoris did not wear the rubies and opals after all, but a harness matching that of her mother, who had donned her most formal garb for this occasion. Its finely chased leather was almost invisible beneath a wealth of sparkling black and white diamonds interspersed with onyx and pearl. As the jed extended his arm in welcome, his many armlets of gold and the jeweled medallions on his harness, marking triumphs in battle and service to his jeddak, flashed like the rays of the sun.

Dejah Thoris posed to receive the admiring glances of all those assembled, then bowed to left and right, as did her mother. The rituals of state occasions were second nature to her. Once the elder and younger princesses were stationed at the jed's side, trumpets rang out again and the heralds announced the arrival of other members of the court. The troop assembled in the great hall glittered like the stars of the Milky Way.

At last the trumpets rang out for the guest on whose account all this pomp had been organized.

"The ambassador comes! Ptar Koro, the messenger of the Jed of Zor!"

All eyes turned to the ambassador and his delegation. At last Dejah Thoris could gaze upon him in courtesy. The man stood out among those of Helium, because his gear was of an ancient make. While the typical harness of a warrior remained much the same throughout class and region, many small differences signaled distinctions to the trained eye of a princess. His blade was of an older style, heavier and less streamlined, with a type of elaborate hilt that was no longer in fashion among the Heliumites. His ceremonial headgear was a thick band of gold filigree, with half a dozen colorful feathers standing upright in chased gold sockets. The effect was to make him appear taller and more stately. It was a style no longer affected among the cities in close communication with Helium. His overall appearance seemed somewhat archaic to Dejah Thoris.

After the usual exchange of courtesies, the company progressed to the banquet hall, to the tune of lively musical accompaniment. Mors Kajak was seated at the high table, with Thoria and Dejah Thoris to his right, and the ambassador on his left. The jed waited until wine and delicacies were served, and the guests had time to sate their first hunger. Then at last he broached the question of what might be the reason for their embassage.

"Mighty Jed, and ladies of enchanting loveliness," Ptar Koro began, with a bow in their direction, "my master, Jan Vajo, the awe-inspiring Jed of Zor, sends me here with an invitation to all the royal family of Helium. Yearly, from time immemorial, Zor hosts the Competition of Valor in our ancient arena. Each year, some notable personage is invited to join the jed as a judge of the games. This year, it is my lord's pleasure to invite the Jed of Helium and his family. It would be our honor to show them the hospitality of the city."

"Tell us more of this competition," Thoria said. Dejah Thoris glanced gratefully at her mother. Her own curiosity was awakened by this novel invitation, but she had not dared put herself forward to question the stranger.

Thoria signaled for a serving maid to refill the ambassador's goblet of wine. He relaxed a trifle, and his manner became more lively as he expanded on the glories of his city and its festivities.

"It is thought that the games came into being as a rite of passage for the newly hatched," he said. "When they have reached their full growth and attained the skills of a warrior, the games give them a chance to display their abilities and to be seen by the whole city. They compete in feats of fighting skill, strength, and grace. The prizes gained assist them in finding a place in adult society. As well, the winners are noted by those of high rank, who may offer them invitations to serve in a position of honor, such as the palace guard.

"And it is not only the newest arrivals who compete. We have added a senior division, for any young persons who wish to take part. It is indeed an inspiring sight. The whole city attends, in company with the jed and his family and court."

Dejah Thoris leaned forward and spoke impulsively. "And is it a competition for men only? Or is there a place for women to show their skills?"

The ambassador seemed startled at her interruption, but when he saw that her parents had no objection to her question, he smiled indulgently. "Indeed, most enchanting princess, there is an opportunity for those of the fairer sex to show their talents. Not, of course, the noble ones of the city, who have no need for such public display. But those who seek prefer-ment may compete. These games are bloodless—or, at any rate, not to the death. Among the men, who compete with real weapons, there may occasionally be some injury. But the ladies are armed for sparring with wooden weapons, so they may show their skill without harming their loveliness. Additionally, the women may compete in tests of agility and marksmanship."

"You would understand my daughter's interest if you knew of one of our city's finest traditions," Thoria explained. "Our Hall of Beauty is a place where the women of Helium find pleasure in exercising such skills."

"What a delightful notion," the ambassador said. "I should be greatly interested to be granted a tour of its glories."

Thoria bowed slightly. "And I would be honored to provide a tour if that were possible," she said. "But the Hall of Beauty is closed to male eyes, save during our own little games and festivities. Sadly, none such are scheduled during your visit, or I would gladly provide you with the opportunity to view them. Perhaps another time, if commerce between Zor and Helium becomes more common."

"As is my hope," Mors Kajak said, "and I am certain that of Tardos Mors, Jeddak of Greater Helium, as well. Tell me, did you see any signs of incursions by the green tribes, as you traveled across the wastes between us?"

From that point on, conversation was confined mostly to the jed and ambassador, the jed's counselors, and the chief officers who accompanied the ambassador. The ladies chatted quietly among themselves, and watched the entertainment. After the dinner was concluded, and a suitable period of time had passed, Thoria rose to signal that the women were retiring. Whether the men continued their discussion in the grand hall, or moved to more comfortable quarters, remained unknown to them.

Dejah Thoris was glad to return to the family quarters and relax. Her exertions at the Hall of Beauty, followed by an evening on display for an occasion of state, left her fatigued. Her injured arm throbbed. She repaired to her mother's rooms in search of comfort, and of news. The invitation to visit Zor filled her with interest and excitement.

She found Thoria divested of her stately ornaments, having her lustrous dark hair brushed by her favorite servant.

"Mother, do please send for Rana Temra and her soothing salves. My arm is hurting me."

Immediately Thoria was all concern. She sent for the healing woman at once. It was not very late in the evening. The messenger returned with the news that Rana Temra was still awake and would take her basket and come at once. Dejah Thoris seated herself on a padded stool and leaned upon her mother's knee as Thoria tenderly unwrapped and soothed the reddened limb.

"What do you think, my mother? Will my father accept this invitation? Shall we all go? I would dearly love to be one of the party."

"You know the jed must ponder such things carefully before reaching a conclusion. It is too soon for any of us to impose our own wishes."

Dejah Thoris sighed pitifully. "It is a glorious thing to be a princess of Helium. And yet, one's feet could root to the ground like an ancient mantalia tree before one is allowed to do anything. My noble father has seen the danger of green men to the east of us, and he does not wait! No, at once the ships are readied and the warriors armed! His word can make it so!"

"Your father's many years of endurance and danger have equipped him to command," Thoria reminded her.

"Just so," Dejah Thoris said. "And how shall I, a daughter of Helium, ever learn to serve my city when my part is always to wait and be patient, to do nothing?"

Thoria laughed and toyed with Dejah Thoris' raven-dark locks, tumbling out of their careful arrangement. "What you call nothing can be a very great something. We are your father's most steadfast supporters, whether in action or in patience. Let me take these pins from your hair, before they create a tangle. Remember how hard it was for you to hold still when you were first out of the egg, while I brushed the snarls from your hair? Impatience caused you pain then."

Rana Temra washed and anointed the wound, carefully rubbing in salve to promote healing without a scar. She wrapped the arm again in silk imbued with healing oils. She was just finishing when the heavy steps of armed men in the corridor heralded the return of the jed. Receiving their thanks, she hastily gathered up her supplies and left the chamber, bowing to Mors Kajak as she passed.

Dejah Thoris rushed to his side and hastened to assist him in detaching portions of his harness, heavy with the metal of a jed. She offered him a luxurious fur wrap to ward him against the encroaching chill of night.

He seemed in a genial mood.

"To what do I owe all this solicitude?" he chortled. "I know what it is. You hope that once I am comfortable, my unguarded lips may let fall some interesting news."

He tapped his fingers on the arm of the massive carved chair. The armlets encircling his brawny sword arm clinked against the stonework. "This embassy from Zor aligns very neatly with the wish the great jeddak and I have often discussed, that of creating an alliance over all these southern lands. We strive to strengthen our connection with Zodanga—so far, so good—but the other cities in the lands that Helium protects, such as Zor and Hastor, remain out of our reach. This could be the beginning of an alliance that might aid us in our combat against the green hordes. If only it had come at some other time! I cannot postpone my raid. These Thurds, or whatever tribe they be, must be given a sound lesson immediately."

"I had considered offering to go myself," Thoria said, "or perhaps asking Vara Martis to accompany me, as representatives of Helium. But if I correctly heard when these games will begin, I am afraid that will be impossible. A visit from a contingent of Zodangan nobles has been in preparation for some time now. Vara Martis and I are in the last stages of planning their entertainment. It would be considered a grave slight to Zodanga if we were not here to receive them."

Mors Kajak rubbed his chin in thought. "I shall take counsel with Tardos Mors. But he has already stated his intention of remaining in the palace to guard the twin cities in my absence, and I know that Vara Martis plans to join with you in your welcome to the Zodangan nobles. While our son is absent, it seems we have no one to send on behalf of the rulers of Helium."

Dejah Thoris sprang to her feet, her cheeks flushed with excitement and her eyes shining. Every inch of her stature bespoke her proud heritage.

"My father!" she exclaimed. "How can you say there is none to send? Do I not stand here before you as a scion of the house of Tardos Mors and all our ancestors? Am I not worthy to represent you? Send me! I will gladly carry out this task."

Her parents gazed at her fondly. She seemed the perfect embodiment of pure spirit and fair form, like the incarnation of one of the ancestors of old.

"Child," Mors Kajak said at last, "no one questions your worthiness to represent your heritage before all Barsoom. But to send you alone to an unknown city is a perilous matter. It is not your worth that is questioned—rather, we question whether it is right to risk it on such a gamble."

Anger deepened the flush on the cheeks of the princess. She stamped her foot haughtily.

"Oh! How many hundreds of years will it take to make me more than a youth in your eyes? Have I not shed blood for Barsoom this very week? Mere hatchlings in Zor will compete for prizes and honor, while I waste my days here, like a—a pet sorak!"

Bright tears trembled in her eyes. Suddenly she turned without ceremony and dashed from the room.

There was silence in the room after her departure. Finally, the jed turned a perplexed brow toward his wife.

"I confess myself vanquished," he said. "What was that all about? In all my days of traveling the lands of Barsoom, one thing I have never learned, and that is to predict the wayward paths of a young and beautiful female, even though she may be my own daughter."

Thoria came to sit by his side. "It is hard for everyone when a newly hatched scion perches at the edge of the incubator, eager to take off on her own. Surely you remember a few years ago, when Kajan Dan first took up his sword as a full-fledged warrior? The half-brained quests he chose! The duels he fought! Yet now he is the steadiest and most valiant of captains."

"I see what you are driving at. Every son must win his own metal. But a daughter is to be cherished, not tossed at risk like the counters in a game."

"Not all women are alike, my chieftain," Thoria said. "The heart of a princess is ordinarily wrought of purest gold, soft and yielding, suitable for adornment with gems. But the hearts of the women of Helium are made of both gold and steel, as befits the consorts of the mighty. How well I remember when I was but a maiden, how the steel sometimes chafed my soul! I sometimes felt my heart would burst with longing to discover something new, to achieve something great. That was before I met you, my chieftain. To rule Lesser Helium by your side has been greatness enough for me. But Dejah Thoris has not yet found her joy. Her spirit craves freedom."

Mors Kajak embraced his lovely consort. "You were ever my best counselor," he said. "Sleep, too, brings good counsel. Tomorrow I shall consult Tardos Mors—though I shall be surprised if even his long life has given him wisdom in this area. He hatched no egg but me."

In her own chambers, Dejah Thoris sat on the wide stone window ledge, only her pale face showing against the furs in which she had wrapped herself from head to toe. The chill night air stole in through the unglazed window opening, and a myriad stars blazed brightly in the thin air of Barsoom. Across the backdrop of the stellar array, the bright spark of Thuria danced her eternal flight, and the more distant disk of Cluros swept less precipitately through the night.

Her servant had come to beg her to go to bed. Dejah Thoris merely shook her head. The servant left hot tea and a plate of little cakes at hand, and crept off to her own bed. Once she was gone, the princess buried her head in the soft furs and wept, muffling her tears. Her pride would not allow them to be seen. Before Thuria had made another circuit of the sky, she raised her head and dried away the tears. She sipped the now-cooled cup, but had no appetite for sweets. She crumbled the cakes and tossed them out the window for night-roaming creatures to find, only to realize that probably an ugly ulsio would be the first to scavenge them.

She chided herself for a little fool, and laughed, sniffing back the last of her tears.

"What a silly princess, whose haughty passion ends by feeding ulsios," she said to herself. She regretted her discourteous exit from her conversation with her parents, and would have liked to go back and apologize. Now she yearned for a comforting hug, but she guessed they had long been asleep after a day of many tiring duties.

"True it is," she said ruefully, "that she who cannot control her own actions will never rule a city."

She stretched her cramped limbs, feeling the chill in the air as the warm wrap fell away. She splashed cold water on her face from a carved crystal ewer, and tumbled into bed.

"I will sleep," she told herself. "And I will not have red eyes tomorrow. If Tardos Mors comes to visit, I will show the jeddak that I can counterfeit serenity as well as anyone in the court. Zor or no Zor, tomorrow I shall be seen by all as the queen I wish to become."

3

A MISSION OF WAR, A MISSION OF PEACE

OMEWHAT TO HER SURPRISE, Dejah Thoris slept late the next morning. The servant entered with mantalia milk and a tray of fruits, her ordinary breakfast. Glancing out the window, the princess saw that the morning was now far advanced.

"Why did you not wake me? Has there been no messenger from my mother?"

Susho Llan smiled. "Yes, indeed there was. Your mother told me not to wake you. She said you'd had a tiring day and there was no need for you to attend the luncheon for the delegates from Zor. However, she also said that by midafternoon, your grandparents will arrive in anticipation of tonight's dinner. They will be entertained in the palace gardens, should you wish to see them."

"Why didn't you say so at once!" Dejah Thoris drained her goblet of milk. "Oh, I must hurry."

"Your bath is already prepared."

Normally, she would have lingered in the scented waters of the bath, a luxury on a world of eons-long drought. On this day, she splashed and scrubbed hastily, while calling for her newest set of festive harness. Today it would be the opals and rubies, she determined. Last night's stately black-and-white was far too severe a costume in which to greet her beloved grandparents. To the rest of the world, Tardos Mors and Vara Martis were revered and majestic presences, but to Dejah Thoris, they were the family she loved best, next to her parents

23

and brother. The opals and rubies would reflect the sparkle and warmth she felt in their company. She added several fluttering lengths of silk, which she hoped would disguise the bandage still wound around her arm.

As she entered the palace gardens, the heralds began to trumpet their announcement: "The princess comes! The princess, Dejah Thoris!" But before they had concluded the fanfare, she had already run across the soft moss to the shade of the fragrant pimalia grove, to embrace her grandparents.

As was the way of Barsoom, Tardos Mors and Vara Martis showed no signs of age. The jeddak stood proud and strong, and Vara Martis was as slender and lovely, her hair as lustrous and dark as it had been hundreds of years before Dejah Thoris was born. Age showed only in a certain deepening of dignity, a distillation of personality.

They greeted her with a warm embrace, and drew her to a carved stone bench to sit with them. She was relieved that her parents had not yet made an appearance.

"I hear you had quite an adventure in your flier the other day," Tardos Mors said. "Your father seems proud of how you handled yourself."

"Really?" Her eyes widened in disbelief. "I thought he was angry because I flew too far."

The great jeddak smiled. "Your father thinks highly of your courage and presence of mind—as he should. You are, after all, *my* granddaughter. Now tell me, what do you think of this embassage from Zor?"

"I think we should take advantage of their offer to learn more of their city," Dejah Thoris replied promptly. "But my honored parents seem reluctant. It seems we have many more pressing tasks at hand."

She lowered her head and sighed. "I would gladly go in the name of Helium, but—I think the jed is not willing. I'm afraid I behaved badly to them last night. But I am far from the day of my hatching, though alas I sometimes behave like one newly emerged from the egg. I simply wish I could do something. My father will risk his life in war, my brother in bold exploration. You, my dear grandmother, along with my mother, undertake to entertain heads of state and improve the standing of our city. I alone am of no use to anyone. I sometimes feel I exist merely to be gazed upon, like a flowering shrub or bubbling fountain."

"Would you truly wish to travel to a strange city on your own?" Vara Martis asked. "Would you not be fearful? Remember, a daughter of Helium must show no timidity in the face of strangers. Helium fears no one!"

"Yes! I wish to go, and I am ready! That is, if my jed commands me."

"Spoken like a true descendant of jeddaks!" Tardos Mors said with approval.

"But it is of no use, since the jed does not wish it," Dejah Thoris said, the fire dying from her eyes.

"Let us see what Mors Kajak has to say tonight at the banquet," Vara Martis said mysteriously.

The banquet was even more splendid than that of the previous evening. Two jeds, equal in strength and vigor, and three lovely princesses now graced the high table. Thoria once again wore her diamonds and onyx, but Dejah Thoris scorned to don the same thing twice. She employed the privilege of youth to display a delicate harness chased with silver and adorned with black and white pearls, hematite and smoky topaz. As well, she was seated next to Vara Martis and could engage in lively conversation with her without fear of distracting her mother from presiding over the feast. Her naturally animated personality showed to good advantage in company with an older though equally regal beauty.

On several occasions, she noted the ambassador's eyes dwelling on her with evident approval. She quickly averted her gaze and tried to conceal herself behind her grandmother's shoulder at such times. She had no wish to win the approval of strangers. She wished only for her parents to observe her as an adult who knew how to conduct herself on occasions of state.

As the evening drew to its end, Mors Kajak rose from his seat, drawing all eyes to himself.

"I wish to offer a toast to our future friendship with the city of Zor, which I hope will be inaugurated by this meeting."

As the guests filled their goblets and rose to their feet, he gestured to them to wait.

"But first, I wish to make an announcement. Jan Vajo, Jed of Zor, has offered us the honor of being present at their yearly games of skill. As your jed, I must regretfully decline, for I go to war with the green men in but a few short hours. Our noble jeddak, Tardos Mors, will watch over Lesser Helium in my absence. But, after due consideration, we have decided to honor his invitation by sending the incomparable daughter of Helium, Dejah Thoris, as our envoy and representative. Her presence will be the most valuable gift we can bestow.

"So let us drink first to the princess, and then to friendship with Zor."

Enthusiastic cries of "Hail the princess!" broke out around the hall. The applause for the Jed of Zor was notably less noisy, but the toasts were drunk with equal vigor. The wines of Helium were exquisite, and the cellars of Mors Kajak exceeded even those of his mighty forebear.

Knowing what was expected of her, Dejah Thoris rose and bowed to the guests, doing her best to cover her surprise and confusion under a stately demeanor. The heightened color of her cheeks made her even more lovely than usual, and goblets were raised high in her direction.

"I had no idea of this," she whispered to her grandmother. She was breathing fast, but tried to collect her thoughts and to look as if she had expected the announcement.

"I spoke with your mother early this morning. Our conversation with you in the garden convinced the jeddak of the wisdom of our conclusions. Your father yielded to our persuasion. I trust that you are happy with this assignment?"

"Oh, yes, of course!" Dejah Thoris said. "It is just the surprise that has taken my breath away."

She longed feverishly to get away from the banquet hall, to return to her own rooms to think, to plan. She could hardly endure the remaining speeches and compliments, even though she knew she should be paying attention to every word.

When the women of the court finally excused themselves, she fled to her chamber, expecting solitude in which to compose herself. She found her mother with some of the servants and one of her mother's most long-standing companions, Ela Dusa, already looking through her things. The servants were swiftly wrapping jeweled harness and delicate slippers in lengths of silk for transport.

Thoria glanced up as she entered. "Ah, there you are. Come and help us. Your father has decided it will be best if you travel with his battle fleet as far as Zor. There he will drop you off and proceed to the field. This will enable you to make a grand entrance, and impress the Zorians with the might of Helium. Your father will then return for you after he deals with the green men. A troop of guards will remain with you, and our dear friend Ela Dusa will accompany you as your companion."

Dejah Thoris made a becoming bow to Ela Dusa. In truth, the older woman had never been a favorite with her. The princess found her mother's friend lacking in charm, not at all the sort of person in whom one might confide.

"I thank you, Ela Dusa, for your kindness," she said. "But would it not be better to ask one of the younger ladies to go with me, rather than to inconvenience you with this journey?"

Thoria knew what her daughter was trying to do, and gave her a severe look.

"Not at all, my dear," she said. "Ela Dusa is well versed in the ways of the court and will be able to advise you should you find yourself in any discomfiting situations."

And will watch me every moment and make a report to you, Dejah Thoris thought crossly. But she quelled her temper.

In truth, she thought more soberly, she might well need some advice. She felt herself being catapulted into a whole new world.

"Now come and help me sort out your best ornaments," Thoria said. "I wish we had time to order a few new things made! But your father thinks a week will be plenty of time to deal with the green tribes, so you need not pack too much. Perhaps you will see things worth purchasing in Zor. You must observe carefully what their customs are, and let us back here in Helium know if they have any niceties that we might wish to employ ourselves. Your father will cover your account if there is shopping to be done. Though I imagine the Jed of Zor will provide you with anything you might need."

Thus, pleasantly enough, they passed the first watches of the night in packing and preparations. Thoria brought out several precious heirlooms of the house of Helium for Dejah Thoris to wear at the court of Zor. It was late, and the stars had moved far in their courses, before the leather satchels were filled and strapped up to Thoria's satisfaction. Then she embraced her daughter and urged her to sleep well.

Before retiring, Dejah Thoris looked over her luggage. She had helped her brother pack for his expedition. She wished that her bags contained more of the useful equipment that had gone with Kajan Dan, and fewer jewels and silks.

She undid one of the packs, and made sure to stow within it her sturdiest flying harness, along with several small but practical items clasped to its fastenings. She had already made sure that her dress harness would accommodate the slender blades that served as the last line of protection for the red women of Barsoom. Her stout guardsmen could not be everywhere, and she did not wish to be found helpless in a strange land.

A mere fraction of Helium's fleet took flight in the first light of morning, but it was nonetheless a brave display. Dejah Thoris' heart swelled with pride as she stood on the deck of the flagship by her father's side. She had embraced her mother before embarking, and had seen the tears in Thoria's eyes as she said farewell to husband and daughter. But proud Thoria had smiled regally and forbidden the tears to fall, and the princess could do no less. Head high, she waved to friends standing on the rooftop, and turned to face the morning wind.

Her spirit thrilled to soar over the rolling landscape aboard the chief ship of this shining fleet. Brasswork and iron-hard skeel wood alike gleamed in the morning light, polished to perfection, and the banners of Helium flared out in the breeze. The handful of fliers that had come with the embassy from Zor accompanied the fleet. Mors Kajak's ship was first in the vanguard. The ambassador's smaller vessel was permitted to fly in the place of honor to his right, but the Jed of Helium's pennon was always first in flight. The sunlight gleamed from the polished arms and flashing metal of the warriors who thronged the decks. Dejah Thoris felt a pang as she thought of her own little craft, but it was still at the repair dock after the destruction wrought by her green assailant.

As the walls of Zor came in sight, Mors Kajak slowed the fleet, so that the Zorian craft might go ahead to properly announce their arrival. The ambassador had sent one of his smaller vessels home the previous night, as soon as Mors Kajak had announced his intentions.

It seemed all Zor had turned out upon the walls to behold the arrival of the Heliumetic ships. Gay banners flew, and sounds of music and cheering wafted up from below. Following the ambassador's suggestions, the fleet hovered just beyond the wall, while the jed's flagship and a handful of smaller craft moved on into the air harbor of Zor. The rest of the fleet could not have found anchorage there. It was a small space compared to the broad sweep of the harbors of Helium and Lesser Helium.

Yet, what space there was had been cleared for the descent

of the flagship. Ranks of Zorian guards stood at attention in full panoply. The jed's entourage stood on the prow as the skilled officers brought the ship to a feather-light landing. Mors Kajak, majestic in the forefront, raised his hands in greeting from the prow. A gangplank was readied, and he descended, accompanied fore and aft by warriors of Helium. Trumpeters sounded a fanfare, and the herald of Zor announced, "The Jed of Lesser Helium comes! Mors Kajak, the jed!"

Next, the princess descended, flanked by her own company of guards and followed by Ela Dusa and the chosen servants of the two ladies. The brazen cry of the trumpets sounded imperiously as the herald announced them. "The Princess of Helium comes! The princess, Dejah Thoris!" And then, "The lady Ela Dusa, chosen friend of Thoria, princess and consort!" The applause of the onlookers sounded yet louder for the beauty of the women of Helium than for the might of their jed.

Guardsmen of Zor formed a double line of salute with upraised swords. Through this archway proceeded the Jed of Zor himself. Dejah Thoris scrutinized their host as he approached. His was a commanding mien, set in proud and fierce lines, but it was hard to judge any nuances of character. A diadem ornamented with gems, vivid plumes, and golden tassels partially obscured his countenance.

"Kaor to the pillar of Lesser Helium, and to its finest flowers," Jan Vajo said. His voice seemed somewhat harsh, but his words were gracious. "We beg that you will allow us to return the hospitality you showed to our ambassador. A feast has been prepared in your welcome."

"I fear we must defer your kind offer," Mors Kajak said. "I am even now on my way to punish a troop of green raiders whose insolence has plagued my borders for too long. Within the week, I shall return to escort the princess home. At that time, we would be more than happy to drink together to our victory, should the offer be extended."

A frown crossed Jan Vajo's face—the look of one who is seldom refused. But his manner remained gracious. "I understand. A warrior's answer! But come, let us at least pledge our wishes for your success. One cup, and we will cheer you on your way."

Mors Kajak bowed to this invitation. "To such courtesy, I must consent, but our stay will be short. The hearts of my band are impatient for battle."

In the banquet hall of Zor, a large company already assembled at the tables rose to salute them. Seats of honor to the right and left of Jan Vajo's high seat were prepared for the jed and the princess. To Mors Kajak's right sat a hard-bitten warrior whose metal marked him as jedwar. Jan Vajo introduced him as Ptang Raxo. Next to him, a man of lean and curious visage introduced himself as Dramus Ugo, counselor to the jed. Dejah Thoris found herself seated next to a lady of extraordinary beauty and presence who was introduced to her as Phortora, sister of Jan Vajo.

"The jed, as you see, has no bride, so it is I who must welcome his guests and preside at his table," she said.

The two squads of Dejah Thoris' picked guard were seated together opposite the high table, among Jan Vajo's own personal guards.

Serving men and girls sprang forward to pour cups of wine for all.

"A toast," Jan Vajo cried, rising to his feet. "Victory to Helium! And a speedy return!"

The men of Zor tossed off their cups as if deep drinking were the order of the hall. Dejah Thoris but touched her lips to the cup, as was proper for a princess. Soon she would be Helium's sole representative, and would need to keep her wits about her.

Mors Kajak's resolve did not waver. In all too short a time, his cup was drained. He rose, and his warriors rose as one with him.

"Hail and farewell, men of Zor," he said. "We go now to

battle, entrusting you with our most precious treasure. In one week we shall return for her and our other ladies, trusting to hear a good report of your entertainment. These two files of guardsmen will be left to your hospitality as well. They will answer with their lives for her safety."

At these words, a thundercloud gathered upon the brow of Jan Vajo. "Am I to suppose our royal court is not to be trusted with the care of the princess?" he growled. "I alone could defend her, and would! And besides that, I have all my loyal warriors at my back. Take your warriors to smite the green men. They are not needed here."

"It is not a matter of trust in your arms, which I doubt not are mighty," Mors Kajak said easily. "The honor of our princess requires that she be attended by the men of her own city at all times. Such is their fealty! If you wish not to host so many, but say the word, and our entire party will be gone and trouble you no more."

Jan Vajo's fist clenched upon his sword hilt. "By the bones of my ancestors!" he exclaimed.

Dejah Thoris observed that Dramus Ugo leaned closer to his jed and spoke some word in his ear, too softly to be heard by others. A sullen calm returned to Jan Vajo's face, and his fingers reluctantly let go their grasp of his weapon.

"By the bones of my ancestors," he repeated more agreeably, "if you are to lose two squads of doughty warriors to your solicitude for our lovely guest, you must allow me to make good that deficiency. I beg you will accept the loan of a similar number of my own men to swell your ranks. Thus shall we have some small part in your victory and prove our good will."

Mors Kajak relaxed his martial stance as well. "I accept your noble offer—provided your men can be ready at a moment's notice. The sun advances across the sky, and we would close with our enemies before night falls."

Dejah Thoris had not been favorably impressed by the Jed of Zor's intransigence toward her father, but she thought it spoke well of him that his soldiers seemed accustomed to instant obedience. In short order, the extra troops fell in with Mors Kajak's warriors, and her father took his leave.

4
QUAINT CUSTOMS OF ZOR

NOW, INDEED, MIGHT THE HEART of the princess have quailed, as she found herself, for the first time in her life, surrounded by none but strangers. Now the hitherto unwelcome presence of Ela Dusa and the familiar faces of her own servants brought comfort. However, as they were seated on the far side of the Zorian princess, Dejah Thoris could not turn to them for a reassuring smile.

Phortora offered no conversational opening. Dejah Thoris supposed the Zorian might consider her of higher rank and be awaiting her initiative. She offered the first polite question that came to mind. "Were you brought up together with the jed your brother, here in Zor?"

She thought there was a touch of frost in Phortora's answering smile. "No, indeed. I was fostered to a family of Hastor, and married to a chieftain of good family there. I did not see my noble brother again until my late husband was assassinated and I returned here with my young son. He has been my comfort. Zu Tith—he is full grown now and sits yonder at the table with other young officers. By rights he should be seated higher, but merit that blows not its own trumpet goes oft unrewarded."

"I see. I am sorry for your loss. I too have a brother, Kajan Dan. He is my elder, and is away on a scientific expedition, or he might have accompanied me."

"Your elder—so you, too, are unlikely to inherit your family's rule. And thus you begin the round of visits whereby your parents may find you a suitable husband and remove you from any possibility of intrigue. I know it well, my dear." Her lips curled in a smile that was not without cruelty.

The hot blood rushed to Dejah Thoris' cheeks before she fully realized the insult. On the verge of an angry reply, she put aside her injured pride and laughed merrily.

"Not at all—my dear," she said. "The women of Helium have no need to go in search of wooing. Indeed, our difficulty is to prevent our ardent men of war from throwing their swords at our feet. We have all we need at home within our own walls."

Now it was the Zorian's turn to bite her lip, her insinuations having missed their mark and rebounded upon herself.

Fortunately, at that point, the first course of the banquet was served. The dishes arrived in a quaint fashion that captured Dejah Thoris' full attention. The serving women who brought in trays of delicacies were clad in harness fringed with strings of beads and bells that clashed musically as they moved their limbs in rhythmic dance. Their long hair was braided behind them and ended with a tassel of tiny bells that chimed as they swung their heads and caused the braids to circle madly. At the same time, they held their trays of delicacies high and steady above their gyrations. Dejah Thoris clapped her hands in delight at their skill.

The first in line came to a graceful halt before Dejah Thoris and offered the tray. Before the princess could accept the appetizing morsel, Phortora interposed her hand. She pointed to one of the tidbits. The serving girl plucked the designated item from the tray and popped it into her own mouth. Phortora watched her closely as she chewed and swallowed. Then the Zorian gestured for Dejah Thoris to make her selection.

"Your pardon, Princess," she said. "Here at court, we practice the old customs of having our food tasted. Assassins are rife in this region. It sharpens the vigilance of our faithful servants to know that if they allow poison to slip into a dish, they will be the first to feel its bite."

This reminder checked the appetite of the princess briefly, but, resolved to honor her hosts, she went ahead and selected a few intriguing items.

"In Helium, too, we have our precautions," she said. "It has been long since a successful assassination was carried out within our walls, and still longer since an attempt was made within the palace grounds."

Phortora shrugged. "My brother allows the guilds much latitude—within reason, of course. He feels that a constant vigilance keeps our people on their toes, and prevents the formation of intrigues against his person. Men dare not assert their views too boldly when they know that those who stand out risk being cut to size by the shadow knives."

Finding it best not to comment, Dejah Thoris bit into an appetizer. It had a salty-sweet flavor she could not recall tasting.

"This is delicious," she said. "I've never encountered this flavor. What is it?"

"It is fish from the unknown waters," Phortora said. "One of the secrets of Zor. Certain families of the city have retained knowledge of the underground rivers that lead to the great sea that lies in the forbidden Valley Dor, from which no one returns. Within those dark waters lie creatures that have not been seen since the great seas perished. When our royal fishermen obtain their flesh, it is brought to us for the use of the court alone. You are tasting what no one has eaten in millennia, save for the court of Zor.

"Naturally, even the fishermen dare not venture too far into these waters. If one becomes lost, he is not searched for. He is considered to have made the last pilgrimage. We dare not risk sacrilege. Zor holds the Holy Things, and their guardians, the therns, in great respect."

Dejah Thoris was about to take another bite, when a sudden commotion broke out farther down the high table: a shriek, a shout, a clamor as guardsmen sprang to their feet. Like the rest of the table, Dejah Thoris also stood and craned her neck to view the alarm. A crash and clangor heralded the collapse of a table with all its utensils. Sprawled upon the table lay a servant in the metal of the court. His face was set in a horrid rictus, with purpled lips and staring dead eyes dyed bloody red. One hand clutched his own throat; the other was frozen in a clawing motion toward the tray of food that lay smashed around him.

Dejah Thoris turned in horror from the dreadful sight.

She heard the man called Dramus Ugo giving orders. A crew of stolid workers entered and carried away the dead man on the table where he had fallen. Serving girls quickly swept up and carried away the debris.

"Good friends," Dramus Ugo announced, "please continue the celebration. There is no need for alarm. A foolish and doomed attempt on the life of your jed has failed, as all such must. The perpetrator is being dealt with, and you may feast in safety."

The jed himself had remained in his seat throughout all the turmoil. Now he but waved a hand to indicate that the main course should be brought in.

Trumpets and drums heralded the march of brawny serving men, moving in step, with golden trays of roasted zitidar hoisted high. They slammed the immense haunches of meat to the tables with a resounding crash, then opened their mouths obediently to be fed random morsels of the meat, lest poison reside therein.

Dejah Thoris looked away, fearing a repetition of the earlier spectacle, but the new course was apparently harmless. Nevertheless, the aroma of the roast meat turned her stomach. She allowed herself to be served one of the roasted fruits that served as garnish, but as she cut it into dainty slices, its color reminded her of the dead man's flesh, and she pushed her plate away.

"Why, what ails you?" Phortora said playfully. "Here is nothing to fear. Surely you, daughter of a jed, have seen many such attempts."

"No, indeed," Dejah Thoris said faintly. "My father is loved by his people. No such incident has occurred within my memory."

"It is over now, and the assassin taken away. Come, do not stint your appetite. You must be hungry after your journey."

Dejah Thoris held her head high, that no tears should spill over and betray weakness. "In the presence of death, I confess I have lost my appetite. No disrespect intended to your cuisine, which I'm sure is excellent."

Phortora laughed. "You have been most tenderly nurtured. By the time I was your age, I was quite inured to the sight of death. I would have expected the same from the daughter of a jed."

The repeated taunting at last brought fire to the princess' eyes, and steel to her spine.

"My father's warriors are far too zealous to allow such disturbances to reach as far as the royal halls," she shot back in reply. "They deal with such schemes long before they can disturb the serenity of their princess. I grieve that your family was less well served. Perhaps your brother the jed can see that you dwell in greater ease."

She beckoned a serving man to the table and made great show of choosing a cut of roast meat and consuming an appropriate portion.

Now Phortora's cheeks must color in resentment of a well-placed verbal dart.

My royal father has often quoted the aphorism that a padwar must consume the rations that are put before him, Dejah Thoris thought grimly, as she forced down the rich meat. *Now I understand what he meant by that. I always believed that the part of a princess was to choose with delicacy and care, and put aside all that is unsuitable to one's rank. Now I see that there are times when the duty of rank means to accept with a smile that which one did not choose.*

Jan Vajo, who had hitherto been much occupied in conversation with his ministers on his right, and had not spoken a word to his guest, now turned to her with a smile.

"Well spoken, my gracious guest," he said. "Indeed, it is now my ambition to see to it that my royal sister may live in peace and cease to concern herself with matters of state. For too long, she has been forced to provide for her own protection. It is now my honor to serve her."

The proud Phortora bowed slightly in acknowledgment of his words, but it seemed to Dejah Thoris that she was less pleased than her manner indicated.

"I see you are enjoying our banquet," the jed continued.

"It was delightful, until Death intervened. As I was just saying to your royal sister, I seldom encountered such sights in Helium. I suppose we have as many assassins as any city of Barsoom, but my father's warriors would never allow them to breach our banqueting hall."

Jan Vajo shrugged. "Perhaps the Assassin's Guild here in Zor is more active than in some locations. I grant them much latitude, for I fear them not. They keep our young swordsmen on their toes, and instill enough caution in our lesser nobles to prevent them from engaging in dangerous intrigues."

"Pray explain further," Dejah Thoris said. "I do not understand how assassination can prevent intrigue. I have always thought that assassins were instruments of intrigue."

Jan Vajo seemed gratified by her interest. "It is simple. Ambitious houses may collude together to overthrow existing rule—my own, for example. In this endeavor, assassinations may indeed be useful. However, when such conspirators realize that they themselves may be picked off at any moment, they begin to question whether the game is worth the risk. If a rash word to a colleague can be followed at any moment by a blow from the shadows, it may seem better to them to watch their step and propose no impetuous action."

"Indeed, I see. You may be right," Dejah Thoris replied thoughtfully. "And yet, this seems a dangerous game for a ruler to indulge. One would have to be very certain of one's ability to observe and control such actions."

Jan Vajo smiled broadly. "To have the ulsio's view of every

detail, and the malagor's lofty oversight of every situation, is the duty of every ruler who would retain his sword and seat."

He gestured for more wine, and insisted that the princess' cup also be refilled. Then he clapped his hands. At this command, troops of armed and gaily plumed warriors ran out from opposite sides of the hall.

"Let our celebrations continue unchecked! We fear not the hand of man nor that of fortune."

The warriors paused to salute, then carried out a magnificently choreographed demonstration, half dance, half combat. Swords and javelins clashed, while drums thundered, and horns squealed as if in imitation of maddened fighting thoats.

Dejah Thoris contrived to appear to drink, while in reality she sipped most sparingly. Her lively interest in the spectacle was not entirely feigned. The performance could not but stir the heart of the descendant of a long line of warriors. It occurred to her, also, that those who could perform so skillfully in mock combat must be formidable warriors on a real battlefield. She noted this for report to her father.

"After the dance of war, the dance of beauty!"

Jan Vajo had leaned in to speak these words into her ear, over the applause still sounding—a little closer than seemed comfortable to the princess. She was accustomed to men who kept a respectful distance from her person. And the fumes of strong wine told her that the Jed of Zor had drunk deep where she had merely tasted.

She was grateful for the intervention of Ela Dusa, who also leaned closer and touched the arm of her princess before rising to her feet.

"Great Jed, I must beg your indulgence on behalf of my royal mistress," said Ela Dusa. "She is wearied with her journey, and ready to retire. Please give order for an escort to our accommodations."

Dejah Thoris inclined her head toward the jed.

"For myself and my ladies, I thank you for this magnificent entertainment," she said. "But indeed, we are weary and must ask to rest now. Alas, the beauties of your city must wait to be viewed by us at some later time."

Since the whole entourage was now on its feet, Jan Vajo had no choice but to rise in courtesy and bid them a good night. Phortora led them to the guest apartments, accompanied by a brace of the jed's guard and another pair of the princess' own cohort.

Dejah Thoris felt tremendous relief when the heavy doors closed behind them and she could relax in the company of people she knew and trusted. Not until now had she fully realized how tired she was. Her plea of exhaustion had been no ruse. She longed to divest herself of her heavily jeweled harness and recline on the couches provided. But before she could do so, she felt a responsibility to accompany Ela Dusa in a tour of the apartments, to ensure that her entourage was properly accommodated.

The rooms were less spacious and more fortress-like than the guest apartments of Lesser Helium. The room they had first entered seemed to be a leisure or entertainment area, equipped with the usual seats of wood or stone, curiously carved and made comfortable with rare furs and silken cushions. A table long enough to entertain a group stood against one wall, while smaller tables and lamps were scattered about the area in a manner suitable for reading, games, and private pursuits. An ornate jetan board with figures of pale and dark jade stood on one table. Two curtained archways opened in the far wall.

Passing through the embroidered hangings, Dejah Thoris saw that each doorway led to a chamber of similar size and shape, and these two chambers, in turn, were connected by another arch and separated only by more curtains. The latter feature added to the archaic feel of the rooms. Dejah Thoris recognized the remnants of a past where servants had been bound for life to their lords and mistresses. They were treated as mere instruments, and thus it was not thought necessary to provide for privacy between servant and master.

One chamber was clearly designed for the mistress. A massive sleeping platform was built into the corner. This was loaded with luxurious furs, and the wall behind it was carved and decorated with twining flowers whose stems were gilded and whose petals were precious stones. The wall next to it was pierced with a window to let in a fresh breeze. On the far side of the room, next to the archway that connected it to the other inner chamber, a more modest couch had been provided. It was comfortably furnished, but lacked the florid ornamentation of the other bed.

In the next room, sleeping platforms occupied most of the wall area, providing flexible space for a number of servants or companions. Ela Dusa's possessions had been placed by the smaller bed in the mistress' chamber. It was an awkward moment for Dejah Thoris. She would have preferred the privacy to which she was accustomed at home, but to banish her mother's friend to the servants' room seemed rude and peremptory.

It is only for a few nights, she told herself. *Soon my father will come for me.*

The servants were comfortably situated and occupied in unpacking and putting away their possessions. Seeing that her own pack was placed near her bed, Dejah Thoris returned to the living area and sank into a comfortable seat. Before she could summon one of her companions to assist her in removing her harness, Ela Dusa followed. The older lady sat next to her, bolt upright and in no attitude of relaxation.

"My princess," she said in a low voice, "It is my responsibility as your adviser and companion to warn you of my perceptions, as your royal mother would, if she were here."

A frown dimpled the smooth forehead of the princess.

Now by my blessed ancestors! she thought fretfully. *This is just what I feared. Now begin the incessant admonitions! As if I were not woman enough to draw my own conclusions.*

Yet, she was grateful to Ela Dusa for so smoothly managing their exit from the feast. She resolved to listen patiently.

"I know you have little experience with the insinuations of men, particularly those who are older and more masterful," Ela Dusa began impressively.

At this, Dejah Thoris could not help interrupting.

"I would have you recall that I have already had occasion to refuse several swords thrown at my feet," she said. "Certainly, I do have experience with the impetuosities of the male species."

The older woman brushed her comment aside in a most provoking manner. "True enough—but in your father's house, you are hedged about with extreme watchfulness. None would dare press his suit past your gracious refusal. Moreover, thanks to your father's and grandfather's care, you are surrounded by only the finest specimens of warrior youth. You have not been acquainted with the ways of those who would seize what they desire with an unscrupulous fist."

At this, Dejah Thoris, too, sat upright, unconscious pride tinging her cheeks with crimson.

"Of whom do you speak?" she demanded. "Surely you do not imply that the Jed of Zor, who has been honored by my father's company, could be such a man!"

Ela Dusa bowed her head. "I see that my words are like the raindrops of a former era—vanishing in the sand as soon as they are formed. I ask only that you be very sure of your own limits, my princess, and take care to give no encouragement to Jan Vajo to pass beyond them. I see that he is a masterful man, and one who is not used to accepting any bounds not set by himself. You are the pride of the house of Helium. Do not permit that to be forgotten."

"I assure you I have no such intention," Dejah Thoris replied haughtily. "Please, summon one of my servants. This harness vexes me with its sharp-edged gems, and my throat is dry and in need of cooling drink. Never has a guest been so poorly satisfied at what was meant to be a feast."

Ela Dusa sent Susho Llan, Dejah Thoris' favorite among the young women who had come with her, to bring refreshments. She returned shortly, followed by one of the palace servants bearing a tray and golden vessels, dewy with chill, bearing cold fruit juice enough for all the Heliumites. Ela Dusa insisted on tasting the drink herself. Dejah Thoris' heart again softened toward the older lady, on seeing her devotion.

"Is there anything else I can bring you, noble lady?" the servant inquired humbly. Dejah Thoris had noticed that the servants of Zor were treated much less as equals than those of Helium, and actually seemed to go in some fear of those above them in rank.

"Thank you, we are well provided for," she replied. "Yet, stay—I do have one question. I see no bath in our apartments. In Helium, we are accustomed to bathe daily."

"It is not the custom," the servant replied timidly, with downcast gaze. This was answer enough, for on Barsoom, custom is the supreme ruler of all. Dejah Thoris expected no further explanation, but the girl ventured one.

"Perhaps water is not so abundant as it is with you," she said. "We have the public baths at the hostels. And for the court, there is a garden terrace north of the palace. There one may find fountains and pools."

"Very good," Dejah Thoris said. "I shall inquire of the Lady Phortora. You may go."

A cold drink soothed her irritation somewhat, but she still longed for a refreshing plunge. She had to content herself with washing away the dust of travel with basin and ewer. These vessels, too, were of precious metal decorated with inlays of gems, but she reflected that they were not half so precious as the liquid they contained. Gems were plentiful on Barsoom, but life-giving substances, such as water and air, were rare and to be cherished with care. Dejah Thoris thought of her brother and sighed, hoping his expedition was proving more fruitful than her own had been so far. But tomorrow was another day, when she would see the spectacle for which she had come this far. The optimism of youth enabled her to plunge at last into the refreshment of sleep on an ancient planet.

5
THE GAMES BEGIN

IN SPITE OF BEING FAR FROM HOME, Dejah Thoris slept well, and awoke refreshed. She was sure that a tour of the city would provide more interest and excitement than being stuck between unsympathetic companions at a state banquet.

At her request, Susho Llan summoned the palace servants, who brought the princess a large golden basin and filled it with steaming hot water. With this, Dejah Thoris made shift to refresh herself. She apologized to Ela Dusa and her other ladies for the less commodious arrangements made for them.

"Before we engage in another dinner, I promise I will find out where noble ladies may bathe in this city," she said.

For this important day of the festival, she determined to wear a harness that was lighter in weight and less formal than her banquet garb. It was made not from leather straps, but rather of slender thongs gilded in several shades of gold and silver and braided together. Small gems were incorporated into the braids, so that they twinkled and shone without the ostentatious weight of large jewels. The harness included numerous hooks and fastenings, to which precious objects could be clipped. Thus, the wearer could adorn herself to suit the fancy of the day. Dejah Thoris selected a pleasing variety of precious heirlooms and more modern designs to decorate her harness. Since the jewels hung from small chains, they twirled about and caught the light as the wearer moved, accentuating her grace rather than impeding it with their weight. Delicate links of golden bells and pendants made a soft chiming sound as she moved. She was surrounded by a sparkle of light and melody that she found very pleasing. Her mother frowned on this outfit, and had put it aside while packing as being too informal, but Dejah Thoris had smuggled it into her baggage at the last minute.

She could see that Ela Dusa also frowned upon her garb, but chose to ignore her disapproving looks.

"Ah! This is so much more comfortable than my court harness," she exclaimed, shaking out her glossy dark locks before crowning them with a matching headdress, also adorned with golden bells. "I surely could not endure another day encrusted with several weights of diamonds!"

She chose some gauzy silks in delicate colors and arranged them artfully to float around her as she moved, and considered her toilette complete. Light sandals slipped onto her feet to protect them from the stones of the city streets.

Prepared for the day, she waited until trumpets announced the arrival of the princess Phortora to escort her to join the jed's procession to the arena of the games. The other women of Helium formed a guard of loveliness around her, and she felt her pride equal to the greatest splendors of the court of Zor.

Much to her relief, they were not escorted back to the banqueting hall. A cold collation of fruits and drinks awaited them in the courtyard. Just beyond, Dejah Thoris could hear the stamping and bellowing of war-thoats under saddle.

With an additional portentous braying of trumpets, the jed's contingent formed ranks and began to move forward. A cadre of warriors mounted on thoats led the way, each riding double with a banner-bearer or a trumpeter, as the parade swept into a deeply cut gateway through the walls of the palace. They emerged from its shade into the sunlight, and proceeded down the street to the sound of deafening cheers that echoed from the stone walls on either side.

Dejah Thoris craned her neck in vain to see more of the city. The Heliumetic ladies were flanked on either side by tall, well-armed guardsmen in tight formation. It was difficult to see past their ranks. She was able to catch glimpses of the upper stories of the buildings that lined the street, and could see that their balconies were thronged with citizens in festive garb, waving lengths of many-colored silks and tossing down showers of brilliantly hued flower petals to brighten the way of their jed and his guests. She lifted her hand and waved in acknowledgment of their tribute, hoping that some of those above might see her.

Their way descended from the eminence of the jed's residence, but soon began to wind upward again, until it reached a broad, sweeping ramp. There, the thoats ceased to accompany them, and stood guard on either side of the upward-curving way. "Stood," of course, being a relative word, as the irascible beasts trampled back and forth, jockeying for position among their fellows, and being constantly compelled to hold their positions only by the most strenuous mental exertions of their riders.

After ascending several turns of the spiral, the procession passed through a portico, and came out at last on a viaduct that arched over the street, and finally gave Dejah Thoris a vantage point. She was ushered to the front, along with Phortora, the jed, and his jedwar and counselors, so that the populace might view them and do homage. In turn, she enjoyed for the first time a panoramic view of the city. Like so many other aspects of Zor, its architecture seemed rooted in an archaic mode. The streets were narrow enough that it was difficult for riding beasts and cartage to pass in opposite directions. She saw none of the effortlessly gliding vessels that carried the people of Helium to any destination too distant for easy pedestrian access. If the families gathered on balconies at all levels were any indication, most of the dwellings of Zor had been built into its walls of solid stone. There were few homes surrounded by gardens and constructed around a pillar upon which they could be raised at night to avoid assassins.

No wonder the Assassins' Guild runs rampant here, she thought, all the while smiling and waving graciously. *How can these people sleep at night?*

As she scanned the upturned faces in the street, her eye was drawn to one figure that resembled nothing she had seen before. An endless sea of lustrous dark locks and red-bronze faces, familiar to her throughout her life, was interrupted by a shadow given solid form. As the crowd swept toward her, the shadow-shape moved too, walking like a man. Her body tingled as if with a chill. As the shadow drew closer, she thought she could perceive an indistinct, manlike form hidden within a shroud of impermeable black silk. This, surely, must be a thern—one of that most secretive of the races of Barsoom, the hidden guardians of the way to eternal bliss in the Valley Dor! Dejah Thoris, like all the children of the Red Planet, had been told of the therns and their sacred duty. Yet, although she knew, too, that they moved invisibly through every city of the red race, she had never seen one, even in this all-concealing disguise. Her skin crawled at the thought of being cut off from the free air by a confining shroud of fabric. *Therns must be very different from myself*, she thought, *if they can endure such a discipline.*

She stared, paralyzed, not knowing whether she should bow in submission, or hide her face and pretend she had not seen. Her mind tingled as had her skin, with a sensation she recognized as the attempt of one Martian mind to read the contents of another. Instinctively, she resisted. All of the red race were capable of some degree of resistance to the telepathy endemic to Barsoom. The princess had learned from her parents in her youngest years that the ruling family of Helium had an unusually strong capacity for erecting such mental barriers. This talent served them well in their role as leaders of their city, and Dejah Thoris' parents had taken pains to see that it was well developed in their daughter. The intrusive, prickling sensation faded as she blocked it.

The dark apparition below billowed out like a sail, or like

a flag being raised. Moments later, as if in response to a signal, a spatter of fist-sized projectiles hurtled toward the procession. Before Dejah Thoris could react, several of her Heliumetic warriors surrounded her with raised shields. The projectiles crashed against the shields, as she was snatched away from the balustrade, back to the center of a protective phalanx.

She struggled to see what was happening, but dozens of well-muscled warriors blocked her view. As they double-timed around a corner, she got a glimpse beneath the arm of one of the guards. She could see no sign of the shadow-apparition. It had vanished as mysteriously as it had come. The crowd was pushing and shoving to get away from a dense mist of purplish hue that concealed the spot where it had stood. A whiff of the smoke, ascending to her nostrils, made her cough painfully and brought tears to her eyes. She heard others coughing in the column behind her. Ahead, she heard the penetrating voice of the lady Phortora protesting against her unceremonious handling by the guard.

"This is not the way to protect the sister of your jed! Shame on you, feeble excuses for fighting men, afraid of a little smoke! Let go of me at once! I demand it!"

The column slowed to a more decorous marching pace as it reached a broad terrace, surmounted by a high wall broken only by a set of antique bronze doors, now standing open. Here the close ranks of their escort parted, and once again Dejah Thoris beheld an intriguing vista. Descending a shallow incline, she found herself on the balcony of a large arena. The crowds she had seen in the streets were already pouring into the rings of stone benches on the lower level. The thoat-riders who had accompanied the parade took up positions of guard at the main doors. Again, the members of the royal party showed themselves and received the adulation of the audience. Dejah Thoris noted, with a satisfaction that was not entirely kind, that Phortora's hair arrangement had been partially disheveled by their unexpected encounter. The Zorian princess snapped at her ladies as they attempted to repair the damage. Dejah Thoris chose to smile pleasantly as she was escorted to her seat, between Phortora and Jan Vajo himself.

The jed seemed in an expansive mood in spite of the disturbance.

"How are you enjoying the prospect of our fair city?" he said, gesturing to the scene before them.

Dejah Thoris attempted to frame a courteous answer, one that did not reflect her impression that Zor was a survival of an antique era.

"I confess I have seen much less of Zor than I would like. My view this morning has been much obstructed by the shields and brawny thews of your doughty fighting men. I could not understand from what we were fleeing. Was this yet another ploy of the assassins?"

Jan Vajo leaned back at his ease, toying with a large golden medallion that formed the centerpiece of his glittering harness.

"Mists and vapors," he said carelessly. "Who can say what their purpose might have been? My jedwar, Ptang Raxo, is ever zealous for my safety, and it is he who ordered my men to form the protective phalanx. I give you leave to scold him at your leisure."

The hard-faced warrior on the far side of Dramus Ugo bowed stiffly. He seemed resentful of his master's jesting mood.

"I saw one sight today in Zor that I have never seen before," Dejah Thoris mused.

"And what might that have been?"

"In the street below us, a manlike form shrouded in silks as black as a night without moons, covered from head to toe as no other person I have ever seen. By this mysterious appearance, I could think it nothing other than a thern. Your sister Phortora has told me how greatly the men of Zor honor the Holy Therns, but by my honored ancestors, I never thought to see one with my own eyes. This form appeared just before the projectiles scattered purple mist, and after that I could see it no more."

The man named Dramus Ugo, seated at the right hand of the jed, leaned forward to fix his gaze upon Dejah Thoris. His fist clenched upon his breast as if her words disturbed him. She saw that what his fingers clasped with such force was a medallion similar in design to that which adorned the harness of his jed.

Again she felt the inner pressure that indicated someone was trying to penetrate the veil of her thought. Again she resisted automatically and forcefully. But this time, although the sensation diminished, it did not vanish.

"Phortora speaks truth," Jan Vajo said. "We men of Zor have honored the Holy Ones in a special way since before the seas withdrew from our shores. I do not wish to cast doubt on any observation of my honored guest, but it seems most unlikely you could have seen one of those beloved of Issus on the street today. Permit me to suggest that the excitement may have been too much for you. This may have been an apparition or a vision, not a real thing."

Dramus Ugo, frowning, bent a dark look upon her.

"No thern would so demean himself as to walk the streets unattended, in such a crowd," he said. "Yet the princess may not have been mistaken. Some foolish fellow may have disguised himself for merriment at the festival. Worse yet, an assassin may have thought to take this honored form to assist him in approaching the royal party. Give me leave, O Jed, to search for the perpetrator and punish him."

The jed frowned in turn. "Do as you please, my good counselor. But pray restrain your indignation until after the festival. I wish our games to be a time of pleasure for my people and our honored guest, not an opportunity for another of your inquisitions."

Dramus Ugo settled back into his chair begrudgingly.

"I meant no harm to the people of Zor," Dejah Thoris said. "I thought it a strange occurrence that might intrigue the jed. Please don't punish anyone on my account. I know not what I saw. I may have been mistaken."

She felt certain that she was right, but she had no wish to engage in conflict between the jed and his counselor.

Jan Vajo smiled upon her, evidently pleased by her conciliatory tone. He rose to his feet and offered her his hand to do likewise. Raising his other hand in command, he silenced the buzz of the crowd that now filled the arena to capacity.

"People of Zor, and honored guests," he boomed in a strong baritone, "I hereby open the Games of Zor. Let all who would compete stand forth! And let the referees conduct our competition in good order. Behold our chosen Supreme Arbiter for this year's games—Dejah Thoris, Princess of Helium and daughter of its mighty jed, Mors Kajak, son of Tardos Mors! Let the presence of such grace and beauty inspire all combatants to reach the heights!"

With a flourish, he presented her with a baton, carved of ivory that might have come from the tusk of a green warrior, from the horn of one of the beasts of the far north, or from some sea creature of ancient times.

Dejah Thoris thrilled to the roar of approbation that followed the introduction. She bowed to all sides as the audience threw flowers in her direction. Trumpets sounded a fanfare, and from gates in the lower level of the area, the first wave of contestants marched forth to salute.

The arena had been marked off into a dozen separate rings. In each of these, a pair of fighters faced off for a hard-fought duel. Thus, all sides of the arena could view a fight at close range. Those in the royal balcony had an overview of all rings. Dejah Thoris glanced eagerly from one to another, hardly able to choose which was more exciting, and which warriors more merited her attention and admiration. Unconsciously, she bit her lip and pressed her hands together in suspense. Her quickened breathing and her upright posture on the edge of her golden seat highlighted her vitality and youth. Unknown to her, the Jed of Zor watched her more than he watched the games, and took evident pleasure in the sight.

Wave after wave of contestants took their places in the ring.

Soon, the less skilled dropped out, and the favorites battled for victory. The jed was not too distracted by his lovely guest to wager in animated style with his jedwar, Ptang Raxo. The two of them shouted in joy and grimaced in defeat as their chosen champions rose or fell. Dejah Thoris could not help taking a lively interest in their choices, learning from them which fighters were most outstanding, and soon she too was cheering on those who struggled to be the best of the best. Privately, she thought she had never seen so many examples of handsome youth sparring for glory, and wondered if her father might be moved to institute such a spectacle in Helium.

Surely, she thought, *our own men of Helium could outdo these fellows, and how glorious that would be to behold.*

Dramus Ugo seemed indifferent to the joys of the game and placed no wagers, but he was soon pressed into service as scorekeeper, as the winnings changed hands at a great pace.

As the sun rose toward the zenith, the number of rings in action dwindled, until only the center ring still held contestants. Their battle was prolonged, for both were fine swordsmen, and both, it seemed to Dejah Thoris, were attempting that most subtle of victories—to dominate one's adversary without killing him. Nonetheless, they were at each other hammer and tongs, neither one giving ground. Although no crippling blows were dealt, again and again they marked each other, until blood flowed with the sweat that gleamed along their limbs and was shaken from their harness. The audience rose to its feet, cheering wildly. At last the swordsman who, to Dejah Thoris' eyes, had been slightly the weaker of the two made some error in his footwork that passed almost too quickly to see, and his opponent closed with him, wrung the blade from his hand with a powerful stroke, and had his own blade's tip at the man's throat. The loser yielded, dropping to one knee, and a shower of blossoms nearly obliterated the winner as the audience roared its approval.

Hesitant, Dejah Thoris looked to the jed for instructions as to her function as Arbiter of the games.

"Simply rise and extend your baton toward the winner, and declare him champion," he said. "He and the winners of lesser prizes will take some moments to compose themselves and have their injuries tended. Then they will approach to receive their rewards."

This was speedily done. The fighters then retired from the arenas, and the sellers of refreshments flocked into the stands to regale the now-thirsty audience.

Jan Vajo laughed. "I feel myself almost as much out of breath as if I had fought that bout myself." He called for a round of chilled wine to be served to all on the balcony. "And send some, with the compliments of the jed, to the fighters down below. I'll wager their need is greater than mine."

When the wine arrived, he raised his cup to Dejah Thoris. "And I have you to thank, loveliest of arbiters, for my successful wagers. My jedwar will pay me tribute tonight."

He toasted her, his gaze ever fixed on her face.

Blushing, she pretended an interest in choosing sweetmeats, and turned to Phortora to ask what came next.

Unlike the rest of the audience, that lady seemed distracted and ill-pleased. She answered Dejah Thoris' query, but with little grace.

"Now comes an intermission entertainment. It has nothing to do with the competition. It is merely a crowd-pleaser to allow the contestants a breathing space. And the audience as well—these games seem more endless every year. To be sure, some find them exciting, but for my own part, I would rather be at home in my garden as befits a lady of standing, not showing myself to the crowd in this vulgar manner."

For a moment, Dejah Thoris was stung by her words, and wondered if she had been putting herself forward in an unseemly fashion. But in the next moment, she forgot anything Phortora might have intended to say.

The gates in the lower level opened once more, and a contingent of six well-armed warriors swarmed out, to form a semicircle in the middle of the arena. As they stood on guard, a central and larger gate opened to let in a monstrous creature.

It took a moment for Dejah Thoris to realize its size. Bounding forward, it uttered an ear-splitting howl of rage. Answering shrieks sounded from the audience, as many of the fair sex covered their ears. Even some of the male spectators flinched and paled.

The massive white ape advanced on the warriors with its upper limbs outstretched. Two of the fighters fell back a pace to bring their bows into play. Their first arrows struck the ape's torso, but failed to stop it for more than an instant. The creature paused to pluck the irritating darts away, but then attacked with yet more speed and fury.

Two more warriors intercepted its charge with javelins hurled at close range. The spearheads penetrated deeper, and the ape howled, batting at them ineffectually. In one more bound, he was upon the fighting men.

The first of the javelin throwers was hurled through the air with a single blow of the ape's clawed hand. He crashed to the ground, bleeding from a dozen wounds dealt by its talons. This was the first serious injury Dejah Thoris had seen. She leaned over the rail, her heart in her mouth.

"Will no one help him!" she cried, turning toward Jan Vajo in the expectation that he would send someone to rescue his subject. But the jed's eyes were fixed on the battle, with enjoyment but little alarm.

Two more warriors attempted to engage the beast with their swords. They jabbed at the ape, dancing to and fro, unwilling to close with it to deliver a killing blow. One of them tripped over a spent arrow. He lost his balance for only a moment before regaining his feet, but it was long enough for the ape to cover the ground between them in one careless bound, and to seize the luckless fighting man between the two fists of its middle arms. With these, it hugged him to its rank and bloody torso. He uttered one cry as it squeezed the breath out of him. His convulsive struggles were useless. With its upper arms, the ape slashed out with its talons, warding off rescue.

The princess' hands were at her throat, in unconscious sympathy with the breathless warrior. Her own panting respiration agitated her fair bosom. Had she seen the reactions of those around her, she might have been yet more agitated. Far from pitying the plight of the combatants, Jan Vajo's eyes were once more drawn to his guest, finding pleasure in the play of lively emotion that animated every limb. Phortora's gaze, beneath lowered eyelids, also rested on Dejah Thoris, and her face, too, was animated by emotion, but not a countenance of sympathy. The long fingers of the jed's sister unconsciously twisted the strands of her ruby necklace to the breaking point, and its gems showed against her clutching hands like drops of blood.

6
PRINCESS AND ARBITER

DEJAH THORIS HAD NO THOUGHT for how others perceived her. Her eyes were fixed on the combat below. The bowmen regrouped and again sent a hail of arrows toward the ape. At risk of striking their comrade in his death struggles, they aimed at the creature's head. Most of the arrows struck against the ape's impenetrable skull, opening gashes in their flight but falling aside. One lucky dart reached the ape's eye and buried itself deep. The ape shrieked, but did not let go its prey.

The javelin wielders scrambled to retrieve their weapons. As they jabbed at the ape's feet in hopes of toppling it, the second swordsman ran at the ape. In an acrobatic feat of courage, he sprang upward, gaining brief purchase upon the ape's bent knee for long enough to climb its torso and grasp the arrow protruding from its eye like the rung of a ladder. The ape flailed at him, but could not see him clearly. With powerful blows from his sword, the warrior slashed the ape's neck nearly in two, and adroitly leaped away as its massive bulk tottered toward the ground and fell.

A raucous cheer thundered from the stands. Once the ape had been blinded, servants approached with blunted hooks and nets and towed away the first wounded man. The second victim was recovered, with some difficulty, from beneath the ape's body. A second cheer went up when he was found to be still breathing, and able to be carried off in a litter to be treated for his bruises and cracked ribs.

The remaining fighters accepted the plaudits of the crowd and turned to retire.

Before they could leave, Dejah Thoris leaped to her feet, raising the Arbiter's baton.

"Stop!" she cried. "The Arbiter commands it!"

Startled, they looked toward the source of the ringing tones.

"Dejah Thoris, Princess of Helium and Arbiter of the games, asks the name of the swordsman who slew the white ape."

The swordsman saluted her. "Kan Vastor, at your service."

"By my power as Arbiter, I declare you worthy of the same prize as the champion of these games. For your valor, you are ordered to attend the awards ceremony and receive the reward of your merit."

He and his team bowed low before leaving the arena.

Jan Vajo's gaze was fixed on Dejah Thoris again, but in surprise and indignation. "By my glorious ancestors, you take much upon yourself."

She extended the baton to him, with a smile.

"I thought that when you gave me this, you extended your royal powers to me, while the games lasted. If I have done amiss, pray take back the baton and your place as judge."

His frown lingered for a moment, but then he shook his head and waved away the offered artifact of authority. "No, no, you say well—I had given you that power. You but took me by surprise."

"May I explain myself?" she inquired, with charming deference designed to turn away displeasure.

He could not but yield with a smile. "I confess that at first I was motivated simply by admiration for so bold a deed. But then it occurred to me that your purpose as jed, in hosting these games, must be more than amusement for your people. I surmised that you seek to recognize examples of merit and service to the city, so that all may admire and emulate those virtues. Thus you stir up the spirit of the city and its fighting men, to the benefit of all."

By this time Jan Vajo was beaming again. "You say well. Continue!"

"In such case it seems obvious that the man who dared true combat with a deadly creature, and risked his own life to rescue a comrade, has shown the highest virtues of a fighting man, and should be rewarded along with those who merely won a contest through superior skill. As much as the city benefits from ambition and training, raw courage is yet more essential. Would you not agree, O Jed?"

"Certainly," he responded enthusiastically. "Young Kan Vastor shall receive the same reward as today's champion—fine weapons, a place in the palace guard, and a gold armlet as a token of his jed's favor."

Ptang Raxo was the one to frown now. He spoke a muttered complaint in the jed's ear, but Dejah Thoris' ears were sharp enough to catch it.

"O Jed," he said, "Perhaps you had forgotten my reasons for placing this Kan Vastor in the ring with the ape. It was to punish him for being too forward in his rash actions, for seeking too much glory. Shall we now reward the same?"

"Come now, my good jedwar," said the jed, "if you call this kind of valor 'rash action,' perhaps it is you who should rethink your assessment. Let's have no more of this quibbling. It is time we took some refreshment and relaxation before the contests of the afternoon begin."

The royal party left the balcony for a richly appointed inner chamber, where comfortable couches and a buffet were provided. The common people in the bleachers were left to eat their lunches and stretch their legs.

In the refreshment room, Jan Vajo proved all too attentive, with repeated offers of food and drink that Dejah Thoris had to find increasingly inventive ways of declining courteously. She found the Zorian wine too strong, and chilled juice was all she really craved. To prevent Jan Vajo being always at her elbow, she chose to stroll about the room with Phortora.

By now, she neither liked nor trusted the jed's sister, but Phortora often inadvertently revealed facts of interest.

"What may we look forward to in the afternoon's entertainment?" she asked, as Phortora paused to look out on the loggia at the rear of the room.

"Hopefully to no more surprises from our impetuous Arbiter." Phortora spoke lightly, as if her words were meant as a jest, but her expression was sour. Seeing her brother's eye upon her, she continued hastily.

"The afternoon is more relaxing. It is reserved for the women's competitions. These are, for the most part, exhibitions of skill in archery, pistol marksmanship, gymnastics, and so forth. Pretty, but not so engaging as the morning's combat. At the end, however, there will be something more interesting. There are a few young women who choose to exhibit their martial talents, and these bouts provide the climax to the games. The winner is rewarded with honors, like the winner of men's games. They too are offered a place at court, if they desire it. I always take an interest in these matches, since I may gain an addition to my entourage. They seldom stay long, of course. Usually they are married off within a year. Indeed, I think that is the chief inducement to enter the contests. Young women hope to catch the eye of some eligible fighting man of rank."

She popped a plump fruit into her mouth. "My royal brother will probably wager less on the afternoon's entertainment. But I have a favorite in the games—a daughter of friends who would be welcome among my ladies. I believe she is quite likely to be victorious.

"And speaking of eligible fighting men—" She beckoned imperiously to someone on the far side of the room.

A warrior approached, and greeted them with a flourish.

"Kaor, my mother! And you, honored guest!"

"My son, Zu Tith," Phortora said.

On Barsoom, where men and women hatch from eggs and speedily attain their full growth, remaining in the halcyon state of youth and vigor for a thousand years thereafter, barring some accident, it can be hard to assess the age of a stranger. Dejah Thoris conjectured from Zu Tith's sleek red-bronze skin and bright eyes that he was not long out of the egg, and was perhaps younger than she herself. Either he had not reached his full growth, or he was small of stature for some other reason, for he stood somewhat less than eye to eye with her, where most men of Barsoom are taller than their female counterparts.

She noticed a second anomaly in his appearance. The women of Barsoom often arrange their hair in fanciful yet becoming shapes, but the men wear their locks unconstrained. Zu Tith's head was shaved in a wide swath on one side, and adorned at the end of that swath with a pair of tiny braids.

She hastily turned her curious gaze away from Phortora's son, for he was looking her over in a manner that disturbed her. She was used to looks of admiration, but in the city of Helium, respect and deference were mingled in such a gaze. Zu Tith surveyed her up and down with a cool arrogance that spoke more of one shopping for a decorative item or a tender haunch of thoat than a warrior beholding a sovereign. She had sensed some of this cool acquisitive air in Jan Vajo, as well. Perhaps it was more pardonable in a jed, but it was not to her liking in either case.

Customs certainly are different in other cities, she thought. Not for the first time, she felt homesick for the towers of Helium.

"I see that you have chosen to offer favor to Kan Vastor," Zu Tith said. "If my mother has not already done so, I would caution you, by your leave, to walk carefully with that one. He is not in favor with Ptang Raxo, and hence with the jed, who takes from the jedwar all the advice he does not get from Dramus Ugo."

Dejah Thoris found his tone offensive, but decided to practice statecraft.

I am here to learn, she reminded herself.

"Why is this young warrior out of favor?" she asked.

Zu Tith was pleased to adopt a confidential tone that could not be overheard. "He puts himself forward too much. He takes too many risks, always seeking to demonstrate his courage rather than obediently remaining in the ranks behind his commanders."

Dejah Thoris questioned him with wide eyes of innocence. "How should a young warrior win glory, if not by demonstrating his courage, as Kan Vastor did today?"

"Glory is for the commanders, not those in the ranks who obey. The duty of a warrior is to submit and follow."

"And how does one rise from the ranks to be one of those who are obeyed, without showing courage and winning glory?"

To this, Zu Tith did not reply.

Dejah Thoris tossed her head disdainfully. "I should think it a poor, colorless world without brave young men who take too many risks."

Let him consider her a silly girl who thought only of well-ornamented young men! She would do her best to keep her judgment of him to herself. She wished briefly that she were at home where she could tell her mother about the odious people she had encountered in Zor.

The earlier sensations of pressure on her skull had returned. Again someone was trying to find access to her thoughts. She had no fear that whoever it was would succeed, but the pressure was unpleasant. The jed was looking in her direction, his hand on the medallion that decorated his chest. She thought he was displeased to see her in conference with Zu Tith. It seemed Phortora's son was not in favor with his uncle, either. She smiled and moved in Jan Vajo's direction. His expression immediately brightened.

"Come," he said, "it is time to return to our seats. You have seen our fighting men. Now you will behold our beauty in action."

The crowds streamed back into the arena. All signs of combat had been swept away, with fresh ring markings placed on raked sand. A brief fanfare of trumpets summoned all to attention, followed by stirring airs from pipes, cymbals, and the intricately coiled Barsoomian woodwinds. To the sound of this music, a score of young women ran lightly forth from the lower gates.

They were armed with bows and radium pistols. Through a choreographed interweaving of their paths, they divided into three groups. Two of these immediately began a marksmanship competition with their respective weapons. The third group rolled out a variety of apparatus and launched into gymnastic evolutions that would almost have caused the spectators to believe that the red race had learned to fly. Dejah Thoris could hardly keep up with all there was to see. She wondered how the judges in the ring could keep track of the points awarded. The three groups traded places until all had exhibited their skills. This phase of the competition culminated in all of the contestants performing acrobatic feats while aiming their weapons at the targets at one end of the ring. Not all of their shots reached the goal, but the mere attempt was a pleasure to watch.

Dejah Thoris was particularly engaged by one of the young women who seemed to her outstanding not just for skill, but for the vivacity and impish exuberance that seemed to radiate from her every move. If the contestants were jumping, she would jump highest. If arrows were in play, hers would be the swiftest. The princess hoped that the judges were seeing things as she did, and that she would have the opportunity to bestow an award on her favorite.

The contestants then divided into pairs to face off within the rings for the sparring competition. For this they were armed with skeel-wood practice weapons. Dejah Thoris' preferred candidate defeated one opponent after another, until she battled in the center ring against the sole remaining foe. This was a lovely young woman whose winning appearance could not be denied, but whose sword skill seemed unequal to her other graces. Dejah Thoris was perplexed by how she had achieved this final ranking, and expected her smaller opponent to defeat her handily.

It seemed the bout would end as the princess expected. But, as the more skilled young woman pressed her opponent back to the very edge of the ring, events took an unanticipated turn. One of the defeated competitors, who formed an audience to the bout, moved too close to the ring, appearing to stumble, and in so doing, thrust out a foot at the exact spot where one of the swordswoman's nimble leaps must land. The fighter could not check her momentum, and tumbled head over heels to land with her opponent's sword at her throat.

She who had been so close to defeat raised her hands in a gesture of victory over her fallen foe. The audience leaped to its feet, some cheering, others shouting indignantly. Dejah Thoris saw that Phortora was one of those who were on their feet applauding with approval. The girl in the ring bowed to right and left, assuming triumph and scorning even to glance at her fallen opponent, who by now had risen to her feet and stood looking at the judges in vain for succor.

Fired with indignation, Dejah Thoris again raised her baton.

"Silence!" she cried. "Silence, for the judgment of the Arbiter!"

The roar of the crowd died away. Dejah Thoris found herself alone, the target of all eyes, while Phortora's venomous gaze bored holes in her back. Only her indignation supported her.

"I declare a foul committed upon this competitor," she said. "What is your name?"

The young woman who had fallen, her bosom heaving, caught enough breath to declare herself.

"I am Parvia, Princess, of no other name or nation. I bow to your judgment."

And bow she did, gracefully as she did all else, while her erstwhile opponent stood with clenched fists, looking past the fair Arbiter to Phortora.

"Let the opponents face off again!" Dejah Thoris cried. "Let them continue until a fair decision is achieved, without interference! Let all spectators step back ten paces and dare not to transgress the ring again! I have spoken!"

All eyes turned to the jed, who extended his arm and nodded his assent.

The jed's sister swept past Dejah Thoris, elbowing her in passing, to speak in the jed's ear. He turned away from her and resumed his seat.

"Let the match begin!" he commanded.

Dramus Ugo took the arm of the incensed Phortora and led her aside, whispering to her.

Dejah Thoris remained standing, leaning over the parapet, her attention fixed on the games.

The match began, and ended almost as swiftly. As before, Parvia drove her opponent to the edge of the ring. Not content to push the loser out of the ring, Parvia nimbly stepped inside her opponent's guard, seized her by arm and harness, and flipped her over her head to land asprawl on the sand. Parvia set her foot upon the other woman's arm, twisted the sword from her hand, and stood in triumph with her sword's point at the other woman's throat.

A roar of approval for her reversal of the previous circumstances arose from the audience. Even the privileged viewers in the royal box cheered her—with the exception of Phortora and Dramus Ugo.

In that moment, when all eyes were turned to the ring, a flicker of movement caught the attention of Dejah Thoris. Before she could turn to her right, one of the male warriors from the earlier tournament had already climbed the wall of the balcony, and was in the act of vaulting over its parapet, drawing his sword as he landed.

Dejah Thoris' hand went to her hidden blade, as the powerfully built swordsman moved with lightning speed toward the royal seats.

Jan Vajo, equally powerful and a hand taller, rose to his

feet, blocking the attacker's way toward the princess. But, instead of engaging the swordsman to defend her, he turned swiftly and bounded away as Ptang Raxo followed to protect his jed.

Dejah Thoris stood alone before the assassin.

Alone—until a whirlwind in human flesh appeared from the far end of the balcony to knock her aside without ceremony and fall upon the intruder with a flashing blade. Picking herself up from the floor, Dejah Thoris moved away from the clash of swords, to avoid being trampled by the swift-moving feet.

Tossing back her disheveled hair, she was astonished to see the face of her defender. It was Kan Vastor, the young warrior she had commended for his courageous defeat of the white ape. His arms still bandaged from the wounds of the arena, he had seen the onslaught and sped to the defense of the princess.

From a mere arm's length away, Dejah Thoris viewed the cut-and-parry of hot battle between two skilled combatants. She feared for the young man, for his enemy outweighed him and fought with aggressive fury. Kan Vastor showed a cool head and acrobatic dexterity. The attacker aimed a fierce blow at his body, but Kan Vastor, with a mighty leap, attained the next row of stone seats, and from there struck at the other man's head, slicing open his scalp. Stunned, the attacker wavered and let his guard drop a fraction. Kan Vastor sprang upon him from above, bearing him to the ground, where he slashed the man's sword from his hand and laid his own sword across the man's throat.

"Yield, and I spare you!"

The fallen warrior convulsed in an effort to head-butt the younger man. Kan Vastor's sword cut into his throat, and he convulsed again, in his death throes.

Dejah Thoris turned away her eyes. She shuddered as she recovered from her frozen state too late to avoid the flow of blood that besmirched her feet.

Kan Vastor made as if to assist her, but recognized his own bloody and disheveled state.

"Someone, see to the princess!" he cried.

Dejah Thoris sank down on a more distant bench as some of Jan Vajo's guard returned from their master's side to aid her. Haughtily, she waved them away.

"I am well," she said. "Kan Vastor has seen to that."

Her own Heliumetic guards pushed forward from the rear benches where they had been constrained to sit by Zorian protocol. Falling at her feet in apology for their tardy arrival, they were assured of her well-being and then took up positions of belligerent vigilance behind her.

Jan Vajo returned, walking with his usual commanding stride and appearing not in the least disturbed by his display of what any Barsoomian would consider contemptible cowardice—to leave a woman in the path of destruction.

Before Dejah Thoris could resist, he took her hand and drew her to her feet.

"I regret that you had such a fright," he said. "You were in no danger. The assassin's attack was intended for me."

Had Mors Kajak been there, such insolence would not have gone unpunished.

"Then I am pleased to see you in good health," Dejah Thoris replied coolly. "You will surely wish to reward Kan Vastor for his valiant deeds in defense of your person."

"He shall be rewarded as he deserves," Jan Vajo said, bestowing but a nod to the young warrior who stood with breast still heaving from his exertions.

"Remove this carrion from our sight," Jan Vajo commanded. Guards lifted the body and tumbled it over the wall, into the arena, as the swiftest method of disposal. Others came with sand and brooms to clean the blood from the stones.

The jed guided Dejah Thoris to another seat, where the interposed bodies of her guard shielded her from the site of carnage.

"Be seated, all," he ordered his entourage. "This interruption shall not be allowed to interfere with our ancient customs, nor to disturb the enjoyment of our people. Have the contestants anoint and attire themselves as befits those to be honored. The awards shall proceed shortly."

He still kept his hold on Dejah Thoris' hand. Much as she desired to free herself, she scorned to struggle.

"Preceding all other awards, I desire to reward her whose judgment and courage have made these games exceptional." He spoke more tenderly than she had heard before, and attempted to look into her eyes. She averted her gaze.

He snapped his fingers, and Dramus Ugo, upon one knee, offered him a wooden box, intricately carved and inlaid with precious metals.

Jan Vajo relinquished her hand to reach for the contents of the box. Dejah Thoris immediately folded her hands in her lap, hoping to avoid a recurrence of unwanted contact.

Jan Vajo lifted from the box a medallion of gold and jewels, marked with an archaic symbol of unknown meaning. He lifted it high so that all might see.

"Behold the medallion of service to the city of Zor," he intoned, "a device that has descended to us from our revered ancestors. On this day, I award it to Dejah Thoris, Princess of Helium, in token of her valuable service as Arbiter of these games, and in honor of her friendship for our city."

He turned to her again.

"As you see," he said, "this medallion is identical to that which I wear upon my own breast as Jed of Zor, and that which also is borne by my most trusted advisors, Dramus Ugo and Ptang Raxo. I bear it very close to my heart."

He leaned closer to point out the medallion that occupied a central location in his ornate harness. She pulled away, but he pressed in to clip the award to her harness. His fingers came near to brushing her flesh. Heart pounding, she shot to her feet, mere inches between himself and her person.

"Such a task is not for one of your lofty rank," she cried. "Where are my ladies? Ela Dusa! Your princess requires you!"

The faithful lady in waiting pushed past Phortora and hastened to Dejah Thoris' side. With the older woman present, Jan Vajo was forced to take a step back. Dejah Thoris took the medallion from his hands and gave it to Ela Dusa.

"I accept your gift in the spirit in which it was given," she said. "May the friendship of Zor and Helium be a lasting one. Ela Dusa, please attach this gem properly to my attire."

When Dejah Thoris seated herself again, she made sure that Ela Dusa sat beside her. She hoped that with the lady in waiting at her side, the jed would not attempt further familiarities.

Jan Vajo's gift was certainly a handsome one, inlaid with many a curious gem, some of which were unfamiliar even to the refined taste of a princess of Helium, and carved with antique symbols that she could not read. And yet, it brought with it a feeling of discomfort. The oppressive sense of some stranger attempting to gain access to her thoughts intensified as soon as the medallion was fastened to her harness. A buzzing, tingling sensation pressed upon her heart and spread over her limbs. Her head ached. She longed to escape the sun that still shone unchecked upon the balcony.

Jan Vajo's brow was beclouded by her refusal of his ministrations.

"Your gift is a royal one," she said, forcing animation into her voice. "Tell me more about it."

He brightened immediately. "These medallions are heirlooms of the Jed of Zor, passed down from the times before the oceans were lost. Each Jed of Zor wears one, and the others are given to his closest advisers. And to his princess, as well, when he finds and wins her."

The attempted smile, too like a leer, which she had seen on his face before, gleamed out once more. Had she but known the history of his gift, she would not have accepted the medallion at any price.

"Can you tell me the meaning of the symbols?"

"It is believed that this was the language of Zor in ancient times. We no longer hold the secret to its interpretation. Or some hold that it is the language of the Holy Therns—may Issus prosper them—and bears some great blessing from the keepers of the Valley Dor. We cannot know, unless the Holy Ones deign to read it for us at some future time when we are found worthy. But be assured that whatever the symbols manifest is of great honor and worth."

"I see," she said. "I thank you again for this honor. But is it not time to honor the victors of the day? I would not keep your worthy subjects waiting longer."

Mollified, the jed bowed magnanimously and addressed his guards.

"Bring the winners before us," he ordered, "that they may receive their awards in the view of all."

7
PRIZES AND FORFEITS

T HE WINNERS, WHO HAD NO DOUBT been waiting impatiently, were duly assembled and brought to the balcony, lining up from lesser to greater, with the final winners of the men's and women's competitions arriving last.

In spite of her increasing headache and weariness, Dejah Thoris found great pleasure in handing out prizes and congratulations, while the stentorian voice of Ptang Raxo announced the names to the audience. Rewarding merit had always been one of her favorite duties as Princess of Helium.

Finally came Kan Vastor and Parvia. A quick clean-up could not entirely conceal the marks of their exertion. Victory medals were clipped to their harness, gold rings slipped upon their limbs, and soft tooled-leather cases containing fresh weapons and harness were given to them. It was left for Jan Vajo to bestow the highest accolade.

His invitation to Parvia was gracious and enthusiastic.

"My sister Phortora and I extend our best wishes for your future success, and ask that you attend us at our banquet hall tonight, to meet the court and make your decision as to whether you will choose to serve among the highest and noblest of our city. It is the hope of your jed that you will grace us with your presence. Accept this armlet in token of our invitation. It will guarantee your admittance to our presence at any time, even should you decline tonight's banquet."

To Kan Vastor, his manner was less welcoming. The same invitation was extended, and the armlet given to him was of

71

rich gold and superb craftsmanship, fit for a warrior of high honor. Yet the jed's tone was cold. Nonetheless, the young warrior saluted his jed with head held high.

Dejah Thoris had not been invited to speak, but she stopped the winners before they could leave, to reiterate her praise. She thanked Kan Vastor again for his bold defense of the jed, and spoke a few words to Parvia, asking that she come to see her at the banquet. When Parvia made her final bow to the princess, her eyes lingered on the face of Dejah Thoris, as if she would impress her with some silent communication. Dejah Thoris wondered if Parvia had been trying to communicate telepathically. Perhaps that was the source of the persistent feeling of some mind pressing upon hers. She resolved that she would speak to the young woman at all costs that night.

As the royal party left the arena, Phortora walked swiftly ahead, speaking to no one. Dejah Thoris burst ahead of her guards to catch up with her. Phortora ignored her in a manner that would have been unforgivably rude in Helium.

"My ladies require bathing facilities," Dejah Thoris said, without waiting for a cordial word. "Yesterday, your servant kindly suggested that you would show us to the royal baths. Might I ask that you do so before the banquet tonight?"

Phortora spared her a glance.

"Certainly," she said begrudgingly. "I will order my servant to conduct you there."

On reaching the palace, they parted company without further speech. Dejah Thoris found some relief in the cool shade of the ancient stone walls. Whatever the reason for Phortora's bad temper, she was as good as her word, and sent the same servant who had helped them the preceding night to conduct them to the terrace where the royal bathing grounds were located.

Here Dejah Thoris allowed her entourage to relieve her of her ornaments and bring her a cool drink before she plunged herself into the baths. Almost immediately, her headache faded, and she felt more like herself.

She looked around with pleasure on the bathing area, which consisted of several linked pools set in lovely gardens rich with flowers and bordered by shady bowers and bubbling fountains. From her seat, she could look down on the airship harbor and the walls to the broken country beyond. A cool breeze lifted the heavy locks of her dark hair, freed from the ornaments that had bound them up in festive style.

She extended her hand to Ela Dusa. "Come, let us wash away our cares!"

They joined the other women in the refreshing waters. After some of the day's disturbing moments, Dejah Thoris was inclined to greater appreciation of Ela Dusa's counsel. Indeed, she thought to take advantage of the privacy of the bathing pools to seek further advice.

"Forgive me for my earlier heedlessness," she said. "I now understand more of the pitfalls of diplomacy. This day I have found the jed's attentions intrusive. I wish with all my heart that my father were here! Can it really be possible, do you think, that Jan Vajo seeks to win my hand? In the absence of my mother, I pray you give me your thoughts!"

Before Ela Dusa could speak, the young woman Parvia appeared at the water's edge and plunged in. She splashed without ceremony to Dejah Thoris' side.

"Princess, I must speak with you." She glanced behind her, and blurted out, "The lady Phortora is not to be trusted."

Dejah Thoris, startled, glanced past Parvia to see what she had been looking at. She beheld Phortora herself, arriving in great state, attended by servants and court ladies. Dejah Thoris turned to assure Parvia that she, too, desired communication, but too late. The young woman had plunged beneath the surface to reappear at some distance, as if she had never sought conference with the princess.

Phortora, too, swept toward Dejah Thoris, but less impetuously than Parvia. She circled beneath a cooling fountain before deigning to speak.

"Forgive my ill temper in the arena," she said. "You see,

the competitor in second place was a favorite, a daughter of friends, and one whom I had long hoped to see at court. I believed her deserving of the victor's prize. When your interference demoted her to second place, I was disappointed on behalf of her numerous admirers."

"I held the baton your brother gave me," Dejah Thoris said. "I did as I thought best to uphold the honor of Zor."

A smoldering anger flared in Phortora's eyes, warning the princess to place little trust in her barbed apology.

Phortora tossed back her wet hair, scattering a shower of sparkling drops. "Fear not," she said with a shrug. "My brother agreed that I might invite Lalaro, the second-place competitor, to join us in the court. She has the true prize—the favor of her jed. She lacks only the competition metal, a thing of small worth as time passes and this event fades from memory. Perhaps you would like to have your favorite attend you during the remaining days of your stay, as I shall not be needing her."

She extended her arm and snapped her fingers in Parvia's direction. The young woman moved obediently toward her.

"Now that you are here at court, I presume you will accept my orders," Phortora said. "Since I have no need of a new attendant, I desire that you serve our guest."

Parvia bowed gracefully to Dejah Thoris.

"I will be most happy to attend the princess," she said. "What is your command?"

"None at present," Dejah Thoris said. "I desire only that you refresh yourself from the stress of battle, that you may appear well among my ladies tonight."

Thanking her, Parvia moved out of sight among the other young women.

Having delivered her darts of venom and washed her hands of Parvia, Phortora soon left the pools with her entourage. Dejah Thoris stayed only a little longer, to allow her ladies to enjoy the waters.

She now had two private conversations she wished to conduct, with Ela Dusa and with Parvia. But the presence of each prevented her having confidential talk with the other. Moreover, there was much scurrying about for all the women of Helium to ready themselves for yet another banquet. Jewels, combs, and ointments were called for and traded about, and it seemed that each young woman needed help arranging her hair.

Dejah Thoris chose a simple style, with braids of pearls adorning hair left long and flowing, and crowned with a diadem remarkable for its beauty rather than its ostentation. For harness, she again chose a design of lighter weight, though more formal than that she had worn to the arena. It was adorned with smaller stones of glimmering white and palest pastel hues: rare pink pearls, pale topaz, moonstones, and opals of light, elusive colors like those of earliest dawn. The silks she chose were pure white shot with silver, like moonlight sparkling on desert sands.

Ela Dusa had clothed herself in midnight colors of deepest blue, with an occasional diamond sending forth its rays among the sapphires.

"You must sit next to me at this banquet," Dejah Thoris said. "You will complement me most excellently. Together we shall appear as stars in the night sky."

She sighed. "I suppose I must wear the medallion Jan Vajo insisted on giving me, although it spoils the color scheme.

"Parvia!" she called out. "Please go to my harness of the day and fetch me the medallion at its center."

The young woman came promptly, bearing the heavy golden round, and fastened it securely to the harness of the princess. Dejah Thoris felt its weight immediately.

"Ela Dusa," she said, "I must speak with you privately."

"But Princess, our escort to the banquet will arrive any minute. Can it not wait until later this evening?"

"Not one more instant," Dejah Thoris said. "Parvia, please leave us. And make sure we are not interrupted by anyone else."

"I hear and obey."

Dejah Thoris pulled Ela Dusa to the far side of the room, to make the task of eavesdropping as difficult as possible for anyone who might try. With every step, she felt the weight of the medallion, and recalled the insidious hand of Jan Vajo transgressing her space.

"I see now why my mother insisted you accompany me," Dejah Thoris whispered rapidly. "And I am in sore need of your wisdom and experience. I find this Jed of Zor's attentions most repellent and intrusive. I never expected to encounter such behavior. I know we were to wait for my father, but I have completed my task as Arbiter, and I desire only to return to Helium as soon as may be. Yet how shall I accomplish this?"

Before Ela Dusa could answer, a clangor and a blare of trumpets outside the door announced the arrival of their escort.

"Consider it!" Dejah Thoris concluded hastily. "And be ready with your answer when we return here, for every additional moment within these walls is an oppression to your princess."

The banquet hall was even more opulently appointed than it had been on the first night. The princess' own staunch Heliumetic guards were once again separated from her, seated beyond the press of guests and attendants, at the lower end of the long tables. She entwined her arm with Ela Dusa's, to make sure that one familiar face would remain within reach.

Phortora tried to usher her to the same seat as before, between herself and the jed. Dejah Thoris stuck tight to the side of her mother's friend, forcing the jed's sister to sit beyond them, farther from the center of the table. Phortora wore a gaudy harness bedecked with red coral and carnelian carved into fantastic shapes, with chunks of red topaz blazing out among their convolutions. Clearly, her intention had been to outshine all others, but with Dejah Thoris and Ela Dusa seated side by side in perfect harmony, she merely looked out of place.

No untoward events marred the festivities, but Dejah Thoris took care to choose only those foods served to the jed, after his tasters had showed them to be free of poison. Her headache and discomfort had returned in full force while she was dressing for the event, so her appetite was small. Again, some weight from outside herself pressed upon her mind. It cost her an effort to maintain her composure. She spoke little. Dramus Ugo watched her intently, as if he noted something amiss.

Jan Vajo sought her attention frequently, forcing her to engage in conversation.

"I am glad you wore the medallion tonight," he said. "It becomes you well."

"Indeed, it is a precious heirloom," she said. "I wore it tonight because I thought this might be my last opportunity. Surely, you would wish such a treasure to remain with your house, not to journey far away to Helium. I have been honored to wear it, and will likewise be honored to return it."

"I hope your journey to Helium will not occur for some time yet," he exclaimed. "You must do me the honor of wearing the token of our city until then!"

Again, he dared to place his hand upon her arm as he leaned closer to her.

"Indeed, I hope that you may defer your return to Helium indefinitely. There is much to show you here in Zor—not least, the favor of its jed."

Dejah Thoris' thoughts swirled in tumult. Instinctively, she tried to pull away from this unwanted contact.

Her head ached fiercely. The jed's eyes, his smile—surely, he was a well-favored man. His stature and strength were suited to his princely power. Might not such a warrior be pleasing to a princess? Was it not appropriate to acquiesce to his will? She felt the pressure to yield, to bow, to smile.

Suddenly she remembered how he had fled the assassin's blade in the arena, leaving her to face its edge alone. Such was not the action of a prince! The most unworthy calot of the streets would better defend a woman!

Through the turbulence of her thoughts came one clear beam of light: someone was trying to control her mind. And they had come very close to succeeding. Never had she experienced such a powerful intrusion. It was unthinkable for a daughter of Helium to be so controlled. With the strength of rage, she repelled the influence, as she would have parried a dart cast at her in the sparring ring.

Withdrawing her arm from Jan Vajo's reach, she pulled herself upright. She plucked the medallion from her harness and placed it before the jed. The chill of the northern ice caps frosted her words.

"Such delights must wait to please the next to wear this medallion. You must forgive us; my ladies are wearied with today's exertions, and we must thank you for your gracious hospitality, and retire. Until tomorrow!"

Ela Dusa rose in unison with her. Dejah Thoris feigned weakness, stumbling and clinging to her attendant's arm as she left her seat.

Jan Vajo half rose and extended an arm as if to stop her.

"Princess! Are you unwell? Do you require aid?"

She repelled him with a queenly gesture.

"Do not concern yourself. I am weary and must rest. I need nothing more."

The musicians faltered in their merry tunes as the ladies of Helium filed from the hall.

The baffled jed glared about him, but seeing that all eyes were upon him, he turned off his disappointment with a bellowed toast. Raising his cup of wine, he drank deeply. All were forced to follow, and by the time they had drained their draughts, Dejah Thoris and her entourage had left the hall.

A babble of surprise and concern came to her ears as the other women hastened in her wake. Susho Llan spared her the need to concoct an explanation for them. The young woman approached her princess as soon as they had gained the privacy of their apartments.

"Thank you, my princess!" she exclaimed. "I thought that banquet would never end. The jed's guards are none too respectful of a young woman's preferences! The one behind me stood so close that his ornaments became entangled with my hair. To unsnarl them was both painful and embarrassing. I have never been so grateful to be excused."

The other women laughed, and joined in the chorus of complaint and merriment. The disconcerting moment had passed. They trooped off to their own chamber, where their conversation was muted beyond the curtain. Only then did Dejah Thoris give way to her true feelings.

She sank down upon her sleeping silks, extending an arm to Ela Dusa, that her lady might begin to unwind the straps of her harness.

"Fear not, I only feigned to stumble," she said. "But truly, I am weary. I long for our home in Helium. Have you thought of any way to hasten our return?"

Ela Dusa shook her head. "Your father expects us to await him here. I am sure he would not want you to return without a proper escort."

"I have my troop of guards! A dozen true-hearted Heliumites would be escort enough for anyone!"

"Yet the vessels that remain with us would scarcely accommodate even that many. And they are not ships of war."

"They have armaments enough on board!" the princess flashed out. "If any are bold enough to defend their princess, rather than offering timid counsels."

Ela Dusa completed her disrobing in silence, while the princess sat frowning.

She wished that Jan Vajo might lend her ships for the journey home, but something told her it would be best not to ask, perhaps best not to let him know she desired to leave.

She waited until Ela Dusa had fallen asleep. Then, with infinite care, she retrieved the package she had stuffed into her bag at the last minute, in her own dear room in Helium, and extricated from it her supple flying leathers. To don a court harness would risk the clink of gold or sparkle of gems in a stray beam of light.

She stole forth into the outer passage, arresting the alarm of the guards at the door with a stern command to silence, and swiftly passing by before they could think to stop her. Once out of sight, she walked briskly, head high, so that no observer would suspect a furtive purpose. She followed her best guess for the direction of the air harbor. She passed occasional guards idling before some gate or entrance, but none were of sufficient rank to dare approach her.

The many unoccupied and even dusty passages showed that the palace of Zor had once held a much larger court. The light of radium lamps showed great halls with walls carved and painted, now pitted and faded by time. The city had once been home to a strong and bustling population, fed by rich, well-watered lands, and by fleets of merchant ships and fishing fleets. Now even the air was thin and scarce, compared to the days of Barsoom's glory. Dejah Thoris knew this to be true, from her lessons in history, but she had never experienced it so keenly. Under the rule of her father and grandfather, Helium thrived. Especially in the well-tended centers of its twin cities, it had been easy for her to remain oblivious to the emptying of Barsoom's lands and dwellings. The eerie shadows of forever-empty halls cast a chill over her heart.

She was overjoyed to see the lights around a broad opening ahead of her, and to hear the voices of sailors and craftsmen about their work among the fliers. Since night had fallen, those who still had tasks worked in a relaxed manner, talking among themselves. The Zorian guards on duty were engaged in a lively game, seated around a small brazier. They glanced up, uncertain of her identity, and only sprang to their feet when someone recognized the guest of their jed.

"It is the princess!" one of her own crew exclaimed. Immediately, the handful of Heliumites present gathered to hear her wishes. She beckoned to the captain who had accompanied her in flight.

"I have come to inspect the airships of Helium that remain here," she announced, "and to make sure we will be ready to leave at any moment when the great Mors Kajak shall return. Let it not be said that we have delayed him for even a moment."

She requested that the captain show her around the various ships that lay at their moorings in the harbor. When they were on the far side of the largest, a light cruiser, where it was less likely they would be overheard, she inquired of the Heliumetic ships' readiness, and was satisfied to hear that they were fully fueled and in good trim.

"It is my wish that from now on, my sailors and warriors shall consider themselves on standby. Have messengers ever ready to summon those guards who sleep within the palace. It may be that we shall not await my father here. It may be that we shall go forth to greet him. And above all, it is my desire that our travel plans shall not be discussed by all and sundry here in Zor. Hold yourselves ready, but say nothing to our hosts. I have spoken."

"As you command," the captain said, saluting her.

To plunge again into the darkness of the deserted stretch of corridors between her and her quarters required extra resolve, but with head high and one hand on her hidden blade, she hurried onward.

I am a princess of Helium, she assured herself. *I fear nothing.*

Her flying harness held a small radium torch, but she resolved to do without it, for it would make her a clear target for anything that might lurk in the shadows, out of range of the lamps that glowed high above. Her bare feet were nearly silent on the stone floors, polished by thousands of years of passing steps.

Voices sounded ahead. She was not yet near enough to her own chambers for the voices to be those of friends. Still more stealthily, she approached the sound.

In the abandoned audience chamber whose antiquity had

so impressed her as she passed it before, someone was seated beneath the dim rays of a carved lamp. It was Phortora, still clad in her blood-red harness, and posed regally on the chamber's throne. Beside her stood her son, Zu Tith.

His voice, pitched low, expressed anger, though the words were indistinct.

Phortora laughed.

"Fear not, my son. You shall be jed, as is your right. Though not before I myself claim the throne as your regent."

Her hand caressed the carved arm of her seat. Dejah Thoris held her breath.

"Every attempt against my uncle is thwarted! The last, by that upstart Kan Vastor. And now that the Heliumite wears his accursed medallion, it is only a matter of time until he secures a bride, and the expectation of an heir—which will bump us both away from succession."

His words subsided from wrath to petulance. Phortora spoke with soothing assurance.

"I remind you that inheritance of the jed's throne does not run through blood alone. Sometimes the succession is determined by the shedding of blood—through valor, your role as a warrior, or through cunning and strategy—and that is a skill that a woman may also wield. You will rule, in time. And when you do, you will be free to act, not enthralled by a medallion worn by such as that sneaking ulsio, Dramus Ugo. As for the Heliumite, I've paid well for the certainty that she will never wed my brother."

Dejah Thoris' hand went to her breast, with an involuntary intake of breath. No—the medallion was not there. Whatever its properties, she was free of them for the moment.

Zu Tith, though a traitor and schemer, was also a warrior, and his battle-sharpened alertness sensed her presence.

He touched his mother's arm in warning.

"What was that? Something lives in the shadows. We should not be found here."

Phortora shrugged his hand away.

"It is nothing," she said. "But you are right. Go to your quarters, and I will go to mine, there to await the news that will cause me to express great surprise and consternation. I will send you a message when all is secure."

She laughed softly but wickedly.

8
ENCOUNTERS IN SHADOW

DEJAH THORIS FROZE IN THE SHADOW of a pillar as they passed within arms' length of her. Their torches then flickered away toward the far end of the chamber, where a second exit must lie. The princess took a moment to calm her racing heart before stealing forth. She could only conclude from the few words she had heard that Phortora had hatched some plot to remove her. Anger at the injustice of it boiled within her. She wished she could run after the jed's sister and inform her that nothing would induce her to wed Jan Vajo. Whatever price Phortora had paid to discredit or drive away an imagined rival had been wasted. Dejah Thoris would gladly have paid to remove herself from this ulsio's nest.

She stole toward her chambers as quickly as she dared. Her heart jumped in her throat as she darted glances around her, fearing to be accosted at any moment. She could have sworn she heard footsteps at times, yet could see nothing.

Just before she reached the better-lighted area where the guest quarters were located, a sharp whisper from the shadows arrested her.

"Hsst! Princess!"

Her hand went to her blade again. Turning to face the sound, she peered into the darkness. A portion of shadow detached itself and moved into her vision. It was Parvia, a finger held to her lips.

Parvia beckoned the princess to join her in the shadowed region.

Dejah Thoris started to ask what Parvia was doing there, but the young woman this time placed a warning palm across the lips of the princess. She leaned close and spoke almost into Dejah Thoris' ear.

"Here is danger! Be still and wait."

Stepping noiselessly and delicately, she drew Dejah Thoris into the deepest part of the darkness, a nook behind a great pillar of stone.

With a soft puff of sound, hardly louder than a gust of wind blowing aside heavy draperies, something fell from the ceiling far above. From their vantage point in deeper shadow, that which fell was silhouetted against the dim light from the lamps of the guest quarters ahead of them. It was a humanlike form, but black as ash, and swathed in lengths of black silk that partially camouflaged its outline. It seemed similar to the form she had seen in the city that day, yet it was not the same. Unlike that shape, its limbs were unencumbered and moved freely and visibly. It stole crouching to and fro, like a banth seeking prey. One arm was held out as if clutching a blade, though the weapon could not be seen.

Careless footsteps and banter in loud male voices approached from the direction of the harbor. The dark shape leaped away nimbly and soundlessly.

"Come!" Parvia pulled Dejah Thoris back into the corridor to follow close behind the warriors until they reached the lighted entrance to the guest quarters.

Once safely inside, Parvia continued to grasp Dejah Thoris' arm in a way that was both unbefitting a court lady and physically painful.

"Princess, I am doing my best to protect you," she said, "but I beg of you, do not walk the corridors at night! Many disasters lie in wait. Do not make my task difficult."

"Protect me? From what? What was that thing?"

"That was an assassin in concealment silks," Parvia said, in the same harsh whisper she had used in the corridor.

"An assassin? What? Yet another attempt on the life of our host?"

"No, foolish one! On *yours*!"

Offended by this manner of address, Dejah Thoris managed to extricate her wrist from the grasp of the other woman.

"It is you who speak foolishly," she said. "No assassin, however bloodthirsty, would seek to slay a woman, for any price."

Parvia lowered her eyes and appeared to blush.

Perhaps, thought Dejah Thoris, *she at last realizes the impropriety of her behavior.*

"No honorable person," Parvia said. "But for a high enough price, even honor may be sold."

Ela Dusa emerged from the bedchamber, her hastily donned harness askew.

"Princess! What is the meaning of this?" she exclaimed. "I woke and found you gone. Imagine my distress! Another moment and I would have called the guard to search for you."

Again Dejah Thoris reflected on the inconvenience of having people watching over her. It would indeed have been humiliating to be brought back by the guard, like a stray thoat. But she knew better than to speak unkindly to one's loyal entourage. Such rudeness might be acceptable to Phortora of Zor, but would be intolerable in a princess of Helium.

She was about to speak when Parvia forestalled her.

"Your pardon," Parvia said. "After the banquet, the air seemed stifling. The princess wished to walk as far as the harbor to find a cool breeze. As she did not wish to wake you, I thought it best to accompany her."

"I am so sorry to have awakened you," Dejah Thoris said meekly. "As you see, we have returned without incident. Perhaps it would be best for all of us to sleep now. There is much to consider tomorrow."

Her scolding disarmed, Ela Dusa yielded to the suggestion, and the subject of what Dejah Thoris had been doing in the corridors was dropped.

Awakening did not bring her the usual joy in a new day.

A frown clouded the princess' brow as she anticipated another tiresome round of fetes and banqueting, of repulsing veiled advances from Jan Vajo and ignoring veiled insults from Phortora. Only the thought of hastening to the walls of the city to watch for the return of her father's fleet impelled her to rise and complete her morning routine.

Servant girls of Zor came to conduct them to a terrace on the far side of the banqueting hall, where breakfast was being served in a pleasant garden. This was much more to Dejah Thoris' liking than the stiff formality of the banquet hall, especially since Phortora and the jed were absent. While the servants were bringing in trays of food and drink, Dejah Thoris strolled through the flowering trees to a wall overlooking the lower sections of the palace and its surroundings. She noticed the arrival of a small scout ship that she was certain was of Heliumetic make, although it was flying a pennant of Zor.

In high excitement, she hurried back to her group to send one of them for news.

"Find out who has arrived. If he is a man of Helium, ask him to come to me at once. If he be Zorian, give him my greetings and ask that when he has made what report is needed to his own sovereign, he accept my invitation to attend me. Tell him not to stand on ceremony, but to come at once. We will gladly offer him refreshment at our own table."

Too agitated to eat, she paced the gardens in anticipation. Perhaps a messenger had come from her father, and her wish to leave Zor would soon be granted.

She was dismayed when her servant returned, escorted not by the messenger alone, but by the Jed of Zor and a number of his guard.

"I am in haste to gratify any wish of Dejah Thoris," Jan Vajo said with a courtly bow. "And in hope to be repaid with an invitation to breakfast with you and your ladies."

Dejah Thoris seated herself with the best grace she could muster. But when she heard the messenger's tale, she found she had bought bad news at a high price. The man had indeed come from her father, in a scout ship lent to him for the purpose, but only to relate that Mors Kajak had found the Thurd incursion more extensive than expected, and that he had yet to engage with its main force. It would still be several days before he could fight his way to their base camp and conclusively defeat them. He requested that Zor's hospitality to the princess and her party be extended, as his return must be delayed.

Jan Vajo seemed in high good humor at this news, but Dejah Thoris, for all her efforts at self-control, could not help showing her disappointment. In vain the jed summoned attendants to ply her with the most delicate cakes, the ripest fruits, and most sparkling juices. She might as well have been chewing ochre moss with the thoats. She found no joy in anything but thoughts of a return to Helium.

Jan Vajo chose not to take her consternation seriously.

"Come, come," he said, "surely our court cannot be so distasteful that you would not stay an extra day or two. We shall put our heads together and find some additional festivities to interest you. Let us meet again at midday that I may suggest some diversions for you to consider."

Dejah Thoris thanked him. "Give us leave to bathe and make ourselves ready, and we will join you then," she said. She was ready to snatch at any reprieve, however short, from his irksome presence. She ended the meal as swiftly as possible, and hurried with her servants and ladies to the refuge of the bathing gardens.

She plunged into the waters, while Ela Dusa divested herself of her accoutrements more slowly. Parvia joined her and sought her ear immediately.

"I believe there is great danger for you here," she said. "Now that the assassins have come for you once, there will be more attempts. They cannot brook failure. Your instinct to leave is correct. To stay several more days is to court death."

Dejah Thoris rose to her feet and shook the water from her hair.

"I cannot believe that any of us are in danger from

assassination," she said. "Even in a place like Zor, surely the basic decencies are understood. My father would never have left me in a place where women are at risk of being killed."

She considered the unthinkable only briefly, then shook her head.

"I can well believe that if Princess Phortora could kill me with a look, she would," she said, laughing. Recalling where she was, she looked around hastily to make sure no one had heard her. "But your fears of trained assassins picking me off must surely be misguided," she finished in a more sober tone.

Parvia bit her lip. Her frustration was apparent. She almost spoke, but seeing Ela Dusa and the other ladies approaching, she moved away, looking dejected.

Yet her words had not been without effect. They lent emphasis to Dejah Thoris' strong desire to be gone from this place. While she did not fear assassination, she was certainly uneasy.

She heard Ela Dusa's voice, and realized the older woman had been speaking for some time, unheard.

"You are thoughtful today, my princess," she said.

"You are too courteous," Dejah Thoris replied. "In truth, I am brooding, and did not hear what you said. Forgive me. My heart is consumed with longing to be at home again. I see nothing to be gained from a longer stay. Since my father's arrival is delayed indefinitely, I believe we must take matters into our own hands and return to Helium."

"Should we not respect the plan Mors Kajak made, and wait for him?"

"If my father knew our situation, I think he would not wish me to stay."

Dejah Thoris did not wish to speak more openly of their hosts, but the look she gave her lady in waiting said volumes. Ela Dusa's nod said that she understood.

"I will tell the jed of my decision," the princess said, "and give orders to our faithful guardsmen to prepare for our departure. I leave it to you to supervise the other women in packing and preparations, but make sure they say nothing to anyone else in the city until I have informed our host."

The party quickly returned to their quarters to dress for the events of the day. Soon they found themselves led by court ladies and messengers to an opulently appointed reception room, where Jan Vajo awaited them. Dejah Thoris planned to save her announcement for the evening banquet. The jed was in high spirits over his latest plan to amuse the guests—a ride through some picturesque canyons to the south of the city, where one could view carved glyphs and images from ancient days.

He carried with him a small antique box that he presented to Dejah Thoris with a flourish. Within was an object wrapped in delicate silks. When she unwound the wrapping, the princess saw that it was the medallion she had hoped to be rid of.

"Since your stay with us will be a little longer, I beg that you will consent to wear this for the days that remain. It will give my people great happiness to see this token of friendship with our city as you walk among them."

Dejah Thoris longed to spurn the ornament once again, but knowing that she planned to leave Zor as soon as possible, she thought it wiser not to anger the jed more than necessary. Reluctantly, she placed the medallion upon her harness.

The ride was fully as interesting as the jed had promised. The fresh air was welcome, as was the fact that with both of them mounted and riding free, the jed could not intrude himself upon her personal space so easily. She felt at once the malign influence of the medallion, but the focus of mind needed to control her thoat gave her some relief. Jan Vajo drew near to her all too often to show her points of interest or suggest a different route, and at those times the effect of the device became most difficult. The whisper in her mind grew louder and more insistent, suggesting that she extend her stay, that she allow the jed to press his suit, that his words were kind and winning. Yet the pressure of that voice caused such pain that she was never tempted to give in. Ideas that brought such discomfort could not possibly be for her benefit.

As the shadows lengthened, they rode uphill toward the city. The thoats slowed their pace, allowing Jan Vajo to draw even with her and ride side by side. He was exultant in the success of the day's recreation, and eager to discuss the next day's activities. Dejah Thoris decided to take the banth by the tail, as it were, and to tell him at once of her change in plans, lest he build his expectations higher and be still more displeased when they were dashed.

"This day has been most pleasant, a fine capstone to our visit," she said. "But pray, do not expend more of your valuable time on planning additional entertainments. I fear this day must be our last in Zor. Since my father cannot come to escort us home, we shall have to make our way on our own. My royal mother did not expect so long a stay. She will be anxiously awaiting my return."

His countenance grew grim. With ill-concealed wrath, he tried to persuade her to change her mind, but she remained adamant. When the cavalcade of thoats rumbled through the palace gates, he dismounted, and with little ceremony, excused himself.

"Since you insist on leaving so precipitously, there are matters I must attend to. We shall say our farewells at tonight's feast."

Rejoicing to be so easily rid of him, Dejah Thoris accompanied her retinue to their quarters. Here she assembled them for instructions.

"Dress for the evening as usual," she said, speaking softly and briefly. "But before the banquet tonight, let all your possessions be packed for travel. Appear carefree; show no signs that you suspect the Zorians of any malice. But follow my lead at dinner. Eat and drink nothing but what you see me or the princess Phortora consume. Assassins seem to be everywhere in this city, and I would not have any mishap postpone our departure. We will leave first thing tomorrow morning."

She then summoned the most trusted guard at her door, and sent him with a message to his commander to prepare his men for an early departure in the morning.

She had feared that her warning would make some of the younger women visibly fearful and downcast. However, the news that they would soon be homeward bound seemed to put everyone in a merry mood.

Strangely, the same was true of Jan Vajo. Based on his reaction to her news, the princess had expected a reversion to the surly and rude demeanor she had glimpsed at times, but at the feast, he seemed untroubled. He continued to pay court to her as if she had said nothing. The entertainments at dinner were on a grand scale, and an endless supply of sweetmeats and delicacies were offered at the table. Dejah Thoris did not permit herself to be disarmed by this spectacle. She followed her own advice and tasted nothing unless she had seen the jed or his sister consuming it first.

To avoid provoking the jed, she still wore the medallion. Its pressure on her mind and heart continued unabated. Whatever force lay behind it still pushed her to submit to the Jed of Zor and embrace his proposals. From this, she concluded that the jed had not resigned himself to her refusal. She wondered briefly how he could remain undaunted in the face of the fact that she would leave tomorrow.

On this occasion, she remained for the whole of the banquet, seeking no excuse to depart early. She felt it was the least she could do on their final night. She declined to drink toast after toast. When the final ceremonies arrived, she was exhausted, and would have been quite incapacitated had she pledged with every cup offered to her. She noted with displeasure that many of her young women seemed to have taken a sip too much.

Jan Vajo made a farewell speech, touching upon every proper courtesy and expressing a heartfelt wish for greater intercourse between Zor and Helium, though saying nothing of formal alliances. He then offered her the parting cup, which she felt compelled to taste, at least. His farewell was grave, and yet she was puzzled by a disconcerting spark of merriment in his look, as if he were not taking his own words seriously.

It matters not, she said to herself, dismissing further thoughts of him. *Tomorrow I shall be at home in my own city and palace. I need never think of this time again.*

On their return to the guest quarters, Dejah Thoris urged all to go immediately to their rest, to be ready for an early start. After the strenuous ride and the lengthy banquet, the other women fell asleep quickly. Even Parvia seemed lost in slumber. The princess, however, unable to rest, rose again and donned her flying harness. For safety's sake, she ordered one of the door guards to go with her this time. She returned to the harbor, to make sure the ships would be ready to leave. She no longer feared discovery, since she had declared her intention to leave openly, and no one had opposed it.

At the harbor, her ships sat at anchor, well secured. As she ran her eye over them, they seemed in good trim. Even the war-battered scout ship that had carried the previous day's messenger had been repaired. But the harbor itself, which had been busy with artisans, crew, and warriors just two days ago, stood silent and empty. Far down at the other end of the paving, near Zor's ships of war, a contingent of Zorian warriors stood on guard. Elsewhere, an uncanny silence reigned. There was no sign of the Heliumites whom Dejah Thoris had ordered to be always ready for departure.

She turned to her companion.

"There must be some misunderstanding," she said. "Go with speed to the quarters of our warriors and remind them of my command. They are to keep guard over our ships until we are ready to embark. Send the officer of the day to me at once, in my apartments. I shall return there to await him."

"Princess, I beg you," the guard pleaded, "allow me first to accompany you to safety. Then I will speed on your errand. It is not proper for me to leave your side and allow you to walk unattended in this place."

"Not proper? But it is my command," she replied. Bowing, he obeyed.

She hurried back through the darkness of the corridors. Now more familiar with their turnings, she was less fearful, and moved faster. She reached the point where she could see the lighted area of the guest quarters ahead, without encountering anyone or hearing sounds of pursuit.

Yet, as she drew closer, she halted in surprise. Something about the entrance did not seem normal. No guards stood watch by the door. Instead, an indistinct mass lay across the threshold.

Approaching cautiously, she saw that the guards were still present—but they lay sprawled on the floor. A dark liquid pooled beneath their bodies. Horror seized her, but she forced herself to bend closer to ascertain their wounds. Her cheeks paled, then reddened with indignation as she recognized the scent: not blood, but wine. The men still breathed, though stuporously. Cups lay tumbled at the tips of their outstretched hands.

Stepping disdainfully over their bodies, she entered the room, and opened her lips to call for a servant to make an ill report of these doings to the captain of the guard.

A small whirlwind entered behind her, wrapping her face in her own silks so tightly that she could barely breathe, let alone utter a cry. Fierce hands covered her mouth and eyes, while her legs were tightly enwrapped by the limbs of another, so that she might not struggle to escape.

A voice whispered in her ear.

"Promise me silence. Any sound will endanger your life. Nod your head, and I will free you."

She managed to give the required sign. Hands slipped from her face, and the silks fell away. She whirled to face the attacker, and gasped in spite of her promise. It was Parvia.

The girl laid a warning finger on her lips.

"I came to warn you," she mouthed almost soundlessly. "They are coming for you."

Dejah Thoris' first thought was for Ela Dusa and her ladies, sleeping defenselessly in the next room. She clapped her hand to her mouth in horror, then pointed toward the sleeping chambers, her face beseeching. Parvia shook her head, drawing Dejah Thoris back toward the entrance and the shadows beyond.

Suddenly, the woman froze, as if hearing some sound beyond Dejah Thoris' perception.

"Too late!" she cried aloud. "My princess, I—"

Projectiles spattered around them with a shattering sound like the breaking of eggs. A purple mist with an overwhelming, harshly sweet scent choked Dejah Thoris' lungs and clouded her eyes. Metal and weapons seemed to swirl and flash around her as she sank to the ground, bereft of strength and her senses.

9
ESCAPE BY NIGHT

SHE AWOKE IN A NEST OF SILKS, and thought for a moment that she was at home in Helium. But she opened her eyes not to a delicately carved and painted roof, but to the spangled sable of the Barsoomian night sky, and the ever-changing dance of lights and shadows in the wake of restless Thuria. The breath of the night wind chilled her. A move to arise revealed that her hands and ankles were tightly bound. Turning her head, she saw that Parvia lay beside her, bound and unconscious. A pair of brawny legs and a scabbard swinging at the end of its belt were all she could see of the man who stood on guard beside them.

She closed her eyes hastily, feigning continued unconsciousness, as the man bent down to scrutinize his captives. But it was in vain. Parvia's eyes opened, and she began to struggle against her bonds, signaling to the guard that whatever drug had stupefied them was wearing off.

The hard-faced panthan appeared far too close to the princess. His calloused fingers caressed the softness of her cheek. She tried to scream, but she was gagged with the same silk that bound her wrists.

He laughed most unpleasantly, enjoying their helplessness at his leisure. Finally, he loosened the gag on her mouth and Parvia's.

"Now you may scream all you like," he said. "We are far from any assistance. Your screaming will only disturb the thoats. But please go ahead. My ears have never been caressed by the shrieks of a princess before. I wonder if they are sweeter than the cries of a commoner in distress."

Dejah Thoris stared him down.

I am a daughter of Helium, she reminded herself. *I fear nothing.*

When no screams were forthcoming, the man shrugged.

"Ah well. Since you refuse to scream, I may as well tell you that no harm will come to you. My clients desire that you be kept in the best condition. They have paid my masters well, or I would be sorely tempted to tamper with my instructions."

He raised Dejah Thoris' head and offered a cup of water. Her throat was dry, but she attempted to refuse it, recalling the prevalence of poisons in the region of Zor. True, if he meant to kill them he would probably have done so already, but nevertheless she did not wish to be drugged.

Resistance was in vain. He roughly pinched her nose and forced the liquid into her mouth. Much as she struggled, she was forced to swallow most of it. He carried out the same procedure on Parvia.

Dejah Thoris felt her head swimming. As she feared, there was some potion in the water. Soon she lost consciousness again.

When she awoke once more, it was to full awareness of her plight. Her limbs ached from their cramped position. The same sights met her eyes. The guard stood nearby, a shadow silhouetted against the sky, leaning on his lance. Thuria had passed, for the time being, beyond the horizon, and the light of old Cluros was dim in the west. It was the darkest and coldest time of the night.

Parvia stretched her legs to poke the princess with her toes. Having her attention, she wriggled close enough to place her head near Dejah Thoris and whisper to her.

"I thought we were dead. These are no assassins I have ever seen. If you turn your back to me, I can untie your bonds. But quietly!"

Back to back, they could not speak, while Parvia undid the

tightly knotted cords. Drawing a fold of silk across her body to conceal her movements, Dejah Thoris then untied Parvia's hands, and they made short work of their ankle bonds. They lay side by side, as if still bound.

"What shall we do?" Dejah Thoris whispered. "I see the guard still standing. Beyond him, there may be others."

"True. If we get his attention with pretended screams, we'd only summon the rest. We need a quiet plan."

From a slit in her harness, she pulled out a gossamer length of fabric, and a vial with which she dabbed the cloth. The aroma was sharp and made Dejah Thoris' head swim.

"Now I shall pretend to be ill," Parvia said, "Pretend distress in your daintiest manner—no screaming."

Wadding the wisp of fabric up in one hand, she writhed as if still bound, with lips agape. Her breath became stertorous, and her face swiftly assumed a disturbing pallor.

"No, no!" Dejah Thoris sobbed pitifully. "My friend! There was poison in the drink!"

The guard blundered toward them with a startled exclamation that indicated he might not have been fully awake until that moment.

"Oh, help, help," he mocked. "You'll not catch me with that old trick."

"Do but examine her, if a heart beats within your breast," Dejah Thoris whimpered. "My eyes darken. Perhaps I too am poisoned. Oh, my ancestors! Oh help me—I am not ready to meet Issus."

Scowling, the man bent over Parvia. His expression changed. He uttered an oath and grasped her by the chin, seeking to force her eyes open.

In the twinkling of an eye, Parvia's hand came from beneath the silks to press the cloth to the man's face. With a grunt, he started back, but she twisted out from under him, and leaped to bestride his back, pulling the ends of the cloth tight behind his neck so that the fabric clung to his mouth and nose. Like a speared thoat, his bulk collapsed to the ground. Parvia tied the piece of cloth as a gag around his mouth.

Dejah Thoris assisted her in trussing the man's hands and feet to his own spear, whose point Parvia jammed among some rocks so that he would find difficulty in wriggling to his feet if he awoke. The princess deduced from this that he was still alive. They drew a length of silk over his body. At a distance, his contours would appear as if the prisoners still lay there.

All this had been done as the women stayed as close to the ground as possible. They hid in the moss behind their captor's form, eyeing their surroundings.

No landmarks were visible. They lay in some pathless segment of the endlessly rolling dead sea bottoms. Off to their left, the stamping and snorting of thoats, and the familiar scent wafting toward them on the night breeze, indicated that mounts were picketed nearby. Dejah Thoris did not know how long she had been unconscious. It might be still the same night they had been taken, or a whole day might have passed. She guessed it was the former, and if so, it seemed likely they had been brought here by flier. Traveling by air lent itself to stealth and distance more easily than travel by thoat. She reasoned that this must be a camp already established, to which they had been brought by its inhabitants. But for what purpose? That she could not guess.

Straight ahead of them, a dim glow showed a campfire nearby. A low rumble of voices indicated a circle of additional members of the band enjoying the warmth. To the right of the fire, a flier floated at anchor. If only they could find their way there without being discovered, they might yet escape.

Dejah Thoris pointed to the flier. Their eyes met and Parvia nodded. She drew the guard's heavy sword from his belt and secured it to the back of her own harness. Dejah Thoris drew her slender woman's blade from where it had been cleverly concealed, thanking her stars that she had changed into her flying harness before leaving her room the preceding evening. From the rock outcropping, Parvia also secured a conveniently fist-sized stone to carry with her. Together they crawled toward the flier, moving in a circuitous path to give the gathering by the fire a wider berth.

The earth beneath them vibrated with the impact of running feet. They looked wildly in all directions, but saw nothing in the darkness until, without warning, a hurtling body ran directly into them, tripped, and crashed atop them. By the weight of it and the feel of metal, they knew at once it was a warrior. Such was their fear of discovery that even in this extremity, they were able to stifle their shock. The warrior, either stunned by the fall or equally wary, uttered only a muffled grunt of pain. He had no opportunity to do more, for Parvia found his skull and struck it with the rock in her hand. He slumped into unconsciousness, and before he could recover, she had him gagged with one of her handy strips of silk.

Between them, they were able to drag him a little way into a slight depression in the moss where they would be less likely to be spied if the scuffle had been heard by any of their captors. Dejah Thoris held out the mini-torch she kept clipped to her flying harness.

"Should we look upon his face?" she breathed.

"No light—we dare not," Parvia whispered.

And yet, since they now had a captive and potential resource, it seemed desirable to know if he were friend or foe, and whether they should abandon him and continue swiftly toward the flier and possible escape. Both women paused, as if by mutual agreement, to consider the dilemma.

Fortune took the decision out of their hands. Thuria, returning on her eternal round, appeared above the horizon again. Their position was now more perilous. But the light that threatened them with exposure also touched the face of their captive. Their eyes widened in surprise. It was the young warrior who had won honor beside Parvia at the games, he who stood accused of excessive valor by Zu Tith. Kan Vastor lay unconscious beside them.

Parvia touched his bruised forehead in pitying regret.

"What have I done?" she whispered.

"Dare we believe he is a friend?" Dejah Thoris said.

"I'd stake my life on it."

Parvia pressed her hand against his chest.

"His heart still beats. I have not killed him."

From another pocket in her harness, she produced a tiny vial that emitted a sharp-smelling mist when she pressed its cap beneath Kan Vastor's nose. He gasped and opened his eyes. He threw Parvia aside with an impatient gesture and ripped off the gag.

"What—where—"

Both women signaled desperately for silence. His head turned from one to the other. He subsided, pressing himself into the moss, as his consciousness of his situation returned.

"Friend or foe?" Dejah Thoris questioned.

"What? Friend, of course! I came to rescue you!"

"Sh!" They pushed him back into the moss.

"We are escaping," Parvia whispered, close to his ear. "Can you help?"

He nodded vigorously. "I left my flier back there. Perhaps safer than taking theirs?"

The two women nodded affirmatively also, and as one, the three of them began retracing Kan Vastor's steps, creeping slowly and almost silently, pausing at random intervals so that anyone who chanced to gaze out at their path would not see purposeful motion.

As they crept forward, eyes vigilantly trained at the level of the moss, Dejah Thoris sensed a motion oddly similarly to their own, between them and the encampment. Before she could speak, Parvia grasped each of her companions in an urgent signal to stop. They froze, watching.

Shadows rose up like wisps of smoke from fading embers. They danced across the space to the fire circle. The silhouetted figures of panthans taking their ease around a campfire threw out arms and legs or arched and fell like comic figures in a puppet show, all in silence. Only the shadowy newcomers remained. They gathered into a circle, like a dark flower. Then a part of the circle broke off and moved toward the place where Parvia and Dejah Thoris had awakened.

A shudder went through Parvia and was communicated to Dejah Thoris through the hand that rested on her arm.

Kan Vastor started to get up.

Parvia yanked his arm from under him so that he rolled on the ground again and did not arise.

"Assassins!" she whispered. "I know this crew."

She pulled the guard's sword from its fastening on her harness and rolled to her back, pointing the sword back toward the darkness behind them.

"Prepare," she said. "They will follow our trail."

Her companions rolled to right and left of her, drawing their weapons as quietly as possible and preparing for attack. As Dejah Thoris grasped her light blade, she wondered if her fate was to die far from home, and lie undiscovered on this hillside—at least until some wandering scavenger carried off her bones.

If it is to be so, I will die in a manner worthy of my ancestors, she vowed. *Even if none lives to carry the tale. No doubt many of them died thus, in lonely battle, yet they are no less honored.*

Unlike the booted feet of Kan Vastor, the steps of the assassins made no sound. The princess waited in suspense for the stealthy, unheard attack.

Before it arrived, the sky above them suddenly blazed with light. The kidnappers' fliers came to life as they were fired upon by unknown, flying assailants. The silence of the night was rent by cries, explosions, and rifle fire. Flares dropped near the encampment lit up the whole scene and set the dry moss ablaze.

One of the fliers touched down, and a troop of warriors

poured forth, leaping from the deck to the ground with weapons at the ready. The other ships continued to lay down covering fire. By the light of the flares, Dejah Thoris saw that the grounded flier bore the sigil of the city of Zor.

"Warriors of Zor," she said. "They have come to rescue us! Let us make our way to their lines and fight alongside them."

Even as she spoke, a doubt came into her mind as to their intentions toward her. When last in the palace of Zor, it had been the jed she feared. Should she now place herself in his hands? Yet among the jed, the assassins, and the kidnappers, Jan Vajo seemed the lesser evil.

"Wait, Princess," Kan Vastor said. "Strange as it may sound from one recently enrolled in his service, I am not sure you should trust Jan Vajo."

"Why do you say this?" she asked.

"I have not yet explained how I came hither, and the battle-field is not the place for explanations, yet I must tell you. After the banquet, I noticed that Parvia, my fellow honoree, had left the hall. I went in search of her, hoping to assure her of my friendship and learn her plans for the future."

He glanced at Parvia, who seemed captivated by his account.

"Having searched in vain, I found myself in the halls near the guest quarters. What should I see there but a furtive troop of armed men who had gone unchallenged by the jed's guard. They carried two burdens, of the size and shape of maidens of Barsoom, rolled in silken wrappings and making no outcry. I stole after them, unwilling to attack, since I knew not their business.

"They went straight to the harbor and took their strange burdens aboard a swift ship, again unchallenged by any guard of Zor. In fact, the guards were withdrawn from the harbor and the place was deserted. They vanished quickly into the night. As I searched and called for help, I stumbled across a handful of bodies lying on the stone near the flier of the princess."

Dejah Thoris gasped in horror.

"My guardsmen! My trusted captain! I set them to guard our ships! What has happened to them?"

"Fear not, Princess. I took a moment to examine them, and they were not dead, merely rendered unconscious by some secret means. I continued to raise the alarm, and at last encountered some members of the jed's guard. Their dwar took me aside and let me know, with bellicose mien, that this was not my affair, but business of the jed's, and that if I knew what was good for me, I would forget what I had seen and say no more of it.

"I feigned to agree, but I fear not convincingly. I was rushed from behind, and after a heavy blow to my head, knew nothing more until I woke up in sore pain in a remote area of the palace, to which I assume I had been dragged. Once I found my way back to the light, I could think of nothing better to do than take a ship and search for these mysterious intruders. Now that I am here, I am reluctant to place myself again in the gentle hands of the warriors of Zor."

He rubbed his head ruefully. "Not that your hands, fair ladies, were gentler. My poor skull has been so knocked about, it's a wonder that it retains any thoughts at all."

"Do you mean to say our abductors were known to Jan Vajo?" Dejah Thoris said.

"I see no other explanation."

"And yet he comes to save us. I do not understand."

Parvia slapped the earth in impatience. "This is not the time for pondering! I understand one thing: we are in danger here and must depart."

"The battle rages between us and the ships," Dejah Thoris said. "But there is another way."

The squealing and bellowing of agitated thoats sounded a constant background accompaniment to the clash of swords and shouts of men.

"To the thoat pen!" she ordered, and received no objection.

Again they crawled to escape detection, although this time they moved quickly and with no concern for silence. The noise of battle and the trumpeting of thoats easily covered the sound of their movements.

Near the thoat pen, shadow still reigned, and the creatures jostled about in semidarkness, illuminated only fitfully by the flare of flames on the other side of the encampment.

Dejah Thoris moved deftly among them, fearless of their trampling. The mind training that permitted her to resist the probing of other thoughts had well equipped her to communicate her wishes to her riding mount. She trusted these would be as easily dominated as those in the herds of Helium.

In moments, she had selected a strong steed and swung herself onto its back. With the help of her mount, she cut a second thoat from the herd. Their combined charge easily flattened the gate to their makeshift pen. Kan Vastor mounted the second animal and extended an arm to Parvia, who mounted neatly behind him. The thoats were eager to run away from the noise and confusion, and they were soon far out into the silence of the dead sea bottoms. The rest of the herd scattered behind them, some running with them for a while before gradually dropping off to graze.

"Well done," Parvia said. "The others will confuse our tracks, in case anyone should seek to follow."

For a time, they rode in silence, taking solace in the peace of a quiet night, the steady rhythm of pounding feet, and the spectacular glory of the Barsoomian skies. If they were pursued by air, they had nowhere to hide, but while the darkness held, there was some surcease from vigilance. They had come far enough from the battle site that its sounds could no longer be heard. The thoats slowed to the point that conversation was possible.

"Does anyone know where we are?" Dejah Thoris asked.

Neither Parvia nor Kan Vastor could answer.

"We of Zor seldom travel to these southern zones," explained the latter. "Sometimes we journey westward, in the direction of Helium, but the sea bottoms south of the city are unknown to us."

"Neither do I have any familiarity with this area," Parvia chimed in. "I have traveled west as far as Hastor, but never in this direction."

"Well, then, perhaps more to the point," Dejah Thoris said, "where are we going?"

"The thoats seem to know where they are bound," Parvia said. "Ordinary thoats would stop to graze. These seem determined to reach some destination, like a home ground where they are accustomed to being fed."

"In the absence of a map, perhaps we should let them run."

"Is that wise, Princess?" Kan Vastor asked. "Those who own them will be those who kidnapped you."

"Indeed," Dejah Thoris said grimly. "That is my hope. I must know who is responsible. I cannot safely return to Zor until I know if Jan Vajo is trustworthy. At present, it seems he is not. Also, I will need a flier. I think my father would be most displeased if I were to attempt the distance to Helium on thoat-back, without provisions."

"A good point," Kan Vastor said. "Yet, what if the owners of these thoats are not just kidnappers, but assassins?"

"Unlikely," Parvia said. "I told you, I know that crew. They are not the ones who took us."

Kan Vastor twisted in his seat to cast a puzzled look at Parvia.

"So you said before—yet, how could a maiden so young and beautiful know aught of assassins? They are a vile crew, the spawn of the gutter, not the sort of company you would keep."

"I feared it would come to this," Parvia said, in a low voice scarcely to be heard. "This is not how I would wish to tell my tale, having my words jolted out of me by the gait of a thundering thoat. But I have cast my lot with you, so I will tell you the whole truth."

She raised her head and spoke with pride.

"My parents sold me at a young age into apprenticeship with an assassins' band."

Kan Vastor uttered an exclamation. "This cannot be. Women do not practice that trade!"

Parvia laughed. "As long as that is believed, we are all the more effective! This band is so highly skilled that very few know of its existence. We—that is, they—take on the tasks that others fear to attempt. Or, in some cases, assignments so shocking that other bands would refuse them. Such as, with your pardon, Princess, the killing of women found inconvenient. Even women of high rank.

"Such was my assignment. I was trained from the time I could handle a blade in all the arts of the assassin, as well as in the arts of pleasing speech and manner. My masters believed that using me to slay you, Dejah Thoris of Helium, would be their crowning achievement. I was assigned this job, and my victory in the games would have made it so easy. I was placed at court, and by the malice of Phortora, was even sent to wait upon you. A knife in the night . . . poison . . . the silken cord to your slender neck!"

Kan Vastor uttered an imprecation, and his mount reared and stumbled as his rider's mind faltered in guiding him, under the influence of his strong emotion. Kan Vastor made as if to hurl Parvia from her seat behind him. She clung to his strong arm, preventing the action.

"Peace, peace, my friend. You behold the princess unharmed. You see that I was unable to carry out my assignment.

"Princess! Your kindness and justice as Arbiter of the games allowed me my victory. Without you, Phortora would have seen to it that I lost. All that I saw of you at court confirmed your incomparable beauty and nobility. How could I take advantage of your trust to murder you? Even the child of assassins could not stoop so low. I renounced my task, and with it, my very identity. And most probably my life as well. My old crew will punish my treachery with instant death whenever they find me. From this day forward, I will not sleep or drink water in peace. Death for me may hide in every shadow. But it has been worth it to have the trust of the Princess of Helium and to ride as her companion.

"And as yours, noble warrior," she added in a lower voice, resting her head for a moment on Kan Vastor's shoulder.

"It is not the custom of Helium to let loyal service go unrewarded," Dejah Thoris said. "When I go home, you can come with me. My father would never let you suffer retribution for the crime of saving my life."

"I thank you—but I do not believe that even the great Mors Kajak can prevent my old mates from exacting their revenge."

"You have not met my father," Dejah Thoris said. "When you do, you will understand my confidence. But meanwhile, we have to get out of our current predicament and find a way home. Tell me, since you know so much, who hired you? Who wanted me dead?"

"Alas, Princess, that I do not know. We are never told. Only the chief of the guild knows who has hired us, and what price they paid. The less we know, the less we can tell, should we stumble into capture and interrogation before we can take our own lives. We are not even told the names of most of our fellow guild members. We know only those few with whom we work on a regular basis, five or six at most."

"This ignorance is frustrating," Dejah Thoris said. "I suggest our first objective, should we find ourselves in an inhabited location, is to obtain a flier. Our second must be to try to get information. We must know our enemies to have any chance of survival."

"This seems the best plan we can have, at the moment," Kan Vastor said. "We are at your command."

Dawn touched the eastern horizon, and the moons were fading into the pale light. Snuffing the morning wind, the thoats bellowed at each other and broke into a gallop again. They rocketed over the moss as if they had scented their destination. There was no more conversation. The fugitives clung to their saddles and had no breath for talking. Dejah Thoris found it difficult to keep any control over her mount. Kan Vastor's thoat dashed ahead even more recklessly. Soon Dejah Thoris had to abandon the attempt to slow her steed or risk being left behind in the wastes.

They careered over a flat, featureless plain. Perhaps it had once been the abyssal plain of the vast, vanished sea. Nothing ahead seemed to indicate human habitation. Yet the thoats thundered on. Suddenly, a dark line appeared ahead of them. Before Dejah Thoris could even wonder what it might signify, they were nearly upon it, and it was revealed as a gash in the earth, stretching far across their path.

"Stop!" Dejah Thoris screamed. She mentally clutched at her thoat's simple mind, but he did not heed her. It seemed he would hurl himself over the edge. Ahead of her, Kan Vastor and Parvia abruptly disappeared from sight, Parvia's faint cry trailing out behind them. Dejah Thoris thought of hurling herself from the thoat's back to save herself, but she hesitated a moment too long, and her mount plunged over the edge.

10
DWELLERS IN THE CLEFT

AFTER ONE HEART-STOPPING MOMENT of terror, the thoat landed with a jolt. Beyond the edge was not a precipice, but a steep, twisting path that was only near-vertical. Sure-footed beyond most of their kind, the thoats skidded and blundered their way downhill, raising clouds of dust and scattering pebbles to rattle down in miniature avalanches about their feet.

When they stopped abruptly, their riders tumbled off with a stunning impact onto hard, sandy ground intermittently punctuated with moss and shrubs. Unfortunately, they had not fallen on the more cushioned portions of the area. Dazed and groaning, they sat up and brushed the dust out of their eyes. Dejah Thoris spat out sand. Although, like most Barsoomians, she could travel a long way before feeling the pangs of thirst, she wished for water.

Her wish was granted. Wincing from her bruises, she stood up slowly and heard the tantalizing sound of running water. It was a rare sound on Barsoom, something she normally heard only in the palace gardens where man-made fountains had been created. She looked up. The sky was a blue streak between steep, sharp-edged walls of sand and rock. She could just make out the trail by which they had descended. It looked like a crooked thread hanging from the cliff's edge. At the very bottom of the cleft, there was another thread: a thread of water, reflecting the sky's blue. The intermittent stream sometimes showed itself only as a damp patch in the sand. Other times, a trickle of moisture seeped from the rock walls to join the stream, and a pool formed, to bubble out over the stony ground. The sound came from those miniature cascades.

Kan Vastor joined her.

"Imagine the days when the ocean rolled over this spot," he said. "This would have been a crack in the seafloor. Nothing but lightless water, up to the edge of the cliff. And that point would be the ocean floor, with miles of water still above us!"

"Why frighten us with tales of the times of our eldest elders?" Parvia grumbled. "I find our current state disturbing enough. Oh, my head. I swear that stupid beast stepped on me when I fell."

She limped to the small rivulet and plunged her head into the water. Dejah Thoris followed suit.

"If I had known what was coming, I would have eaten more at the banquet," she said.

"I too have a hollow stomach," Kan Vastor said. "My flier was well provisioned, but I brought nothing with me. So eager was I to rescue you!"

"Next time you hasten to a rescue, pack a lunch," Parvia said playfully. She examined the foliage beside the water.

"I see the moss grows here, as everywhere, and the thoats are happy with their grazing. But many of these plants are unfamiliar to me. I see no usa, no mantalia trees."

A scattering of pebbles falling from the cliff's edge alarmed them. They threw themselves to the ground behind some low shrubs, seeking concealment. A thudding and scrambling heralded the arrival of more thoats. To their relief, the animals were riderless. They trumpeted a greeting to the two who had already arrived, and soon a small herd was milling about, seeking to sate their hunger and thirst.

"That settles it," Kan Vastor said. "Clearly, Princess, you are right. They seem quite at home here. This must be the hiding place of some of those miscreants who carried you off."

Parvia splashed a final palmful of water into her mouth and checked her weapons. "I suggest we move away from this spot. It seems to be the main point of entry to the valley, and we might not wish to loiter here to be spied by foes from above."

As the herd blocked the narrow passage before them, and they had little taste for further mingling with thoats, they turned to follow the stream downward and see what lay in that direction. While scanning the cliffs for signs of enemy presence, they also kept a lookout for potential sources of nourishment.

Save for the ubiquitous moss, which had found its way down from above to grow on the valley floor, the vegetation was unfamiliar. Vines with tough, fleshy leaves trailed from the rocky cliffs wherever a trace of moisture showed. Beneath their stems, the rocks were encrusted with lichenous orange scales. Neither plant offered much hope of edibility.

As they followed the path of the stream, fibrous mounds of red-orange tendrils appeared at the water's edge. Some were small, merely fist-sized, but they increased in height until finally Dejah Thoris stopped to examine one as large as a grown man's torso. It had an internal structure composed of tough-looking stems like smooth red wood, intricately interwoven. To her eyes, it resembled a type of decoration found in the palaces of Helium, a sphere of semiprecious stone carved into a filigree effect, permitting one to see through its latticework to a second carved sphere within, and so on. Whatever lay at the center of this patterning was invisible beneath so many weavings.

As she gazed upon this remarkable growth, she noticed movement going on within the structure. Reddish buds were swelling before her eyes, until they reached the size of a large bead or a small ball. Then, with an audible *pop*, they parted from the stem and rolled into the stream where they floated along, sometimes encountering an eddy where they bumped into each other and formed a small floating cluster.

"These appear like fruits of some kind." Cautiously, she touched one swelling bud with a fingertip. No sting ensued. There was no reaction. She bent and scooped up a few of the fallen buds from the water.

"Princess, no!" Kan Vastor exclaimed. "You should let one of us test these for you."

Dejah Thoris shrugged off his counsel. "I would not act like the court of Zor for the world," she said. "They allow others to risk poisoning for them, as if their lives were of more worth than those of their faithful friends. I choose to taste for myself."

Placing one gleaming scarlet sphere close to her lips, she took a tiny nibble. The skin or rind was firm, but thin enough that her teeth could pierce it. She dared to bite more deeply and taste the juicy pulp within. The flavor was salty, yet with a hint of sweetness. The rind was crunchy, while the interior had a pleasing softer texture. She consumed it with unexpected enthusiasm and reached for another.

"I feel no ill effects," she said. "These bud-berries are delicious."

"Should we not gather a few and see if the thoats will eat them?" Kan Vastor said. "We will not die of hunger if we take precautions first."

"Try just one," Dejah Thoris said. "Look at me—I am well. I see no reason to wait before refreshing ourselves."

She had already swallowed a handful of the berry-like spheres. They were strangely tempting, and so easy and pleasant to consume.

Kan Vastor frowned, but not to be outdone in boldness by a slender young woman, he also tasted. A smile spread over his face. He offered a palmful of the shiny red objects to Parvia.

"The princess is right," he said. "I feel strengthened and more alert already."

Soon all three were kneeling at the river's edge, plucking the berries from the water as they floated downstream from the parent plant, and swallowing them with gusto.

Parvia, more slight of body than the other two, was the first to feel the further effects.

Her hand opened and let the last few red spheres float away from her trailing fingers.

"What is this I feel?" she murmured. "I can eat no more. Let us be on our way . . . after a small rest. Just . . . a tiny . . . respite . . . ."

She pitched forward and lay prone, her face dangerously close to the lapping waters.

As Kan Vastor reached out to her, he toppled over too. He lay curled up as if sleeping, one hand immersed in the stream. Dejah Thoris rose to her feet to step back, as his body fell at her side. Her head swam with vertigo, and she found herself sinking to the ground not far from her friends. A wave of sleep overwhelmed her, even as she fought against it. She knew not how long she lay in a daze, her body whispering insistently that she must rest, while some corner of her mind continued to sound the alarm.

A sharp bit of rock was her salvation. It landed on her cheek, stinging, as the ground shook beneath her. The small, sharp pain said *here is danger*, as the quaking ground jolted her out of somnolence. With a tremendous effort, she pulled herself once more to her knees. Glancing behind her to learn what had struck her, she saw another group of thoats scrambling down the steep trail and thundering down the valley, shaking the earth with their footfalls and scattering pebbles in their wake. She recalled vaguely that there was some reason to fear the arrival of more beasts. She dared not try to stand, but pulled herself forward on hands and knees to warn her fallen friends.

Something about the scene was not right. Parvia's harness was adorned with gleaming red baubles, each the size of a fist. She had not been wearing such gaudy garb at first light, had she? Dejah Thoris shook her head to clear her vision. As she watched, more of the red spheres floated down the stream to cluster around her friend. They also clung to Kan Vastor's arm where it lay in the water, and were moving up his arm toward his body.

Dejah Thoris' first thought was to drag her friends away from the water. She succeeded in pulling Parvia to a dry location where she was no longer in danger of being drowned. But try as she might, she could not shift the greater bulk of Kan Vastor and his warrior's accoutrements.

Her efforts were not completely without effect. The warrior groaned and stirred.

Encouraged, she shook his shoulder vigorously.

"Get up! Get up! You must wake up!" she cried in his ear.

He rolled over heavily. Opening his eyes, he caught sight of his own arm, and sprang to his feet in horror. He tried to shake off the red things without success. Then he caught sight of Parvia, and forgot his own plight.

"What has happened?" he cried. He tried to pull the red basketwork creatures away from her body. At first his efforts were in vain. Then, with a cry of pain, he snatched his hand away, with a red sphere adhering to his fingertips. He tried to shake it off, but it would not go. Dejah Thoris took hold of his hand and pressed it down against the rocks by the side of the stream. A thrust of her knife against the red sphere had no effect. She took up another stone and smashed it repeatedly. Finally it lost its grip on Kan Vastor's flesh and lay inert, oozing a blood-scented ichor. Its fellows still stuck tight to his arm.

He extended his arm toward Dejah Thoris.

"Smash them," he begged.

"I cannot—I might harm you," she said.

"I care not! Remove it! And remove them from her!"

Still fighting the soporific effects of what she had consumed, Dejah Thoris knew that time was of the essence. She told Kan Vastor to lay his arm across the rocks again, and smote the parasites with the flat of her blade. The basket-creatures were too resilient, bouncing back from her blow. She could not smash them effectively without using such force as to damage

Kan Vastor's arm as well. Certainly she could not smash them away from Parvia's ribs without injuring her.

With the point of the blade, she prodded the remains of the creature she had killed with a rock. In the center of the smashed strands, she found a teardrop-shaped node that was oozing ichor from the cracks sustained in her attack. She turned her efforts to the remaining creatures clustered on Kan Vastor's flesh, piercing the basketry of tendrils to seek the central node. When her blade found its target, the creature contracted and quivered. As she sliced through the node, the intricate basketry collapsed, and the tendrils slackened their attachment to his skin. The red sphere lost its grip and fell to the ground. Her experiment succeeded on several more of the spheres before Kan Vastor stopped her.

"Enough! I live! Parvia's plight is far worse! We must help her!"

He too seized his blade, and the two of them bent over their companion's body. Dejah Thoris' slender blade had a finer point, and she was more easily able to pierce the creatures' core. His larger sword was less effective, and his wounded and numbed arm made it harder to aim the point, but he cut away valiantly. Soon they had cleared away a number of the creatures, revealing puffy abrasions where they had secured themselves to Parvia's skin. Tiny pinpoints of her blood oozed out.

"They tempt their prey to eat until they fall asleep, then extract their lifeblood!" Kan Vastor said.

"Indeed, it would seem so," Dejah Thoris agreed. "Shame upon me that I allowed my belly to lead my head astray! No seasoned warrior would have done so. I ask your forgiveness for my error."

"I ate as eagerly as any famished ulsio," Kan Vastor said. "I can only hope there is no lasting harm."

Both were so intent on their work that they failed to notice the scarlet reflection in the stream. They glanced up only moments before the writhing tentacles of the parent creature engulfed them. The large basket-creature that had originally dropped its buds into the stream to lure them had arisen in wrath at the destruction of its scions. Surging out of the water, its full size was revealed as it slithered on pseudopods to attack them.

One immediate advantage ensued: the remaining smaller spheres immediately loosed their hold on human flesh, to be swept back by the tentacles to rejoin the parent body. As the thrashing tentacle-creature absorbed the fluids its emissaries had drained, it flushed a deeper red. Their adversary had been strengthened by their own blood, as they were weakened by its loss.

The outer layer of its structure unwound itself from its protective basket shape to lash out with abrasive tentacles. Their once-smooth surfaces extruded thousands of tiny prickles that scratched and gripped. The two combatants were fortunate that their swords had already been drawn. The scarlet tentacles sought to constrain their limbs and bind their arms at their sides. Standing back to back and each slashing at the tentacles that menaced the other, the two kept themselves free enough to fight back.

While they battled the onslaught at human height, the pseudopods below the water's surface crawled ever closer to Parvia, who still lay unconscious on the shore. Having tasted her blood, the creature was bent on assimilating her entirely. In vain Kan Vastor hacked away at the tough, tenacious limbs. Where one was severed, another unwound to take its place. Its sphere-within-sphere structure made it near-impossible to reach the vital organ at its core. Taking her cue from the structure of the smaller units, Dejah Thoris assumed that piercing the central bud would incapacitate the creature. But her repeated thrusts never reached their mark. The creature pressed them ever back, reaching greedily for Parvia.

"Cover me," she said to Kan Vastor. She stepped away from him, and into the lashing maelstrom of the tentacles. He did his best to strike away the limbs that strove to immobilize her, but soon she felt the sting of half a dozen scarlet strands enveloping her. Through the woven screen, she caught a glimpse of a red, pulsing organ, shaped like those of its smaller copies, but as big as the head of a warrior.

She knew she would have but one chance. Ignoring the needlelike pain of the red appendages piercing her skin, she watched the ceaseless motion of the swaying basketry. As the creature reached out to seize her, an opening appeared. She lunged and fully extended her arm through the opening, trapping herself in its meshes, but plunging the point of her blade into its central organ. She wagered her life on the belief that this was the creature's heart. As she pierced the organ, the creature convulsed in a paroxysm of rage. Its tentacles thrashed madly, knocking Kan Vastor to the ground and crushing Dejah Thoris in a final embrace. A horrid shrieking, like a pressurized vessel about to explode, filled the air.

From what orifice it was emitted, they never knew. As suddenly as it had begun, it leaked away. The flailing tentacles sank to the ground, and the intricate structure of the creature collapsed into a disheveled heap. Groaning, Kan Vastor got to his feet and plucked the encircling strands away from Dejah Thoris with the flat of his sword. As they peeled away, they left red welts behind to crisscross her delicate skin. She had been partially protected by her harness, so it was mainly her limbs that suffered injury, but the welts were nonetheless painful.

Tears of pain brimmed her eyes as she attempted to rise, but she resolutely suppressed them. It seemed in another life that her least discomfort had been eagerly solaced. Now it was her duty to hearten her companions, and bear her own pain as best she could.

Kan Vastor offered a strong arm to help her to her feet. He did not wince at her grip, but she saw the puffy abrasions that covered his skin.

"Are you well?" she asked.

"My hurts are trivial," he said. "And you, Princess?"

"I am well enough. Fortunately that thing died before its

seizure could crush my ribs. I felt concern for a moment as its grip tightened."

She took a deep breath experimentally, and found herself still able both to breathe and to move.

"What of Parvia? She suffered longest from our greedy foe."

Tenderly lifting their fallen companion by her knees and shoulders, they moved her to a patch of soft, dry moss and examined her injuries. Her back was covered with the same kind of swelling that marked Kan Vastor's arm. It seemed there was no serious hurt, yet she remained unconscious. They chafed her hands and feet, but she did not stir. Dejah Thoris wished in vain for the reviving tonics and the healing practitioners available in abundance in Lesser Helium. She feared that the creature had drained Parvia to such an extent that she needed expert help to wake again.

Kan Vastor gripped her shoulders and shook her with a fervor that Dejah Thoris thought might go beyond the normal concern of one warrior for another.

"Parvia!" he cried. "Awake! Your princess has need of you! Wake up!"

Such rough handling succeeded where gentler ministrations had not. Parvia's eyelids fluttered and she stirred. Suddenly, her eyes opened wide and she struck out fiercely, landing one glancing blow across Kan Vastor's nose. He dropped her involuntarily, clapping one hand to his face.

Caught between laughter and tears of relief, Dejah Thoris sought to soothe her, as their warrior companion backed away, rubbing his nose.

"All is well! Fear not!" she cried. "The monster that attacked you is slain! We are safe."

Parvia sat up, patting her own arms and shoulders as if to assure herself that the predatory spheres were gone.

"I do beg your pardon," she cajoled Kan Vastor. Abashed, she tried to peer around Dejah Thoris to be certain that the warrior was not offended. "I felt something grasping me, and feared it was an enemy. I had such horrid dreams while

I was unconscious. Dreams of a maw that drew me ever closer! I tried to shout a warning, but could not make a sound. What happened?"

She shuddered at the sight of the tangled mass of scarlet tentacles, now fading as the currents played with them at will.

"Don't look," Dejah Thoris said, helping her to her feet. "Have you strength to stand? I fear we are all the worse for wear after that encounter. And still as empty of belly as before. Those tempting red lures, whether they were bud, berry, or I know not what, contained much sleeping-juice and little nourishment."

"What shall we do now?" Kan Vastor asked.

"To sample more unknown fruits would be unwise," Parvia said.

"I agree," Dejah Thoris said. "I suggest we do what we probably should have done in the first place. We must follow the thoats upstream and find out who their masters are. What saved me from the same sleep that took you was the arrival of another group of riding thoats. As you warned, Parvia, sooner or later thoats still possessed of their riders will descend into the valley. We would be better off to gain some knowledge and concealment before they show up to identify us. Let us move on, as you are able. Kan Vastor can tell you of our battle as we go."

They followed in the direction the thoats had taken, and soon caught up with them, even at the slow pace they used to allow themselves some recovery. The herd was browsing as it went, and they were able to shelter behind the beasts. The valley was a crooked cleft, so they could not see far ahead before encountering some abutment of rock that blocked their view. The thoats ambled at a leisurely pace. After following them through several zigzags, Dejah Thoris was the first to spot a sign that they were on the right track.

Floating just below the edge of the cliffs, undetectable from above, a couple of fliers were tethered. Immediately, the small party moved close to the valley wall for cover, in case someone was aboard and surveying the valley from above. They parted company with the thoats and moved on as stealthily as possible in the shadow of the rocks. The sun was close to zenith, and soon that shadow would be reduced to a mere scrap.

They began to see signs of previous habitation. There were portions of walls, built of stone blocks weathered by unguessable ages. Most lay tumbled to the ground, but the stretches of wall that still stood provided convenient cover. At one point, their path was blocked by a mass of stone shaped like a column. As they scrambled over it, they saw that it was not a plain column, but a statue carved in the shape of a giant diving fish. It seemed these walls could not have been built until the oceans had completely dried away, yet the column had been carved by an artist who remembered the former denizens of the seas. Dejah Thoris tucked the mystery away for consideration. It could not be solved this day.

Abruptly, the remnant walls and fallen stones ceased. The ground was bare and cleared of rubble. Around the next bend in the valley loomed a fortress. One wing lay in ruins, but the central section and its adjoining towers stood tall and sturdy. This seemed the logical destination of the scavenged stones. Builders had carried them here to fortify the existing structure. The fliers they had seen earlier still floated at anchor behind the building. Between the cliff wall and one of the towers, a third vessel was now visible. It lay awkwardly placed, as if its crew had cast anchor and disembarked in a hurry.

The lower part of the building was partially concealed behind a little grove of sompas and sorapus trees. The trees must have been planted only recently, for they had not yet reached their full growth.

"Pity," Parvia said, measuring the distance with her eyes. "If only those trees had a bit better growth, we might get to the rooftop that way."

"Why would we want to be on the rooftop?" Kan Vastor said. "Would we not do better to make our way at once to the fliers and escape before we are seen?"

"I would like nothing more than to commandeer a flier and return at once to Helium," Dejah Thoris said. "But we must first go to Zor and learn what has become of the brave men and women I left there. I would forfeit the honor of my people if I allowed them to languish as captives for a moment longer. Before we go to Zor, we must learn who we can trust there. We must learn what part those who dwell here had in our abduction, and whom they serve in Zor."

Kan Vastor's hand went to his sword hilt, and his eyes flashed at the promise of daring deeds. Yet he frowned at her words.

"Your plan is bold," he said. "But, Princess, you should not hazard your own person in such an endeavor. We should first make our way to the fliers and see you safely aboard. Then Parvia and I can carry out a surveillance raid. If we fail, you can still seek refuge in Zor."

"My father and my father's father were not entrusted with the rule of Helium so that we could hang back while others risked their lives for us! Their blood flows in my veins and urges me to the forefront."

Kan Vastor could only bow to her. "Princess, it shall be as you command."

"Enough conversation," Parvia said. "To action!"

The trees that grew around the fortress provided the benefit of concealment for those within. However, they also promised cover to visitors who might want to enter unseen. They were too convenient to be unguarded, so the trio proceeded cautiously, belly-crawling across the open space left by the clearing of rubble.

The thoats arrived at the same time, and made a welcome distraction as they milled around the building, squealing querulously. They drew out the guards whose presence Parvia had suspected. The trio froze, hugging the ground, not daring to look up, as rough voices approached.

"Riderless thoats? How have they returned so soon?"

"Look! That's old Sovus Kor's mount! I'd know him any-where, by that scar on his snout."

The squealing became cacophonous as the two men who had spoken tried to drive the thoats to their pen by smacking their flanks with spear shafts.

Parvia risked raising her head to locate them. As they had guessed from the voices, there were only two guards present. She unwound a length of silk from her arm. Its hue, once bright, was now dulled with dust. Seizing a stone from the ground, she rose to her feet, dropped the stone into the doubled silk, then swung it around her head and let fly. The slung stone flew true. It slammed into the skull of the guard standing nearest to her, with his back turned, and he dropped to the ground. Her action took place in seconds, and in silence.

The other guard was on the far side of the thoat. It took a moment for him to note the absence of his companion. Kan Vastor gathered himself to rush the man before he could realize his danger. Parvia unslung her captured sword from its place on her back. Dejah Thoris chafed at her own inaction.

If only I had my bow, she thought.

She had only her slender woman's blade. It was no match for the weaponry of the grim, experienced guard. She feared that if she joined the fray, she would only be a distraction, as her companions tried to protect their princess.

Yet there was something she might be able to do.

"Wait for my signal," she commanded her friends.

She crept swiftly closer to the restless thoats, heedless of the stony ground chafing her bare limbs. As she moved, she reached out mentally for the dull minds of the thoats. She had never attempted to control them at a distance, without the assistance of physical contact and guidance. She attracted the attention of the nearest animal, just touching his dim consciousness. The thoat uttered a grunt of surprise and rebel-lion, rearing half upright with four of his limbs pawing the air. He landed with an earthshaking thud, squealing his dislike of this new attempt to tame him. His club-like tail, lashing about, connected with the guard who had been trying to herd him away, and knocked the man to the ground.

Dejah Thoris beckoned with an upraised arm. Parvia and Kan Vastor hardly waited for the signal. In a crouching run, they dodged full speed across the bare space and darted behind the bulk of the thoat. Kan Vastor clubbed the fallen guard with the hilt of his sword. The man joined his fellow in unconsciousness.

In the meantime, Dejah Thoris had vaulted aboard the thoat. Once in physical contact with the animal, she soon established command of his movements. Although he stamped and bellowed, he obeyed.

"Quick! Climb on!" she ordered her companions. Kan Vastor and Parvia clung to his broad back precariously. They had not far to ride. Dejah Thoris urged her mount close to the fortress wall, where a particularly large sompas tree raised its branches. The lowest accessible bough was already high above the ground, too high to climb, but within reach from a thoat's back. Kan Vastor rose to one knee, steadying himself on the princess' shoulder, as she held the thoat in check with firm control. Parvia placed one foot lightly on Kan Vastor's shoulder and leaped for the branch.

Then, lying full-length upon it, she reached down to give Kan Vastor a hand up. He, too, vaulted into the tree. Dejah Thoris rose to her full height, balancing for a moment on the thoat's swaying back with delicate bare feet. From thence, she sprang for the branch, and in an instant, was atop it, steadied by the strong arm of Kan Vastor. Had anyone glanced down from the vantage point of a flier or a rooftop, they would have been likely to miss the whole affair. It had been but a short interval from their leaving the concealment of the shadows to attaining a hiding place among the foliage.

11

FORTRESS OF MURDEROUS INTRIGUE

WITH OCCASIONAL AID FROM THE STRAPS attached to their harness, they quickly ascended a few more rungs of branches, until they were level with the first windows. As was customary in Barsoomian structures, the lower levels were windowless, to deter entrance by assassins and other dangers. The denizens of this building had unwarily allowed the shading foliage to grow a little too close to the lowest aperture for perfect safety. Measuring the distance with her eye, Dejah Thoris considered that it might be possible to gain entrance.

The tips of the branches nearest the window were alarmingly thin. Parvia ran out on the slender limb fearlessly and sprang onto the broad sill, with no more sound than the falling of a ripe nut. Hugging the edge of the window, she peered within, then waved the others on. Dejah Thoris, determined not to be outdone, imitated her movements and also landed safely, albeit with a thud that might have aroused suspicion. However, when Kan Vastor edged closer to the end of the branch, it bent dangerously low. He retreated, to unwind to its fullest extension the hooked strap Barsoomians use to swing aboard a flier. Swinging this above his head, he moved forward again. As the branch bent double beneath his weight, he used it as a springboard. His grappling hook caught the sill's edge as he leaped, and soon he was scrambling up to take his place beside the two women.

"'Tis well this room is empty," Parvia said. "The sound of

your landing might have alarmed a listener, who would think a giant ape had perched here!"

She was about to jump down into the room below, but Dejah Thoris restrained her.

"We cannot be sure the room is empty," she said. "It has the appearance of an audience chamber. I see a dais and chair at this end. There may be guards at the interior door, which we cannot see."

Moving to the other side of the windowsill, where she might have a broader view of the room, would take her out of the shade of the tree and allow her to be seen by watchers below. Nevertheless, she began to creep along the ledge.

She was checked by Parvia's hand on her arm.

"I hear someone coming," Parvia said. Dejah Thoris heard nothing, but trusting to the ears of the trained assassin, she froze.

Moments later, voices and footsteps were audible to all of them. The unseen door clanged shut, and guards stamped as they came to attention. Two shapes quickly crossed the length of the room, backs to the viewers. One turned and flung himself into the chair of audience. Dejah Thoris stared into the relative gloom of the chamber, hoping to see his face. But the sun had now moved across the sky far enough that the end of the room was in shadow. She could dimly make out a seated form, but nothing of his features.

His companion was of lesser rank, for he fell to one knee before the throne-like chair. His face was still turned away from them, but his harness, metal, and weapons appeared to denote a warrior of some standing. It seemed he had been summoned to report on an urgent matter.

"Why are you here without the girl? And why are our thoats returning riderless?" the seated man demanded.

The warrior attempted an explanation. With his head bowed and turned away from her, it was difficult for Dejah Thoris to hear every word. She hoped that Parvia's keen hearing would fill in anything that she missed.

"We subdued the girl easily enough," he said. "Both girls, in fact, for there was one close to her at the time, in similar harness, and our hired panthans feared kidnapping the wrong princess. They were drugged with the agents you supplied, and taken to the rendezvous, as you ordered."

"And where are they now?" The seated man's tone was that of one who would be dangerous when crossed.

"Our agreement with the jed was that he would allow them to remain for some days, long enough to be really frightened, and then set out to accomplish their rescue. In gratitude, the Heliumetic girl would then have thrown herself into his arms, as planned. But the foolish jed could not wait for the agreed time. He arrived to the 'rescue' too early, before they had even awakened. Word has it that some impetuous courtier saw the kidnapping, and the jed feared his deception would be discovered."

"So, then, the Princess of Helium has been returned to Zor?"

"I fear not, Holy One. A gang of assassins arrived before the jed could secure the camp. They killed several of our hired men, as well as some of our own guards. They engaged the men of Zor as well, and damaged their forces before vanishing into the night. In the confusion, both of the girls disappeared. Their current location is unknown. I took a flier under pretext of searching for them, and came at once to make my report to you."

"You dare to bring me this news?" the seated man burst out. "You dare bring me the tale of your failure? I should send you to Issus this very day! This moment!"

He paused to gain control of his anger.

"Perhaps you can still prove your usefulness and salvage something from this debacle. What is your explanation for the princess' absence?"

The warrior remained in his submissive pose, muttering something in an even lower voice, which Dejah Thoris took for a demurral of knowledge. He spoke again in a stronger tone.

"There was much blood in the camp, and the thoats had trampled the ground so that no tracks could be found. Thoat tracks departed in all directions. The kidnapped girls were both helpless under the influence of your powerful soporifics. They could have made no resistance. It is my belief that the assassins carried out their mission and removed the bodies as proof to those who hired them. It is not known whether the princess or her companion was their target. The companion was a nobody, but had recently incurred the displeasure of the jed's sister."

"And what of the jed himself?"

"When last I saw him, he was searching the area for traces of the princess. Whether it be our influence or his own folly, he is truly enthralled by her. After she spurned his advances, it was not difficult to convince him that having her kidnapped, so he might play the rescuer, would be a sure way to her heart. Now he blames himself for her death, but if I know him, he will soon find another target for his wrath. "

"Arrogant bumbler!" the seated man said. "He will soon give up the search and slink back to Zor like a wounded calot."

He remained silent for a moment, still near-invisible in the shadows.

"I never had much faith in this plan," he said at last. "Obedience is easily obtained from weak minds, with the aid of our device, but the Princess of Helium is a different matter. She and her kind are far too independent. Such minds cannot be affected so quickly—particularly in matters of love, where resistance of the heart is joined to resistance of mind. However, the jed was instantly besotted with her beauty, and there was no great harm in making the effort. It would have been great gain to our cause to have subdued a princess with the power of the medallion, and introduced our control into the heart of Helium.

"But if she is truly dead, we must move to our next plan— the one that was always more sure. The loss of his daughter will be a blow to Mors Kajak, but not sufficient to humble him. Nothing short of his own death can do that. Return to Zor at once, assemble an armed force of men you can trust, and find Mors Kajak. Contact the guards you embedded in his force, and have them kill him as the battle rages. Make it seem an accident if you can, but by whatever means necessary, he must die. Let him fall from his airship, to be hacked to pieces by the green men. I have spoken. Go now!"

Dejah Thoris gasped in horror. Her muscles tensed to spring out of concealment and slay those who would threaten her father. Before she could do so, a second revelation left her stunned. The kneeling man rose, saluted, and turned so his face was toward her. It was Ptang Raxo, Jedwar of Zor. His seated overlord stood and moved out of the shadow, but became no more recognizable than he had been before. Like the shadowy figure Dejah Thoris had seen in the streets of Zor, his identity was concealed entirely by a shroud-like veil of night-dark silk.

Was Mors Kajak to die at the behest of a thern? All her life she had been taught to respect, if not revere, the therns, custodians of the mysteries. Perhaps this creature merely wore the disguise of a thern. It must be a trick. Assassins she could deal with, but her mind could not grasp the idea that her father could be condemned to die by the guardians of the Valley Dor.

She nearly cried out "It is not possible!" but came to her senses in the nick of time as Parvia insistently shook her foot, the only part of her still within the young woman's reach. A hubbub swelled in volume nearby. More survivors of the raid on the kidnappers' camp were arriving, and had discovered the disabled guards and the agitated thoat herd. Dejah Thoris moved to seek better concealment, but it was too late. She flattened herself to the window ledge barely in time to escape a lance hurled from below.

The lance sailed past her, through the window and into the

room beyond. A shout of alarm sounded there, from the unseen guards at the door. A glance at the scene below revealed that it was too late to try to summon a thoat to carry them away from the tree. Only the milling about of the angry thoats stood between them and immediate death or capture. Once the warriors shoved their way through the herd, they would be at the throats of the princess and her friends.

"We're in for it now," Parvia said. "Princess! Your orders?"

Dejah Thoris felt the awful responsibility of a commander for the first time, though her troop was composed of only two.

"Into the fortress," she ordered. "We know we are outnumbered here."

She slid over the windowsill and dropped to the ground within. Parvia and Kan Vastor followed. Immediately, they confronted two angry guards, running to the window to see who had hurled a lance at them. The lance itself lay on the floor. Dejah Thoris, first to regain her footing, picked it up and hurled it at the oncoming adversary. Its point pierced the man's throat with deadly accuracy, and he fell to the ground in a welter of blood. Kan Vastor dispatched the other man with a sword thrust.

"Where to now?" He looked to the princess for direction.

One thought filled her mind.

"We must warn my father. Did you hear what they said? The veiled one—be he false thern, assassin, or whatever—plots with Ptang Raxo to kill him!"

"To the fliers, then?"

"Yes! But how?"

"We need another exit," Parvia said. "That pack outside will be after us in a moment."

Weapons drawn, they ran full tilt through the chambers and corridors of the fortress in search of escape. The building held few inhabitants. The outer walls had been stoutly repaired, but indoors, it was still partly ruinous, and rubble frequently strewed their way as they passed through empty rooms.

Some chambers, however, were meticulously appointed. Dejah Thoris slowed her pace briefly to peer through an open archway into a place of strange smells and stranger devices, where machinery hummed and clicked. Some type of manufacturing was being carried on. She longed to know its nature and purpose, but had no time for exploration.

At an intersection of corridors, the princess had to make a split-second choice of direction. She sprang toward the path she believed would lead away from the armed men lying in wait for them.

When they turned the corner, they came face to face with a score of warriors, heading toward them with swords drawn. Just behind the vanguard strode Ptang Raxo, and sheltering prudently behind him, his veiled master.

"The girl lives!" screamed the shadow-man. "Take the women alive! Kill the male!"

"Slay them!" Dejah Thoris cried. She had no thought but to charge the betrayers of Mors Kajak, and slay them at the price of her own life if need be. But her companions prevented it. Kan Vastor held her back with his left arm, while his strong right hand continued to wield the sword that the foremost rank of their adversaries feared to engage. Parvia cast about for some avenue of escape.

Down the passage perpendicular to the one they had chosen, she spied a ramp spiraling upward. Fleet-footed, she ascended to the first turn while Kan Vastor, shielding the princess, backed in that direction. Contrary to appearances, she had not retreated to save her own skin. Once arrived at a vantage point, she pulled one more device from the repertory of tricks concealed within her harness.

The sphere she hurled toward the oncoming warriors looked like the perfumed sudsing balls that women of refinement used to scent their baths. But when it landed at their feet, it exploded in a hail of sparks and thick smoke. Panic ensued as those in the front rank turned and tried to force their way back against the men behind them. As the smoke spread, the entire troop turned and ran. Those whose harness included enough silk to wrap their faces did so.

The confusion lasted long enough for the three to ascend the ramp and reach a door that led to the rooftop.

"What did you do to them?" Dejah Thoris panted, as they emerged into the sunlight again. "Was that a device like those our kidnappers used?"

Parvia laughed.

"I wish it were so, but it was harmless, just a simple explosive designed to strike fear and throw men off their guard. I've used up most of the toys I packed for this trip. They'll recover and be after us again in a twinkling."

Kan Vastor looked for something heavy to block the door, but there was nothing. He hammered the lock shut with the hilt of his sword, jamming the latch. Even now, footsteps thudded below them, and in moments, the door shuddered under the onslaught of the warriors' pounding.

"That will not hold them long," he said. "We must get off the roof."

They ran to the edge of the roof and glanced over the parapet, only to be met by a shower of arrows. They ducked back behind the protecting stones. On all sides it was the same. Enough men remained from the kidnappers' band and the garrison of the fortress to surround them on all sides. To descend would be impossible.

"If we cannot go down, we must ascend," Dejah Thoris said. The flier they had seen from afar still hung tethered between fortress and valley wall, tantalizingly just out of reach.

"A good plan, if only we could fly," Kan Vastor said. He measured the distance with his eyes, then backed toward the opposite wall, to get a good run for a desperate leap.

Parvia stopped him. "Wait—let me."

Kan Vastor scoffed. "I know you are nimble, but this is a leap that would be a risk for the strongest thews, certainly not a chance for a young woman to take. Let me go. The time is short."

"I am a trained assassin! Many a bruise I have taken in just such exercises. Your strong thews will help us, indeed they will be essential, but not for leaping."

She made Kan Vastor bend at the edge of the parapet, holding to the stones, in such a way that his broad back created a platform. Then she ran at him with the speed and lightness of a meteor tearing through the sky. Never losing momentum, she made a handspring to his back and hurled herself upward and outward in a tight-tucked somersault. More arrows darted toward her, as if she were a target in a training game, but her lithe body wheeled past them to land unharmed on the deck of the flier.

She ran crouching to the controls, and guided the flier toward the rooftop. Kan Vastor linked his hands together to give Dejah Thoris a boost over the parapet. She half fell onto the deck. Kan Vastor made his own leap to join them.

Dejah Thoris took the controls from Parvia. "I may not be a trained assassin, but I can fly."

Parvia yielded reluctantly, but her doubts soon vanished as the princess pointed the nose of the flier skyward and ascended so swiftly that her companions were forced to cling to the deck rails to avoid being thrown to the stern. This airship lacked the speed and the fine-tuned responsiveness of her own vessel, but she forced it to her will, ducking and dodging until she shot forth from the crack in the earth and sped across the plains beyond. Arrows rattled against the ship's hull, but by the time the sound of radium rifles was heard, they had left the fortress behind.

Without the guidance of a map or a beacon, she leveled off and headed east, hoping eventually to ascend to a height from which some landmark could be seen. They sped along for some time—long enough for the excitement of flight to wear off, and the ache of exertion to be felt in their weary limbs.

The princess angled the airship's nose upward to rise higher, when she heard exclamations from her lookouts.

"Below there!" cried Parvia. "A downed flier!"

"The ship bears the jed's symbol!" Kan Vastor said. "Hold! Our help may be needed!"

Dejah Thoris swung the flier in a wide circle to get a better look at the circumstances on the ground. She took the opportunity to glance back in the direction they had come from for signs of pursuit, but so far, no vessels from the fortress had appeared.

The ship below them lay on its side upon the moss, a trail of debris extending from its resting place. Half a dozen small figures gathered on its deck, swarming the area where the controls lay. From that direction, they could hear the faint reports of a radium pistol. One of the group of figures staggered and fell.

"More bodies lie nearby," Parvia said.

"Some brave defender battles unequal odds," Kan Vastor cried, as always eager to see glory in each new situation. "We must go to his aid!"

"I see danger in confronting more unknown assailants," Parvia said. "If our most vital goal is to protect the jed, your father, we must speed onward."

"All true," Dejah Thoris said. "And yet I could not face my father, knowing I had failed to render aid where it was needed. To pass by one in need of help would dishonor my ancestry."

"We are but three. How can we best approach without endangering ourselves and our ship?"

They had already lost the element of surprise. One of the attackers on the wrecked ship pointed upward and hallooed to his fellows. Dejah Thoris quickly ascended again to a greater height.

"Do any of them have pistols or rifles?" she asked.

"From here, I see none in their hands. It seems only our unseen defender is so armed," Parvia said.

"Search this ship for weapons," Dejah Thoris ordered. "We ought to have done so before."

They searched in haste, but in vain. They discovered some stores that might be welcome later, but all armaments appeared to have been commandeered by whomever had last flown the ship.

"Drop low enough, and I shall leap over the side, sword in hand!" Kan Vastor proposed. "I'll deal with them speedily enough with my blade. Hurry! If we delay, their prey will be slain before we arrive."

"No, you must not leave the ship," Dejah Thoris declared. "I have a better idea. Stand by, with weapons in hand, one to each side. Fasten your harness to the rail lest you be thrown overboard."

She put her vessel into a steep dive, whistling downward through the thin air. They passed above the wreck, clearing it by what seemed a mere hand's breadth. Parvia and Kan Vastor, leaning from the rail with extended blades, each cut down an attacker. The velocity of their ship added force to the blow, cutting the adversaries nearly in two. The nose of the ship struck a third man in the back of the head as he attempted to escape, striking him down with a crushed and bloodied skull. As Dejah Thoris wrenched the ship back to near-vertical and ascended, drops of blood sprayed back from the hull and spangled her smooth skin with a deeper red.

She dodged and swerved to avoid potential fire from below. No one tried for revenge. Two remaining attackers leaped from the tilted deck of the wrecked airship and ran. The warrior who had been defending himself stepped out of the bows and fired his radium pistol after them. One fell at once. The other staggered, but continued to flee, until a second, more carefully aimed shot brought him down as well. The little figure on the deck collapsed to his knees and then fell prone, to lie motionless, either dead or senseless.

Dejah Thoris circled the site once more, to be sure no

enemies still lurked in concealment. Then she brought the airship down, allowing it to hover mere feet above the ground.

"Go and get him," she ordered. "Hurry! I shall remain here at the controls in case we need a swift departure."

Kan Vastor bent to lift up the fallen man. He uttered an exclamation of shock and recognition as he hoisted the man to his shoulders and carried him to the ship. Strong as he was, he staggered under the burden, for the warrior was tall and muscular. Parvia remained a moment longer, searching the storage of the wrecked ship. Unrolling a canvas sunshade, she piled items into it and dragged it behind her as she made haste to catch up. Kan Vastor deposited his rescue on the deck of their ship, and then turned to help Parvia hoist her booty aboard.

As soon as both her companions were safely on deck, Dejah Thoris took the airship up to an altitude where the dead sea bottoms below were just a blur of reddish-yellow. She set the ship to continue slowly on its eastward course. Then she turned to examine the unconscious man.

She found Parvia using a soft cloth and a container of water from the wreck to wash away the grime and blood so she could see what injuries would need treatment. Gazing upon the man's newly cleaned visage, Dejah Thoris uttered a soft cry of surprise.

"It is Jan Vajo! It is the Jed of Zor!"

12
UNEXPECTED RESCUES

REVIVED BY THE COOL WATER, the man groaned and struggled to get up. Parvia gently restrained him from rising farther than a sitting position.

"You are safe," Dejah Thoris assured him. "You are aboard my airship. Those who attacked you are dead."

"Princess! How can this be?"

As he stared at her, in shock, she met his eyes with a steely gaze.

"Yes," she said, "I know that you had me and my friend kidnapped and held against our will. As you see, we have freed ourselves. You can make some reparation for this incomprehensible insult by telling us what happened between then and now. How came your pretended rescue to fail so badly?"

The jed rubbed his aching head, bewildered. "I hardly know. We meant to wait until the following day, but someone—" His eyes lit upon Kan Vastor, and he paused in shock, again. "Yes! This very fellow, this—" He swallowed words of insult. "This man. I received word that he had learned of your kidnapping and had left in pursuit of the party. I quickly summoned my forces to overtake him, set you free, and get the credit. As you know."

As he spoke, his hand moved repeatedly to his chest.

"Are you in pain?" Parvia asked. "Princess, give me permission to continue wrapping his wounds as you speak with him. Otherwise, he may lose consciousness again."

"What? No, I am well," he said, clutching again at his chest. "My wounds are nothing to a warrior. Save for my head, which aches most fiercely."

He rubbed his skull again, but soon his hand returned to the place where his harness straps crossed.

"Tell me what happened after you arrived," Dejah Thoris insisted. "We were attacked by assassins. What do you know of them?"

"No more than you. I had never seen those men before. The battle raged fiercely. Once we had subdued them, Ptang Raxo brought me the terrible news of your absence. He believed you killed by the assassins, your bodies dragged away as proof whereby they might receive their pay. All scattered in search of you.

"With a few trusted warriors, I took my ship up to search. As soon as we were out of sight of other vessels, assassins swarmed forth and attacked my men. I would not have thought it possible for them to conceal themselves as they did. They clung to the hull and contorted themselves into storage lockers. Nothing seemed impossible for them. My crewmen were taken by surprise, stabbed with stilettos, poisoned with dust, thrown overboard. They died protecting me. In the struggle for control, the ship was wrecked."

Grim laughter split his battered features.

"And now I, who sought to rescue you, am rescued by you! The Jed of Zor, ruler of legions, owes his life to a pair of slender women and a mere panthan. This is the reward of my ambition."

He struggled to his feet.

"Leave off your ministrations. I am well enough to go on, if I had my sword in my hand."

Again he clawed at his chest, frowning.

"Something else is missing, not merely my weapon. What is amiss? Gods of my ancestors, my head aches fit to split. I cannot think what is wrong."

He looked down at his harness.

"The medallion! The sigil of the ruler of Zor! Where is it?" His hand went to a nonexistent sword hilt.

"You have taken it from me while I lay helpless! What have you done with it?"

"It ill befits a swordless man to accuse those who have saved his life," Dejah Thoris said. "Your harness was bare of ornament when we picked you up. It must have been lost in the struggle."

Suddenly, her eyes opened wide in alarm. She pointed astern. "Ships come after us!" She leaped to the controls to wrest all possible speed from the engines.

"Ruler of Zor!" she cried. "Your help would be welcome, if you can tell me where we are."

Jan Vajo came to her side and gazed out over the expanse beneath them. "We travel lands I have not seen before. But wait—why are we speeding eastward? Zor lies to the west! I command you to turn around!"

"What gives you authority to issue commands here?" Dejah Thoris said coldly. "I pilot this ship. Our destination is of my choosing. Knowing that in Zor, I was kidnapped and treated with disdain, and that my trusted guards have suffered some vile fate, I prefer not to return there. I go to seek my father."

Jan Vajo moved as if to seize the controls, but Kan Vastor took a warning step toward him, sword in hand.

The jed glanced back and forth between Kan Vastor and Dejah Thoris. His lip curled.

"Ah, I see how it is," he said. "You, an upstart panthan, offered the favor of my court, have taken advantage of your undeserved position. Now you desert allegiance to Zor, to woo the faithless daughter of Helium!"

Dejah Thoris spoke quietly, but her eyes flashed fire and her grip tightened on the wheel.

"If my father were here, lord of Zor, you should answer for those words with your life."

Kan Vastor also restrained himself with difficulty. "And if you were not at present a swordless man," he said, "I myself would seek satisfaction for this insult."

"You speak as a lover," Jan Vajo sneered.

Kan Vastor flushed beneath his bronze hue. "My words are those of a man of honor," he said. "Which you would recognize, had you not fallen so far from that rank. The Princess of Helium is as a star to whom all must look up in wonder at her beauty. But my heart is vowed elsewhere, to a gem whose luster seems no less bright to me."

Dejah Thoris caught the glance of adoration that he directed toward Parvia. Such was love, she supposed. And Kan Vastor was a man worthy of her friend's love. For a moment, she wished she might inspire such devotion from one of similar nobility. And yet, it was not Kan Vastor whose love she wished. And it was certainly not the attention of a jed. With all her heart, she detested Jan Vajo and his schemes.

"Enough!" she ordered. "This conversation will not continue in my presence. Such words are unfit for my ears. Jed of Zor, if you can inform me of the way to the canal, do so. Otherwise, be silent. You are a passenger, and one who is obligated to my friends for his very life. It behooves you to speak respectfully."

Jan Vajo scowled. He retreated from his accusations, but without acknowledging her order of silence. "What are these ships that follow?" he demanded.

"Ships of Zor, I believe," she said. "Another score I place against you. Your jedwar, Ptang Raxo, is aboard, I wager, and he pursues me with intent to do me some further dishonor in your name."

If she had not known better, she would have thought the jed was truly surprised. His surly expression turned to consternation.

"Ptang Raxo? But he searched for you only to aid you. Turn back! If my jedwar follows us, we could have no better assistance. He has always been faithful to my house."

"Then it would surprise you to hear that when last I saw him, he was plotting to slay my father—not in open battle, but by treachery, like a common assassin."

"Impossible!" Jan Vajo cried. "I gave no such orders!"

"Ptang Raxo cares nothing for your orders. He kneels at the feet of one who has the appearance of a thern, like the one I saw at the festival. They have a secret fortress within the boundaries of your lands. It was there that I saw your jedwar. Ptang Raxo obeys him and scorns you."

"Impossible," Jan Vajo repeated, but in a weaker tone. He swayed and sank to a sitting position against the hull.

"If Ptang Raxo is your loyal retainer, then how do you explain his actions? Indeed, they match your own. Your invitation was meant to lure me here, where you could force me to accept your suit by giving me a medallion that could bend me to your will. To kill Mors Kajak would be in accord with this treachery."

Jan Vajo's hand felt again for the missing medallion, then moved to his head.

"Hold your fire!" he said. "You hurl your accusations at a man without sword or shield. Indeed I am not myself today. Blame that knock on the head if I spoke amiss. It taxes me more than I thought at first. I am bewildered. I have some memory of Dramus Ugo urging that you be taken from the palace—for your own safety, I thought he said—but I swear on the bones of my ancestors I have no knowledge of a plot to kill Mors Kajak. Why should I bring the wrath of Helium upon my city?"

"It would better befit the Jed of Zor to own his actions," Dejah Thoris said, "rather than to plead ignorance like a youth at lessons." She felt the inexpressible contempt of a woman of Barsoom for a man who flinches from responsibility. An outright villain is more respected than a weakling. She had not expected feeble excuses from a powerful warrior. And yet—

"Whence came this medallion of yours?" she asked.

"Dramus Ugo, oldest and wisest of counselors, placed it

upon my harness when I became jed, more than one hundred years ago. It is an heirloom of the city, as I told you."

"An heirloom—or a trap for the mind?"

To this Jan Vajo made no answer. He had fallen into a stupor.

Parvia moved closer to him to examine his wounds. The bleeding was stanched. His breathing was regular. Yet he seemed greatly weakened.

"A blow to the head can do harm our best medicines cannot reach," she said.

"I wonder," Dejah Thoris replied. "Is it a blow taken in battle today, or is it the damage done by one hundred years of wearing that device? Glad am I that I left the medallion he gave me behind! Else I might be turning back even now to join Ptang Raxo and suffer a fate unknown."

Kan Vastor had been gazing behind them for some time. "We may see Ptang Raxo again whether we wish to or not," he said. "I am sure now—the ships are gaining on us."

"I have felt it," Dejah Thoris said. "I sense a sluggishness in the controls. We are losing altitude. The gauges warn of a lack of buoyancy. I fear those volleys we endured while fleeing may have had some effect after all. We have a slow leak in our tanks."

She had done her best to keep the ship in the air by increasing its velocity, but as they sank unmistakably earthward, it was no longer safe to maintain speed. The ships behind them gradually came closer. Soon they were no longer mere dots against the sky, but could be distinguished by their shape. Kan Vastor confirmed that they were ships of Zor.

"What shall we do?" Kan Vastor asked. "I will stand and fight for you, if such is your command. But I must advise you that our chances of victory are small."

"Your courage becomes a warrior," Parvia said. "But as an assassin, I think it better to feign submission and hope for a chance to escape later. However, my loyalty now lies with you, Dejah Thoris, and I will follow your lead."

"Since we can no longer hope to outrun them," the princess replied, "I will land while they are still at some distance. We can at least try to conceal ourselves."

"What of him?" Parvia pointed with her chin to the still-unconscious jed.

Indeed, what of Jan Vajo? Dejah Thoris thought. Would he honor his debt to them, for saving his life, or, once again with warriors at his command, would he treat them as captives? Would Ptang Raxo, if he were indeed the commander of the pursuers, treat his jed as master, or would he show the same contempt he had shown in the fortress of the false therns?

There was no time to decide these thorny questions. Even as Dejah Thoris guided the ship lower, seeking for a safe landing space, the whistle of radium projectiles passed to either side of them. Parvia and Kan Vastor instinctively ducked, and thus were close to the deck when a second volley struck their ship in the stern and sent them sprawling. Dejah Thoris was thrown against the controls with bruising force, but never lost her grip on the wheel.

The leaky buoyancy tank was now ripped wide open, she guessed by the speed with which they plummeted toward the ground.

"Stay down!" she cried, as she wrestled with the wheel. The keel struck the moss with a squeal and a shudder of metal. The little craft rebounded, skipping like a stone over the dead sea bottom. Each succeeding bounce rose less high, until the remaining velocity was expended in a wild skid that rattled every bone in her body. Leaving a long furrow ploughed into the moss, the ship wallowed and then settled, canted sideways.

Parvia and Kan Vastor had been thrown together against the gunwale, beside Jan Vajo. Shaken but uninjured, they looked to their leader and were relieved to see her running lightly along the slanted deck toward them. The impact awakened the jed, who cast about for his weapons, before realizing what had happened.

"Who dares fire upon the Jed of Zor?" he cried. "My sword! Give me my sword!"

"It is Ptang Raxo who fires on us," Dejah Thoris said. "But I would guess he does not know you are here. He thinks you safely back in Zor. He only seeks to harm your guests."

Jan Vajo clambered to the highest point of the crashed ship and waved his arms.

"Cease fire, you fools! You treacherous calots!" he roared. "It is I, Jan Vajo! It is your jed!"

Kan Vastor pulled him down, as another volley whistled past. "They cannot recognize you at this distance," he said. "He knows you not. If you would live to see your city again, follow the princess."

"Quick," Dejah Thoris panted. "Over the side and seek cover! They will fire on the ship. We must get away."

She had chosen her landing area for its broad and smooth features—ideal for emergency landing, but quite the opposite for concealment. Long ago, the sea that covered this place had spread out, smooth and calm, with easy sailing and no hidden obstacles to snag a ship. Now the springy, yellowish moss spread far and wide, without a trace of declivities or vegetation in which to hide. To burrow deeply into some cranny of the moss would be the best they could do.

Jan Vajo clung to the side of the ship, unwilling to leave its deceptive shelter. "Give me a sword!" he cried again. "I cannot meet an unknown fate so disgraced, a weapon-less man!"

Dejah Thoris darted back into the cabin and threw a sword over the side, before vaulting down herself. Jan Vajo caught the hilt and set the weapon in its place at his side. Where once a gilded and bejeweled blade of the finest forging had hung, he held a workmanlike sword fit for a panthan or the lowest of his guards.

As Dejah Thoris' feet hit the ground, she felt a trembling in the earth, and a growing thunder met her ears. She thought at first that the ships of Zor had deployed an unknown explosive weapon.

"What is it?" Kan Vastor said, frowning. Dejah Thoris had meant to flee the spot immediately, but paused to learn first what lay ahead of them.

Moving shapes appeared over a gentle rise in the ground, and then she knew.

"Too late to flee!" she cried. "Take cover behind the ship."

The shapes grew rapidly as the thunder increased. A herd of maddened zitidars charged past them. On the open sweep of the dead sea bottom, their downed ship was the only obstacle to the trampling feet. The herd parted like a tide that sweeps around a single stone.

But they were safe enough, until one member of the herd, swept against the ship by its stampeding fellows, trampled right over the deck. Its massive soft pads splintered the wood, and it floundered forward with ear-piercing squeals. The zitidar was only a few strides away from them, looming like a mountain above them as they cowered. They could not spring away, for the herd milled around them on all sides.

Kan Vastor leaped out of hiding. Nimbly, he climbed the ship's stern and hurled himself upon the zitidar's flanks. It still bore the caparison of the Thurds, marking it as once domesticated, to the extent that the monstrous creatures ever could be tamed. Clinging to those straps, Kan Vastor climbed to a point behind its head. He drew his sword and stabbed repeatedly, striving to find a vital point.

The zitidar shrieked and reared up, its first two pairs of legs pawing the air and threatening to crush the planks that remained between its massive bulk and the princess below. Parvia, too, vaulted to the zitidar's back and added her blade to the battle. Jan Vajo did not hold back, but being older and of a less agile build, he struggled to climb to a vantage point from which he could attack. All of their efforts had a counter-effect to their intent. Rather than stopping the beast, the hornet stings of their blades caused it to charge onward to escape.

Dejah Thoris faced the charge alone. The reddened eyes of the behemoth, each the size of her fist, scarcely beheld her, except as a petty obstacle to be swept away in its headlong flight. No radium pistol hung at her side. Only one slender blade stood between her and the zitidar's crushing feet. She had but a moment to decide: Wait, and attempt to stab the beast? Or risk everything on a single throw? Her eye had been honed on target practice with pistol, bow, and spear, but only on delicately carved, immovable targets, not on a maddened beast whose breath she could feel hot against her face.

She drew back her arm and hurled the blade. It struck one eye of the zitidar and buried itself to the hilt. The beast reared up with one final howl of woe, nearly throwing the princess' friends from its back, and crashed to the ground at her feet, an ochre rheum oozing like posthumous tears from its pierced eye. Pausing to pull her sword free and wipe it on the moss, she felt a moment's sadness for the giant creature, swept up in a catastrophe it could not understand.

A portion of the herd had galloped far away down their path, but others, arrested by the cries of their herd mate, still milled about the wrecked flier. What remained of the vessel was much less effective as a bulwark than it had been, and the companions were in danger every moment of being crushed by a stray footfall.

"These beasts still wear the harness of the Thurds," she called out, making her voice carry above the noise of the herd. "Let us climb up on their backs, and I will do my best to direct them back the way they came. I believe they are fleeing the battle. By backtracking their path, we may find my father."

She darted into the herd, emboldened by the unexpected chance to escape Ptang Raxo's rapidly approaching ships. With her blade at the ready, she pricked the feet of any beast that threatened to step too close, until she found an especially broad-backed animal, still wearing harness with many fastener rings and cargo pockets. Leaping, she caught a harness strap and pulled herself to a commanding position in a saddle meant for a much larger green rider.

The zitidar proved more difficult to control than the riding thoats to which she was accustomed. Although the thoat is never more than half-tamed at the best of times, the riding thoats of the red man become accustomed to their duties and fall in with their rider's will in part by habit. The zitidar's consciousness, by comparison, felt inchoate and heavy, like moving a boulder with one's will. In addition, the beast was used to the mind of a green master. Dejah Thoris had to amplify her mental commands repeatedly to match the sheer brute force of the mind of one of those savage warriors of the wastelands. At last she bent the great beast to her will, and turned it back toward her friends amid the wreckage. She brought her mount close enough to the ruins of the ship that Jan Vajo was able to clamber up. Parvia and Kan Vastor had no difficulty seizing a strap and swinging themselves up as she had done.

They thundered back along the trodden way, clearly stamped out on the moss by the feet of the herd. Used to moving in a caravan, a dozen or more of the great beasts turned to follow them. Dejah Thoris directed the other passengers to conceal themselves as far as possible in the panniers strapped to either side of the zitidar's harness. Within one such pouch, they found the former owner's supply of sleeping silks and furs. Dejah Thoris took one large fur and fastened two of its corners to the harness. She crept beneath it, and was able to lie atop the zitidar's broad back, concealed from the view of any ship that might follow them, and also secured to the beast so she need not fear falling.

She dared not look out to see if Ptang Raxo was following them, and the silent passage of the Barsoomian vessels gave her hearing no clue. After some time had passed, she called in a low voice to her companions, asking them to search the sky if they were in a convenient position. Kan Vastor assured her that he had been watching from beneath a veil of silk. The two ships had spent some time searching the wreckage and the surrounding area, and had then flown off southward to follow the other portion of the herd.

"Given that they are out of sight for the time being," the panthan said, "I propose that we warriors climb out of these bags to a more comfortable position. My legs are cramped, and I fear I am crowding my fair companion. I am sure the mighty jed is also experiencing some inconvenience."

A grunt from Jan Vajo signaled his assent. The two men climbed somewhat stiffly to the zitidar's back and took up positions behind Dejah Thoris.

"I have another suggestion, if it please the princess," Kan Vastor said. "Parvia can now stretch out comfortably in the baggage pannier, with ample silks to cover her from view. Dejah Thoris is safe enough where she is. Let the jed and myself take turns keeping watch while the others get some rest. It has been a long day, and twilight approaches. The chance that friend or foe can see us in the dark is slim. Until then, one may keep watch as easily as four. We may need our strength later."

Indeed, Dejah Thoris felt a great weariness stealing over her limbs. "But who will guide the zitidar, if I sleep?"

"I believe I can do so," Kan Vastor said, "now that you have the creature headed in the right direction. I had some experience with supply caravans during my time in Zor. I believe the beasts are easily herded toward familiar territory. The fear of battle has faded, and it will take only a nudge or two to keep them moving. If they show signs of rebellion or come to a stop, I will surely wake you."

To this she assented gratefully. The warmth of the zitidar's broad back and its rocking gait provided more comfort than she had experienced since being stolen away from her guest chamber, and she slept deeply.

Dawn found the small herd scattered across a slope that curved upward toward a line of bluffs. Dejah Thoris climbed out from beneath the concealing furs and shivered in the chill of the early morning. The pale, swift Martian dawn put the darkness to flight. Thuria was a bright spark disappearing in the eastern sky.

"Why have we stopped?" she said to Kan Vastor, who sat on watch.

"Look to the north, beyond those bluffs," he said.

More sparks than Thuria danced in the sky, low down near the horizon. Sounds of battle, too, came faintly to her ears. The zitidars raised their heads from their grazing and grumbled uneasily, low in their massive throats.

"The herd has been resting only since the first light touched the sky. I did not want to proceed toward battle without consulting you. Undoubtedly, your father's fleet is fighting there. But how shall we reach him, from the ground we now occupy? Our way will certainly be barred by the hordes of the green men."

Parvia thrust her head out of the pannier where she had been drowsing.

"I have found a pouch of dried usa and some preserved fruits," she said, through the mouthful she was already chewing. "Also a flask of some liqueur, brewed by Thurds no doubt, but it smells acceptable. And the fighting potato is hard chewing with nothing to wash it down."

Dejah Thoris stood upright, balanced on the zitidar's back, contemplating the horizon, as the flask and handfuls of victuals were passed around.

"You did well to pasture our beasts of burden," she said. The zitidars, with their immense bulk, could not go as long as the nimbler thoats without satisfying their hunger by grazing on the abundant moss.

"I would not want to walk to battle," she continued. "And it is well to feed ourselves too, preparing ourselves for the greatest exertion. I have no other thought than to come to Mors Kajak's aid with the utmost speed. I risk my own life gladly to save my father, the champion of our people."

"I must advise you, with the greatest respect," Kan Vastor said, "that the mind of Mors Kajak may be otherwise. As a champion of Barsoom, no assassin's blade could wound him more deeply than an injury to the fairest flower of Helium. Like any true man of Barsoom, he would gladly embrace his own death rather than win life at the price of a woman's sacrifice."

Dejah Thoris stamped her foot on the zitidar's back, a gentle blow that moved the great beast not at all. Her eyes flashed fire.

"What would you have me do? Stand by while a craven foe stabs my father in the back? Never!"

"I would only suggest that we proceed with caution."

"I have no time for caution!"

The morning breeze blew her dark hair streaming behind her, as she lifted one graceful hand toward the line of battle. Balanced atop her massive steed and silhouetted against the dawn, she was a magnificent sight, one to inspire any warrior to reckless valor.

Without entirely meaning to, her urge to speed onward had communicated itself to the zitidar. Thrashing its tail back and forth and leaving its latest morsel of moss unchewed, the beast half-reared and charged forward.

Dejah Thoris dropped to her knees and seized one of the rings affixed to the zitidar's harness, to keep from tumbling off. Kan Vastor and the jed arrested their falls with less agility. Parvia, who had once again seated herself comfortably in the oversized saddle bag, laughed merrily at their gymnastics.

"As we are apparently hurtling into battle, perhaps you've had enough of the Thurds' cordial," Kan Vastor grumbled, rubbing a spot that had connected rather too abruptly with the zitidar's tough hide.

Dejah Thoris merely lifted the flask and offered a toast with the last swallow. "Forgive me. The beast caught my mood. It is becoming as pliable as my riding thoat."

She patted the creature's neck, though it seemed unlikely

he could feel such a light touch. "I feel sorry we must abandon it to its green masters when we arrive at our destination."

Half a dozen of the other zitidars also lifted their heads from grazing and galloped alongside. Dejah Thoris was pained to see that at least one of them had suffered injury in some earlier battle. A large portion of its hide had been scorched to charcoal so it could not bear a harness. The beast they were currently riding was handsomely colored and seemed healthy. She hoped no such fate would befall it.

Their pace slowed somewhat as the slope grew steeper. The line of bluffs approached rapidly. Perhaps, when water filled the great basin, this had been a bay in some island kingdom. Though she had acted impetuously to speed to her father's side, Dejah Thoris knew Kan Vastor was right. To simply charge a foe vastly superior in arms and numbers would be worse than useless. She must find some practical way to breach their lines.

"Luck favors the brave," she said, quoting one of her father's favorite proverbs.

Parvia wrinkled her nose. "When I was an assassin in training, our master put it somewhat differently. He used to say, 'Luck favors the clever.'"

"It is best to have all three—courage, cunning, and luck," Kan Vastor said. "When I was a young one, I had a sword master who taught us his proverb:

"It is good to be valiant and brave;

"It is good to be faithful and true.

"But the panthan who wishes to see many days

"Will use his intelligence too."

"Courage and cunning are weapons close to hand that may be grasped by any," Jan Vajo chimed in unexpectedly. "Luck is an elusive charm. If our ancestors approve our actions, they may bestow a bright destiny on us."

The jed seemed to be recovering his spirits after the loss of his medallion, the knock on the head, or whatever it was that had brought him low on the previous day.

As they reached the foot of the bluffs, Dejah Thoris prepared to dismount and seek some way to climb up. But indeed, luck seemed to be favoring them. A fan-shaped fall of sand lay before them, and as their mount moved across its drifts, they saw that it had spilled down from the edge of the cliffs, traversing them diagonally and forming a steep but navigable path to the top. The zitidar plodded gamely upward, sometimes slipping back or sinking in the loose drifts, but always making progress. Its herd mates persevered in following.

Weapons in hand, the princess and her companions steeled themselves for the first glimpse of what lay beyond the end of the path. They expected to be greeted at once by enemies. The only question was, how many Thurds would surround them: would there be few enough to offer some chance of survival, or would they face odds that were insurmountable by any red warrior, however dauntless?

13
THE FALL OF A JED

THE FACT THAT A SMALL HERD still accompanied them inspired a thought that might increase their slender chances.

"Let us once again conceal ourselves," Dejah Thoris said. "The green men may see only a few strays from their herd, and so we might pass at least their first lines."

Kan Vastor and the jed put up a token resistance to this subterfuge, but the princess won them over quickly. Assured that they should keep a firm grip on their swords and be ready to spring upon the enemy as soon as they were discovered, they consented to duck beneath coverings and harness again. Parvia enthusiastically complied. Subterfuge was second nature to the former assassin.

Dejah Thoris urged the zitidar onward with all the mental force she could focus. There was no room for fear in her mind while she projected only thoughts of moving onward. It took all her concentration to quell the fear in the zitidar's mind, as the sounds of battle came ever louder and closer.

They crested the top of the bluff. The plain before them teemed with green men yelling their war cries and urging their giant thoats onward at a mad speed. Radium projectiles whistled through the air as the ships above closed with the horde. Somewhere, in one of those vessels, Mors Kajak stood directing the battle. If only his daughter could cry out to him and be heard!

The zitidar's fear of the din of battle worked to their advantage.

As soon as its pads were free of the encumbering sand, it broke into a thundering gallop, scattering any green men who stood in its way. The rest of the herd clustered close behind. They ran at random, zigzagging across the field until they were directly beneath the airships.

It was now or never. Dejah Thoris threw off her covering and stood upright again on the zitidar's back, waving her slender blade until it flashed in the light of exploding projectiles and burning debris.

"Men of Helium! Help us!" she cried.

Parvia darted to her side, unfurling a bright length of silk that flew out like a banner.

After a moment of stunned silence among the ranks of the green men, this sudden appearance incited a volley of pistol shots, accompanied by a bloodcurdling chorus of yells. Clinging to each other, Parvia and Dejah Thoris fought to keep their balance. Only the erratic plunging of the panicked zitidar prevented the marksmanship of the Thurds from having its deadly effect.

Kan Vastor and Jan Vajo clung to the harness straps, in great anguish of spirit. Without pistol or rifle, they could do nothing to defend their lovely companions. They, too, brandished their swords and shouted, hoping to attract the attention of those who flew above them.

They had come so close to the ships that the green men were reluctant to close with them, for fear of being fired on from above. Yet this was a perilous advantage, for it brought the companions into the danger of friendly fire. One Thurd chieftain, a particularly large and ferocious warrior, saw a chance to win glory for himself by charging them single-handed. He bore a curved sword in either hand of his upper pair of arms, each blade already dripping with the blood of previous victims. His tusks had grown to such size they reached almost to his brow, and they were adorned with rings of gold, no doubt signifying some feats of vicious

hostility, while his face was set in a grotesque grin of anticipation of the slaughter to come.

The red men shouted out battle cries as they awaited his
attack. Dejah Thoris could understand their eagerness to
find work for their blades at last. To bounce like baggage on
the back of a pack animal, unable to protect their fair companions, must go against every instinct of the fighting man.
The princess believed that Jan Vajo could be trusted to look
out for himself, but clearly Kan Vastor was ready to give his
all. Dejah Thoris could do nothing to cool his reckless
chivalry. She had all she could do to hang on and exercise
even a modicum of control over their plunging beast.

The Thurd drove his scarred thoat into the flanks of the
zitidar. The rider's snarling face loomed so close that the
defenders could almost feel his hot breath.

Kan Vastor braced himself to leap from the zitidar's back
and grapple with the Thurd.

"Wait!" Parvia cried. Dejah Thoris felt the assassin tugging
free of her steadying grasp to rashly follow the young swordsman. The princess clung to her companion's arm. "Stop,
both of you!" the assassin commanded.

All of them danced on the brink of falling from the danger
of their perch on the zitidar's back to certain death on the
ground below. The grotesque visage rushing toward him was
suddenly obscured by a rush of blood, before toppling and
disappearing. The riderless thoat squealed and galloped
madly away. Kan Vastor ducked involuntarily as the hull of
an airship passed over them, mere inches from his head.

Shrill cheers burst from his companions as the ship came
about and hovered just above them. They had been seen!
They were saved! The intrepid gunner aboard the ship had
brought down the Thurd just before he could attack.

"Quickly!" "Get aboard!" her crew cried out, as they
lowered ropes.

It was a lightly armed scout ship that had come to

their rescue. They were already taking fire from the green lines, and had no large radium cannons with which to effectively return fire. As soon as Parvia and Dejah Thoris had a grip on the ropes, the sailors on board began to reel them in. Kan Vastor and Jan Vajo swarmed up behind them.

Dejah Thoris was the first to gain the deck. She was just in time, for a lucky shot from some distant Thurd marksman struck down the steersman. Disabled, he crashed to the deck. Dejah Thoris sprang into the wheelhouse and took control just as the ship began to veer toward the ground.

She steadied the ship as her friends kept climbing. Relative safety was within an arm's length, when another pair of Thurds galloped toward them to take up the exploit at which their leader had failed. They shook their weapons at the ship on seeing that the fugitives were out of reach. Then, with surprising enterprise and agility for savage warriors of the wastes, they vaulted from their mounts to the zitidar's back. From thence, their arms were just long enough to catch the trailing ends of the ropes. The ship lurched and sank lower under their weight.

Dejah Thoris gave a desperate glance behind to catch sight of her friends' progress. Parvia had reached safety. Jan Vajo was just an arm's length from the gunwale, but Kan Vastor had waited for all his companions to grasp the ropes before he left the zitidar's back. He was still far enough down the rope to be within the grasp of the Thurd who had seized the rope's end. One of the green warrior's massive hands wrapped itself around his leg. The Thurd was unable to use maximum leverage, for fear of losing his own grip, but his sheer weight threatened to drag Kan Vastor away.

The panthan could not draw his weapon, for both hands were needed to retain his grip on the rope that was his only hope. He kicked at the Thurd's face in vain. He could not land an effective blow.

Jan Vajo leaned out from the gunwale, sword in hand, trying to strike the green man, but could not reach past the struggling red warrior. He was poised to hack the rope in two, below Kan Vastor's grip, but if the Thurd fell, still clutching Kan Vastor's leg, the massive weight of the green man would drag the red warrior to death along with him.

Dejah Thoris grasped their situation in brief flashes while struggling to steer a level course. There was nothing she could do from her position at the helm. All depended on Parvia. The quick-thinking assassin took in the deadly dilemma at a glance. Darting to the storage locker that held the ship's tools, she seized the axe provided to cut away debris in a ship-to-ship engagement. As well, she snatched up one of the grappling hooks and clipped it to her harness. With the axe in one hand, she set the hook and hurled herself over the edge. Swinging level with Kan Vastor, she chopped the green man's hand off with a single well-aimed blow. There was no need for a second. Grim face agape in shock, the Thurd dropped to his death. The scarred green hand retained its clutch for a moment. Then the severed nerves relaxed, and the hand fell away to join its master in oblivion. Kan Vastor hauled himself up the last few feet and dropped to the deck. Moments later, Parvia swung herself aboard brandishing the bloody axe to let the princess know that all was well.

Dejah Thoris had not dared to maneuver, lest she dislodge her friend. Freed from the weight on one side, the ship lurched and tilted perilously sideways. All aboard clung to any available handhold, as the second green warrior continued to drag himself doggedly toward the deck. Parvia still held the axe, but could not get to her feet to use it against the ropes that held the attacker. Dejah Thoris stopped fighting the pull of the Thurd's weight. Instead of trying to rise, she banked the ship in a steep curve. Following the contours of the landscape, she flew so low that the ship hung perilously close to its shadow that grew and shrank as the terrain rose and fell beneath it. The clinging Thurd roared in anger, but could not climb fast enough to avoid his fate. Dejah Thoris scraped him from his perch against the first rocky outcropping that flashed beneath the speeding ship. His crushed body slid down to the plain, to move no more.

The flier leaped skyward as if joyful to be freed of its encumbrances.

"Which of these ships carries Mors Kajak?" Dejah Thoris cried.

Only then did the crew realize that their princess was on board. Awestruck, they saluted her. She saw that they wanted to ask questions, but brushed them aside.

"Show me the way to my father!"

"The jed is aboard his flagship, as always," they said, pointing to the foremost and greatest of the warships, proudly flying the symbol of Helium.

To reach the flagship, they would have to pass through the thick of the battle. Radium bullets whined and whistled about them, sometimes impacting the hull and exploding into spurts of flame. Crew members dashed about the deck, dousing those fires. Spare radium weapons were handed to the rescued three, so they might help defend the ship, while the remaining crew members fired the light artillery. They did not at first offer to arm Dejah Thoris. Barsoomian chivalry demanded that they protect their princess; they did not expect her to defend herself. But when she reached a hand imperiously for a pistol, they would not gainsay her. It was good to feel the weight of the pistol hanging from its proper place on her harness.

The captain of the craft respectfully offered to relieve her at the helm, but she refused his offer.

"I will continue to pilot," she said. "Be my lookout and direct me. Fear not to command your princess! Treat me like any other crewman."

Hesitant at first, he was soon shouting his orders as he guided her through the fray. Dodging and darting among the ships of Helium, evading the fire of the green men, while raining bullets on them from above, Dejah Thoris experienced for the first time the exhilaration of battle, the thrill her mighty forefathers experienced in combat. She felt herself at one with the forces of Helium.

She experienced the terror of battle as well. She feared not for herself, but for her father. Ever she searched with desperate gaze for the ship that bore both Mors Kajak and his nemesis. It seemed they would never reach it. When at last they drew level with the flagship, she saw to her horror that Ptang Raxo's ship was just pulling level with it on the far side.

"Father!" she screamed. The powerful figure in command stood transfixed in astonishment. He turned his eyes from the ships of Zor to the unanticipated apparition of his daughter.

Ptang Raxo's ship cast out grappling hooks to board the flagship—unopposed, since all assumed that Zor had changed its mind and come to aid their struggle after all. While Mors Kajak stood distracted, Ptang Raxo barked out a command.

Two of the guards he had lent to the Heliumetic force, standing close to the Jed of Helium, turned upon Mors Kajak, with swords drawn to cut him down. Kan Vastor jumped the gap before the crew could secure one ship to the other, and intercepted the foremost of the guards. The Zorian guard fought like a madman, as if possessed by one command: to kill Mors Kajak. The swords of the two men flashed together like flames of fire. Kan Vastor forced his opponent back, away from his intended target, but he had no blows to spare for the second assassin, who lunged forward with blade raised to slash the Jed of Helium's throat.

Too late Mors Kajak reached for his sword. Even the most seasoned of warriors may be disarmed by the simultaneous appearance of an unexpected ally and the treachery of a trusted associate.

"Take the wheel!" Dejah Thoris cried to the captain.

Letting go the helm and balancing upon the pitching deck, she aimed her radium pistol with deadly accuracy. The rule of combat demanded that, in a fair fight, blade must be met with blade. She felt no compunction in escalating to the more deadly weapon, for the Zorians had attacked two to one, and without warning. This was no fair fight. Her bullet sped to strike the attempted assassin between the eyes. The Zorian fell almost at her father's feet, as Kan Vastor at last triumphed over his opponent and sent him sprawling with a lethal thrust to the body. At once, Kan Vastor found himself under attack from warriors of Helium, who had failed to understand that he battled in defense of their jed.

Dejah Thoris jumped to the deck of her father's ship, and in one more leap, interposed herself between Kan Vastor and her father's warriors.

"Stop! Your princess commands that you spare this man!" she cried. As they lowered their weapons and looked to Mors Kajak for an explanation, she turned to her father and gasped out her story in as few words as possible—the tale of treachery by assassins bearing the metal of Zor.

As quickly as she uttered her warning, it was not in time to prevent Ptang Raxo from stepping aboard the ship. As soon as the jedwar was on board and saw Mors Kajak and his daughter, the Zorian drew his sword and advanced on them.

Jan Vajo thrust himself between his jedwar and the Heliumites.

"It is I, your jed!" he cried. "What folly is this? Sheath your sword, I command you! Look about you! It is the green men we battle, not our allies from Helium."

"Do you attempt to command me?" Ptang Raxo said. "Only the medallion commands. You have no authority over me now. Stand aside, or you shall be the first to fall."

"Old friend!" Jan Vajo said. "Take off the medallion. It has poisoned your mind. I am your jed, with or without that treacherous device. Stand by my side, as you used to, and even now all will be forgiven."

"Old friend?" the jedwar sneered. "Old fool! You have failed our masters, but I shall not."

He sprang at his former commander with reckless abandon. The two seasoned warriors clashed with the force of two maddened banths. Steel rang on steel as those on deck stepped back to give them room. At first, Ptang Raxo overbore the jed, aiming blow after blow at his head and forcing him onto the defensive. He thrust at Jan Vajo's right side, attempting to turn him so that he might get past him to strike at Mors Kajak. He drew blood—and on feeling the sting of his blade, Jan Vajo burned with battle rage and ceased to give ground. Confusion at this betrayal no longer weakened the jed's hand. The onlookers had a brief glimpse of Jan Vajo as he had been in youth, before the corruption of power and the medallion's bane had dulled his edge. Once he had been a warrior worthy of rank.

Dejah Thoris could only cling to her father's side and watch. Even knowing her own danger, she thrilled to the skill and ferocity of the combat. And yet, how terrible that it had come to this, that two men who had once fought side by side now battled to take each other's lives.

Jan Vajo pressed Ptang Raxo back and back, giving no ground and allowing no escape, until the jedwar's back was against the ship's gunwale.

"Yield," Jan Vajo panted, "and you may yet live."

"Never!"

Ptang Raxo continued to turn aside his opponent's blade in a flurry of desperate parries and feints. Jan Vajo struck a downward blow, attempting to get past his guard, and by some sleight that happened too fast for Dejah Thoris to see how it was done, Ptang Raxo locked hilts with his jed and twisted the sword out of his grasp. It flew overboard.

Jan Vajo immediately closed with him and grappled him with the power of a white ape. Ptang Raxo's sword was rendered useless, for he could not turn it to stab his opponent while Jan Vajo was crushing the breath out of him. He struggled weakly. *Surely he will have to surrender now*, Dejah Thoris thought.

In a final act of treachery, Ptang Raxo drew a vicious stiletto from concealment in his belt. Again too fast to comprehend, it flashed before their eyes and was buried between the ribs of the Jed of Zor.

Jan Vajo gasped but did not let go his grip. He turned his head toward Dejah Thoris.

"Incomparable princess," he said in a choking voice, "believe but this—the man I was—would have thrown his sword at your feet in honor."

With his last strength, he overbore Ptang Raxo, and the two of them, locked together, plummeted over the ship's side.

Before Dejah Thoris could catch her breath, Mors Kajak ordered his men to disarm and bind the remaining warriors of Zor.

"Harm them not if they yield," he said. "We will dispose of them later. Now, turn our eyes and our blades back to our true foe! We have a battle to win."

He beckoned to Parvia. "Go with the princess to the cabin, and remain there until we have finished with the green men."

"But, Father—" Dejah Thoris protested.

"Silence!" he said. "You chose to come here as a warrior. Therefore, I am your jed and you must obey me. I cannot concentrate my will on the enemy if you insist on placing yourself in danger. Go!"

Still rebelling in her heart, but chastened by his words, she took Parvia's hand and ran through the noise and confusion to the ship's cabin. There she and Parvia huddled in a corner where they were as safe from a random shot as they could be onboard a battleship.

"I could fight at his side," she said indignantly. "He allows Kan Vastor, a Zorian, to join the fight, and I am his own daughter. We have faced worse perils in these last few days."

"True," Parvia said. "But I am told that even the most hardened warriors find it difficult to focus their energies when they know that beloved family is in danger." She shrugged. "So I have heard, anyway. I would not know from experience. My father and mother sold me to the Assassins' Guild without a second thought. There are worse things than a father who loves and protects you."

Parvia rose and searched through the supply lockers for

food and drink. "Here, I have found water and usa. At least the usa is fresh and not dried this time. Come, refresh yourself. It is a soldier's duty to take rest when he can. When we are needed, we will be ready."

Still indignant, Dejah Thoris consented to take food and water and at last to relax her aching limbs. She sighed.

"I confess I am weary."

Sleep was impossible amid the sound of cannon, the impact of projectiles against the hull, the rocking of the ship, and the shouting of warriors. Often, the princess clutched at her companion's arm in fear.

"You seem to fear nothing," she said. "Would that I too had training as an assassin! My life as a princess has not prepared me for this day."

"Do not wish it," Parvia exclaimed. "Until the day we first met, my life meant nothing to me. That is why I fear nothing . . . save, perhaps . . . the loss of a cherished comrade." Here she blushed. Then Dejah Thoris squeezed her hand in sympathy rather than fear.

"I understand," she said. "Remember that my father is a man of honor. He owes his life to Kan Vastor. I am sure he will do everything in his power to see that Kan Vastor lives to be rewarded."

"And do not say that your life as a princess has not prepared you," Parvia said, after a few moments with eyes cast down in reverie. "You look to the future, to a wider world, and you see much that I do not, even though my eyes are trained to perceive the smallest detail. You think always of your responsibilities, and the good of others. You people of Helium fight not for yourselves alone, but for your family and city. I have never had anyone to stand at my side."

"But now you will come to Helium with us," Dejah Thoris said. "You will stay as long as you wish. I hope you may decide to stay forever."

Parvia smiled, but a little sadly.

"The decision may not be mine," she said.

The sounds of battle diminished around them, and the motion of the ship steadied. No longer did the voices from the deck shout in anger or warning. They waited to hear themselves summoned, but no one came. At last, they dared to step out to the open doorway and look about—having first used a few handfuls of water to splash away the grime of battle from their faces.

Kan Vastor hurried toward them as soon as he saw them.

"Praise be to our ancestors! We all live!" he shouted. The three of them joined briefly in a warm embrace. Then, shocked by his own impetuous action, Kan Vastor stepped back to a respectful distance.

"Your pardon!" he said. "The Jed of Helium asks for your presence. Many are wounded, and would welcome your care."

"Is the battle done, then?" Dejah Thoris said.

"Yes! Done and decided! Helium is victorious! And by the bones of my ancestors, never have I fought beside such excellent warriors. It will be my boast long after this day that I went to war alongside the men of Helium."

Parvia grinned mischievously. "Do not forget that you have fought beside two other excellent warriors—ladies of Zor and of Helium! It will be a still rarer and more impressive boast that you went to war with an assassin and a princess as your comrades!"

Plumes of smoke rose past them from the ground where the camp of the green men lay in ashes. Far in the distance, the disorderly ranks of the remaining Thurds retreated. Many green men's bodies lay heaped upon the ground. Intermingled with them were bodies of the red warriors who had fallen when their ships were brought down by enemy fire.

Mors Kajak sent his smaller ships to bring up the bodies of their dead and wounded. Those who still had life in them were laid on the deck of the flagship, which was also to serve as the hospital ship. Where the bodies had been dismembered by the savagery of their enemies, or where they were too greatly disfigured in their falls, their comrades stripped their metal and weapons from their limbs and wrapped it tenderly for delivery to their families.

A solemn set of bearers carried a stretcher draped in silks, laden with the bodies of Jan Vajo and Ptang Raxo, still locked together in death. The draperies, stained with blood, concealed their injuries from view. They were placed far away from the living who might still benefit from care. Dejah Thoris steeled herself to look beneath the coverings. She needed to make sure they were dead, even though their fall left no real hope of life. The faces were an awful sight. Their features were rendered nearly unrecognizable by the crushing force of impact, and veiled in congealed blood. Their bodies were cold, and no pulse of life remained in them. With a shudder, she drew the silks over them again.

14
THE FALL OF A PRINCESS

DEJAH THORIS AND PARVIA scarcely noticed when the fleet completed the mournful task of recovering the bodies and began to move again, this time on a course for Zor. For the entire flight, they were occupied in giving first aid, and they used up every resource of healing that the ships possessed. They could do no more until they reached home, but they had achieved much to preserve life and ease suffering. Wounded warriors of Zor were treated side by side with the Heliumites. Not all were tainted by the duplicity of their jedwar. Most had fought with honor.

Mors Kajak placed the two ships of Zor at the forefront of the fleet, under command of his own crews, but flying the banners of Zor. With this precaution, they sailed into the harbor of Zor without challenge, though the warriors guarding the harbor watched them arrive with puzzled looks. It was a far different entrance from the pageantry of their first sight of Zor.

"We welcome you, Jed of Helium," the captain of the guard said. "But we were awaiting the return of our own jed. Is he with you?"

The captain looked hopefully toward the ships that bore the banner of Zor. Then, startled, he saw Dejah Thoris descend from the flagship and approach.

"The Princess of Helium is here!" he exclaimed. "How is this possible? Jan Vajo went out to search for her. Has he found her? But where is he?"

"All shall be made clear to the princess Phortora," Mors Kajak said. "Our news must go first to her ears. Where can we find her?"

"She awaits the return of Jan Vajo in the great audience room," the captain said, stammering. "Let me go and announce you."

"I fear our errand cannot wait," Mors Kajak replied. "We have many wounded on board. Some are men of Zor, who have been tended by our princess and her companion with as much care as if they were Heliumites. Will you give orders for your men to carry your wounded to your own infirmary? Our own will remain aboard, for we do not intend to stay long."

The captain, somewhat reassured by hearing that Helium did not intend a permanent occupation, gave orders accordingly, and hurried ahead of Mors Kajak's party to give Phortora at least some warning of their arrival.

It could only have been a few moments, for the Jed of Helium burst into the audience room on the captain's heels. Phortora sat on the throne of Zor. On her lap she held a medallion and a sword, richly adorned with gold and jewels. Behind the throne stood her son, Zu Tith, heavily armed as if he were a jeddak going to war, and bedecked in jewels and honors as if he were about to attend a feast.

"Where is my brother?" she demanded. She held the medallion and the sword high, one in each hand. "Long have I awaited his return, but I received only these fragments. You offer friendship, but I believe your treacherous daughter has lured him to his death!"

Mors Kajak frowned and placed his hand upon his sword hilt. But he recalled that he was speaking with a woman and controlled his wrath.

"You speak in ignorance," he said. "Yet the news I have for you will be no better. The Jed of Zor has died honorably in battle, fighting the treachery of his own jedwar, who would have slain us both. We have brought both of their bodies with us, that you may see the truth with your own eyes."

Warriors of Helium carried in the bier on which Jan Vajo and Ptang Raxo had been laid, now draped discreetly with additional unstained silks and overlaid with a flag of Zor.

Phortora turned a pleading look toward her son. Zu Tith stepped forward to let her lean upon his arm as she approached the bier, exhibiting a faintness that Dejah Thoris, watching unnoticed from behind a screen of tall warriors, was sure the woman did not feel. She drew back the cover, and uttered a piercing shriek.

"It is he! Jan Vajo is dead!"

She staggered back to the throne, and sank upon it, clutching at the emblems of her brother.

She drew herself up then, sweeping the room with a steely look.

"If it be so," she said, "as I have feared these past two days since he disappeared, then I must act in his place and guide the chariot of Zor in his stead."

Dramus Ugo, Jan Vajo's former counselor, approached the foot of the throne. He still wore upon his chest the medallion that had signified his office.

Before he could speak, Phortora threw out her arm in a dramatic gesture.

"Behold his face! Satisfy yourself! Your master is dead."

Dramus Ugo took a cursory look at the bodies, and like Phortora, feigned horror and shock, though Dejah Thoris thought he seemed like one to whom the news was no surprise.

"It is not our custom to give the title of jed to a female relative," he said. "The warriors of Zor must acclaim their new leader as a trusted guide in battle."

Phortora nodded to her son, who stepped forward.

"As they now proclaim the princess Phortora!" he announced. A few dissenting voices were heard from the back of the hall. Zu Tith raised his arm in a commanding gesture. Men of Zor, strategically placed on both sides of the hall, drew together in battle lines, placing hands menacingly on their sword hilts. A commotion at the back of the hall was abruptly silenced, as several inert bodies were dragged out. The warriors under Zu Tith's command raised a deafening cheer, while those few who did not join in stood silent and cowed.

Dramus Ugo surveyed the hall, bristling with supporters of Phortora and her son, and licked his lips.

"Then, since Zor claims you for its ruler, as jeddara you must don the medallion of your office. The honor that Jan Vajo once wore is yours."

Dejah Thoris sprang forward, abandoning the safety of her father's guard.

"Stop!" she cried. "That cursed medallion is the very thing that led Jan Vajo to his death and caused the treachery of his jedwar! This man, Dramus Ugo, is the one who can explain all. By the power of the medallion he wears as chief counselor, he has clouded the minds of your great men. Speak, calot! Tell your princess, and your people, what you have done, that they may render judgment on you."

Phortora sneered.

"Speak, indeed—you she-calot!" she said. "My brother is dead, and do you still live? It is intolerable!"

Before Dramus Ugo could speak another word, Phortora whipped a small, gleaming dagger from her bosom and hurled it toward the front ranks of the assembly. Parvia, with a cry of horror, leaped to the defense of her princess. Before she could reach Dejah Thoris, the princess bent and swept her arm up in the protective arc she had practiced in the sparring ring. The dart glanced off her armlet of gold, and buried itself in Dramus Ugo's breast, just above the medallion.

"Poison," he croaked, and fell heavily, striking his head on the edge of the dais where Phortora stood. All eyes were drawn to his fall, as many rushed to aid him.

The dying chief counselor clutched the medallion spasmodically and tried to speak, but consciousness fled before he could say another word.

A woman of Zor who had come to help the wounded as

they were carried from the ships hurried to kneel at his side. She tried her best to stanch the blood that flowed from a gash in Dramus Ugo's head. Soon she recoiled, looking up in frightened confusion.

"I do not understand. Something terrible has happened to the honored counselor. Look—his hair is not natural hair. See how it has slipped from his skull, and beneath it, he is bald! And this wound, where I have cleansed it with healing ointments, shows skin that is white and pale! Is it a disease? The effects of the poison?"

She wiped away more of the blood, revealing his face to be white as snow. She stepped back in horror, scrubbing at her hands as if she feared contagion. A hubbub ensued as the lords of Zor pushed forward to see, while others tried to hold back the crowd.

"Enough!" Zu Tith commanded. "Stand back, all of you."

He knelt beside the body. After a cursory inspection, he rose again.

"Whatever he was, he is dead, and his bad counsel with him. Dramus Ugo is dead, Ptang Raxo is dead, Jan Vajo is dead. None remains to question the rule of our jeddara."

Before another compulsory cheer could be raised, Mors Kajak stepped forward and raised his arm for silence.

"I am here to question it," he declared. "No one who attacks the Princess of Helium shall be suffered to assume the throne in my presence. Phortora has sought one life and ended another. All of you here are witnesses. I demand that she be tried for her crimes."

"Helium does not rule here," Zu Tith sneered. "You have no standing to bring an accusation."

Mors Kajak did not reply to the Zorian youth. He turned to the ranks of the older warriors.

"Men of Zor! I call upon your wisdom and justice. I ask not that Helium should rule you. Rather, I appeal to the laws of Zor. Will you be ruled by the law of your own land, or by murder and tyranny?"

The tension in the room was palpable. Would the men of Zor set upon the Heliumites? Or would they turn on their own would-be rulers? Phortora's eyes blazed like flames, but as she opened her lips to speak, a loud and solemn gong rang out. All eyes turned in surprise to the source of the thrice-repeated sound.

A procession of a dozen spectral figures approached from behind the throne. No one had seen them enter. They had been neither announced nor challenged. They came with silent steps, appearing like shadows coalescing out of shadow. All were veiled in black from head to toe. The foremost bore the gong that sounded. Behind him came another, to whom the rest gave reverence. A golden circlet bearing a brilliant gem crowned the darkness where his head might have been.

Hushed murmurs swept through the crowd.

"It is a Holy Thern!"

"The therns!"

"The therns are among us!"

"Issus preserve us!"

The crowned one spoke, his voice issuing sepulchrally from within the veil.

"Through the wisdom of Issus, it has been revealed to us that our faithful servant, the meritorious Jan Vajo, is no more."

"Indeed, Holy One, his body lies upon that bier," Zu Tith said, his customary insolence cowed by the appearance of the therns.

The thern crossed to the bier and gazed down on those who lay upon it. He drew the cover back across their faces.

"I see that it is so. May his journey to Issus be swift."

He glided on noiseless feet—if feet there were beneath the impenetrable veil—to stand above the corpse of Dramus Ugo.

"Issus has also informed us of the iniquity that led to the death of your jed. You need not fear infection from this body. This is his natural appearance, not a deformity. The man you know as Dramus Ugo was one of those who serve us and have this form. He cleverly disguised himself as one of you."

His hearers gasped.

"How can this be?" someone cried out.

"Alas, I must regretfully inform you that such things occur. On very rare occasions, one who has been favored to serve the therns turns to evil, betraying our trust for his own gain. This one obtained by wrongful means a curious treasure, made by the Orovars in a distant age, and used it for his own ends. Be assured that his vile scheme is now ended, and the people of Zor will be free of his influence. The object shall be returned to its proper place, to be guarded in the vaults of the ages and never more profaned in this manner."

He bent and removed the bloodstained medallion from Dramus Ugo's harness, passing it to an acolyte. He motioned for the same acolyte to approach Phortora.

"We will take charge of the medallion of Jan Vajo. It must return to Issus with him."

Phortora instinctively clasped the medallion closer, turning away from the messenger.

"I am Phortora, sister of the jed, and acclaimed as the new ruler of Zor! The medallion is mine, and it is mine to say what shall be done with it!"

More black-clad figures approached, silently encircling her. Intimidated by their faceless menace, she let go the medallion, which disappeared beneath a black robe.

"Bring a litter for your fallen counselor," the Holy Thern ordered. "The bodies of our servants, Jan Vajo and Ptang Raxo, shall be taken to the hidden river and sent with honor to the blessed valley where Issus reigns. Not so this treacherous one. Not for him the peace of Issus or the joys of the Valley Dor. His body we shall remove to be dealt with according to our holy rites."

Acolytes came forward to take up the body.

"Wait!" A warrior of Zor came forward, holding up a hand in appeal to the therns. "An accusation has been made just before your arrival. Phortora, who now claims rule, stands charged with murder and attempted murder. Will you not hear and judge this case before you go?"

It was Ptor Koro, who had been ambassador to Helium, who spoke. Seeing so powerful a man stand forth emboldened those who had previously been cowed by Zu Tith and his adherents. A chant swelled from the back of the room.

"Justice! Justice! Justice!"

The gong sounded.

"Silence!" said the Holy Thern. "These contentions among mortals are of no concern to us. Such petty matters are for you to settle among yourselves."

The acolytes lifted the biers to carry away the bodies.

Before they could depart, the insurgents in the rear ranks broke forth, attempting to reach the dais while Zu Tith's men were still constrained from open conflict by the presence of the therns.

"Seize her! Hold her for judgment!" they cried.

Phortora clutched at her son, but he eluded her grasp and stood aside, unwilling to serve as her champion.

A flash of rage crossed her face at the treachery of her own offspring, but as half a dozen men of Zor reached out to lay hold of her, she threw herself at the feet of the therns in supplication.

"I appeal to the Holy Ones! I will go with my brother to Issus and make the pilgrimage by his side!"

The therns drew back their skirts from her grasp.

"Enough!" the crowned thern proclaimed. "No living man or woman may trespass among us. If you go to Issus, you go alone. Our conference with you is ended. There is nothing more to discuss. The people of Zor must now determine for themselves who shall rule here. Mors Kajak, we commend your courage and invite you to return to your own city forthwith. I have spoken."

As the procession began to move, the gong sounded again, over the wailing of Phortora.

"Avert your eyes," an acolyte intoned. "None may know the way of the chosen of Issus."

Dejah Thoris lowered her eyes, but looked all the more curiously from beneath her eyelids, greatly desiring to know how these therns had entered the hall unseen. A sudden, soundless puff of purple mist filled the great hall, stinging her eyes until they were forced to close, and filling her head with a dizzy vertigo. When the mist cleared, she found herself on her knees, near swooning. All around her, even the strongest of warriors had been brought to their knees, or even sent sprawling. All traces of the therns had vanished—and Phortora, too, had disappeared.

Nor could any sign of Ptor Koro and his supporters be seen. Their departure, at least, was no mystery to Dejah Thoris. It seemed obvious that, seeing themselves to be outnumbered, they had prudently taken flight before the inhibiting influence of the therns could be removed.

Zu Tith had fallen on the steps of the throne. He rose scowling, an expression not unlike his late uncle's.

"Mors Kajak," he said, more abruptly than was courteous, "you have heard the words of the Holy Thern. Every visit has its terminal point. As you have wounded men to carry home, I am sure you would not wish to stay longer. You need not linger on our account. The people of Zor have our own affairs to arrange. I wish you a pleasant journey."

Mors Kajak stepped forward until he was too close for comfort to the shorter man.

"Not so fast," he said. "I am told you hold my guardsmen in confinement. Bring them to me, and then we will discuss the terms of my departure."

"And we are not your only guests," Dejah Thoris said, moving to her father's side. "The ladies of Helium are still in pleasant accommodations, I trust? Until I see my friends and am assured of their well-being, I shall not leave this spot."

Zu Tith's frown deepened.

"Why bring these reckless accusations to me? I know nothing of all this."

"Before assuming authority, it is well to clear away the wrongful deeds of one's predecessor," Mors Kajak said. "Or else you might find their debts coming home to roost."

Zu Tith shrugged angrily, and rudely. Before he could speak, one of his entourage spoke urgently in his ear. Zu Tith chewed his lip for a moment, and then dismissed the man with an impatient gesture.

"Very well then—go and do it," he said.

He had not deigned to speak to Dejah Thoris.

"I know my way to the guest quarters," she said.

"There is no need," Zu Tith said. "I can give orders to summon your women."

"They shall not be summoned," Dejah Thoris said. "I will go myself to be assured of their well-being, as befits their sovereign."

"So you will not leave this spot, but now you will leave it," Zu Tith jeered. "It is the privilege of a female to change her mind, I suppose."

"Follow me," she said to the warriors of Helium nearest to her. She swept out of the room and did not hear whatever words were exchanged between her father and the upstart Jed of Zor in her absence.

When they reached the guest chambers, the heavy door would not open. Dejah Thoris pounded upon it with the heel of her hand.

"Open up!" she cried. "Your princess, Dejah Thoris, is here and desires entrance."

Something heavy scraped across the floor. A lock clicked. Finally the door opened a crack. With a cry of joy, Ela Dusa flung the door wide and burst through it to embrace Dejah Thoris. For a moment, she clung to the princess, in tears, but then glanced fearfully up and down the hall.

"Quickly! Quickly, come within," she said, tugging at Dejah Thoris.

The princess yielded and stepped into the room. She was immediately mobbed by weeping ladies and servants. With difficulty she made herself heard, and blocked them from slamming the door shut again.

"There is nothing to fear now!" she said. "My father, Mors Kajak, has returned victorious. He is here to take us home. I beg your pardon for leaving you here alone. I was taken against my will—but all is well now, and you shall hear the full tale when we are safe again in Helium."

The women had already assembled their gear in anticipation of needing to flee, though they knew not whither. As they distributed their luggage among the guards to be carried away, Ela Dusa quelled her tears to give Dejah Thoris a brief report.

"On that dreadful night, we did not know we had fallen unconscious until we awoke to find you and the Zorian girl gone! We were bewildered. We demanded to see Jan Vajo, only to be told that he was gone as well. That repellent she-banth, Phortora—pardon me, but I must speak as I feel—came here, but only to show her contempt. I will not sully my lips with the words she used of you. I wish that I could cleanse my ears of every trace of her voice. She offered no assistance. We requested guards of our own city, but were told that no one knew where the men of Helium had gone. We took counsel with each other, and determined that we must protect ourselves. So we bolted the door, and blocked it with the heaviest chest we could move. We have lived on such provisions as we had among us, and on tears, and on desperate hope."

Dejah Thoris removed one of her own golden armlets and placed it on the older woman's arm.

"You have done well, protecting my ladies when I could not. This is only a token of the honor that is due you. I am sure my parents will add to it a thousandfold when they hear your tale. My mother indeed was wise to send you with me, most trusted of friends. Come—let us not remain away from Helium one moment longer than we must. You need not fear encountering Phortora. She is no longer among us."

15

SWORDS OF HONOR

THEY HURRIED BACK TO THE GREAT HALL, and arrived just as the remaining contingent of Heliumetic guards emerged from their detainment. The men were disheveled and famished. They had received no water for washing, and little food. Zorians carried in several armloads of their weapons and accoutrements, and cast them in a heap on the floor before them, like food for calots.

As Dejah Thoris entered the room, her father raised a shout.

"Dejah Thoris comes! The princess, Dejah Thoris!"

The rest of the Heliumites took up the cry, beating sword on shield, to make up for the lack of trumpeters and heralds. Zu Tith stood sullenly as proper honors were accorded to the princess for the first time in days.

"Take them to the ships immediately," Mors Kajak said to the warriors assisting Dejah Thoris' entourage. "Await me there."

"Wait, father," Dejah Thoris said. Breaking away from her escort, she ran to Parvia's side and took her hand. Kan Vastor stood beside the former assassin.

"These are my treasured friends, with whom I survived many disasters," she said. "Will Helium take them under its mighty protection? My friends, will you go with me? I do not wish to leave without you at my side."

"There is room in Helium for all who love our princess," Mors Kajak said.

"There is no place for me in the court of Zu Tith,"

177

Kan Vastor said. "But I would not wish to leave so long as one friend remains."

Color rose to Parvia's cheeks. "I stand by my princess," she said.

She followed Dejah Thoris, and Kan Vastor followed both, guarding their backs.

As the men of Helium reclaimed their weapons, Mors Kajak turned to Zu Tith.

"I shall take my leave now. If ever you send embassy to Helium again, come with black flags of sorrow, and with abject apologies for the disrespect you have shown my people, for if you come in any other way, you may expect the rain of fire from my battle fleet to be the first greeting you receive."

With swords naked in their hands, the warriors of Helium left the halls of Zor, and none dared to stand in their way.

Dejah Thoris stood again on the foredeck of the flagship of the fleet of Helium as the day faded. It was her father's wish that she remain close by his side. She too preferred to be near him, where she could watch over him until they had returned to Helium. No more adventures must come between them.

How high her heart had beaten with excitement when the fleet set out! How fresh and bright the ships had gleamed in the morning sun! Now they flew into oncoming night, yet no less proud for all their battle scars. They returned victorious, and she had her share in that victory.

Wrapped in fur against the chill of the Barsoomian night, she watched the stars brighten against the violet hue of sunset. Blue Jasoom and bright Sasoom had risen along the ecliptic. She thought of all the times she had amused herself by gazing through the telescopes that brought the far worlds near and showed the strange capering and costumes of their uncommunicative inhabitants. She smiled, wondering what those far-off neighbors would think if they could see all that she had experienced in the last few days. They would probably find it as hard to comprehend as she had found their puzzling antics as a child. *And truly*, she thought, *the behavior of men and women five hundred years old can still lack all sense.*

Her smile faded as she thought of the treachery and cruelty she had seen on venturing beyond Helium. But then she threw off these sad reflections. It was her hand that had saved the life of her jed and father, her hand that had uncovered the malice of the false therns and revealed the curse of the mind-controlling medallion. A princess of Helium indulged no regrets.

The whole force was on deck again, and in the best array they could muster, as the lit towers of Greater and Lesser Helium shone out ahead. The cry of trumpets ascended toward them, heralding their return. Late as the hour was, it seemed all of Lesser Helium turned out to welcome them. Dejah Thoris had eyes for her mother alone. To see her parents re-united was the greatest happiness she could imagine. And once the tumult of welcome had died down, to be escorted to her own apartments, there to enjoy every luxury of rest and refreshment after her privations, was delightful indeed.

Soon enough, the new day had come, and she found herself once again bathed, perfumed, and contemplating her store of court-worthy adornments. She chose a simple and modest harness, an heirloom from ancient times, appropriate for a celebration of homecoming. The primary stones were large, dark blue sapphires that brought out the sheen of her glossy raven hair. The sapphires were interspersed with cloudy blue agates from the southern wastes, reminiscent of vanished seas and clouded skies.

Since Parvia possessed no more than the harness in which she had traveled, Dejah Thoris invited her to choose formal garb from her own treasury. When Parvia, bewildered by such riches, hesitated in confusion, Dejah Thoris and her servants selected becoming items and pressed them upon her. She sat by her princess' side in silver and sparkling emeralds that became her well.

At the hastily convened banquet, Mors Kajak in his most

resplendent regalia handed out honors with a lavish hand. Many a jewel and golden armlet adorned his warriors in honor of their brave deeds. Thanks to the wonders of Barsoomian healing, even most of the wounded were present for the celebration. As the culmination of the ceremony, Mors Kajak unexpectedly summoned Dejah Thoris to stand forth. He presented her with a woman's blade of exquisite and ancient craftsmanship, its pommel a star sapphire.

"This blade has been handed down through generations of the women of Helium," he said. "Your grandmother bore it in her youth, and now it passes to you, in honor of your vigilance and valor. Without your swift action, Lesser Helium might now be lacking its jed!"

As the hall resounded with the crowd's acclaim, he bent to secure the blade to her harness.

"I pass on to you the words of your grandmother," he said in her ear. "'Wear this in honor, and use it with skill. But try to stay out of situations where you will need it!' I could not agree more with my honored mother."

When the wine was drunk and the music and dancing concluded, and the guests made their farewells, Mors Kajak invited Parvia and Kan Vastor to join the family party in the jed's private quarters. Tardos Mors and Vara Martis had arrived from Greater Helium to hear the news.

Additional refreshments were provided, for there was still much to discuss. Now, at his ease and able to pay close attention, the Jed of Lesser Helium wished to hear his daughter's adventures again, and in more detail. Thoria had not yet heard the tale, and listened in shock to what Dejah Thoris had endured at the hands of the royal family of Zor. Parvia and Kan Vastor added their own observations to make a more complete account.

Their tale of the false therns and their fortress at the bottom of a crack in the earth caused much interest from Tardos Mors, oldest of those present.

"Only twice or thrice in my long career have I encountered therns in the flesh," he said. "One hears of them, but their guidance remains unseen. Their strong presence in Zor is unusual. This may be information worth remembering."

"And what of these false therns, wielding an artifact from the ancients? This, too, is unheard of!" Vara Martis said. "Do you think the true therns will hunt them down and extirpate them?"

"If not, they would pose an unusual danger," Tardos Mors said thoughtfully. "For who among the red men could tell false from true? Their influence could spread unknown to us, under the cloak of the reverence that is felt for the servants of Issus."

"Were the veiled ones indeed therns?" Dejah Thoris said. "We were told many things by the people of Zor, but I cannot tell which statements were true and which were intended to mislead. I can think of no one that I could trust within those walls—save, of course, our friends who have left Zor behind. I have wondered whether the veil served as disguise for more of the assassins. Perhaps we have still not seen the true therns."

"I am less angered by the hidden crimes of inscrutable therns than by the open contempt shown by the red men of Zor," Thoria said, turning to her mate. "You should have razed their city to the ground! Such treatment of our daughter is a crime against all custom and chivalry, as well as an unforgivable affront to our family."

"Truly, it went against the grain to allow Zu Tith to remain standing, with a smirk on his face," Mors Kajak said. "But since I had in my care both ladies of Helium and wounded warriors, I denied myself the pleasure of destroying him in fair combat. Our daughter had suffered enough from the perfidy of Zor. I decided to risk no more of it."

"I suppose you are right," Thoria said. "I doubt that he was worthy of your blade."

Dejah Thoris shuddered. "Indeed not. I thank you, Father,

for sacrificing the natural feelings of a warrior for long enough to remove me speedily from that place. Jan Vajo was bad enough, but of his nephew, the less said the better. It hardly seems possible that he will remain for long as Jed of Zor."

"Certainly not without his mother to advise him," Parvia said, with a curl of her lip.

"Yes—what of Phortora?" Mors Kajak said. "Was it she who ordered the assassination of the princess? According to our customs, all women must be respected, so it is well that she took to flight. By the bones of my ancestors! Had she remained in my presence, I would have been hard pressed to observe custom and not to punish such an offense."

"What do you think, Parvia?" Dejah Thoris asked. "Could she have been the one to order the assassins? It is hard for me to believe, even of one who so viciously disliked me."

"She seemed to strike at you, at the end," Parvia said. "So it would seem logical that she was the one who wanted to strike you down at the beginning. And I suppose that it would have made sense to prevent you from wedding with Jan Vajo and producing an heir to supplant her precious son."

"But it is impossible that she could have believed that I would accept his advances!" Dejah Thoris interrupted.

A sad little smile played on Parvia's lips.

"Not all women of Barsoom have been raised in such conditions of honor as you," she said. "Phortora no doubt grew up in circumstances where a woman might barter her beauty for power and profit. She could not have known how different are the ways of Helium. In any case, it is impossible to know whose hand invisibly directed the assassins. The Guild is always secretive, with many layers of concealment masking their operations. And this arrangement was the most clandestine that even I have seen. I can find no clue that might help to unravel the conspiracy."

There was a brief silence. Then Tardos Mors smiled.

"All this is food for thought on some future day. But for now, I am content to see that my son and granddaughter have returned victorious. Let us put aside those memories and rejoice in a bright future here in Helium."

"Well said," Mors Kajak agreed. "And, to speak of the future, I am sure we are agreed in offering a place among the warriors of Helium to one who has so faithfully befriended the city's best-loved denizen. Kan Vastor, there will always be a welcome for you here."

Kan Vastor leaped to his feet, all weariness apparently dispelled.

"Gladly will I cast my sword at your feet!" he cried.

Mors Kajak retrieved the blade and buckled it in its rightful place on Kan Vastor's belt.

"I will be your jed and Helium will be your city, for as long as your heart finds contentment here," he said.

Yet, no sooner had the well-worn blade returned to its accustomed spot, than the young red man drew it forth again. Presenting it on his open palms, he held it out toward Parvia.

"I have placed my sword at your feet in fealty, Mors Kajak," he said. "Now, in the presence of the greatest captains and ladies of Barsoom, I seek permission to place it at the feet of one who has been my star of hope since first I laid eyes on her."

He laid the sword at Parvia's feet.

The woman's wistful expression was replaced by a look of such joy that all present could not help smiling. With trembling fingers, she hastened to return the blade, hilt first, to Kan Vastor, who sheathed it swiftly, with an air of triumph.

"And there may it stay for a while," she said laughing.

He placed his arm lightly around her waist, as one who had won that right.

"I never thought, when I entered the lists of competition in Zor, that I would find such a reward," he said.

"Nor did I—my chieftain!" Parvia replied.

Finally, even the family had departed, and Dejah Thoris found herself again in the comfortable companionship of her parents. Thoria sat beside her and drew her close.

"Now, having heard the tale of your adventures as a valiant warrior and representative of our city, I must ask you of the adventures of the heart. It seems Jan Vajo courted you at first. I would not have you wounded by his treachery."

"No, indeed! I disliked him extremely from the beginning of our acquaintance! Nothing could have induced me to favor his suit at any time!"

She leaned pensively against Thoria's shoulder.

"It is true that, before he died, I saw the man he might have been without the malign influence of that cursed medallion—rough and grasping perhaps, yet not without honor. He met his death with courage, protecting my father. We must grant him our gratitude for that. But even as his true self, he could never have won my love."

She laughed ruefully. "No, no, I was not born to be consort in Zor! I would far rather stay here in Helium with you."

"I am relieved to hear it," Thoria said. "And yet, when we see such a happy couple as passed before us tonight . . . do you not feel how delightful it is to be thus courted?"

Dejah Thoris shrugged. "Parvia feels it, and that is enough."

"But, my dearest daughter, when you have spent much time in the company of a courageous, and if I may say so, a very well-favored young man, one who has the esteem of your father . . . did you never wonder why his eyes would turn elsewhere?"

"Oh!" Dejah Thoris sat upright and frowned at her mother in playful chiding. "Now I see the meaning of your questions! You think my poor heart must be wounded because Kan Vastor's blade is laid at my friend's feet and not at mine. Surely you know me better than to think I would pine away in jealousy. Kan Vastor has become a trusted friend, but I never thought of him for one instant as a suitor. If Jan Vajo was too old, Kan Vastor is too young. He and Parvia are meant for each other. He could never be my choice."

Thoria sighed. "Well, I am glad that your feet are not

shadowed by unattainable longings. And yet . . . would you not wish one day to be married?"

"You and Father—not to mention Grandmother and Grandfather—have given me such unattainable visions of perfection that I believe I shall renounce all attempts to find a lesser relationship," the princess teased. "Perhaps at the end of a very long life I may find some ancient worthy with whom to make the last long voyage."

"Oh, you are incorrigible," Thoria said, laughing in spite of herself. "I was trying to speak seriously with you."

"I will speak seriously, then. My father, I shall be ever grateful and will never forget my joy in having some part in bringing you home, for myself, for our family, and for Helium. But as for the court of the Jed of Zor and his untimely affections, I beg that you would never again send me forth for that kind of diplomacy, nor countenance any such embassies to me."

"But, my child," Mors Kajak said, "your mother is right. Surely you will wish to marry—one day. And how will you do so without suitors?"

"One day, perhaps," she said. "But recent events have shown me that I would not wish for a suitor any time soon. I have so much to learn, so much to see and do, to serve my city and my people. All I ask is that you will allow me to choose my own time to be courted. And I know that time is not yet."

"My pride in you is so great that at this moment, I would find it hard to consider any man worthy of you," Mors Kajak said. "And since I owe you my life, this seems a reasonable boon to grant in return. Truthfully, in the past few days, I have wished many times that I had sent you with your brother as you desired, instead of this excursion that I imagined to be so much safer!"

The evening ended in shared laughter and a warm embrace, before the princess retired at last to the peace of her own chambers, and her own thoughts. For a long time, she remained on the balcony, lightly wrapped in silk against the chill of the night. She smiled fondly as she recalled the look on Kan Vastor's face when Parvia returned his sword. That was love— not the greedy gaze of such as Jan Vajo. Yet, not for worlds would she desire such a look from any warrior she had met so far. She gazed into the limitless skies, where the curious blue gem of Jasoom blazed high, and her thoughts wandered far into the unknown. Her heart whispered to her that it might be moved one day, but only by one as far different from any she had known as that beckoning sapphire star lofted high above the gems quarried from the rocks of Barsoom.

EDGAR RICE BURROUGHS UNIVERSE™

JOHN CARTER®
OF MARS®

SWORDS OF THE MIND

Transcribed by Geary Gravel

From Gridley Wave Transmissions received at the offices of
Edgar Rice Burroughs, Inc.,
Tarzana, California

ERB
INC.

1
MYSTERY IN THE AIR

TIME AND AGE ARE THE STRANGEST THINGS, and nowhere is this more evident to me than here on Mars. At least on Barsoom I am not the odd man out for having a life span that has so far encompassed centuries rather than mere decades.

One of the unforeseen consequences of a life as long as mine can be too much time to think. It is true that I am by nature a man of action, and often engaged in pursuits in which my attention is wholly focused on discovering the best route to deliver the point of my sword to an opponent's vitals—yet no matter how filled with peril and excitement are the vast majority of my days, there inevitably occur those quiet periods during which I may easily fall prey to an attack of rumination. So it is that every now and again I find myself pausing to take stock of my numerous responsibilities as both Prince of the House of Tardos Mors of the great nation of Helium and Warlord of all Barsoom, not to mention my duties as husband and father, and now—impossible as it may seem as I examine the vigorous and youthful fighting man in the looking glass— grandfather and great-grandfather. That is when I solemnly resolve to comport myself as the elder statesman and mature family man I am in every aspect but spirit and appearance by swearing off all further adventure.

In the end, of course, both pondering and resolution come to naught—for as soon as I leave off seeking adventure, it eagerly comes in search of me.

Such was the circumstance when I found myself winging

my way home through the thin atmosphere of dying Mars to Helium's twin cities in a trim one-man flier, following my first return visit after nearly a year's absence to the site of one of my more recent brushes with death in a hellish underworld not far from Barsoom's ice-clad southern pole. Lying in a series of interconnected caverns some ten miles below the surface of the planet, the Perfect World (as its inhuman rulers, all unacquainted with the concept of irony, had seen fit to christen it) had once contained over a million captive men and women, who languished there as slaves until I spearheaded the rebellion that toppled their cruel masters and returned them to freedom.* Now those few souls who—perhaps internally scarred by decades of horror trapped below ground—could no longer bear the thought of returning to the sunlit world above were looked after by my friend and ally Xodar of the First Born, who also ruled in the Valley Dor as jeddak over the new nation of mingled races forged decades ago from the chaos left behind after the downfall of the false goddess Issus.

Near the end of my visit, whose main goal had been a reinforcement of the ties of friendship between Helium and Xodar's two realms, now collectively known as Pravenoom, I had been on a solitary walking tour of the very cavern wherein I had spent my own confinement the year previous. Suddenly, out of the dimness, thundered three of the eight-foot-tall beast men known as Long-arms, who had originally been bred in the laboratories of the Perfect World by certain unscrupulous human scientists in the employ of the monsters who ruled there. Those few of their number who had not perished in the great battle that unseated their masters, or fled the caverns through secret ways, had been made to understand they would be allowed to continue to abide there for only so long as they comported themselves with civility. Apparently these three had chafed under such restrictions and chosen the

---

* See the Edgar Rice Burroughs Universe novel *John Carter of Mars: Gods of the Forgotten* by Geary Gravel.

moment of my appearance in what they obviously still regarded as their own fiefdom to express their indignation—though whether they recognized me as the principle architect of their reduced circumstances or simply another detested human careless enough to wander unaccompanied in their domain, I do not know. Whatever the case, they fell upon me without warning from the shadows of a great carven stalagmite with fangs bared and great arms swinging.

Had I been unarmed things could have gone a different way, but few male Barsoomians go abroad without a full complement of weaponry buckled to their harness, and so I had a dagger, as well as swords both long and short, at my instant disposal. Nor were my would-be assassins weaponless, for in addition to their natural defenses of muscle, tooth, and claw, two of the three bore great wooden bludgeons. A year ago I had battled for my life against their ilk in an arena reverberating with cheers of encouragement as hundreds of slaves looked on with rising hope. Now I fought without an audience in a silence punctuated only by the grunts and snarls of my savage opponents.

Once I had knife in hand my first thought was to get some use out of my enemy's own weapons. This I accomplished by charging head on at the sole Long-arm unencumbered with a club, racing up to within a foot of his mammoth bulk, and then leaping up to plaster myself against his hairy chest. Clinging to his fur, I dodged rapidly back and forth, up and down, as the others swung their cudgels in a furious attempt to brain me, but instead succeeded only in raining blow after blow upon their hapless comrade as he bellowed and shrieked while striving to dislodge me. Anticipating a mighty swing aimed at separating my head from the rest of me, I dropped like a stone to the ground, heard the crunch of bone as the club connected with my victim's own cranium, then turned swiftly to put him out of his misery with a dagger to the heart. I stepped back to face the two who remained with my longsword drawn. Three of the formidable creatures continuing to attack from all sides might have given me some close calls, especially had I been reduced to fighting barehanded as had been the case in the arena, but a pair of them were no match for me fully armed, and it was not long before I had relieved the nearest not only of his bludgeon but of the hand that clutched it and then, a moment later, of his life. I could see my final antagonist wavering for a moment as he entertained the idea of returning to the shadows in one piece, but in the end his fury got the best of him and he hefted his weapon and barreled toward me with a terrific roar. My blade flashed to meet his charge and soon he too was lying at my feet, his lifeblood mingled with that of his predecessors on the rough cavern floor.

Xodar met me as I emerged from the cavern still wiping the dark blood from my sword. He was visibly unsettled when he learned what had transpired, but knew me better than to offer an abject apology for what might have spelled my end, and merely noted that I seemed no worse for the wear after my several minutes of vigorous exercise, promising that he would henceforth maintain a tighter rein on the less savory elements of the underground population. When we parted as friends the next morning, I extended an invitation for him to visit Helium in the near future, where I promised I would do my best to put together as diverting an experience for him as I had enjoyed in his new realm.

I was still a day or more out from my destination, and contemplating a pleasant interval of peace and quiet with my beloved princess once I arrived home, when I became aware of a flicker of brightness in the corner of my eye caused by sunlight reflecting from a metallic object some distance behind me and to starboard. I turned to see another flier, a vessel larger than my own, though of familiar configuration, coming up from behind me on a course that I reckoned would soon bring it close to my own. Before long it seemed clear that we were in fact converging on an identical path, and I wondered if this flier was also on its way to Helium and—more importantly on warlike Barsoom—whether it was piloted by friend or foe.

I swung the ship's spyglass before my eye and was both surprised and pleased to see mounted upon the vessel's bow the proud insignia of the House of Tardos Mors, and blazoned on a scarlet pennon above it the personal device of my son. I would have recognized the *Susstos* even without those identifiers, since Carthoris had chosen to humor a request of his own young son to have the sides of the sleek craft embellished with a striking pattern of stylized golden sunbeams.

I knew that he had been planning to set out on a routine aerial mission of his own, this to undertake the long-delayed delivery of a pair of Gridley Wave transceivers, one to Exum, the scientific installation located on Barsoom's equator that functioned as the planet's prime meridian, and the other to the far mountain kingdom of Gathol where his sister Tara ruled with her husband Gahan. I was puzzled, however, as to why he would only now be returning from his journey. I did not know the exact date of my son's departure, as his trip was still in the planning stages when I left Helium. Yet my own stay in the southern regions had lasted roughly five weeks by earthly measurement, which was surely enough time for him to drop off the needed equipment both at the Exum communications station and in Gathol, and even allowing for a family visit in the latter case, I had assumed he would be back in Helium long before my own return.

I immediately ran up my own colors accompanied by a flag of greeting. When no response was forthcoming after a minute or two, I employed my ship's annunciator at full volume to hail the other flier, thinking that perhaps Carthoris had decided to engage his controlling destination compass—a marvelous device of his own invention that would not only automatically guide an airborne vessel to its destination, but could even land it without human assistance if need be—thus allowing him to stray from the helm if he chose, to enjoy a meal or maybe a brief nap in the ship's small cabin.

My stentorian hail also failing to evoke a reaction, I increased the magnification on the spyglass and reexamined the ship, becoming immediately aware of a pronounced tilt to port and making out several deep gashes along that side of the hull. Now convinced the flier had undergone some sort of serious assault, whether by an enemy airship or the large guns employed by certain hordes of the green men that roamed the dead sea bottoms, and fearing that Carthoris might have sustained a grave injury during such an encounter, I altered course by a few degrees and reduced my speed in order to drop back and more swiftly intercept the other vessel.

Soon I had fallen abreast of the *Susstos*. In spite of the other ship's damaged state, it appeared that its throttle was wide open; I gained several yards of altitude so that I might more easily survey the ship from above. I winced at the damage to the hull, which had obviously resulted in the rupture of one of the main buoyancy tanks carried there, thus allowing the Eighth Ray stored within to escape in a slow leak and accounting for the ship's sloping posture. This flier was Carthoris' newest pride and joy; fresh from the Hastor shipyards, it had been constructed of the finest materials and personally outfitted by my son with all of the latest aeronautical amenities and aesthetic adornments. The deck was of skeel planking that had been polished till it gleamed and framed with a burnished hand rail of gold filigree, the cabin constructed of dressed sorapus ribbed with narrow panels of overlapping carborundum aluminum and forandus, while the instruments at the helm were embellished with dozens of tiny jewels.

With no one visible on deck, and the steep angle at which the wounded craft currently rode the wind preventing me from seeing into the portholes of the small cabin, my concern for my son's well-being was growing. It was imperative that I board the other ship and investigate as quickly as possible.

The one-man flier I favor when venturing out alone is a comparatively modest conveyance, its basic design little altered from the model I once flew some eight decades ago as an air scout in Zodanga: sixteen feet from pointed stem to pointed stern and a mere two feet wide. The pilot's seat, adjustable so one may choose to sit upright behind the curving windscreen, recline at an angle, or even stretch out prone, lies above the small, magnetically energized motor that has replaced the radium-powered engine of the older model. Its own store of the Eighth Barsoomian Ray, that remarkable substance whose manipulation is responsible for maintaining the craft's buoyancy while propellers fore and aft drive it through the air, resides in reservoirs located within the thin metal walls that constitute the narrow hull.

Unfortunately, a one-man ship such as this is not equipped with more than the most rudimentary boarding tackle, and this presented me with a challenge. It is true that my earthly muscles allow me to perform prodigious leaps in the lesser gravitation and lower air pressure of Mars, and I briefly considered attempting to span the gap between the two vessels in a single bound—had not the wind generated by our high rate of speed convinced me it would be nigh impossible to do so with any guarantee of success. Instead I decided to employ what stout cordage I had in an attempt to lasso a stanchion on the larger craft, at the least providing myself with a sort of tightrope over which I might crawl between the speeding ships.

I gained half a ship's length on the other vessel and brought forth the lines, which were studded here and there with hooks. Loosely braiding them together, I formed a temporary noose on one end that I proceeded to hurl across the gap. My first several attempts went widely astray and I was close to abandoning the effort when finally, more by chance than design, a pair of hooks caught on the deck bolts of the *Susstos* and the ships flew in tandem, now roughly twenty feet apart. Recognizing that this was still far from a safe venture, for the damage to Carthoris' vessel was causing it to lurch and swerve unpredictably, I wrapped the remainder of the cordage about my ship's railing and started to inch across. Not long after my sandaled feet left the gunwale, one of the hooks let go and a strand of cable flew back to catch in an inconvenient location on my own craft, which then veered sharply behind me. A moment later the other hook came loose as well, sending me flying back into the gulf and causing me to miss by mere inches the swiftly churning aft propeller on my ship as I dangled precariously a few feet behind its tapered stern.

Muscles straining, I pulled myself hand over hand up the slender cable against the fierce wind until I had regained my craft. I reconsidered my strategy with a rueful shake of my head and a smile of determination playing on my lips. The smile was genuine, for I have found that it is simple human nature to enjoy most that which we do well. By contrast, this is why I am often forced to conceal the grim expression of stoic endurance that would otherwise disfigure my face when I find myself compelled to engage in such activities as the grand and stately formal dances required by my station. Though I can now perform the intricate movements with passable skill, it has been a long road for one seemingly blessed at birth with as many left feet as a newly hatched calot, and I salute the courage of my patient mate for remaining by my side through endless practice sessions, though I fear her own feet were often left bruised and trampled as a result. All this simply to say that piloting an aircraft through its own intricate dance high in the skies of Barsoom is one of the activities I have always truly enjoyed as a proficient practitioner. Now, using my destination compass to fully synchronize my flight path to that of the *Susstos*, I secured my throttle at maximum and employed a trick of the gearing perfected by the Heliumetic navy that I had learned from my friend Kantos Kan many decades ago to shoot far out ahead of the flier racing below me. Attaining a lead of about two miles, I halted my ship and set it to float nearly motionless in the air. Then I took up my post at the bow railing and fixed my eyes upon the other vessel. Just as the *Susstos* once more soared beneath my little craft, I leaped out and over in the direction of its flight with all the force I could muster. A moment later I was tumbling onto the deck of my target, my own forward momentum just enough to prevent me from being splattered across that highly polished skeel planking. I quickly lashed myself securely to the deck, playing out enough line to allow me to push up to my feet on the canted surface and, much in the manner of a mountaineer negotiating a severely angled cliffside in a driving wind, hastened to the helm, where I gradually cut the motor until the ship was now also suspended nearly unmoving in the air, some half a mile ahead of the flier I had just deserted.

Not waiting to catch my breath, I next made my way to the door of the small cabin, slipped the latch, and stepped inside to find with a mixture of great relief and disappointment that the beautifully appointed chamber—now in jumbled disarray due to the impact of the shell that had left the ship listing so heavily to one side—was unoccupied. Naturally I was relieved not to find Carthoris seriously injured or worse within, but dismayed and not a little mystified that his whereabouts remained unknown. I took a few moments to sift through the jumble on the floor for some sign of a message from him. Finding nothing, I went out on deck again to inspect the bejeweled helm more carefully. As I had surmised, the controlling destination compass had been set to guide the ship unerringly to Helium at top speed.

I turned the ship around in a wide circle, returned to where my little flier waited obediently for us in midair, and nosed up directly alongside.

Now I found myself faced with a choice. Assuming Carthoris had sent the *Susstos* on its pell-mell flight to Helium in a plea for assistance, I could abandon one of the two fliers and resume my journey home aboard the other one, there to acquire reinforcements and go in search of my son. Or—what now seemed to me the more sensible option, considering that Carthoris might very well be in dire straits, in which case time would most certainly be of the essence—I could more quickly discover the location from which the craft had been dispatched by turning my son's ship about and engaging what Carthoris, who enjoyed the occasional use of phrases from his father's tongue, had whimsically designated the "homing pigeon" function of the destination compass, thus ensuring that the *Susstos* would faithfully retrace the path it had been following straight back to the place where he had first sent it aloft without its pilot.

There was one problem with the latter option: the ship's port buoyancy tank had been irreparably damaged and the *Susstos* was tilting heavily to that side, which would at the very least make for an awkward flight. Indeed, should the store of the Eighth Ray left in the punctured tank soon be completely exhausted and the amount in the starboard reservoir then prove insufficient to keep the flier aloft, there was a good chance we might not make it all the way back to its mysterious point of origin—or, for that matter, the rest of the way home to Helium.

Necessity is a breeding ground for ideas, some strokes of genius and others of more dubious quality. It was then that I had the rather outlandish notion to employ the larger craft's more extensive grapples and boarding tackle to tightly bind the two ships together, thus stabilizing the larger one in the manner of the outrigger canoes I had once seen employed during a brief stay in the Pacific islands. With both fliers floating nearly motionless side by side, in less than an hour I was able to secure the tackle between them in a manner I hoped would form a more or less reliable connection. By the time I was finished, my one-man flier had been firmly grafted to the side of the larger craft—admittedly more in the fashion of a jury-rigged motorcycle sidecar than the graceful outrigger of my memory—its own full buoyancy tanks now compensating for what had been lost from my son's vessel to bring us level once more. The result was a serviceable mode of transportation, if a decidedly unconventional one. Smiling as I imagined Carthoris' reaction to the effect of my rough-and-tumble handiwork on his beautiful new vessel, I activated the *Sussto'* "homing pigeon" and the battered ship began to race back along the path it had just flown.

Without knowledge of when or from what starting point the ship had been sent on its lonely journey, I had no idea how long the return trip would last, nor to what part of Barsoom it would take me. As the long hours dragged by I alternated between gazing out over the deck railing for some identifiable landmark below and busying myself in the small cabin as I attempted to restore order now that we were once more traveling upright, and made a more thorough search through my son's effects for some clue to what had transpired. Among the articles that had been scattered across the floor in the attack I discovered a small item I had overlooked in my first cursory inspection, recognizing it as one of the more interesting creations of Heliumetic scientists, cast in the form of two five-inch golden cylinders fastened together side by side.

As I have noted on more than one occasion, my adopted planet of Barsoom is a world of profound paradoxes. Here is a globe strewn with the monumental ruins of once magnificent ancient cities now overrun by primitive hordes, where most warfare continues to be conducted at swordspoint. Though many unparalleled scientific achievements were lost forever with the collapse of these ancient centers of culture and learning, yet new metropolises have risen in their stead, along with technological marvels far beyond what we had accomplished on Earth at the time of my departure. Indeed, during my first sojourn here in the year 1866 I flew in a gigantic aerial battleship held aloft by invisible rays, shouldered rifles that could accurately fire an explosive projectile over a range of two hundred miles, and supped in an eating establishment where the touch of a button caused a mechanical apparatus to convey to one's table a sumptuous meal prepared from raw ingredients totally untouched by human hands from the time they entered the building until the moment they were set in final form before the diner. A decade later I stood in a glass-domed hothouse principality near the planet's northern pole before a mechanism that instantly transmitted my likeness and description to five different locations in cities several miles distant from one another. So it was that I was able to recognize the instrument in the cabin as a compact reading and writing device known as a *teeltjor*, a miraculous combination of portable library and typewriting machine in one.

It is my experience that the young are more apt to embrace the new, and my first encounter with such an implement had actually been in the hands of my only grandson, Djon Dihn being seldom found without the device. When unlocked by the touch of its owner, the two golden cylinders could be pulled apart as one would open a scroll to reveal between them something that outwardly resembled a single sheet of gilded parchment, yet could serve as a repository for millions of words in the pictographic written language peculiar to Helium, all to be stored away or summoned forth as if by magic through the manipulation of the tiny knobs and buttons affixed to the undersides of both cylinders. Djon Dihn had eagerly demonstrated for me how even diagrams and drawings could be preserved in the instrument by use of a tiny stylus. If at any time a palpable record of something contained within was desired, the touch of a button would cause the surface of the central sheet to slough off an exact duplicate of itself that had the appearance and feel of stiff paper. A voracious consumer and would-be producer of the written word, with an especial fondness for sweeping sagas and tales of adventure, my grandson had amassed within his device innumerable volumes comprising many of the great epics of Barsoom's past, as well as detailed descriptions he himself had recorded of the memorable exploits—several of my own included—of his own fighting ancestors both ancient and contemporary.

I was a bit puzzled to find the toy—for such I deemed it,

finding little practical value in such things myself—among my son's belongings here aboard the *Susstos*, for so far as I knew Djon Dihn was currently in Ptarth at the court of his other grandfather, Thuvan Dihn, no doubt plying the great jeddak with endless questions concerning his own feats on and off the battlefield. Deciding that Carthoris must have acquired one of the instruments for his own use and wondering if he had possibly stored some sort of message in it before sending his ship off in search of aid, I attempted unsuccessfully for a time to pry the device open with my fingers, finally leaving off my labors for fear of damaging whatever might lie within.

Since my engagement of the "homing pigeon," we had been following a southwesterly course that increasingly had us flying over territory still largely unexplored by the nations of red men. Miraculously, my stitched-together vehicle was functioning better than I had predicted, with only the occasional shudder or jolt to remind me that we were probably riding on borrowed time. The daylight hours passed in relative calm as I roved the deck, anxious for some sign that we were nearing the end of the trail; at night I took to the cabin for a few hours of restless sleep.

With no more evidence than a strong feeling to back it up, when the second morning dawned in our flight I awakened with the conviction that we were closing in on our destination. We were speeding high above the endless miles of ocher moss that constituted the dead sea bottom where once Thurdus, least pacific of the five great oceans of ancient Barsoom, had challenged those stout-hearted sailors of old who dared brave its famously stormy waves, when the excitement began.

The sounds of gunfire drew me out onto the deck. Far below was a sight to inspire awe in one's breast—as well as deep concern. I trained the spyglass on a huge convoy of green men, comprising some five hundred of the ponderous three-wheeled chariots favored by these nomadic giants. Each vehicle was drawn by a single mastodonian zitidar, flanked by dozens of warriors astride the outsized thoats bred exclusively by the green race, and followed by a single calot, that faithful ten-legged Martian hound whose ferocity made it the equal of half a dozen armed fighters. At the head of the cavalcade rode no less than three hundred warriors, with a similar comple-ment bringing up the rear, each fighter bearing swords, dagger and rifle. It was the sporadic discharge of the latter weapon that had attracted my notice.

Few ever venture knowingly into the skies above a green caravan lest they become a convenient source of target prac-tice for gunners wishing to advance their reputation as defend-ers of the horde at the cost of knocking a red interloper out of the air. In recent years this had become somewhat less true in certain regions as Tars Tarkas, Jeddak of Thark, as well as my long-time friend and a staunch ally to Helium, continued his work of consolidating the disparate nomad nations of green men beneath a banner of peace. Unfortunately, not all tribes evinced an interest in abandoning the bloodthirsty habits of millennia, many clinging tenaciously to their animos-ity not only toward the red race but to all other living beings outside their own horde. My spyglass confirmed that the standards and insignia of the caravan beneath me belonged to just such a group, as did the radium bullets that were already whizzing past our bow. These were the Thurds, their name derived from that long-vanished body of water whose mossy bed they now claimed as their own.

I had been half-expecting such an encounter, figuring that whoever had blasted holes in the side of my son's ship might be found somewhere along the path we now flew and would likely attack again. I raced to the controls and began to dip and roll the ship as we flew into range above the convoy, executing a series of maneuvers I hoped would render the *Susstos* almost impossible to hit, despite the renowned marks-manship of the green warriors. After a lucky shot grazed the hull I reluctantly swerved widely to the east and dipped lower in the sky, putting the rising sun in their telescopic sights and hoping for the best. Soon we had left them behind. What alteration this wild though brief deviation might have wrought to the recording of the path of its previous flight stored in the craft's controlling destination compass, I was not sure. I reengaged the device, hoping against hope that we had not strayed so far from our prescribed course that the vessel would insist on swinging about and carrying me back over the caravan once again in an effort to resume our original path. To my relief the ship made a few minor lateral adjustments, gained more altitude, and then continued on what I estimated to be the same course we had been following before the interruption.

Unfortunately, my relief lasted no more than a few hours, as shortly past noon I spied an encampment of yet another group of hostiles, this one situated directly between us and the mounting rim of the seabed some miles ahead. The Torquasian horde, famed as the superlative marksmen of a people known for their uncanny aim, had lately surpassed their brethren from the other green nations in the field of armaments, refining the long-range rifles traditionally employed by their race to produce a lightweight, easily carried rocket launcher that closely resembled a similar martial device nicknamed the "bazooka" back on Earth. A few miles west of us a range of steep cliffs loomed beyond the gradually upward-sloping sea bed. Once more taking evasive maneuvers, I was confident we were going to make it past this barrier—right up to the moment those below trotted out one of these big guns and an ambitious sharpshooter managed to blast away most of my carefully arranged connecting tackle with his very first shot, leaving only a few stout lengths of cordage between the two ships. With a terrific jolt my sturdy sidecar suddenly devolved into a semidetached caboose trailing some thirty feet behind the larger ship, where it commenced twisting and rolling wildly like the tail of a kite being flown by a running child. Fortunately, I had lashed myself to Carthoris' ship using the fasteners on my flying leather and the various hooks and eyes that studded the deck for that purpose, or I would have been tossed overboard at once as the *Susstos* also heeled violently over, first to the one side and then more deeply to the other, while I strained at the helm and fought a losing battle to bring us back to something resembling an even keel, the loss of the added buoyancy provided by my original craft having left the larger ship listing heavily once more to port.

Besides threatening to afflict me with a severe bout of airsickness, at first the new arrangement actually functioned as an asset, for it presented us as a target of weird and unfamiliar conformation that seemed to confuse the shooters below. Once they got over their initial consternation, however, the various riflemen began to concentrate their fire on one or the other of the dipping, swerving ships, and before long the sharpshooter shouldering the Martian bazooka—the man was clearly deserving of a medal, though my own inclination at that moment was to throttle him—once more demonstrated his eagle's eye and a powerful blast struck my errant kite-tail broadside. Now the little flier pitched and veered even more wildly, throwing the craft I occupied nearly out of control.

The edge of the dead sea bottom was rising within my sights as I clung to the hope that we had a chance of limping over the approaching mountains and perhaps coming to ground for repairs somewhere the green men could not easily access. The Eighth Ray was not my friend this day, however, as a moment later I became aware of a more serious consequence of the damage to my former ship: the radium shell that had exploded upon contact with the one-man flier's hull had demolished that ship's main buoyancy tank and the little craft began to plummet to earth as its own store of the miraculous substance dissipated into the atmosphere, while the craft I was now aboard, already lacking in sufficient aerial support of its own, opted to follow it to the ground, swiftly becoming almost vertical as the additional weight dragged its stern downward. Before we could flip over backward I leaped from the controls and brought my longsword down with all my strength on the remaining ties that bound the two ships to each other. The last rope split and the rear of the *Susstos* bobbed upward again as the smaller craft, its propellers churning madly, shot past us, just cresting the cliff tops before it vanished into the woods beyond them.

I gunned the motor again and the *Susstos*, now free of its former encumbrance, darted forward, once more flying nearly sideways as I clung to the helm. I was startled to find that the range of mountains was actually part of a vast circle of towering cliffs enclosing a forest-ringed level plain within its protective embrace. I had a quick glimpse of what appeared to be a sizable structure near the center of the plain as we flashed over a small arc of the inner circle, then once again flew beyond the cliffs, almost grazing the highest peaks, after which I used all my skill as a pilot to bring us to the sort of extremely rough touchdown that an uncharitable observer might have classified as a crash landing in a small clearing.

2
FIREWORKS

IT WAS GOOD TO BE ON SOLID GROUND again after such a harrowing flight. As the ship shuddered into silence I unhooked my harness from the deck riggings and stepped to the railing to survey the surroundings, wondering if we had come down anywhere near the point from which Carthoris had launched the ship. Here, away from the monotony of the moss-carpeted dead sea bottoms, was a different side of Barsoom, where gentle hillocks of black loam and scarlet grasses were host to a variety of shrubs and a riot of colorful wildflowers.

The broad ring of cliffs reared up like an impenetrable wall before me, with boulders great and small strewn about its base. With no signs of human habitation in the immediate vicinity and the tantalizing glimpse I had had of what might have been a good-sized city, it seemed my best bet would be to prosecute my search for my son on the other side of this barrier—if I could only find a way to surmount it. The *Susstos* was clearly no longer in any shape to assist me in my quest. Accordingly, I removed the sleeping silks from one of the pallets in the cabin and used them to fashion a pair of small sacks, into which I stuffed whatever items from the ship I thought might come in handy, including a waterskin and some cubes of usa, the nearly tasteless mashed fruit that is a staple of the armies of Barsoom. On impulse, I also brought with me the small construction of golden cylinders,

just in case I was able to figure out how to open it with some
more experimentation.

The cliffs rose in a nearly vertical wall before me, the portion
within my view clearly impossible to climb, though I hoped
this would not be the case everywhere. I craned my neck until
it ached as I roamed the perimeter, staring upward for some
sign of handholds I might use to scale the daunting barrier.
The solution when it finally came was not to be found above,
however, but below, for when I chanced to peer behind a large
boulder lying close to the base of the rocky wall, I noticed a
previously hidden opening leading downward into the ground
at a gentle slope. My longsword drawn and my radium torch
in my other hand, I made my way cautiously into the dim
tunnel, my light revealing floor and walls of such smoothness
that it was soon obvious I was traversing a man-made construction rather than the natural cavern I had first assumed.
I paused here and there to examine ancient carvings in bas-
relief upon the corridor's sloping walls. Though timeworn,
these had been afforded enough protection from the elements
that I was easily able to make out the sculpted images of
graceful human figures clad in flowing robes, the archaic
styling of which confirmed their great age.

I was beginning to feel as if the downward-sloping tunnel
would descend forever into the bowels of the planet when the
floor leveled off for a short space and then to my relief began
slowly ascending. Light grew in the distance and before long
I emerged to find myself on the sunlit forested slope of the
huge valley, bounded on all sides by the towering cliffs over
which I had recently flown. I was certain that, other than by
means of aircraft or through passageways such as that from
which I had just emerged, no outsiders could have found their
way across that formidable barrier, so steep and treacherous
were its sides. In fact, the ring of cliffs forming the bowl-shaped
depression had seemed of such regular circularity during my
brief flyover that I wondered if I now stood in the vast crater
of one of the planet's long dormant volcanos. The view before

me was obscured by thick clusters of the gigantic, smooth-barked trees whose presence is usually confined to the narrow strips of arable land bordering Barsoom's mighty waterways, their trunks rising above a carpet of brilliant scarlet sward dotted profusely with blossoms of mingled purple, yellow, and vermillion. I stood for a moment, struck again by the contrast between this lush landscape and the endless dead sea bottoms of yellow moss that covered so much of this planet of breathtaking extremes.

With no "homing pigeon" device to guide me on this portion of the trip, I could only hope that my son had made the same trek through the tunnel and onto the hillside. I headed downslope, following what seemed to me to be the most direct route to the plain I had seen from above. The farther I descended the more difficult it became to see past the huge boles and the rank underbrush clustered at their bases to anything beyond my immediate surroundings, and I moved with caution so as not to be suddenly confronted by an unwelcome surprise. If it had not been for a stray shaft of early afternoon sunshine falling upon a reflective surface far off to my left, I might have walked right past the wreckage of my one-man flier. After a quick inspection to confirm that the little craft, now a mass of twisted metal, would never take to the sky again, I removed a few supplies I thought might prove useful from this ship as well, stowed them with the items from the *Susstos* in the sacks tucked into my leather belt or attached them directly to my harness, and moved on. Soon I began to get glimpses of a broad, flat stretch of land up ahead. Peering through a final line of trees, I beheld the level plain I had seen briefly from above. There, set like a fabulous jewel at its center, was a magnificent high-walled city of shining domes and colorful minarets. Perhaps equally fascinating as this unexpected vision was what lay directly outside those towering marble walls.

From my vantage just within the line of trees I could see two encampments of about a thousand green warriors each, one to the north of the city and another to the south. The colorful pennons flying high above each camp indicated that these fighting men were not derived from the same tribe, the battalion camped to the north made up of members of that same Torquasian horde I had lately encountered to the significant detriment of my flight over the dead sea bottom, while those on the southern side bore the insignia of their age-old rivals, the Thurds.

There was a great circular gate set in the western wall toward which I faced, its construction of a sort not employed since the earliest days of Barsoom's recorded history—a discordant note I could not reconcile with the lack of any signs of obvious age and wear in the besieged city. Perhaps my imagination was playing tricks on me, but I was fairly certain I could see a few tiny figures atop the wall above the gate. Still within the edge of the forest, I was too far away to make out any details of color or conformation, but I had little reason to believe the watchers were of the same race as their assailants. Those of the nomadic green tribes make their temporary dwellings exclusively in the long-deserted cities that border Barsoom's dead sea bottoms, scorning the construction of any permanent habitations in favor of occupying the remnants of the once grand abodes of those peoples that had fled or suffered near extermination at the hands of their ancestors millennia ago. Raising my gaze once again to the walls of the enigmatic city, I could see clearly that here was no crumbling ancient ruin, but a glorious monument to the architects and builders of millennia past, somehow still standing proud and unbroken in spite of the passage of time, the polished gold, azure, scarlet, and silver of its minarets and the unblemished white marble of its walls gleaming as if only recently erected.

I turned my attention from the city back to the twin encampments that bracketed it. Could the two armies have united to stage an attack on the city? As far as I knew there had never been aught but bitter enmity between the green men of Torquas and those of Thurd, and I quickly dismissed that scenario as all but impossible. This left the much more likely explanation that they were competing for the city, and were currently engaged in a mutually agreed upon temporary cessation of hostilities. Due to the often deadly accuracy I had recently witnessed for myself on the part of the Torquasian marksmen, and their determination to prevent outsiders from making inroads into their territory, very little was known of this area of Barsoom, save that the hordes of Torquas had historically claimed the entire region as their own. There had been rumors of late that the Thurds were seeking to expand their own domain westward, which would have them encroaching upon their unfriendly neighbors. Was this part of a Thurd incursion to gain a foothold in established Torquasian territory? And yet the Torquasians seemed no more in possession of the city than did their rivals. I did know that both hordes had rebuffed the earnest attempts by the Jeddak of Thark, my noble friend Tars Tarkas, to welcome them into the peaceful union of the many tribes of the green race he was working to establish.

I needed to decide on my next move. As eager as I was to gain entrance to the city in order that I might discover whether or not my son had done the same and perhaps found sanctuary there, I harbored no illusions as to the likelihood of my successfully making it past thousands of green warriors to do so. I slipped quietly through the trees, keeping well back from any open spaces where sharp-eyed sentries might spot me, and determined that the sparsest concentration of warriors occurred both on the western end of the city, where I now stood, and the eastern. Even at those two locations, guards from the northern and southern camps maintained constant vigil, glowering at one another across the few hundred yards that separated them.

What I needed was a distraction.

Deep in thought, I retreated from the edge of the plain and retraced my steps through the forest to the crash site of my one-man craft.

Fliers both great and small typically carry a well-stocked tool kit in the event repairs are required on the fly. Finding mine intact in an undamaged section of hull, I set about using it to extract components from the wrecked vessel, removing several elements of the engine itself, as well as a section of the aft buoyancy reservoir, which still retained a tiny fraction of its store of the Eighth Ray. Goaded on by urgency, I worked tirelessly for most of the afternoon, the rapid Barsoomian dusk just beginning to unfold by the time I completed my task and carried the object I had cobbled together back down through the forest and to the edge of the plain. Carefully positioning the device on a flat rock just inside the wall of trees, I breathed a prayer to whichever of my ancestors might happen to be within earshot, activated the thing with a spark from the fire-starter in my pocket pouch, and stood back.

The patchwork missile shot into the darkening sky in a silent arc that peaked high in the air just beyond the far eastern walls of the city. I held my breath in anticipation, half afraid my afternoon of fevered labor had resulted in nothing more than a high-flying dud, but a second later my unlovely creation exploded beautifully. I did not know what day or even month it was back on Earth, yet that evening the skies above this lost valley of Barsoom were briefly illuminated by as impressive an exhibition of pyrotechnics as had ever graced an Independence Day picnic in Virginia, before what was left of the disintegrating hodgepodge fell to the plain in flames.

As I had hoped, my dazzling display instantly captured the full attention of both opposing camps, and hundreds of warriors deserted their posts at either end of the city to stampede in the direction of the conflagration, converging at about the same time around the smoldering remains of my improvised missile. Guttural war cries began to echo throughout the valley, followed by wild gunfire and the clang of swords as the hereditary enemies—each camp no doubt assuming the spectacular phenomenon represented the onset of a sneak attack from the other side—closed in heated battle, while I took full advantage of the melee to slip out of the forest and bound at top speed across the plain toward the temporarily deserted western wall of the city. I had earlier spied the remnants of a siege ladder that had been broken in two during some previous attempt at breaching the city's defenses. Propping the larger portion up against the wall, I climbed swiftly to its pinnacle some forty feet above the ground. From there the summit of the wall loomed another twenty feet above me. Fortunately, that distance is as nothing to my earthly muscles and, bracing myself against the top of the rickety structure, I sailed upward, kicking the ladder as I took off so that it fell back to the ground. An instant later I was crouched atop the wall.

I stayed there for a good quarter of an hour, surveying the silent metropolis beneath me and listening to the continuing commotion to the east while I waited for the Martian sundown to complete its rapid transition from day to night. I was reasonably certain I had not been observed by the green troops outside the walls, nor yet by any of the still unseen inhabitants within—and I desired to maintain that status for the time being. Though I believed that those who dwelled in the city were most probably human beings like myself, at this point I preferred to keep them ignorant of my presence, not yet knowing anything of their philosophy concerning hospitality or whether they would be more inclined to greet an outsider with open arms or the point of a sword.

At length I located a narrow stairwell—itself an indicator of the city's great age, for Martian construction has eschewed stairs in favor of sloping ramps for many thousands of years—and climbed down the inner wall to street level. I moved cautiously along empty thoroughfares, seeing no lights in the nearby buildings and no signs of the inhabitants, yet finding it difficult to believe the entire population had taken to their sleeping silks and furs at the very onset of evening. The nearer moon rose to start her swift journey through the heavens as I skulked through the shadowed streets, and I soon noticed a curious change had come over the city with nightfall: under Thuria's flashing radiance the towers and domes of the soaring edifices I had admired from the plain now appeared tarnished and in sad disrepair, the whole more resembling the many long-abandoned cities of ages past I had visited during my time on this dying planet than the gleaming metropolis I had earlier viewed. The deserted streets through which I wandered were filled with rubble, while the bright moonlight illuminated the crumbling facades of the buildings I crept past. Perhaps I had imagined the figures I thought to spy on the battlements after all. Yet if that were true, why had not one or the other army of green men already scaled the walls and taken possession of this untenanted realm?

I spent my first night in the city searching building after building for signs of life and some clue as to the whereabouts of my son, finally retreating into a vacant ground-floor chamber in what looked to be some sort of storehouse just before dawn to sleep, for I still felt uneasy about wandering abroad exposed in the light of day. I decided to make the building my base of operations, taking care to stow the supplies I had brought from the aircraft along with some fresh fruit I had picked up on my way down the forested slope in a cupboard near the back of the room, though the atmosphere of disuse made it doubtful anyone would come across them in the near future even if they were left sitting in the open. I emerged at dusk on the second evening to begin my exploration of a different neighborhood, this one nearer to the center of the city, and that is when I saw the first sign that I was not alone.

I was wandering somewhat aimlessly about the darkened streets and feeling discouraged by my lack of success, when a bright glow of light from high above attracted my attention. The first suggestion of any current human habitation I had yet seen, it emanated ten stories above ground level from the rear of a tall building across the broad avenue from where I stood. I made a quick count of the floors and windows to fix the location of the chamber in my mind. Then, choosing a tower on my side of the street I judged to be of roughly the same height, I climbed the stairwell to a floor slightly above the level of the light I had seen. Entering a deserted room where dust lay thick on the floor, I hurried to the window and peered out. Facing me across the avenue was a large semicircular aperture, perhaps five feet from side to side at its base and the same in height from the sill to the top of the curve, from which the warm and welcoming golden light streamed forth. Framed within its borders I was amazed to see an image of luxury worthy of the grand palaces of Helium, with glimpses of gilded furniture and sumptuous wall hangings sparkling with jewels. Two male figures were visible against this extravagant backdrop. The one faced in my direction had pale skin lighter than my own and golden hair. He was clad in flowing blue robes not unlike those I had seen in the ancient carvings on the walls of the tunnel through which I had gained ingress to this hidden realm.

My mind raced. Was this another Orovar enclave such as the one I had once found in the dead city of Horz, where survivors of one of the original three races that had populated Barsoom millennia ago had sequestered themselves in utmost secrecy? Or could the man before me be a thern from the land at the south pole I had but recently quitted, for that inbred offshoot of the age-old light-skinned race, though now completely hairless, habitually wore yellow wigs to conceal the bald pates of both males and females? I could not be sure of his origin from this distance—yet whichever race claimed him, the fellow was not in a good humor, for he paced the chamber back and forth, gesturing all the while in great agitation. The other figure, apparently the object of his ire, was seated with his back to the window and only partially visible, but my heart leaped in my breast as he moved further into view and I clearly made out the copper skin and black hair of a red man, leaving little doubt to me that I had at last found my son! I watched the fascinating scene for another minute, then descended hurriedly to the ground and darted across the

broad avenue. Making my way through an alley to the opposite side of the structure, I ducked into the once grand main
entrance. To my surprise, in contrast to the richly appointed
chamber I had viewed from across the street, the ground floor
of this building seemed quite as shabby and dilapidated as I
had found the rest of the city. I located a stairwell and quickly
made my way up to the tenth level.

I crept down the dark hallway, noting again the air of
general disuse and deterioration as I neared the place where
the corridor branched and I knew I would find the richly
appointed chamber I sought. I heard faint voices and saw a
flicker of light as I peered around the corner. As I watched,
someone exited a doorway near the far end of the corridor
and for a moment the entire hallway was filled with golden
light, appearing to my dazzled eyes every bit as splendidly
ornamented and well kept up as the chamber I had observed.
The person turned a far corner and the light vanished, but
for a spot of diminished radiance that marked the doorway
from which he had emerged.

I went softly down the corridor in near darkness and stepped
cautiously before the open doorway. The room was large with
few furnishings, with a few small candles burning on a table
in one corner. My eyes adjusted gradually to the dimness as
I looked around to make sure there was no one standing guard,
and I saw with puzzlement that the chamber that had appeared
so elegantly appointed from across the street was in fact as
dilapidated and neglected as the rest of the building. Could
I have gone to the wrong floor? But no, there was the red man
I had seen before. He lay facing the wall, his back turned
toward me, on a worn couch near the open window.

Moving silently to within a foot of the couch, I realized
with a sharp pang of disappointment that the figure before
me was but a youth, too slight of build to be my son.

The young man rolled over with a groan at my touch on
his shoulder. The surprise that then greeted me was as great
as any I had encountered on this unexpected journey, for the

individual that occupied the couch was not my son Carthoris—
but my *grandson*.

"Djon Dihn?" I exclaimed in amazement.

A surprise of a different sort followed a moment later when
the boy opened one eye to regard me with seeming disinterest.
"Do go away," he said in a tone of weary irritation. "I need
to get some rest." And with that he shut his eye once more
and turned back to the wall.

3

THE MISSING DOORWAY

OMPLETELY DUMBFOUNDED, I shook the boy's shoulder and repeated his name. "Djon Dihn, do you not recognize me?"

This time he opened both eyes to examine me, his eyebrows rising in bemusement. "Now this is an unusual development," he murmured as if to himself, "for never have I seen my esteemed ancestor in this particular state of dishevelment." He propped himself up on one elbow on the worn couch and stifled a yawn. "How then could he appear to me here like this, unless—" His eyes widened, squarely meeting mine for the first time as he searched my face with an expression of dawning hope. "But wait—I felt your touch and heard you speak before ever I looked upon you. By my first ancestor— can it be that you are John Carter after all?"

I had followed the strange monologue with growing consternation. "Such has been my belief these past many years," I said.

He regarded me with an almost comical intensity, the clear gray eyes that were the sole mark of his Jasoomian heritage staring deep into my own until I swore I could almost hear the cogs and levers clicking inside his brain.

"Grandfather!" he cried at last, springing up from the couch and throwing his arms around me, only to drop to one knee before me on the floor, bringing an ornamented bit of my harness to his brow in a display of respect. "O John Carter, forgive me! I owe you a sincere apology for my impertinence."

217

More mystified than ever, I drew him back to his feet and clapped my right hand on his left shoulder in the traditional Barsoomian greeting. He returned the gesture with an expression of relief. Now that the issue of my identity had been established and a touch of normalcy restored, I turned to the next logical topic of discourse.

"Where is Carthoris?" I inquired, just as Djon Dihn demanded: "Please tell me—have you found my father?"

"It seems we have simultaneously asked and answered both our questions," I told him with a frown. "But before we go further, please explain why you did not think I was myself, and then tell me what has persuaded you otherwise."

"It is just that Tario has been subjecting me to this sort of thing for days," he said mournfully, as if that accounted for things. The name rang a faint bell, but I could not place it. Djon Dihn saw the confusion in my expression. "Tario is my jailer and the jeddak of this weird place—of Lothar," he added. "And of course you have to see the image first in order for the suggestion to take hold, so I knew you had to be you."

That name I did recall. "Lothar!" I exclaimed, looking about me with a dawning comprehension. "So that is where we are." I scoured my memory for everything I knew about the place. Though I had never before set foot here myself, some six decades ago it had figured prominently in the lives of my son and the woman destined to become his mate.

Carthoris had found his way within the gates of this isolated city while on a mission to rescue Thuvia of Ptarth, the princess whom I had first met when we were both prisoners of the false gods of Mars in the Valley Dor. Here they had discovered the hidden stronghold of a group of Orovars, one of the few remnants of the ancient pale-skinned race that still survived on Barsoom, and found themselves for a time the playthings of decadent immortals who had somehow mastered the fantastic ability to cast illusions so perfect that they could kill. Untrained in war themselves and pacifistic by nature, they had for centuries defended their city against recurring attacks from the green men who had stumbled upon their refuge, by lining the battlements with phantom bowmen plucked from the Lotharians' own prodigious memories, archers whose imaginary arrows bore such an uncanny semblance of reality that the foes at whose breasts they were aimed literally willed themselves to die when struck by the nonexistent bolts.

Djon Dihn had begun to beg my forgiveness again for his failure to recognize me at once. "Under the circumstances I am inclined to grant you a full pardon," I reassured the boy as we seated ourselves on the couch. "But only if you curb your apologies and tell me how you came to be here and what has become of your father."

Djon Dihn told me that Carthoris had proposed that his son accompany him on this trip, in a manner that the former interpreted as more mandate than invitation. "I had just returned from Thuvan Dihn's court in Ptarth and was working on collating the results of my interviews with him. I am planning to write an epic poem or perhaps a prose saga in the Duhorian style based on the exploits of both of my grandfathers—" He saw the look of impatience on my face and cut himself short. "At any rate, my father said it would be good for me to have more time out in the world. I know that he believes I spend too much of my day reading about the great heroes of the past and too little of it practicing to be like them. He likes to tell me that one day I will find myself with a permanent inkstain on the end of my nose if I keep it always buried in a book."

"Barsoom is a world of constant strife and battle," I told him. "Carthoris wants you to be able to defend yourself and those you care about when the need arises."

In truth, I had had my own questions about the boy's seeming preference for flights of fancy, whether the product of his own or another's imagination, above those martial pursuits beloved by most youthful Barsoomian males.

Unlike his older cousin, the spirited Llana of Gathol, Djon

Dihn had always been rather shy and diffident around me. I had gotten the notion that he feared I considered him a disappointment, an impression I strove to negate whenever possible. In truth I found him to be something of an enigma. On Earth he would have been described as "bookish," and he was most often to be found on the periphery of the group at family gatherings, his face hidden in a volume of stirring tales of derring-do from Barsoom's ancient past, or scribbling away furiously with his stylus as he concocted his own imaginative scenarios. Although he had been given a heroic name— Djon Dihn translates loosely into English as "Sword in Hand"—in contrast to the majority of his contemporaries on this warlike world he evinced little appetite for the life of a fighting man, preferring to exercise his imagination rather than his sword arm. Lately I had even begun to harbor the suspicion that my young grandson might have set his own sights on that most dubious of professions—that of author. While it was true that over the course of my long life I had known at least one writer who was a truly exemplary human being, by and large I had little understanding of those who seemed to willingly forsake a more active role in the wider world in order to spin tales about the real or fanciful accomplishments of others.

For myself, I had long been of the opinion that a powerful imagination can be at once a blessing and a curse, a double-edged sword as likely to bring ruin as success to the one who wields it. To the disciplined military commander, the ability to formulate and execute complicated strategies can mean the difference between sweeping victory and ignominious defeat for the nation he serves; conversely, the incurable daydreamer may find himself lost in realms of fancy, sitting paralyzed in contemplation of an infinite array of fascinating possibilities while the precious years of his own life pass by unheeded.

"I understand how to wield a weapon and I will do so when I see the need," Djon Dihn averred. "But spending the day striking the flat of my blade against that of a feigned opponent simply to hear them ring has always seemed like a waste of good sunshine."

"Sunshine that might be put to better use when it falls on the printed page?" I inquired with a wry smile. "But continue with your tale."

"My father and I went first to Gathol, where we delivered one of the Gridley Wave transceivers and then stayed to visit my father's sister and her family for a time. I was able to speak at length with Llana's mate, Pan Dan Chee, about the hidden Orovar enclave in Horz that was once his home, a fascinating conversation that afforded me great insight into his culture that I intend to explore in my saga of ancient Barsoom. Then we flew to Exum to hand over the second device. We were on our way back to Helium when we spotted two great masses of green men on the march. My father was curious as to their purpose, as they seemed to be converging on the same destination. Extrapolating their course, we landed not far from here, on the other side of the cliffs that ring this valley. He instructed me to wait for him and left the ship. I was happy to have the time to spend reading and working on my saga. Yet one day passed and then two more. By the end of the third day I decided it was time to leave the ship and go in search of my father in spite of his instructions, convinced that he would have returned to the *Susstos* by now if he were free to do so.

After a while I came upon a sompus tree growing beside a small stream where I stopped to slake my thirst and eat some fruit, as we had only bland warrior's rations on board the ship. From a rise I had been able to spy glimpses through the trees of what looked to be open land and a great edifice of some sort. Figuring that Carthoris might have seen this as well and gone to investigate, I was heading downhill in that direction when I began to hear loud noises of the kind made by a group of men tramping carelessly through the underbrush. Soon I could make out bits of loud conversation in the harsh gutturals characteristic of the green race. Knowing that the green hordes travel almost exclusively on the open plains of the dead sea bottoms, it made sense to me that they would not be skilled at traversing heavily wooded areas with any degree of circumspection.

Moving cautiously forward, I saw a party of about a score of warriors whose metal identified them as Torquasians, and I wondered if they were a scouting party for one of the larger bands we had seen from the air. They had scored some game, three or four of them carrying the carcasses of plump dandox in their middle limbs, while some of the others were gathering firewood as they made their way. I believe they had no idea anyone else was in the forest and so they made little attempt to hide their presence. While I found them fascinating to observe, their appearance did cause me some alarm, for I had read that members of their race, although they deem travel through the air to be unnatural and thus have no interest in making use of fliers for their own transportation, will dismantle any aircraft they encounter for parts to be used in the construction of weaponry.

Realizing that the path of their explorations might well bring them within sight of the *Susstos*, I silently circled back so that I would be sure to arrive there first. Once I scrambled onboard I drew up the ladder, then crouched down to await their approach through the trees. One young warrior, walking well ahead of the others, was first to spot the ship, which he pointed out with great cries of excitement to those who followed. It was at that moment I decided it would be better to send the flier on to Helium than to allow it to fall into their destructive hands, hoping there would be a chance it might eventually return with assistance for my father and me."

"A sound decision," I interjected at this point. "But tell me this—why did you not send yourself to Helium along with the vessel?"

Djon Dihn drew himself up to his full height and favored me with a look of stiff reproach. "And so abandon my father?"

he inquired. "I may be far from a seasoned warrior, John Carter, but I could not leave this place so long as there was a possibility I might rescue Carthoris from whatever dire circumstances had prevented his return to the ship."

"Of course. I would expect no less from your father's son," I told him, laying my hand on his shoulder.

He relaxed a bit at my words. "I had just set the destination compass for Helium when the green scout's upper arms appeared at the railing. Naturally, the fifteen feet between the deck and the forest floor were no challenge to his twelve-foot height, and I ducked back behind the cabin as he clambered on board, a sword brandished in each of his intermediary limbs. I moved about stealthily so as to keep out of his sight while he examined the deck and peered into the cabin, and then, having satisfied himself that the ship was abandoned, he turned back to the railing to call out the good news to his fellows. I crept quietly from behind the cabin. Then, extending my arms before me, I rushed full speed at him from behind and collided with his posterior, throwing him off balance and propelling him more by luck than by strength over the side. While he was thrashing back to his feet on the forest floor, I swiftly loosed the mooring cable and engaged the propellers. An instant later the *Susstos* shot upward to the accompaniment of shouted curses from the rest of the green warriors—most of them directed at the hapless scout, whom they loudly berated for his clumsiness, having been unable to see me expedite his sudden exit from the deck. I set my sights on a high branch as the ship rose like an arrow through the trees, hopped off with a prayer to my first ancestor, and clung there out of sight of those below, waiting several long minutes till the party moved away, still in noisy argument, before making my way down the trunk. I had seen what looked to be the towers of a city from my lofty vantage and circled around through the woods in that direction."

Djon Dihn had hurried though the forest and out onto the plain as quickly and quietly as possible so as to make it to the city before the scouting party, should that also be their destination. As he drew near, a man in a white robe called out to him from atop the towering wall and directed him to run to the city's main entrance, activating a mechanism that rolled back the great wheel-shaped gate enough to let him squeeze through before shutting it again.

"As I found out later, the scouting party had reached the edge of the plain a minute after I did and spotted me. They have excellent aim, you know: one of the green warriors tossed his spear just as the door was rolling shut and it struck me a glancing blow on the back of my head." Djon Dihn raised a hand with a grimace and rubbed the base of his skull through his thick black hair. "I awoke with a terrific headache some time later in a sumptuous apartment to find a golden-haired, pale-skinned man standing over me and staring at me intensely with brilliant blue eyes. And that was Tario."

"I do have some familiarity with this city and the preternatural abilities of its inhabitants through the tales your father has told me," I said, "as well as from many conversations with Kar Komak, the former bowman who was himself one of Lothar's phantom protectors for centuries. That is, until the day he awoke at the end of a particular battle with the green attackers to find he had not returned to the void of memory, but was somehow fully alive again after half a million years. But I still do not understand what made you think that I was a phantom as well?"

Djon Dihn sighed. "It is a result of Tario's plan to weaken my resolve and have me ally myself with his cause. No matter the mental shield I erect about my present thoughts, he delves deep into my mind and plucks figures from my memories that he then brings forth to cajole or badger me, until I am no longer quite sure who is real and who is not. Just this morning your peerless mate, my honored grandmother, stood in this very chamber for three quarters of a zode, sweetly urging me to give Tario my full cooperation in his quest to subjugate the world to his will."

I gave a skeptical smile. "I am hard pressed to imagine my beloved Dejah Thoris advocating the conquest of Barsoom by an addled tyrant with an inflated ego. But Tario is one man. What harm could this mad magician think to inflict upon the world?"

"Of that I am not entirely sure. At times he seems to believe that with my assistance he could reach beyond Lothar to command the members of the lower races—as he names all others save his own kind—to make their way here and thus repopulate his all-but-deserted city as his slaves."

I shook my head at the absurd image of blank-eyed pilgrims from all over the globe marching into the silent city.

"Other times he tells me of his plan to send his phantom bowmen marching out of the gates of this city to exterminate the green race once and for all and thus bring all of Barsoom beneath his heel."

My first impulse was to laugh at this obvious delusion. But then I remembered my son's description of the seemingly endless stream of phantom archers he himself had witnessed pouring forth to slaughter an army of attacking green men when he had come to this city with Thuvia of Ptarth. If Tario alone could summon an army of deathless soldiers to do his bidding, then why not believe that with the assistance of others he might send them out to the far corners of the world? For that matter, I had also seen what appeared to be the migration of a considerable number of green men in this direction—the very phenomenon that had caused Carthoris to investigate. And yet . . . looking at the earnest face of my grandson in the growing moonlight now beginning to stream in through the window of the chamber, I once again had to curb my amusement.

"As I have told you," Djon Dihn continued, "when I arrived at the city there were no green warriors massed outside the gates and just the one small scouting party in the woods. One morning soon after, a battalion of Torquasians arrived to resume their perennial attempts to besiege and ultimately overrun Lothar. As was his habit, Tario called into being scores of phantom bowmen atop the walls and set them to launching their unfailingly accurate arrows, quickly felling a great many of the invaders. When he met with me that evening he told me that after centuries of this unvarying routine he had decided the time had come to do something different. The next day he brought me up to the battlements with him and encouraged me to join him in meditation, staring fixedly into my eyes until I began to feel drowsy. Some unknown while later I awakened to a great din and peered down to see a second cohort of green men, Thurds by their emblems, pouring down out of the forest and into the valley. These took up position on the opposite side of the city from the surviving Torquasians, where they remained until the night before last, when some unknown catalyst incited them to break their uneasy truce and engage in a prolonged and deadly combat with their enemies, resulting in the near eradication of both armies. But whether these newcomers were summoned by Tario or created by his mind with my own unconscious assistance, I do not know."

"They seemed real enough to me, for I saw their banners and heard their war cries," I told him, explaining that I had taken on the role of that unknown catalyst in my effort to gain entrance to the city in search of his father. Something occurred to me. "If these illusions are always products of memory, then how could Tario have recreated a horde he has presumably never seen?"

"By riffling through the pages of my own mind," Djon Dihn responded glumly. "From my reading I am familiar with the metal and insignias of most of the green nations and so it is possible that he pried such information out of my brain. Since my arrival I have strengthened my mental shields considerably when in his presence so that he cannot read my present thoughts, yet I cannot prevent him from nosing about in my memories. This was how he discovered that Carthoris was my father. At the start, you see, he was very friendly to me and offered to help locate Carthoris. It was only later when I declared I would go off and search for him myself that he revealed he had my father captive somewhere in Lothar and he would remain a prisoner until I assisted him in his plans."

This news, while unwelcome, was not completely unexpected. At least I now knew my son had made it to Lothar and was presumably still somewhere within its bounds.

"You have mentioned your own assistance more than once," I said. "But what would make Tario think you are equipped to aid him in the accomplishment of this bizarre goal?"

Djon Dihn hesitated as if abashed. "He professes to admire my imagination," the boy replied at last, his expression a mixture of embarrassment and shy pride.

I blinked in disbelief. "Surely he does not believe you are also capable of these weird feats of illusion he and his compatriots have taken millennia to perfect? From what Kar Komak and your own parents have informed me, that skill is the sole province of this single isolated enclave of pale-skinned survivors from the ancient world, while Tario has but to gaze upon your copper skin and black hair to see that you are no Lotharian. Now I know he must be mad!"

In response Djon Dihn fixed me with a penetrating look for a long moment without speaking. Just as I was starting to wonder whether he had fallen into some form of waking trance, he said: "Do you remember my Korsova, Grandfather?"

I frowned in puzzlement, trying to place the name, which means "Mighty Hunter" in the Barsoomian tongue, and to fathom what bearing it might have on our present situation. "Is that your pet sorak?" I asked at last, not surprised that it had taken me a while to call up the information, for I have no great love for the imperious catlike animals most often found cradled in the arms of highborn ladies of the red race.

With a silent gesture, Djon Dihn directed my attention to the moonlit open window behind me. Sure enough, there to my surprise perched one of the little devils, six limbs, mottled lavender hide, yellow tail-tuft and all. The creature stretched

and yawned languorously under my startled gaze, then began
to preen itself.

"You brought your pet with you?"

At my words the sorak ceased its ablutions and leaped
lightly to the floor of the chamber. Immediately, two others
with identical markings stepped daintily in from outside the
window to take the place of the first on the broad sill. These
also jumped down to the floor, to be quickly followed by four
more, and then another eight—

I looked over my shoulder to stare in astonishment at my
grandson. "Do you mean to tell me you yourself are somehow
conjuring up all of these—"

"Look again, John Carter," he advised me, the hint of a
boyish smile tugging at the corners of his mouth. "Perhaps
you will detect a more familiar face . . ."

I turned once more to see an intruder among the soraks.
"Woola?" I cried in wonderment.

It was my beloved old calot, all right: there was no mistak-
ing that singular countenance, to me both hideous and
beautiful at the same time. And yet it was assuredly not my
faithful companion—for while these faithful Martian watch-
dogs typically attain a height of almost four feet from forepaws
to crown, the specimen I saw before me stood no taller than
a housecat!

Calots are often employed as guardians of the great herds
of thoats raised on Barsoom as both mounts and sources of
food. Now as I looked on in wonder, this miniature incarnation of my old friend sprang into vigorous action on my
behalf, dashing back and forth among the hissing soraks
milling about my sandals as he strove mightily to gather
them into a cohesive group, all the while howling furiously
in a ludicrously high-pitched version of the full-throated
hunting call I knew so well. Herding soraks is a nigh impossible task no matter one's stature, and so the scene before
me quickly became even more chaotic than before, obliging
me to take several steps backward so as not to trip over any

of the sinuous bodies rubbing against my ankles. "Enough!" I said.

Djon Dihn winced apologetically at the expression of appalled incredulity on my face. He gestured again and the sea of soraks at my feet vanished, taking with them the Lilliputian calot and leaving the windowsill and floor once more empty, with nary a paw print where moments ago dozens of animals had been pacing in the dust. "I am still having a problem achieving the proper scale," he said.

I shook my head in bafflement. "How in the world are you able to accomplish this?" I inquired before he could introduce any more phantom creatures into the room.

He shrugged his shoulders. "As to that, I cannot say. As you well know, my noble mother has long possessed the uncanny power to control banths as if they were household pets with but a murmured word, a mysterious ability I have always envied and in fact strove diligently to emulate when I was younger. As we had no tame banths upon which I might practice, I used to spend hours focusing my will upon Korsova in hopes that I might one day coerce him into doing my bidding. Of course I always failed miserably and in the end resigned myself to the fact that I possessed no special skills that set me apart from the majority of Barsoomians. Yet since my arrival here in Lothar I have felt my mind opening up in some indefinable way. Perhaps when Tario went sifting through the contents of my memories he inadvertently unearthed the key to a previously locked chamber." He lifted his hand to gingerly pat the back of his head. "Or maybe it was that blow to the cranium I suffered from the green man's spear that jarred something loose."

I felt a small stab of concern at this statement; from what I had been told by both Carthoris and Kar Komak, the mental legerdemain of the Lotharians was something to be feared rather than imitated.

"Whatever its origin," my grandson went on, "Tario is of the belief that by exercising this power I will steadily improve my ability to wield it, eventually enabling him to add it to his own arsenal. He visits me here at least twice a day, sometimes more often, to gauge my progress and exhort me to greater effort. He also provides me with food and drink at these times, which I have no means of obtaining for myself. He is a strange and frightening man, and very erratic in his behavior," he confided, "though I have come to predict his moods by the cut and color of his garments, which he changes frequently. When he appears in full white robes he seems most clear-headed and determined. Severely cut blue garments like those he wore tonight betoken a quick temper, while robes of *parthral* indicate that he is filled with a cold vehemence." He was ticking the different options off on his fingers. "Clad in yellow he is despondent; when in red he is most likely to bluster and threaten; garbed in *klanamel* he plays the sympathetic confidant, and so forth. I have been trying to compile a list, but sadly I have no writing materials here except those I devise."**

He pulled the couch a few inches out from the wall to reveal bands of minute characters that looked to have been scratched into the faded plaster with a fingernail.

"That reminds me," I said. I reached into one of the pouches attached to my harness and drew forth the golden *teeltjor* I had brought with me from the *Susstos*. "I presume this is yours?"

"My scroll!" he cried, cradling the thing lovingly in his hands. He stroked the object with his fingertip and the two

---

* I have reproduced the Barsoomian words to describe some of these colors because I know of no satisfactory translation for certain hues I have found to be quite common on Mars but entirely absent on Earth. *Parthral* is best characterized as an intense emerald rose-black, while *klanamel* is a sort of pale ambered lavender that reveals glints of silver only beneath the light of both moons—but perhaps these definitions are of little help to one who has never seen the originals for himself. I wonder sometimes if my transits from Earth do not alter the qualities of my optic nerve in some fashion, enabling me to see things here on Barsoom that I would have found imperceptible in my earlier life.

cylinders separated with a small click, each one extending to almost twice its previous length as he drew them apart to reveal a thin sheet of golden parchment suspended between them. "Thank you, Grandfather! At least now I may keep proper records."

I pointed to the cracked and discolored wall with its crabbed lines of hieroglyphs. "When Carthoris told me about his adventures in this place, he described it as both beautiful and ageless, which is how it appeared to me when I first saw it from the edge of the forest two days ago. Yet once inside the walls I have found a deserted city suffering from ruin and neglect, save for this one chamber—or so I thought when I first spied it from across the avenue and was impressed by its luxury. Yet now . . ."

Djon Dihn nodded. "Yes, the city has fallen into considerably more disrepair since the time of my father's visit over half a century ago. As you have seen, wherever Tario goes, he brings glimpses of the old Lothar with him that he may ever be surrounded by its past magnificence. When he leaves an area, however, it soon reverts back to its true appearance. One day, when garbed in his yellow robes and appearing quite morose, he admitted that alone he does not have the power to restore the entire city to lasting beauty."

"How many others of his countrymen are here? I have so far encountered no others souls in my nocturnal explorations of the city."

Djon Dihn looked thoughtful. "I do not know. When my father and mother were captive here, they were told that of those twenty thousand refugees who originally survived the ancient flight from the green men half a million years ago barely a thousand still lived—and not a woman among them, for all had perished upon the long trek. Bound for extinction, once sequestered here in this valley the survivors somehow mastered the Great Truth, as they called it, and developed their technique of creating illusions, at which time they miraculously ceased aging—or perhaps became part illusion themselves, as some of them later came to believe. As you may have heard, there were for ages two diametrically opposed philosophies in Lothar: the realists and the etherealists. The realists espoused the notion that in order to exist they must continue to conduct their lives according to the requirements of normal human beings, periodically eating and sleeping and so forth. The etherealists held that the mind is all and that their existence was no longer predicated upon fleshly needs. Ironically, these apparently radically divergent positions had much in common, for though the realists ate and drank to sustain their lives, the food and water they consumed was itself all illusory, since there are currently no sources of either within these walls and they never venture out of the city.

"Still, these clashing opinions were the cause of continued strife among the inhabitants, with Tario and his etherealist allies being in the majority and so able to hold the upper hand. For centuries realist dissidents who displeased the jeddak and his cronies were sacrificed to satisfy the appetite of the Lotharians' god, the giant banth Komal who later departed the city in the company of my parents and eventually met his own doom while fighting in defense of my mother."

Djon Dihn went on to say that chaos had reigned for a considerable period in Lothar following the dual shocks of the abduction of their god and the near fatal knife wound his mother had inflicted upon Tario in her own defense. Without the threat of Komal to deter rebellion, many now disputed the rule of a weakened Tario—whose susceptibility to physical harm seemed to belie the claims of the etherealists—and the two factions warred among themselves to determine who should replace him as jeddak. Hundreds of them perished in those protracted battles of the mind, with the phantasmal bowmen of one aspirant cutting down the imaginary archers of another, until a phantom arrow would inevitably chance to pierce the heart of a living individual and he died the real death, instantly taking all of his warriors with him."

"Just how does one abduct a god?" I inquired dryly.

"Allowing oneself to be kidnapped would seem to argue against any claim of omnipotence."

Djon Dihn shrugged. "From what I have read of religion, it seems the gods prefer to keep quiet about such controversial matters, leaving their adherents scrambling to justify any inconsistencies for them. Tario told me that toward the end of the uprising the etherealists embraced the notion that Komal had actually departed the city in disgust because the realists refused to accept the one true way of nonexistence. I suppose they found that as good an explanation as any. Personally," he added with a grin, "I believe the great banth had grown tired of dining on the same bland fare each time one of the realists displeased the jeddak.

"In terms of your question about the other inhabitants of the city, just yesterday morning Tario addressed the subject while attired in his robes of brightest klanamel," Djon Dihn told me. "This is always when he is at his most voluble and willing to speak to me of the past. He told me then that all of the realists are now long dead, finally eradicated by himself and the other etherealists—though he did not specify how many of his own supporters followed them into oblivion.

"As for myself," he added, "although I have occasionally glimpsed other Lotharians in their colorful robes from a distance, I have only ever had dealings with Tario himself, along with whatever phantoms he conjures up from my own memory to browbeat me, and the bowmen it pleases him to materialize from time to time to remind me of his power."

Though I found all of this information interesting and hoped to glean from it something useful, it seemed to me that the time for discussion had ended and the time to act had arrived. I said as much to my grandson. "You have described Tario as your jailer, yet I see no obvious signs of confinement. Why have you not left this chamber after one of his visits and searched for your father's place of imprisonment?" I asked. "Why do we not do so at this moment and effect his release?"

"Of course I have wanted to do this many times, but it

is impossible," Djon Dihn said forlornly, "for when Tario leaves he takes the doorway with him, and I cannot walk through walls."

I turned and regarded the opening into the hallway, wondering once again at the state of my grandson's mind. "Nonsense!" I told him. "The doorway is right there before us, and opened wide. Come—we will go now and find Carthoris on our own."

Seizing his forearm, I marched us toward the corridor. I had taken but a single step outside the room when I felt a sudden tug of strong resistance against my arm, hearing at the same time a sharp cracking noise and an *"Ow!"* from behind me. Djon Dihn was standing just inside the open doorway and rubbing his nose, from which a small trickle of blood now issued. Puzzled, I tugged on his arm again.

"Grandfather, please—no!" He raised his hand, his palm seeming to flatten against the empty air between us.

"What has happened to your nose?" I asked. "And why do you stand there? Are you telling me you truly cannot see the doorway?"

"I cannot. On the contrary, I see an unbroken wall from which half your body now miraculously protrudes," Djon Dihn said, drawing a scrap of silk from his pocket pouch and dabbing at his upper lip. "Please do not pull me into it again!"

I shook my head in amazement. "The window then," I suggested, stepping past him back into the chamber and crossing to the great open half-circle on the opposite wall. "Surely you can see this window and the bright beams of moonlight falling here upon the floor?" I leaned out to inspect the marble ledge set a few feet below the sill. It was only a foot wide, but I was sure we could traverse it easily to where it ended about six feet to the left. From there it was another ten feet to a small balcony that jutted forth outside the neighboring room. Looking down, I saw that balconies and ledges alternated in this fashion all the way down to the empty street. Although Djon Dihn was stronger and more agile than the typical Barsoomian, he did not possess the remarkable leaping abilities that my earthly muscles had bestowed upon me here on Mars and that had manifested themselves to a lesser extent in his father. Still, I was confident I could maneuver my way safely to the ground even with my grandson clinging to my back.

Djon Dihn had joined me at the window. "I do see the moonlight," he told me in a tone of resignation, "but its brightness is intersected by the shadows of the stout bars." He lifted his hand and appeared to press strenuously against something solid but invisible in the open space above the windowsill, then turned his palm to me so that I could see the fading impression of a cylindrical length. "They are too narrowly spaced for me to squeeze through and appear to be fashioned of steel, or perhaps forandus. Unbreakable."

"I do not understand," I said. "Of course you know that any bars you think to see there are not real."

"My brain knows that well enough," he confirmed. "Yet Tario says that mind is all, and my mind insists on reacting to the evidence of my deluded senses." He smacked his palm silently against the air. "This looks and feels like solid metal, and it makes a sound like metal when I hit it." He leaned forward and sniffed, then shook his head. "I do not know what steel smells like, nor will I attempt to taste it, but the overall impression is apparently convincing enough to persuade my mind to imprison me within these walls."

I quelled my rising exasperation, recalling an instance years ago when Kar Komak had used his own mental powers to materialize in front of my eyes a goblet of wine, which he then offered me. I had known in my heart that both cup and contents were illusory, yet the metal vessel felt solid in my hand and the wine was of a fine vintage—though according to the former phantom bowman I could drink my fill of it and never become intoxicated.

Frustrated, I passed my arm back and forth in the empty space above the windowsill. Djon Dihn shrugged when I asked him what he had just seen. "To my credulous eyes it looks as if you have gained the power to pass your flesh through solid objects. At any rate, I believe it makes more sense for me to bide my time here for the present. Unbeknownst to Tario I have been slowly finding a way through the shields he has placed about his own mind. When he focuses his mental energy on demonstrating the creation and maintenance of phantoms to me, I am often able to slip inside his barriers. At these times I glean fleeting impressions of my father that make me feel confident I will eventually be able to uncover his exact whereabouts. In the meantime, perhaps you could use your own freedom to embark on some further exploration of the city on the chance that you might come upon him before I do."

"Or I could simply remain here with you to await Tario's next visit," I countered, "and quickly persuade him at swordspoint to tell us where he has imprisoned Carthoris."

Djon Dihn shook his head. "Have you forgotten the bowmen, Grandfather? His brain is very powerful, and even if you managed to evade their phantom arrows, he could trade places with me by means of illusion and have you drive your sword through my heart while convinced it was Tario you were skewering. At the very least he could trap you in this chamber as he has me."

I scowled at his recitation of these unappealing scenarios. "But you say he is teaching you to increase your own mental abilities?"

Djon Dihn nodded. "Naturally I have considered trying to defeat him at his own game, but at the moment all I can muster is a battalion of soraks, and I do not think they would intimidate him and his archers for very long. In terms of attacking him by other means, as you can see he has relieved me of my weapons, perhaps in fear that I would surprise him with a dagger to the ribs as once did my mother long ago."

I was itching to take immediate action against this madman—not only for his current treatment of Djon Dihn and Carthoris, but for his ill handling of my son and Thuvia of Ptarth when they visited Lothar decades ago—yet I had to admit my grandson's reasoning was sound.

"Very well," I told him. "You may continue with your plan for the time being. I will expand my search of the city while you pry at his brain."

Djon Dihn lifted his scroll. "Allow me to sketch you a map. I told Tario that as a simple being composed of flesh and feelings I would quickly become bored and distracted and thus incapable of concentrating on my mental exercises if I were not able to get fresh air and move about, so once every other day he takes me for a brief walk through the city—always accompanied, of course, by a score of bowmen ready to quash any attempt I might make at running off. Later I record where we have gone." In consultation with the network of scratch marks and hieroglyphs on the wall behind the couch, he drew a rough guide to the sections of the city they had visited, highlighting those areas where he thought Carthoris could possibly be hidden. He pressed the buttons that instructed the device to create a separate facsimile of the map and a thin sheet of gilded parchment detached itself from the instrument. I rolled it up and affixed it to my harness, then departed the room by means of the window.

That evening I was back, waiting down on the street for half an hour while the rich golden light once more streamed from the chamber. I had found nothing in the deserted districts I had combed, no sign of any inhabitants and no closed chambers where a man might be imprisoned. Djon Dihn told me that Tario had been garbed in flowing robes of klanamel this evening and, true to form, had exhibited the milder side of his disposition, gently urging him to practice his illusion-casting powers with greater diligence so that he might offer real assistance to the jeddak and thereby earn his father's freedom.

The next day was much the same for both of us, although Tario had visited my grandson in his red robes that morning and issued thinly veiled threats about Carthoris' well-being should Djon Dihn not soon progress past the creation of small animals. His mind was in a state of heightened emotion and so more than usually closed to Djon Dihn's mental probes, which had yielded no information pertaining to the location of his father's confinement.

"It is growing more difficult for me to simply skulk in the shadows while this madman holds both you and your father beneath his thumb," I told him somberly. "Something must change, and soon!"

"It is not just the two of us who are being kept against our wills," Djon Dihn said quietly. "On my first day in the city I met another prisoner."

"What? You have not mentioned this. Was it one of Tario's realist foes? Could he be a possible ally?"

He looked at the floor. "It is an . . . unusual case," he said. "Soon after I awoke in the jeddak's apartments after my encounter with the green man's spear on that first day, there was a great din from outside. After sternly admonishing me to remain where I was, Tario hurried from the chamber. I know now that he went to the city wall to orchestrate the latest onslaught of phantom arrows to be unleashed upon those green men who had followed the scouting party into the valley and begun attacking the city shortly after my arrival. At this point he had been quite civil in his treatment of me, claiming no knowledge of the whereabouts of my father, and so I was inclined to go along with his request. However, as time wore on and I felt more recovered from the blow to my head, I began to be restless. I decided to explore the apartments to see if there was someone else I could speak with and was drawn by a small noise to a great hanging on the wall. Lifting it, I discerned a line that indicated there might be a hidden doorway. I was curious and decided to have a look inside.

"When I pushed open the panel, I came face to face with a young woman, a most beautiful maiden with golden hair and fair skin who shrank back from me in surprise. I told her that I did not mean to frighten her and gave her my name, but when I requested hers in return she could not tell me.

"'How long have you been here?' I asked."

"The question seemed to puzzle her. 'I do not know,' she said at last, 'for each day in these dreary apartments is much like the one before, but I feel that it has been a very long time indeed, with no end in sight.'"

"'You are being held here against your will, then?' I inquired. "'You wish to leave this place?'"

"'Oh yes,' she replied, 'I have wished for nothing else!'"

"We heard some noise in the outer apartments then and she backed away from the doorway with a cry of fright. "'He has returned! You must go or he will punish both of us!'"

"I backed reluctantly from the hidden chamber, but not before I assured her that I would return when I was able and take her from the city, if that is what she still desired. Restoring the wall hanging to its original position, I turned just as Tario was entering the room. I told him I was feeling much better and had decided to stretch my legs and admire the furnishings. He gave me a suspicious look, but I think he believed me. Soon thereafter he and a company of bowmen marched me across the city to this room, where he informed me for the first time that this was Lothar and that he was holding my father captive. It was not until then, when I found out where we were, that I recalled Kar Komak's tales and realized at once who the young woman must be," he concluded with a beatific smile, "for she is none other than the fabled Maid of Lothar!"

I remembered hearing of this fantastic creature myself—the suggestion of perfect beauty Tario had kept hidden in his apartments while he strove to permanently materialize her, as he had inadvertently done with Kar Komak. The embodiment of Tario's memories and longings, to Kar Komak's knowledge she was nonetheless the sole woman in the city, since all were forbidden by royal edict to summon up a female—all but the perfidious jeddak, it seemed, who had concocted the rule himself only to secretly defy it.

"So this young woman was no more real than the phantom archers," I mused.

Djon Dihn looked uncomfortable. "I do not believe that is the case, although I cannot prove it," he said earnestly. "She had a quality about her that was very different from the bowmen—even from the phantoms of my own memories that Tario has materialized. With those it is always easy to tell that they are acting out the jeddak's thoughts. Yet she was most definitely not speaking Tario's words," he said. "Grandfather, she seemed as real and alive to me as do you."

"Well, it is all very strange," I said. "as is practically everything else in this place. And now I will continue my search for your father and hope one of us has better luck." Telling Djon Dihn that I would return to share my findings in two zodes, or about five hours of terrestrial time, I took a step toward the doorway, halting in my tracks at a sudden flare of light in the corridor.

"What is it?" asked Djon Dihn.

"Something is happening," I told him. "I see a golden glow in the hallway, while the walls beyond the doorway are once again decked out in beautiful hangings." A second later the effect had spread inside the room, the mean couch transforming before my eyes into a richly brocaded divan, while gold-framed mirrors and paintings appeared on the walls above an immaculate tessellated floor. It was obvious my grandson could see it now as well. I heard footfalls just outside the chamber.

"It is Tario—he has returned," Djon Dihn whispered in agitation. Seeing my hand move instinctively toward my sword, he shot me an urgent look. "Remember the bowmen! I beseech you, Grandfather: if you value your life—and mine—pretend that you do not exist!"

4
THE JEDDAKS OF LOTHAR

I WAS PONDERING THE IMPLICATIONS of this unusual request when the jeddak himself appeared in the doorway, a sharp-featured man of haughty mien with golden hair and piercing blue eyes, now clothed in a long robe of snowy white.

"Well?" he snapped at Djon Dihn by way of greeting, not yet having become aware of my presence. "Have you naught to show me? The days pass while your father languishes in his lonely cell, awaiting only the actions of his son to free him." Although I could understand the man, I noted that he spoke the common tongue of Barsoom with a marked accent and some of the words he used had an archaic ring to them.

Djon Dihn's eyes darted in my direction and Tario followed his gaze. I stood motionless, my own eyes focused on the far wall between the two of them. The jeddak made a choking sound and took a step backward. *Who are you?* he cried. "Where did you come from?"

I forced myself to show no reaction as a dozen silent, stern-faced bowmen appeared out of nowhere behind him, arrows nocked and ready to let fly in my direction. It took all of my self-control to ignore their presence.

"I have indeed been practicing, as you demanded," my grandson said. "As you can see, today I have progressed well beyond soraks."

Tario looked me up and down with an expression of extreme skepticism. Then he fixed his blazing eyes upon mine and his pale forehead creased with exertion. We remained thus for several minutes, his phantom guards winking out of existence one by one as perspiration beaded on his brow, until at last he turned back to Djon Dihn.

"It is not possible—yet the thing is clearly an illusion, for when I attempt to read its thoughts I encounter nothing but a void." I understood now what he had been up to. All Barsoomians are telepathic to one degree or another, but one of the traits that marked me as a native of another world was my own mind's utter resistance to being broached—or even perceived—by that of another. "But see the pale skin and black hair," he continued. "No such race ever trod the surface of Barsoom, yet I feel I have seen his like somewhere in your memories! How could a lower being like yourself have fabricated a creature so lifelike with so little training?"

Despite my resolve to play the part assigned me by Djon Dihn, I was finding it difficult to bear his supercilious tone to my grandson. "Perhaps his will is stronger than your own," I said softly.

The jeddak's head snapped around at the sound of my voice, his blue eyes fairly bulging from their sockets. "What is this?" he exclaimed. "You dare endow your puppet with speech in order to mock me? You have brought forth an abomination! I command you disperse it into the thin air from whence it sprang at once—or I shall do it for you!" He turned and stalked toward me, his pale face darkening with anger. Suddenly a dagger gleamed in his hand—though whether he had produced it from within the folds of his white robes or the folds of his brain I did not know—and he swiped at me with the sharp blade. I had grasped my shortsword as he neared me and now I brought it up, easily parrying his strike. The dagger rebounded with a clang and the blade struck Tario's face a glancing blow, scoring a small cut along his cheekbone. The jeddak cried out in pain and incredulity, the bowmen appearing again at his back, now twice the number as before, and a score of arrows were trained upon my breast.

Tario pressed his hand to his cheek and drew it back in amazement to regard a droplet of blood. "It is not possible," he repeated. "I *know* the thing to be an illusion—yet its blade repelled my attack . . ."

The troop of grim warriors ranged at Tario's back retreated into nothingness once more as the jeddak swung his gaze back to my grandson, the rage that had contorted his pale face supplanted by a look of avid curiosity. *"How?"* he cried. "How have you done this? In all the centuries of my rule only rarely have I succeeded in giving material form to any of my phantoms. The first was a stalwart warrior formed from my memories of the man who ages ago commanded the seagoing fleets of ancient Lothar, that peerless realm that sat like a treasure chest upon the shores of the mighty Throxus, of which this glorious citadel is the only remaining jewel now that all the rest of Barsoom has fallen into savagery and decay."

"You are speaking of Kar Komak, I presume?" my grandson said. "He is a mighty warrior, indeed."

"You know of him?" Tario's expression of wonder grew quickly to one of pure amazement. "Then it is true! For long ages did I bend my will upon his permanent materialization. I suspected that my great undertaking had finally come to fruition decades ago, not long after your father came to threaten my rule and make off with our great god. The she-banth that accompanied him reacted poorly to my lordly offer to accept her as my consort and left me painfully wounded from her assassination attempt. When next the accursed green hordes returned to harry my city and I attempted to summon Kar Komak from the depths of memory as was my wont to lead his troops of deathless bowmen against the fiends, for the very first time he did not appear! Nor has he ever since, despite all of my efforts, leading me to conclude that he had assumed palpable form at the conclusion of the previous battle and struck off, perhaps dazed, into what would have constituted to him a terrible new world. Since that time I have oft wondered what became of him and why he did not return at once to Lothar to express his gratitude to his jeddak for the great gift of life."

"Could it be," Djon Dihn suggested mildly, "that having dwelled for so long within the confines of your mind, once freed of the shackles of another's will he had the desire to roam Barsoom in search of more congenial habitation?"

I restrained a smile, for the comment had the flavor of a subtle insult. Tario apparently felt the same, for he scowled and moved toward the youth with fists knotted, but I took a single step between the two of them, my shortsword once more at the ready, and he backed away with a snarled oath.

"As you can see," remarked my grandson, "I have no such problems with disloyal creations."

Tario drew himself up with a sneer. "I leave you now to continue your practice. Soon you will assist me in sending my deathless armies over all Barsoom to exterminate the green vermin once and for all, so that I may assume my rightful place as Jeddak of Jeddaks over our dying planet." He paused at the door to the chamber and fixed me with a steely gaze before looking back at my grandson. "If you are still able, it would be better that you sent this one back to the oblivion from which you summoned it sooner rather than later. I do not care for its attitude and it will doubtless turn upon you once its materialization is complete. Remember this: you must heed my commands if you wish to be reunited with your father."

I turned my head a bit and winked at my grandson, then moved my eyes to the window.

"As you command, O Jeddak of Jeddaks," Djon Dihn said, gesturing in my direction with a flourish worthy of a vaudeville stage magician. With a low bow I turned and marched like an automaton to the window, then leaped out. Once on the ledge I immediately sprang to its end and jumped over to the neighboring balcony, where I ducked down out of sight. I heard Tario's exclamations of disbelief as he leaned out over the sill and searched the street below in vain for me. I waited until the room grew silent and then returned through the window to find Djon Dihn sitting once more on his threadbare couch, jotting down notes in his scroll.

"It is fortunate you have a Jasoomian brain, Grandfather, and are thus immune to Tario's attempts to locate your mind," he told me with a wry expression. "He is very impressed with my new abilities. In fact, I think he is now a little afraid of me, not that it will do me much good. This time when he departed he left behind a sturdy door studded with a dozen locks and deadbolts, while the bars in the window have doubled in thickness."

While I crouched outside I had been struck by a possible solution for dealing with my grandson's uncanny incarceration. I waited until evening fell. Then, telling Djon Dihn only that I was off to investigate another of the areas of the city where he believed Tario might have imprisoned his father, and also do some scouting about on my own before returning the next day to share any news, I again departed the room by way of the window and used the ledges and balconies to climb down to the street, careful to keep to the shadows as before lest I be spotted by Tario or one of his fellow etherealists.

I followed the map Djon Dihn had given me to the latest location he thought Tario had likely chosen to incarcerate Carthoris. Alas, if there was a prison cell there, I could not find it. Next, I found my way back to the storehouse in which I had stashed the various items from the two fliers. Here I consumed a small amount of food and water, took some additional cubes of usa from the dwindling store, and removed an item from the compact medical kit I had brought along in case my son had sustained an injury during his stay here. I noticed that both the water jar and the packet of usa seemed lighter than before, but chalked this up to my own imagination—until I was leaving the chamber and spotted a set of sandal prints in the dust leading in and out of the doorway that were not my own. I went back to the cache and inspected it more thoroughly, this time finding a coiled length of harness leather on which a few rows of Heliumetic characters had been hastily carved with a sharp object. It read: "Moving about to avoid detection. We must leave this place! Will return 12th zode each day." My spirits rose. So Carthoris must now be free and roaming the city in secret like myself! It had been three days since I last returned to the storeroom. I checked my wrist chronometer. If luck was with us he would be back here in about five hours. I turned the strip of leather over and used my dagger to write: "See you here 12th zode." Placing it atop the bundle of supplies, I exited the storehouse and made haste back to Djon Dihn, crouching in the shadows of the street to make certain the brilliant golden light that indicated Tario was currently in the chamber was not in evidence, whereupon I scaled the building by means of the alternating ledges and balconies and slipped in through the open window.

I was eager to share my good news with my grandson and to put my plan in motion to free him from his imaginary prison cell. I entered the chamber to find Djon Dihn pacing the floor with excitement.

"John Carter, at last!" he said. "Something very strange has happened. I have been waiting to tell you!"

"I have news, as well," I told him. "But what is yours?"

"This morning when Tario came to judge my progress he seemed much distracted. It was one of the days upon which he grudgingly allows me to walk about the city with him. We were near the palace when I heard raised voices from within. He brought me to a room on the ground floor and bade me remain there until his return, but in his haste he neglected to use his power of illusion to remove the doorway, merely pulling shut the actual door and locking it from the outside.

"I have read a book on lock-picking, and after waiting a minute or two to make sure he had gone, I used a little metal toothpick from my pocket pouch and soon had the door opened. I scanned the hallway to make sure Tario was not lingering nearby, then hurried on my way, thinking he might be heading to where my father was imprisoned. Before long

I began to hear noises and saw a shaft of light spilling from a partially opened doorway up ahead. The entire corridor was richly appointed, with paintings on the walls and heavy carpets underfoot, and I knew this meant Tario must be inside. As I approached, I realized the sounds were the voices of men in heated conversation. I crept stealthily up to the doorway, hoping one of those within might be my father. Sadly, that was not the case."

"I am not surprised to hear that," I said. "But you finally discovered some of Tario's allies?"

"In a manner of speaking," Djon Dihn responded. "When I peered cautiously into the chamber I saw twenty or more individuals, all clad in the colorful robes favored by the Lotharians, most gathered at a long table engaged in games that appeared to be the progenitors of our modern jetan, while the others looked on. Several of the players were arguing with each other while the rest conversed more civilly."

"Did you overhear any of their discourse?" I inquired, eager to know if Tario's men were aware of my son's escape. "Do you believe they knew of Carthoris' whereabouts?"

"I am very certain they did, though they never mentioned him. You see—"

"But this is good news, as is my own!" I interjected, clapping him on the shoulder. "Your father is no longer their prisoner, for I have had a message from him this very day." I detailed my discovery in the storehouse.

Djon Dihn was exultant at the news of his father's freedom, his elation quickly tempered by the reality of his own situation. "If I had but known this, in the morning I could have made my own escape into the city when I picked that lock," he said with a sigh. "Instead I returned to the room where Tario had left me shortly thereafter so that he would not suspect I had been spying on him. Now my father is free and I am not."

"You could not have known," I told him. "But tell me more of this gathering of Lotharians you witnessed. It seems we have more opponents to consider than just the jeddak. Or were they all faithful etherealists? You said they were arguing. If these others are possessed of the same mental powers as Tario and still chafe beneath their mad jeddak's rule, then perhaps we could enlist their aid in staving off his deadly intervention while we make our escape."

Djon Dihn laid a hand on my arm. "You do not understand, John Carter. It is true that I counted more than a score of Lotharians in that chamber—*but every one of them was Tario!*"

5

A WALK IN THE MOONLIGHT

F YOU HAVE EVER HAD THE EXPERIENCE of confidently going along a familiar path only to suddenly find yourself completely lost, then you will understand my feeling at that moment. Djon Dihn could see my confusion and quickly continued.

"You remember, of course, that Tario was grievously wounded by my mother decades ago when she repulsed his unwanted advances by means of a dagger. He told me once that with the realists threatening to depose him and his own allies occupied in putting down the rebellion, he had been forced to call upon someone he could trust to assist him in the rule of Lothar while he slowly regained his health. I did not pay much heed to this statement, naturally assuming that he had summoned one of his phantom bowmen to maintain order in his stead—although knowing them to be the materialized memories of warriors from a bygone age, I should have realized Tario would not believe them capable of coping with the responsibilities of a jeddak. As I listened to the crowd of identical men in that chamber, I began to piece together what had happened."

"And what was that?" I still felt as if I were groping my way through a heavy fog.

"As it turned out, the wounded Tario felt he could temporarily deed his rulership while he recovered only to someone he trusted implicitly to carry out his wishes—*himself!* And so he created a phantom Tario, a man he knew so well—inside and out, as it were—that the substitute eventually assumed a form of independent reality. After some time this surrogate evidently reached a point in the unfolding conflict when he felt the need to do the same, as then did his own creation, and so on and so forth down through the years, each new Tario imbued with the thoughts and desires of the original and the powerful mind required to duplicate the process. In the end, I believe the various Tarios were all that remained of the populace of Lothar."

"One man alone without allies in the entire city," I said. "A jeddak without subjects save those he conjures up from the depths of his own mind. So to add to our obstacles, we now have twenty-odd duplicates of our adversary, each of whom holds exactly the same opinions and sinister goals as their creator."

"I am not so sure of that," said Djon Dihn. "While I listened at the door I heard several altercations erupt over the various contests taking place, with this man or that accusing his opponent of underhanded moves. The white-robed Tario whom I had followed was there among them, and at one point he grew wrathful and rose to his feet, threatening to discorporate one man in green robes and another in parthral who had dared implicate him in dishonest play. The others quailed instantly before him, which led me to think that the one in white is most likely the original Tario—and furthermore that he still holds some power over his brainchildren. At any rate, there was enough dissension and squabbling to prove they are no longer of one mind. Indeed, when the white-robed man informed them that he would retire for a while to his apartments and that none should follow him— thankfully departing through another door from the one at which I listened—those left behind revealed their fear and hatred of him, each one claiming that he was more fit to bear the title of jeddak. Each successive Tario then recounted the circumstances of his own origin and called for support from the next incarnation he himself had felt compelled to bring into the world—with not a few bitter disagreements as to whose creation had preceded whose, the older Tarios showing ill-concealed disdain toward those of the copies they deemed to be of later vintage and thus in their eyes inferior, as an echo must gradually lose the strength and clarity of the original cry."

"Fascinating. I suppose this also explains why Tario's mood and demeanor when he visits you has seemed to alter with the color of his robes," I mused.

Djon Dihn nodded. "Exactly so! What I assumed to be the same man expressing a variety of erratic moods must have been a different Tario each time, depending upon whose lot it was to interrogate me on a given day."

At length Djon Dihn had pulled himself away from the bizarre spectacle and, realizing that the man in white must soon recall his presence in the locked chamber, swiftly returned there, where that Tario found him soon after and escorted him back to his cell.

"And here I sit, still his prisoner," he concluded unhappily, "while both you and my father are free to depart this insane place when you choose." He glanced at his chronometer and took a deep breath. "You must go to him, Grandfather. At least you two can return to Helium."

"And you must stop speaking nonsense, for the three of us will leave Lothar together—and soon, as I am confident we will figure out a way to end your confinement in the very near future," I told him. "But first . . ." I brought forth some water and two cubes of usa, smiling when Djon Dihn wrinkled his nose at the latter. Although extremely nutritious and thus popular as a staple among fighting men, products made from the almost tasteless fruit of the usa tree are for most an acquired taste. "It concerns me that you are subsisting on what is in effect imaginary nourishment. I know this is not princely fare, but it is at least honest foodstuff that has not originated in the mind of an illusionist and it may give you the strength you will need if we are forced to exert ourselves at some future time. Let us share a meal while we make our plans."

I could see from his expression that my grandson found the flavor of the mashed fruit even more off-putting than usual, but I encouraged him to down all of it as there was no telling where his next real meal would come from. After a few minutes his eyelids drooped and he began to stifle yawns, and soon he had nodded off. I waited quietly for an additional minute or two. Then, after first snapping my fingers by his ear to make sure that he was fully unconscious, I lifted the boy in my arms. This was not an ideal state in which to brave the ledge and balcony descent, meaning we must count on Tario's having made his last visit of the day and exit the building by means of the hallway and the stairs. I swiveled carefully to one side as I neared the doorway, thinking that my grandson's sandaled feet would be less likely than his unprotected skull to incur lasting damage should they encounter any unseen barrier. Thankfully, we passed quickly into the corridor as if there were no door—which as far as I was concerned was the truth.

We were back in the storeroom by the time Djon Dihn awakened. He came to suddenly, staring around in great confusion to find himself outside the chamber for the first time without Tario by his side. "How did you do this, John Carter?"

I pointed to my cache of supplies. "Since your mind has insisted on acting in collusion with your jailer, I decided to incapacitate it. In the medical kit is a soporific compound commonly used in field surgery, with which I coated your share of the usa. Naturally I could not inform you of this in advance in case your bewitched brain proved powerful enough to extend its control over your body even while you slept."

"Excellent thinking!" He looked around the dim storeroom. "But where is my father?"

I showed him the note I had found when I got there: "Fear I am followed. Moving to avoid detection." There followed a list of rendezvous locations in the city and the times when he would be there over the next day or so.

Checking our chronometers, we departed the storeroom in search of the next meeting place on his list, which I was certain we could reach by the appointed time.

As usual, the dark streets of Lothar were completely deserted and we were able to make good progress. Things were going surprisingly well, which I have learned from experience is often an indicator that they are about to take an unexpected downward turn. As if on cue, a slight breeze wafted our way as we moved along the back streets, in which I could detect the sharp aroma characteristic of the presence of a banth, the great leonine predator who rules the nights in the hilly country surrounding the dead sea bottoms of Barsoom. Recalling that Tario had warned Djon Dihn that the trained banths the Lotharians had once employed to devour the bodies of fallen green men from the battlefield outside the city walls had reverted to their feral instincts during the chaos of the battle between the realists and etherealists, I hoped that we were not now trespassing on territory claimed by the ferocious nocturnal beasts.

I relaxed a little when the odor began to dissipate and we stepped cautiously out into a deserted plaza that was bathed in the soft light of tiny Cluros, Barsoom's lesser and more distant satellite, the periphery of the open area cloaked in inky shadows cast by the towering structures that surrounded it. We had made it halfway across the square when a low, eerie moan broke the silence of the night from somewhere nearby. Unfortunately, I was all too well acquainted with that particular sound and instantly unsheathed my longsword.

Just then plodding Cluros' swift and wayward mate Thuria broke free of the horizon and began her own ascension into the heavens. At once the plaza was flooded with gaudy brilliance, the second moon's appearance imbuing the scene with motion and color as each of the modest shadows bestowed by her predecessor upon the dusty fountains, the ornamental statuary, and even the clumps of rank vegetation thrusting up from the cracks in the ancient masonry now gained swaying new companions. But shadows were not the only new things brought to our attention by the compounded moonlight, for about fifteen yards from us directly in our path stood a huge banth, its ruff of yellow mane bristling above its otherwise hairless tawny hide.

Momentarily halted by the sudden burst of moonlight, the great creature resumed slinking slowly toward us on its ten sinewy legs, protruding green eyes agleam and powerful tail lashing behind it like a bullwhip. I motioned my companion to get behind me and raised my sword, feeling a surge of near relief to be facing an antagonist of flesh and blood rather than the armed phantoms I had been anticipating. The sensation was short-lived, as just then another mournful moan sounded off to the right, to be followed by a third from somewhere in the shadows behind and to the left of us. Still more of the calls originated from various parts of the square until the air reverberated with their lugubrious notes and a sea of green eyes glimmered all around us.

"We appear to be completely surrounded by them, John Carter," whispered Djon Dihn in awestruck tones.

"Yes. It would be convenient if your mother's gift chose this moment to suddenly reveal itself in you as well, for then you might quickly call these monsters to heel with but a soft-spoken command. As it is, they must be dealt with in a somewhat more time-consuming fashion," I replied lightly, hoping to keep the boy's spirits from flagging. I was weighing our options as I spoke, noting the positions of our adversaries while surveying the plaza behind them for any openings through which we might take our leave. I turned to look my grandson in the eye. "Listen well. At my signal you will make for yon gallery and seek sanctuary behind those closely spaced columns. If you note an escape route at the end of the colonnade, avail yourself of it as swiftly as you can and go to meet your father."

Djon Dihn shot me a look of hot defiance. "And what shall you be doing while I run for my life, Grandfather?"

"I shall be slaying banths," I replied simply, "a pastime I have engaged in more times than I can count since my advent on Barsoom." As his dubious expression lingered, I added: "I do not impugn your courage, Djon Dihn, but trust that you are intelligent enough to concede that I am far better equipped to handle this threat than are you. To be candid, my own chances of emerging victorious will be severely diminished if I must also concern myself with your well-being while exchanging pleasantries with this crew. Therefore: when I engage the three nearest of those who stand before us, move as swiftly as you can into the gap that will appear to the left of the largest. I will join you as soon as I am able."

He considered this for a moment with a doubtful frown. Then to my relief he gave a nod of reluctant assent and poised himself to run.

We two now stood motionless at the center of a ring of razor-edged claws and gaping jaws, the bright moonlight gleaming from the triple rows of fangs. I had to admit that the odds did not seem weighted in our favor. It was true that I had fought representatives of this most awe-inspiring predator of nighttime Barsoom before on a myriad of occasions and lived to tell of it—yet never had I taken on so many at once and from all sides. Still, there was nothing for it in the present situation—and if it provided my grandson with the opportunity to extend his short tally of years, I found myself more than willing to gladly sacrifice however many moments of my own already protracted existence I had remaining.

The banths had been creeping toward us with exquisite slowness while we conducted our quiet conversation, the approach of their long muscular bodies nearly silent save for the soft padding sound of many feet on marble and the lashing of yellow tails. It was the stuff of nightmares, the circle tightening about us like a noose as the leonine predators continued to move in from all directions, those directly in front of us closer than the others, their glistening eyes fixed on the hypnotic motion of the sword I had begun to weave in lazy arcs before us. At last I saw the nearest one tense his massive shoulder muscles and knew that the time had come to act.

"Now!" I cried, at the same moment leaping directly for the trio that crouched ten feet before us, my longsword flashing in front of me. My move took the three off guard and I was able to sink my blade deep into the neck of the leftmost one in the grouping, sending a gout of vermilion blood spurting into the air from severed arteries before his fellows could rally to his side. As I turned to face his companions I saw from the corner of my eye Djon Dihn dash past the great ten-legged flank and disappear into the dark gallery behind the dying beast while I rapped my weapon sharply against the marble pavement to maintain the attention of the others. Incited by the sudden escalation, the two nearest me parted their formidable jaws in the deafening roar designed to paralyze their prey with fear and bounded forward, those behind me echoing the cry, yet hanging back for the time being as I had hoped to allow their pack leaders the right of first kill.

I had previously observed that one of the pair remaining in front of me was moving with a slight limp, favoring two of its foremost right paws. I waved my blade high in the air to coax up its massive head, then ducked low beneath snapping jaws and swung the sword down in a rapid sequence of vicious blows, first to one foot and then the other, dissevering several clawed toes from each and sending their owner howling in pain and outrage. The beast lurched sideward, violently jostling its neighbor, who turned instinctively to sink its teeth into the offender's shoulder, providing me with a neat opening through which I lunged with a downward thrust of my blade so powerful that it nearly parted the great shaggy-maned head from its corded neck. In a flash I spun about and buried my sword to the hilt in the heart of the other wounded animal.

When I turned with renewed determination to face those that had been creeping up behind my back, I found that their numbers had grown in the half minute during which I had dispatched the three leaders, and that now fully half a dozen faced me from that direction. Glancing back over my shoulder at a low growl, I saw with a grim smile that two more had just emerged from the shadows behind the fallen ones; these were closer to me and so I moved to engage them first, my back tingling as I awaited the attack from behind that must surely occur at any moment. With this many of the beasts united against me, my chances had grown slim indeed and I knew that my only recourse was to continue to surprise my assailants. Accordingly, I took two quick steps forward, then vaulted high up into the air, twisting in mid-leap to land lightly astride the muscular back of one of them, from which perch I chopped down in front of me, slicing through the creature's spinal cord before he could shake me off. Bellows of mingled rage and agony from the paralyzed beast echoed through the square as I jumped lightly to my feet.

His companion proved to be a cleverer foe. He faced me squarely, swinging his head back and forth in a short arc that gave me no opening, while I listened to the soft pad and clicking nails of many feet approaching from behind me. When I feinted with my longsword, he startled me by thrusting his head forward instead of flinching away. Closing his mighty jaws on the flat of the blade, he wrenched the thing from my grasp and hurled it with a flick of his head to the pavement behind him. I quickly drew my shortsword and engaged him with that, fanning my blade so rapidly in his face that it became a silver blur in the brilliant moonlight. Undaunted, he leaped at me and succeeding in raking my free arm a deep cut with his razorlike claws before I twisted to the side and, grasping my sword with both hands, ran it the length of his tawny flank as if slicing open a sausage, his steaming entrails pouring out with a sickening sound onto the dusty marble. His death throes were accompanied by an ungodly yowling that sent shivers up my spine.

I had been fully expecting the others to mount a concerted

assault on me while I was engaged with their packmates. Instead the dying banth's howls were succeeded by a sudden wild cacophony of roaring and hissing from behind me. Fearing that my grandson had lost hope in my ability to survive another attack and decided to enter the fray himself, I spun around to behold one of the strangest sights I had ever witnessed: the remaining half-dozen banths were lunging and prancing madly about the square, stepping awkwardly and wild-eyed in the midst of a sea of tiny, lithe bodies, as scores of dainty soraks darted between their legs and hopped upon their backs and heads to bat at the roots of long tails or claw at bulging green eyes. I saw all of this in a few seconds before the banth closest to me, so far unencumbered by any of the diminutive attackers, darted away from the others and attempted to circle behind me, thus putting me between himself and the chaos of little creatures. But as I turned to face my newest adversary a throng of the sinuous bodies streamed past me on either side and hurled themselves upon that bewildered beast as well, swarming up his legs and onto his back. Eyes rolling crazily, he strove to grab them in his jaws and fling them onto the pavement—yet as quickly as one fell to lie twitching on the marble, twenty more burst from the shadows to take its place and soon his tawny hide was covered in a seething purple mass of needlelike teeth and claws.

I could not suppress a deep shudder. Once long ago on the African continent I had watched a troop of army ants overwhelm their considerably larger prey in much the same fashion. Witnessing the stunned helplessness on the wicked countenances of the struggling beasts, I believe this was the nearest I ever came to feeling sympathy for a banth.

As I stood staggered in the midst of this mad scene my eyes alighted on the face of my grandson, who stood peering around the opening to the gallery, waving for my attention. Djon Dihn cupped his hands about his mouth and shouted to me above the din: "John Carter! Shall we continue on our way?"

Stooping to retrieve my longsword, I sidled past the

spasming figures of the leonine giants, most of them now almost completely covered in writhing little bodies, and joined Djon Dihn in the portico. He was soaked with perspiration, his face pale beneath its copper cast.

"I did not mean to interfere," he told me in a shaky voice, "and I am quite sure you could have managed them all handily on your own, but since time is of the essence I thought perhaps it was a good moment for us to leave."

I nodded thoughtfully and matched my stride to his slower one, supporting him with an arm about his shoulder as we headed down the gallery. The noises from the plaza were beginning to grow less frantic, though no less furious.

"I am not very practiced at summoning phantoms that remain once out of my eyesight. The soraks will quickly begin to lose interest in their larger cousins and fade away now that we have left their immediate vicinity," said Djon Dihn, drawing himself up with visible effort and quickening his pace. "We should probably not linger."

At length we reached the second rendezvous point, only to find it also deserted, despite signs of recent visitation. It was obvious that we had tarried too long among the banths and Carthoris had departed for the next meeting place.

Quelling my frustration, I consulted the list my son had left in the storehouse. The next rendezvous was located in the basement of a building not too far away. "We can only follow the trail he has left us. Here are the directions to the next destination. Assuming no further interruptions, we should arrive in plenty of time to meet him there."

Djon Dihn stayed me with his hand as I turned to go.

"Wait. Once we find my father, we will need to depart the city as quickly as possible, correct?"

"Yes, of course."

He straightened his shoulders. "In that case you must go ahead while I return to the palace to free the Maid of Lothar. I am certain that she is real, John Carter!" he insisted when he saw my expression of skepticism. "I told her I would come back for her without fail and I must keep my word as a prince of Helium." He scanned the list his father had left. "If you are not at the next rendezvous when I get back, we will simply make our way to the third meeting place and find you there."

I shook my head. What my grandson proposed was a noble gesture, but obviously futile. "Djon Dihn, the palace may be guarded and you are still unarmed. More importantly, real or imaginary, she will be no more able to leave her prison chamber than were you—" I began.

"Which is why I shall bring this with me." He hefted the small bottle from the medical kit, still half full of soporific liquid. "And this." He brought forth the last of the ripe sompus I had plucked on my way through the forest. "The Maid will be much more likely to accept a few bites of this delicious fruit to fortify her for our escape than that vile-tasting sub-stance you tricked me with," he said with a youthful grin. "I know a quick way to the palace grounds and will need no weapons. As for guards, there were none before and I have no reason to believe there will be any now. Tario may not even realize yet that I have escaped. If he does, the last place he would expect to find me is in his own apartments."

I hesitated.

I have referred to my grandson as both a young man and a boy, but this does not quite capture the situation, as concepts such as age and youth naturally take on different meanings on different planets. Perhaps I should take a moment to remind those who may have forgotten that the human race on Mars differs from its terrestrial counterpart in several striking aspects, not the least of which is the fact that there are no children on Barsoom—at least not as the inhabitants of Earth understand that word.

As every reader with more than a passing interest in Barsoomian biology is by now aware, present-day Martians of all stripes and colors are oviparous, this having been—at least in the case of humanity—a purposeful adaptation made millennia ago to those increasingly harsh conditions of a

drying, dying world that without such radical scientific intervention would have hopelessly stacked the odds against
the survival of the type of helpless infant regularly produced
on Earth. Although the conscious decision was made to retain
most of the ancient mammalian characteristics in this new
incarnation, there is in fact only one small and extremely rare
species of true mammal currently on Barsoom. (Two, I suppose
you could more accurately say, now that I and at least one
other Earthman have taken up long-term residence on the
Red Planet.) Here, the newborn emerges from the gradually
expanding egg in which he has gestated for five long Martian
years at approximately one-third the stature of the adult he
will one day become, though otherwise well-proportioned
and almost fully developed, being rapidly able to walk and
talk, and even to defend himself once someone hands him
his first sword. Over the next few years he grows at an aston-
ishing pace both in body and in mind. The fact that all human
beings on this planet are telepathic assists in the swift impart-
ing of first language and then knowledge, as well as in the
inculcation of societal norms, and by the time five local years
have elapsed from the moment he broke the shell, the youth—
now a mere ten years old by earthly reckoning—is for all
intents and purposes an adult. This was in fact the age my
son Carthoris had attained when we two first encountered
one another as cellmates on an island prison in the underground Sea of Omean at Barsoom's south pole, following my
return to Mars from an involuntary decade-long exile back
on Earth. Relatively slighter of build and half a head shorter
than the six feet and one inch he would eventually achieve,
and therefore recognizable as a comparative youngster, my
son was nonetheless by this age a highly educated man, a
practiced swordsman, and a fierce fighter, and thus deemed
fully competent to conduct his own affairs and explore the
planet in his flier—when had he been born on Earth he would
still have been confined to riding the tilting board in his
schoolhouse yard.

It was this strange juxtaposition of youth and maturity that still sometimes gave me pause when dealing with younger Barsoomians, this being especially true in the case of Djon Dihn, with his demonstrated lack of interest and experience in what I would consider practical matters. However, in the eyes of Martian society my grandson was a man, and I knew that I must treat him as one. Not without a few internal pangs I handed over the items he requested and watched him head off into the night.

The directions Carthoris had left were not difficult to follow and I had no further run-ins with foes real or otherwise. I arrived at the building he had designated and descended as instructed into its cellar, only to find it deserted, again with markings in the dust that indicated someone had indeed been here recently. The tracks led to a second descending stairwell that could only be an entrance to the subterranean pits common to all Barsoomian cities. The pits beneath any city of a certain age are an unsavory region; walking beneath Lothar was like traversing the interior of a long-abandoned tomb.

In this case, the ubiquitous heavy dust was an aid rather than a hindrance, as I needed only to follow the fresh sandal tracks. I turned a corner, my pocket torch picking out the outline of a slumped human figure next to a pillar up ahead. I approached cautiously. Was it at last my son? Had he given way to fatigue and fallen asleep while waiting for us?

I shined my light on the figure to view a shocking sight. It was indeed Carthoris and he was indeed unconscious—but he was also gagged and bound securely in thick ropes. He awoke as I bent and pulled the wad of leather from his mouth.

"Father!" His eyes filled at first with confusion, then gladness, and then suddenly with doubt: "But how could you be here? Is it really—"

"Yes, it is I, John Carter, your father, and no illusion," I interjected somewhat impatiently, eager to be done with this time-wasting period of skepticism so that we might move on to more important matters. "Who has done this to you?" I bent down, reaching for my dagger to cut him free of his heavy bonds when he suddenly stiffened.

"Behind you, John Carter—it is a trap!" I saw the movement of many massive shapes in the shadows, and then a stout net was dropped upon me from above and quickly drawn tight to pin my arms to my sides to prevent me from reaching my weapons. Though I thrashed wildly about, striving to give a good accounting of myself with powerful kicks of my legs, I was set upon by numerous assailants, and finally clubbed unconscious.

6

THE MAIN COURSE

I AWOKE WITH AN ACHING HEAD to find myself securely bound in thick ropes of my own and seated next to my son against a wall in a long, high chamber, the room lit by flaming wooden torches set in crudely fashioned sconces.

As I chased the cobwebs from my brain, Carthoris explained how he had come to be here. Intrigued by the great cavalcades of green men he had seen heading in the same direction, he had not realized until sometime after he landed his ship that he had returned to Lothar. Curious, he had gone into the city to investigate, whereupon he had been tricked by an illusion that his mate Thuvia was also there, and eventually captured by Tario, who had imprisoned him in much the same manner as Djon Dihn—in his own case in much reduced circumstances, in a pitch dark cell with no visible doors or windows, to be visited at unknown intervals by the jeddak who furnished him with small amounts of food and water, all the while railing at him for his attempted invasion of the city. He was left weaponless but unbound, and as the time of his captivity lengthened he inspected every inch of his lightless cell, finally locating a loose stone in one corner where the floor met the wall. Diligently working at it in the dark with his fingers and covering it with his body when Tario visited, finally he had pried it loose and thus triggered a small landslide in that corner of the cell, which he frantically enlarged with his hands until he was able to squirm downward through a tortuous ancient tunnel to find himself in the pits below the city.

When night fell he had emerged from there to prowl the streets, hearing the sounds of a great battle without that must have been the meeting I myself had brought about of the Torquasians and Thurds. Each day he retreated underground, emerging only at dusk to search for food and drink—as well as for some sign of his son, whom he feared might by this point also have become a victim of the illusionists. Following the recent tracks of sandals that he took to be Djon Dihn's in the dust of the deserted streets, he eventually discovered the cache I had left in the storeroom. Struck by the feeling he was being watched, he had left the list of rendezvous points and eventually returned to the pits, where he had been caught in a net in the dark in just the same sudden fashion as I, fighting fruitlessly but just as vigorously, that he might at least have the satisfaction of taking some of his attackers down before they knocked him out. Unlike myself, he had now had ample time to learn the identity of those assailants. To my great surprise, he revealed that we had been taken prisoner by a tribe of Barsoom's feared great white apes.

"What? How are we still alive?"

Bearing a superficial resemblance to the African gorilla of Earth, these colossal six-limbed creatures, their dead-white hide hairless except for a huge shock of bristling fur upon their heads, evince more kinship with the Martian green men in their physiology, the males typically fifteen feet tall and heavily muscled. There are few creatures more expert at striking terror into the heart as these monstrous inhabitants of Barsoom's dead cities, and even a banth will think twice before pitting fangs and claws against their brute strength and legendary savagery.

"Your guess is as good as mine," my son answered. "I have a feeling we will find out before too long, though we may not like the answer. But now, Father, tell me if you have any knowledge of the whereabouts of my son, for Djon Dihn was traveling with me, and I have not seen him for days, thinking to have found the first sign of his presence in Lothar when I came upon that cache of belongings in the storeroom. And then explain if you will what strange quirk of providence has brought you here to this forsaken place—perhaps just in time to share my doom."

I quickly reassured him that Djon Dihn was alive and well, and now also free of Tario's clutches, and then proceeded to provide a summary of my own adventures starting with my sighting of the pilotless flier. "And so you see," I concluded, "it was not providence but your son that brought me here."

"He should have flown back to Helium and safety, although I am touched he chose to remain here for my sake," he said with a troubled sigh. "However, it was unwise of him to attempt to succor this fabled Maid of Lothar on his own."

"He is his father's son," I said.

Carthoris summoned up a smile. "And John Carter's grandson," he replied, adding ruefully: "Although at this moment I wish he had your skill with a blade. But you say that he has learned the secret of summoning up phantoms in the manner of Tario and the other Lotharians. How can this be?"

"I have been thinking about that. The current red race was formed by an intermingling of the ancient white, black, and golden peoples that once ruled Barsoom," I said. "Perhaps Djon Dihn carries some hidden strain of power from his Orovar ancestors. Or maybe it is simply one of those providential quirks you mentioned, such as the one that endowed his mother with her own wondrous ability."

"I have a third suggestion," Carthoris said after a few moments' thought. He told me that after his escape from Tario on the night of my arrival he had spent his nights ranging the city and his days exploring the underground space looking for another means of egress from Lothar, always with the feeling he was being watched or followed. He had only brought enough rations from the *Susstos* for a day or two, leaving the bulk of the supplies in the ship for Djon Dihn, and after his capture had subsisted on what mean viands Tario deigned to materialize for him. As the days passed he had naturally grown hungry and increasingly thirsty.

"I knew there must have been a source of fresh water beneath the city when Lothar was originally constructed, before the inhabitants had learned to subsist solely on the products of their imaginations. At length I came to a subterranean stream where the water passed over an immense, shallow pool floored with humps and involutions of a smooth, glassy material that most resembled a flow of solidified volcanic lava, save that it was transparent and scintillated in many colors from deep within. I felt a queer throbbing in my brain as I stood before it, as if the glassy waves and folds were emitting some unseen rays that penetrated my skull. Parched, I drank my fill, then sat down fascinated at the edge of the pool and looked within, noting for the first time as my eyes grew used to the dimness that its shore was ringed with what I had assumed was a decorative arrangement of white rocks but now recognized as reclining human skeletons." He shuddered. "I do not know how long I tarried there, staring into the shining depths. In the end it was the thought of Thuvia, my mate, of you and of my mother, and above all of my son, who I hoped still waited beyond the cliffs for my return, that gave me the strength to break free of its awful power and make my way farther down the tunnel, until I found a corridor that brought me back up into Lothar, leaving behind the entrancing glow and the remains of those others who had not been so fortunate as I. After a few days of moving furtively around the city I wandered into the storehouse, where I found the cache of supplies from the *Susstos* and naturally assumed that Djon Dihn had stowed them there and further, that he must be somewhere in the city—perhaps by now a captive of the illusionists.

"It is my theory that the Lotharians built their city above the glowing substance, perhaps without even being aware of its existence—save for those unfortunates who stumbled upon the opening to the lava pool and never left to tell about it—and that as the millennia passed its emanations gifted them with both their immense longevity and their fantastic mental abilities," he concluded. "Yet this does not explain why my son is now able to perform the strange feats you have described, after such a short time here."

"True. I myself have not gained the ability to summon illusions," I said.

Carthoris stared straight ahead for a few moments as if concentrating on a point in the air in front of us, then shook his head. "Nor have I, after having spent more time in Lothar than either of you—but perhaps as you suggested, the radiating energy does not affect all in the same way. I think you will notice some unusual behaviors among our captors that may bear this out. As you know, I have been a prisoner of the great white apes before, but never have I seen ones with such advanced, almost manlike habits."

He went on to remind me of his previous experience some sixty years ago with a tribe located not that far from where we currently sat that had adorned themselves with strips of animal hide in clumsy imitation of the harness worn by the green warriors who frequented the dead cities in which they habitually dwelled, commenting that these Lotharian apes had advanced much further, their garments more closely matching those of humans, and that they were speaking with one another in what was obviously some form of sophisticated language.

I was able to observe this remarkable behavior for myself on the infrequent occasions when a pair of the apes would appear to feed us our dinner, squatting before us to use their intermediary limbs to push gobbets of hardened mantalia seepings into our mouths, since they would not free our arms so that we might feed ourselves. They seemed to enjoy the process, commenting to one another amid bursts of guttural laughter in what sounded clearly like a complex tongue, as they smeared the rancid paste on our cheeks and chin. It was obvious that the harnesses in which these had clad themselves, while not up to the meanest human standards, had yet been carefully fashioned from leather strips overlaid with banth hide and even decorated with small pieces of quartz and other shiny rocks, while metal armlets adorned their massive limbs in a grotesque parody of the ornamentation of the green men from whose bodies they had doubtless been filched.

Carthoris nodded to the flaming torches on the wall. "Their use of fire, their attempts to clothe themselves like human beings, their refined communication far beyond the expected meager collection of grunts and growls—it all seems to indicate that the apes of Lothar are climbing upward on the evolutionary ladder at a greatly accelerated rate," he observed, "and I wonder if the glowing pool may not also account for that."

I spat a piece of bark that had been pushed into my mouth along with the mantalia cheese onto the floor and commented that it was a pity our hosts were mounting the evolutionary scale without picking up proper table manners along the way, reflecting that on all levels Lothar was surely not an exemplar of the rules of hospitality adhered to in most civilized regions of Barsoom.

When our giant jailers were not around—which was most of the time, as they seemed to have little interest in associating with us beyond amusing themselves with stuffing our mouths and plastering our faces at feeding time in what I was beginning to suspect was an effort to fatten us up for some unpleasant future use—we occupied ourselves by working to gain freedom from the thick ropes that held us, which in their devilish complexity and strength seemed to provide additional evidence of the apes' upward progress on the path toward civilization.

Our efforts were of no avail. It seemed we had been scraping our bonds against the pillar of rough stone at our backs for most of one day when we were interrupted by the appearance of a particularly imposing male ape who must have been well over fifteen feet in height. Picking me up in his right intermediary paw and my son in his left, he carried us as if we were a couple of handfuls of straw down a rough-hewn corridor and into a cavernous hall with a long shallow pit at its center in which a great fire blazed, where he deposited us with un-expected delicacy on a woven mat and departed the chamber.

Chanting in a weird growling bass alternated with a high-pitched ululation, half a dozen female apes then brought forth and assembled an enormous spit upon which the main course was evidently to be skewered and roasted, while others began to lay out on more fibrous mats a carefully arranged garnish of various tubers and mushroom-like growths in complicated, almost artistic patterns. Carthoris had already endured days of near starvation, followed by an unknown stretch of time being stuffed with the near tasteless mantalia after his capture. Now, staring at the relative bounty of this potential feast which we assumed would prominently feature ourselves in a role other than diners, he licked his lips, then leaned over to me and said: "Is it wrong that observing these preparations is causing my mouth to water?"

My own lips curved in a smile, nor was I taken aback by his comment, an example of the gallows humor that is as common among the warriors of Barsoom—who may face death hundreds of times over their long lives, never knowing which close call will be their last—as it is among the soldiery of Earth.

"Not at all," I replied. "For myself I am looking forward to that moment when the fires burn away these accursed ropes and I can finally stretch my cramped muscles again for a few seconds before we are done to a turn. Who knows—perhaps there will be time for us to excuse ourselves from the feast and wreak some final havoc among the guests?"

We continued to surreptitiously strain at our bonds until the moment the chief culinarian signaled her staff to bring us forth. As they approached with massive arms outstretched, I pricked up my ears at the sound of a great hubbub that seemed to be emanating from the central corridor outside the dining chamber.

"Father—is that a human voice I hear?" Carthoris asked

me, the expression of stoic unconcern on his face giving way to solicitude. It was evident we shared the same fear: that his son had succeeded in tracking us down after his perilous errand of mercy only to be captured himself. I shuddered at the thought that he—and perhaps the Maid of Lothar he had been determined to win free of Tario's imprisonment—might now join us as a last-minute course in the apes' banquet.

We looked on with mounting anxiety as a brightening flicker of orange torchlight approached down the tunnel. At last a group of several dozen of the towering apes came lumbering into the chamber. Diminutive by comparison, Djon Dihn strode in their midst, at his side a beautiful, pale-skinned maiden with flowing golden hair, attired in a long silver robe studded with sparkling gems.

Incredibly, my grandson seemed to be no prisoner. On the contrary, we watched in great amazement as he walked at ease among the massive creatures, who bent low to regard him with an almost fearful fascination as he appeared to converse with them easily in the growling gutturals of their own tongue!

7
DIVINE INTERVENTION

D JON DIHN AND THE MAIDEN departed from their entourage and walked briskly to where we sat with mouths agape, still trussed up in our ropes. Gesturing imperiously, my grandson uttered a few sharp syllables and two of the apes at once fell to fumbling with our bonds. Once we were free, they helped us to our feet as we massaged our stiff arms, and presented us almost timidly to our deliverer.

Djon Dihn dismissed the apes with a wave of his hand and gave each of us a formal embrace before turning to introduce us to his companion.

"I found her waiting for me." He paused to give the beautiful maiden a look that mingled awe and something deeper. "I told her I had come back to take her away with me as promised, she graciously accepted a piece of sompus, and we made our departure. It took a bit of searching once she had recovered from the soporific, but at length we located the marked passage and here we are."

The Maid of Lothar took her azure eyes from Djon Dihn for the first time and turned to us, her perfect lips curving in a dreamy smile. "Have you truly come to escort me from this place, O strangers?" she asked in a husky whisper. "I have grown weary of Tario and his endless improprieties, and I wish to spend no more time in his company. Djon Dihn tells me there is a vast and wonderful world beyond these stifling walls, and I should very much like to see it with my own eyes."

After assuring her that we would do everything in our

power to bring that about, we looked to her rescuer for some much-needed explanations.

"Some time ago I read a monograph by a Heliumetic linguistic researcher who was proposing a grammar and lexicon for a language he had recorded while spending some months in secret observation of a tribe of great apes," my grandson told us cheerfully. "I entertained myself by committing it to memory, hoping one day to discuss it with the author. You can imagine my delight to hear these apes speaking to one another in a more advanced form of the language I had read about!"

Djon Dihn recounted what he had so far learned from the giant apes. In addition to their hereditary foes, the green race, the apes naturally assumed all humans to be their enemies. They had been driven years ago from their previous habitation in the deserted city of Aaanthor by the attack of many bowmen they believed to be real. The latter, Carthoris and I realized, must have been the products of Kar Komak's own illusion-casting when he and my son had fallen briefly into the apes' clutches while going in pursuit of Thuvia's abductors. The apes had struck out across the dead sea bottom, traveling only at night as was their wont, and eventually found their way into this valley. Accustomed to inhabiting abandoned cities and seeking a new refuge in what they found to be a largely deserted metropolis, they had entered Lothar through one of the tunnels beneath the city, only to be relentlessly hunted by the Lotharians themselves. Their numbers grievously reduced by the unstoppable archers, who at times seemed to number in the thousands, they had retreated to the underground ways and established their community not far from the glowing lava pool, which they took to be a manifestation of the moons they no longer saw at night.

Fearing extermination by the implacable bowmen should the Lotharians learn of their continued existence, they had captured first Carthoris and then myself when we stumbled onto their hidden realm in order to prevent word from reaching those on the surface, intending us to be offered to the hurtling moons, which the apes had long ago come to view as gods. They had planned the same fate for Djon Dihn and the Maid until, at once shocking them and gaining their trust by speaking to them in their own tongue, Djon Dihn had assured them that he and the companions he sought were in fact enemies of their enemies, recently come down to Lothar from the sky. This was a fortuitous phrasing of our actual origin, as the apes interpreted his tale to mean that we were emissaries of the moons, calling us, according to my grandson, *eta-goro-mangani*—or "little moon men."

"The Lotharians they call *eta-tarmangani* and the red men *eta-gamangani*. The green men are *wamangani*, while their name for themselves is *zumangani*—"

Carthoris raised a hand to interrupt the enthusiastic language lesson. "What exactly is meant by the phrase 'offered to the moons'? Are you saying they were not planning to devour us, after all?" my son asked, casting a dubious glance at the great spit above the firepit.

"Oh no, Father, they had every intention of eating you," Djon Dihn said earnestly. "After all, they were going to have to kill you anyway to prevent you from betraying their location, and the *zumangani* consider the waste of good meat to be a sign of poor character. While they will dine on members of the green race when famished, they particularly relish the taste of *eta-gamangani*. Now, of course, they have acknowledged us as their friends and allies as well as messengers from their gods, and so they must of necessity curb their appetites. Just to be on the safe side," he added in a confidential tone, "I hinted that as anointed emissaries of Cluros and Thuria, our own flesh would have no more flavor than moonbeams."

When I asked if the apes had inquired as to why neither Carthoris nor I also spoke their tongue—in which case we too would have been treated as honored guests—he told us with an apologetic look that he had explained that the moons had endowed us each with different attributes, that his was intelligence while our own obviously lay in other areas.

"*Zumangani,*" I said aloud. "*Eta-gamangani.* What a strange tongue. I have never before heard its like on Barsoom."

"Indeed!" Djon Dihn's eyes sparkled with youthful enthusiasm. "I am going to write the new vocabulary down so that I may include it in the account of our adventures I am composing. I look forward to discussing my findings with Talo Thoran, the author of the monograph, should he ever return from the far north."

"I am sure it will please him to learn that his scholarly studies allowed us to progress in status from main course to diners at tonight's banquet," I said with sincerity. "Assuming, that is, they are planning to share their bounty with us."

They did that and more, roasting several haunches of deer-like dandox from the forests that ringed the valley on the spit originally intended for us. After we had supped, an ancient female ape diffidently applied a healing poultice to the wound on my upper arm where the banth had raked me with its claws. Later, Carthoris and I spent some hours exercising our cramped muscles, while Djon Dihn educated our hulking hosts on the nature of the phantom archers in the city above and advised them on how to shield one's eyes and thus avoid being pierced by their illusory arrows, while the Maid of Lothar looked on in wonder. At length my grandson informed the leader of the apes that it was time for us to return to the sky, which the towering creature pronounced *vando,* or "good" in their own language, adding a formal request that we convey his tribe's greetings to the moons. Promising to do so the moment we were next in contact with them, we were guided to an ascending passage that terminated in a heavy wooden door that was evidently bolted on the other side. The largest of our guides knelt down before it and dealt it a resounding blow with one of his elbows that left it in splinters. The apes, by nature nocturnal creatures who disliked going abroad by day, drew back at the shafts of sunlight filtering through the broken door and refused to accompany us further. We wished them luck in cohabiting with Tario and his archers, then walked cautiously through the doorway into a low-ceilinged room where the air was stale and the floor covered with hard objects that crunched beneath our sandals. I shined my torch down to reveal a litter of mangled human skeletons. The Maid of Lothar pressed closer to Djon Dihn's side.

"More bones," Carthoris observed, surveying the chamber with distaste. "Yet I recognize this place from long ago. This was once the lair of the great god Komal." He led us through the detritus to the far end of the low-roofed room and forced open a small door. We walked up a steep runway to find ourselves standing in a great circular arena, joined by a narrow passage to a smaller one.

"Yes!" My son surveyed the tiers of empty seats with a look of great relief. "Just across there at the base of the lowest level is another door. Beyond it is a flight of stairs and past that a corridor that will lead us through the palace gardens and thence to the city gates. If we move quietly and our ancestors smile upon us, Tario will not catch sight of us before we leave the city. Then, assuming there are no green legions currently camped without, we should be able to cross the plain unhindered and enter the forest." And so we set forth, my son leading us, the Maid of Lothar hand in hand with Djon Dihn, and myself bringing up the rear.

Unfortunately, our ancestors were not in a jovial mood, as we had not taken half a dozen steps before the door toward which we were headed was flung open and out stepped Tario in his long red robes to greet us with a sharp cry.

8

SWORDS AND ARROWS

NVADERS!" HE SHOUTED, fixing us with a malevolent stare. "Abductors!" He gestured and the first level of the arena was suddenly filled with stern-faced bowmen. I touched Djon Dihn's shoulder, bidding him in a low voice to take the maiden to a place of safety. I watched them hasten to an alcove near where we had emerged from below, then stepped forward to stand shoulder to shoulder with Carthoris.

"You are a fine one to talk," I called to the glowering jeddak. "In your time you have abducted both my son and my grandson."

He grimaced. "Son! Grandson! It is a lie—you yourself are a great lie, for your lack of a mind makes it plain you do not exist!"

I gave a grim smile. "Then draw your blade and meet me man to man," I retorted. "We will see whether my longsword is also a lie!"

"You dare challenge *me*, the last true jeddak in a fallen world, to base physical combat?" came an outraged cry from an aisle several rows above us. Tario stood there as well, this one garbed in dark blue, a score of archers materializing to flank him on either side.

"I shall watch you shall die in agony for your temerity, pierced by a hundred arrows!" Another Tario, this one resplendent in yellow, took up the cry from a tier midway up the arena to our left that was also suddenly crowded with bowmen.

Shouts rang out all over the great space until no less than a score of identical madmen faced us in their variously colored raiment, bowmen appearing by the dozens until grim-eyed archers swarmed the steps around and above us, far too many to count. There followed a short period of squabbling over who should have the honor of taking us down, climaxing with each Tario simultaneously ordering his own legions to let loose.

"Do not look at the bowmen!" Djon Dihn cried out as the arrows began to fly. Both Carthoris and I turned to see him peering out with eyes narrowed in concentration from behind the filigreed screen of the alcove in which he and the Maid of Lothar had taken refuge. "Tario will attempt to plant an image in your mind of each arrow finding its target to deadly effect, but this will be far more difficult if he cannot cause you to observe them leaving their bows. Here, take these—" I felt something thrust out of nowhere into my left hand and turned to exchange a wondering glance with my son, for of a sudden we both hefted great metal shields. A multitude of slender shafts glanced off them with a sharp clanging while the archers advanced down from the stands, all the while cursing and taunting us as cowards, and I found it almost impossible to convince myself that these were aught else than genuine missiles, or those who loosed them other than fighting men of flesh and blood.

Figuring it was only a moment before the jeddak's various duplicates filled the arena with many hundreds of archers attacking us from all possible angles—at which time we would surely catch sight of them and go down before their substance-less bolts, our stout, but equally imaginary shields notwith-standing—I lowered my head and charged forward like a bull, slashing blindly at anything before me.

A second later I heard an exclamation of surprise from my son and looked about, stopping in my tracks at the sight of the figures abruptly appearing to either side of me, then watching in amazement as a host of new warriors joined the battle, each similarly armed with longsword and great shield, some racing past us to bring the fight to the enemy, while others stepped fearlessly into the space directly before us to block the archers' aim. But who were these brave allies who had appeared just at the moment we needed them?

It is difficult to describe the emotions that ran through me as I recognized the warrior closest to me—*for it was myself!*

Surveying the scene with frank disbelief, I saw a dozen other John Carters standing shoulder to shoulder with an equal number of Carthorises, and beyond them multiple incarnations of Tardos Mors, the great Jeddak of Helium himself, marching in ranks with his own son, my wife's father, Mors Kajak. Flanking me on the right with a nod of friendly greeting was Xodar of the First Born, while Talu, Jeddak of the yellow men of the North, swung his peculiar hook and sword combination on my left. I noted that the exigencies of our situation had apparently enabled Djon Dihn to conquer his difficulties with producing illusions to the proper scale, when long shadows fell between myself and the true Carthoris and I looked back and up to see a company of fifteen-foot tall green men striding forward into the fray, each the exact image of my great friend Tars Tarkas, Jeddak of Thark.

The fantastic battle raged on in the central arena, multitudes of fair-skinned Lotharian bowmen against hosts of Djon Dihn's red ancestors, along with myself and whatever black, yellow, and green swordsmen of his acquaintance he could call to mind, in what was surely one of the strangest contests that had ever taken place upon the surface of this ancient world. We were evenly matched for a time. Here the thrust of a sword would snuff out the ersatz life of a bowman, sending him back into the void from whence he had been summoned; there an arrow would fly to its mark in the breast of an illusory swordsman and one of our own allies would topple dead to the pavement—only to wink out of existence in the next instant along with the pool of imaginary gore in which he lay. I can personally attest that there are few experiences as

unique as seeing yourself fall heroically in pitched battle—
especially when you are then privileged to look on as your
corpse fades away into nothingness! I must admit that seeing
both myself and my treasured family members and comrades
meet their doom again and again soon wore on me, making
it difficult to remember that it was in fact only the three of
us Heliumites in combat with a score of identical Lotharians
in the now crowded arena—Carthoris and I with our blades
and Djon Dihn with his mind.

The odds slowly began to turn in our enemies' favor, our
need to approach close to the bowmen to cut them down
increasing the likelihood that one of our allies would catch
sight of an arrow leaving a bow in his direction and thus
convince himself that he had been fatally struck. At my shouted
suggestion, my son and I slowly backed out of the main arena
and maneuvered ourselves into the smaller court, where the
closer quarters made it much more difficult for the archers to
use their preferred weapons against us, while we were able to
plunge forward into their crowded ranks and dispatch them
far more easily. At length Tario and his cadre of duplicates
must have realized this as well, for at some unspoken command
their phantoms discarded their bows and came at us brandishing the short-handled war-axes that were their only other
weapons. This was my hoped-for outcome, as it was quickly
obvious that the ancient bowmen conjured up by our opponents were far more at home with their weapons of choice
than they were with the axes, and soon it seemed that the
only thing we and our own phantom surrogates had to fear
from their onslaught was that the battle would never be
concluded, so long as each side continued to hold the power
to create and send forth an endless army of replacements. In
this regard I began to feel that we were outnumbered indeed,
for I knew the toll this mental effort must be taking on Djon
Dihn and feared he would soon be overpowered by the strain.

It was then that something wholly unexpected occurred.
"NO!"

My grandson's desperate cry came from close behind me.

At that same moment the army of phantasmal swordsmen that had been battling in a protective circle around Carthoris and myself abruptly evaporated into thin air, as did our own sturdy shields, and we found ourselves once more two warriors alone with only our swords against an ever-increasing number of fierce bowmen that now faced little impediment to finishing us off.

Swift on the heels of that first exclamation came a second cry in a different voice, this one a strangled shriek of shock and pain accompanied by the sharp clang of metal on stone. As the archers surged forward in an expanding mass to finally overwhelm us with their sheer numbers, I risked a glance over my shoulder to behold Djon Dihn standing a few feet behind his father, in his hand a shortsword slick with red. On the marble floor at his feet lay none other than the white-clad Tario, his pristine robes now stained with crimson as he clutched at his chest with convulsing fingers, a second sword lying on the pavement at his side. At once I grasped what must have occurred: while his archers and those of his duplicates pressed us ever backward, the jeddak had stolen up behind us through the corridor circling the arena and crept forward, his sword raised to strike Carthoris and myself down in a cowardly attack from behind. Djon Dihn had spied him just in time from where he stood directing our side of the battle in the alcove with the Maid of Lothar and, his intense concentration upon the legion he had formed of his ancestors and other phantom stalwarts shattered, dashed forward to intercept the villain, running a blade of his own through Tario's evil heart before the ancient Lotharian could carry out his murderous plan. Now Tario lay gasping, pale face contorted in furious disbelief, mouth writhing as he tried unsuccessfully to form words. Then before our eyes the Jeddak of Lothar vanished into nothingness.

All of this had taken but the merest moment. Djon Dihn was still staring down in seeming disbelief at the result of his grim handiwork when I turned my full attention back to the fray and charged forward, all the more determined to give a good final accounting of myself after my grandson's heroic act.

Just then Carthoris cried out: "Father—look!" I followed his gaze to where a great gap had suddenly appeared in the ranks of our foes as fifty of the bowmen facing us abruptly disappeared. An instant later the white-clad Tario's death cry was echoed by an identical shriek from across the arena as the Tario robed in blue also fell to the ground and was no more, fifty more of the archers winking out of existence with his passing. The red-robed Tario was next, taking another score of phantoms with him as he cried out and vanished as well. All around the arena the air resounded with the din of inter-mingled death cries, as Tario after Tario shrieked and fell into nothingness on the cracked marble, each immediately followed by his own cohort of unliving warriors.

Soon only we three were left facing the empty arena.

Djon Dihn was still standing over the place where the Jeddak of Lothar had vanished for all time, shortsword un-noticed in his hand. I caught his gaze.

"You wielded a weapon," I told my grandson.

"I saw the need," he answered grimly, looking down at the bloodstained blade as if seeing it for the first time. As I watched, the sword also melted away into the air. Abruptly he straight-ened, his face ashen beneath its copper hue, and spun around with a stricken cry to stare at the alcove in the gallery. "Oh no!" he gasped, racing into the shadows.

When Carthoris and I caught up to him he was kneeling on the marble, the Maid of Lothar's head cradled on his lap. The maiden's form was obscured by a strange shimmering, as if she lay just beneath the surface of a swiftly flowing stream.

"Do not give in!" he implored her in a hoarse whisper, grasping her pale hands tightly in his own as if he could physically prevent her from departing this plane of existence. "Stay with me!"

Slowly the coruscating waves faded and Djon Dihn looked up at us in wonderment.

Gone was the lovely Lotharian maiden of long ago with her golden tresses and skin of ivory. In her place lay a copper-skinned, raven-haired girl of equal beauty. The silver gown had disappeared as well, leaving her shapely form attired in the harness and silks of the latter-day red Martian. She stirred, then sat up slowly and looked about her as if waking from a deep sleep.

The erstwhile Maid of Lothar related her tale to us in bits and pieces as her memory returned to her. She told us that her name was Ptora Bal and that one night in the wake of a heated argument with her parents she had secretly stolen away from her home, a farmstead on one of the fertile strips of land that border the great Martian waterways. Appropriating one of the family's fliers and heading out in a fury at full throttle, she had almost immediately regretted her impulsive actions. I could not prevent an inward smile at this, having raised a daughter of my own who during her early years was possessed of a not dissimilar temperament, being quick to blaze, but then just as swift to cool. There were no moons in the sky when Ptora Bal departed, and she had already been flying over territory unfamiliar to her when she made the decision to swallow her pride, swing the craft about, and return home. What she had not realized, however, was that the flier she had chosen at random from the hangar had been grounded due to a malfunctioning compass, and she soon became thoroughly lost, each hopeful foray in a new direction only sending her farther into the unknown. She flew on through the night and then the following day until, fatigued, hungry, and increasingly terrified that she would never see her home and family again, she had brought her little ship down just inside a range of towering peaks. The next morning she had found her way to a tunnel similar to the one I had taken into Lothar's secluded valley, this one descending from the forest in which she had landed into an underground passage that ran right beneath the plain and parallel to the subterranean river that Carthoris had later stumbled upon. At length she emerged into a beautiful, nearly deserted city of great domes and burnished minarets, where the first person she encountered was a pale-skinned man with golden hair.

"The very last thing I can clearly recall is the look in his blazing eyes," she said in a hushed voice. "They burned into my own like great sapphires set in that strange white face . . ."

Her mind had been wrapped in a misty reverie from that moment until this very day, when upon the death of the former jeddak she had regained her senses—and, all unbeknownst to her, her true outward appearance—as one awakening after a long sleep of half-remembered dreams.

It was a strange reality to which she had awakened: Ptora Bal was bewildered to find herself in the company of three generations of Barsoomian princes, and not a little fearful to learn the national identity of her rescuers, since at the time she had embarked on her reckless flight her own nation of Zodanga had been an avowed enemy of Helium. Djon Dihn gently informed her that this was no longer the case, hostilities having ceased many decades ago when her country's belligerent leader was deposed and Zodanga became a vassal state of the Heliumetic Empire. "Decades!" she whispered, looking around her with half-lidded eyes as if Barsoom had become a strange and alien planet while she dreamed in Lothar. "My parents must have thought that in my foolish anger I embarked upon the last voluntary pilgrimage down the River Iss to the paradise in the Valley Dor." She raised her hand to her eyes and brushed away tears. "At least they will have been granted some solace in the years that have passed since my disappearance, believing that their daughter found her way to the place of eternal reward at the side of the goddess."

Carthoris and I exchanged a look, for here was another profound revelation of which she must eventually be apprised: that the Valley Dor was not now nor ever had been the promised paradise for those billions of Barsoomians who had made the final pilgrimage down the River of Mystery over countless millennia, only to fall into the clutches of some of the planet's most monstrous villains. But that could wait for another day.

9
FAREWELL TO LOTHAR

AGE AND TIME ARE THE STRANGEST THINGS, and nowhere is this more evident to me than here on Mars. Where else but on Barsoom could a man whose brief tally of years would have him judged a mere child on Earth have used the force of his imagination to defeat an ancient tyrant who had ruled for millennia solely by the power of his mind?

A survey of the plain from atop the high wall by the city gate showed us that a new force of Torquasian green men was beginning to gather around the city, and hoarse war-cries filled the air as they once more prepared to prosecute their ages-long attempt to capture Lothar for their own—this time, as they would soon learn, without interference from the deadly phantom bowmen who had repelled them for so many centuries. I wondered what would happen when the new tenants discovered that the pits beneath their long-sought prize were teeming with hundreds of the one creature capable of striking something resembling terror into the hearts of the otherwise fearless green race: the great white ape.

We decided to make our departure by way of a different route. Once she was again in full possession of her memory, Ptora Bal had no difficulty locating the hidden passageway not far from the now deserted grand palace of Tario that would bring us down to the tunnel she had traversed what seemed to her only a day ago, and thence beneath the plain and into the forest. From there she led us to where she had landed her small flier. After we cleared away the vines and underbrush that had obscured it for decades from prying eyes, Carthoris and I gave the craft a thorough inspection. Finding it still shipshape save for the defective compass—little surprise there, since the products of Martian engineering are designed to last—we four crowded onboard and flew over the mountain barrier to the site of my own more recent touchdown with the battered *Susstos*, where my son and I set to work transferring the buoyancy reservoirs to the larger ship and effecting what other general repairs were necessary to get us airborne in style once more.

Finally we were on our way home again, having taken pains this time to choose a route that would give a wide berth to that area of the dead sea bottoms claimed by the green nomads and their troublesome guns.

As we exited the arena earlier in that momentous day, I had noted the longsword that had fallen from the white-robed Tario's hand when Djon Dihn ran him through and still lay there upon the cracked marble after his disappearance. Now I contemplated the strangeness of it all: how an imaginary jeddak with a real sword had been vanquished by a flesh-and-blood prince wielding a phantom blade. It seemed that Djon Dihn would be creating no more weapons out of thin air. My grandson told us as we left behind the great circular valley that the weird alteration he had felt to his mind upon his arrival in Lothar appeared to have vanished; indeed, when he attempted to summon up a phantom sorak to amuse Ptora Bal he had achieved nothing more than a mild headache.

"Real or ethereal himself, after so many centuries Tario must have been truly mad," Carthoris mused as we two stood at the helm. Djon Dihn and Ptora Bal sat close by one another on a bench by the starboard railing, my grandson employing his golden scroll to acquaint the former Maid of Lothar with the current state of the world. "Having cloaked this unexpected visitor in the image of the maiden he had been unsuccessfully attempting to bring to reality for so long, I wonder if over time he himself forgot that she was not one of his phantoms."

"That would seem entirely possible for one whose brain must have been bursting at the seams with memories that stretched back to the days of Barsoom's youth," I replied.

The young woman's name had struck a chord in my mind. Her mention of the country of her origin bolstered my theory.

"If my own memory does not betray me," I told my son, "she may very well be kin to a family of Zodangan farmholders I encountered during my earliest sojourn upon the planet. In contrast to their rulers they were decent and hospitable people, and I have maintained contact with them since Helium's annexation of their nation in order to assure myself of their well-being. I remember hearing years ago that a young woman of the family had tragically vanished one night and never returned. I am sure they will be gratified to find their missing loved one safe and unharmed."

Carthoris cocked an eyebrow at this. "So, Father," he remarked with a grin, "you are telling me Djon Dihn has rescued a farmer's daughter? Knowing how the tales of adventure favored by my son oft conclude themselves, I half-expected to find that the young lady was a long-lost princess."

I nodded with a smile toward Djon Dihn and Ptora Bal where they sat with heads bent together in close conversation as they exchanged shy glances fraught with meaning.

"If I am not greatly mistaken," I told my son, "she may one day find herself a princess, after all."

ABOUT THE AUTHORS

A PRINCESS OF MARS
SHADOW OF THE ASSASSINS

ANN TONSOR ZEDDIES first encountered the ERB Universe as a child, when an old professor who lived down the street allowed her to choose a volume from his shelves. She chose *Tarzan of the Apes*. Later, she read the adventures of John Carter aloud to her young son. She is the author of six science fiction novels, two of which were Philip K. Dick Award nominees. Her short fiction includes stories in *The Ultimate Silver Surfer*, *Magic in the Mirrorstone*, and *Victory Harben: Tales from the Void*. She lives in Michigan with her husband, near the shores of an inland sea.

JOHN CARTER OF MARS
SWORDS OF THE MIND

GEARY GRAVEL is the author of the Edgar Rice Burroughs Universe novel *John Carter of Mars: Gods of the Forgotten*; the Philip K. Dick Award finalist *The Alchemists*; and the novels *The Pathfinders*, *A Key for the Nonesuch*, and *Return of the Breakneck Boys*. He has written several novelizations, including Hook, based on the Steven Spielberg film, and *Batman: Mask of the Phantasm*, based on the animated movie. He lives in western Massachusetts, where he worked for decades as a Sign Language Interpreter for the Deaf.

EDGAR RICE BURROUGHS: MASTER OF ADVENTURE

The creator of the immortal characters Tarzan of the Apes and John Carter of Mars, EDGAR RICE BURROUGHS is one of the world's most popular authors. Mr. Burroughs' timeless tales of heroes and heroines transport readers from the jungles of Africa and the dead sea bottoms of Barsoom to the miles-high forests of Amtor and the savage inner world of Pellucidar, and even to alien civilizations beyond the farthest star. Mr. Burroughs' books are estimated to have sold hundreds of millions of copies, and they have spawned 60 films and 250 television episodes.

About Edgar Rice Burroughs, Inc.

Founded in 1923 by Edgar Rice Burroughs, one of the first authors to incorporate himself, EDGAR RICE BURROUGHS, INC., holds numerous trademarks and the rights to all literary works of the author still protected by copyright, including stories of Tarzan of the Apes and John Carter of Mars. The company oversees authorized adaptations of his literary works in film, television, radio, publishing, theatrical stage productions, licensing, and merchandising. Edgar Rice Burroughs, Inc., continues to manage and license the vast archive of Mr. Burroughs' literary works, fictional characters, and corresponding artworks that has grown for over a century. The company is still owned by the Burroughs family and remains headquartered in Tarzana, California, the town named after the Tarzana Ranch Mr. Burroughs purchased there in 1919 that led to the town's future development.

In 2015, under the leadership of President James Sullos, the company relaunched its publishing division, which was founded by Mr. Burroughs in 1931. With the publication of new authorized editions of Mr. Burroughs' works and brand-new novels and stories by today's talented authors, the company continues its long tradition of bringing tales of wonder and imagination featuring the Master of Adventure's many iconic characters and exotic worlds to an eager reading public.

Visit **EdgarRiceBurroughs.com** for more information.

EDGAR RICE BURROUGHS AUTHORIZED LIBRARY™

Build you library today at ERBURROUGHS.COM

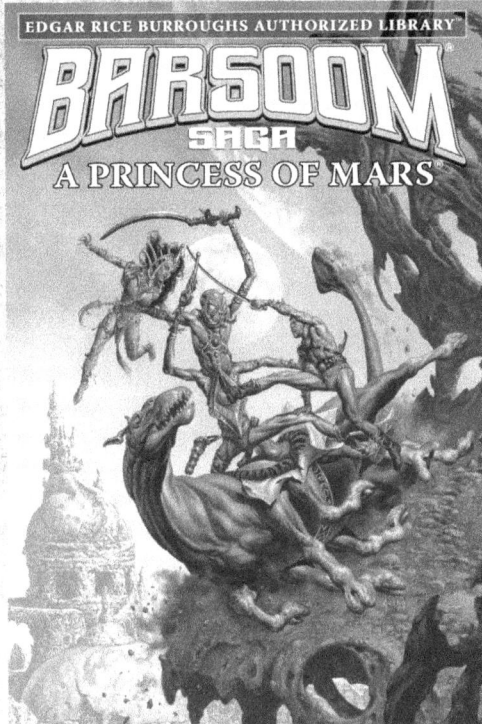

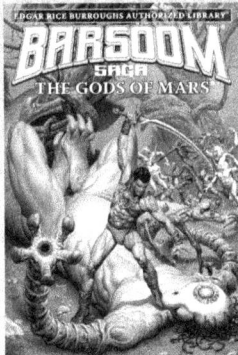

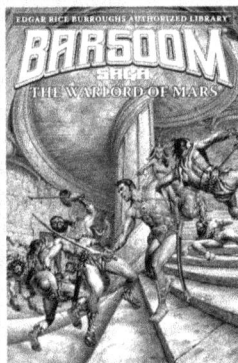

Uniform hardcover editions of Burroughs' classic novels

New cover art and frontispieces by Joe Jusko

Forewords and afterwords by ERB scholars and luminaries

Rare and previously unpublished bonus materials from the archives of ERB, Inc., in Tarzana, California

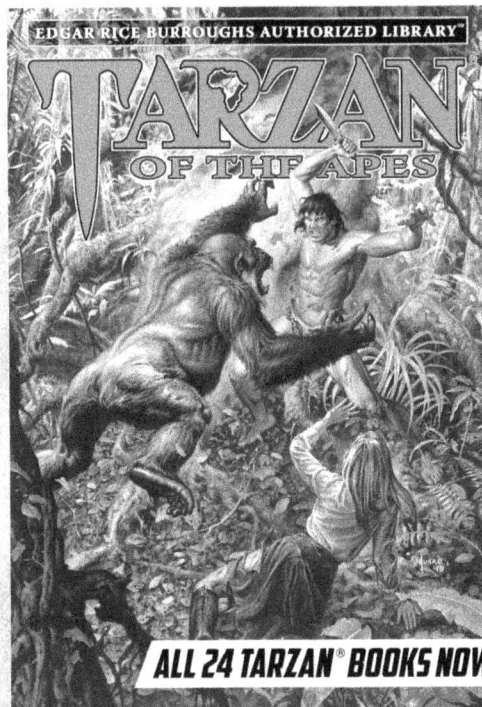

ALL 24 TARZAN® BOOKS NOW IN PRINT!

Edgar Rice Burroughs, Inc.

A whole universe of ERB collectibles, including books, T-shirts, DVDs, statues, puzzles, playing cards, dust jackets, art prints, and MORE!

Your one-stop destination for all things ERB!

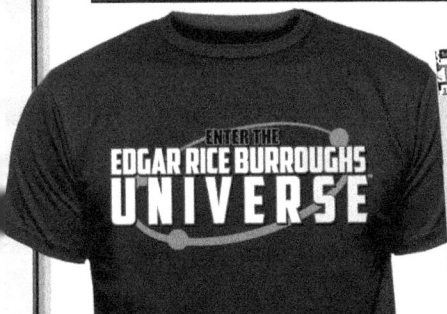

VISIT US ONLINE AT ERBURROUGHS.COM

Milton Keynes UK
Ingram Content Group UK Ltd.
UKHW030949260824
447446UK00001B/176